Fable of the Fatewave

Volume Four of the Joel Suzuki Series

Brian Tashima

Prism Valley Press logo by Purnima Prasad

ISBN: 0998775568
ISBN-13: 978-0998775562

To T & M

CONTENTS

ACKNOWLEDGMENTS

Mahalo to: Karen & John at Autism Empowerment, Susan at Indigo Editing, Jill Colbert for her amazing art and feedback, my fellow authors from NIWA and SCBWI, everyone who has helped me spread the word about Joel's story, and, of course, all the fans and supporters. Remember to breathe, believe, and follow your own wave of fate.

CHAPTER 1: GIVING THANKS

Joel put his fork down. "I'm done," he said, standing.

"Are you sure?" Alison—Joel's mother—asked.

"Yeah. I'm going to my room."

"Well...okay. But could you take your plate to the sink first, please?"

"Sure." Joel picked up his plate, which was still covered with a mound of mashed potatoes and two barely eaten slices of turkey.

"Can I have his pie?" Taylor—Joel's eleven-year-old sister—asked.

"Let's just save it for him, sweetie," Alison replied.

"Aww."

"You feeling all right, bud?" Art—Joel's former music store boss and now soon-to-be stepfather—asked.

"Yeah." Joel walked the short distance to the kitchen and set his plate down in the sink. "I'm fine."

"He's still depressed because his girlfriend quit the band," Taylor said.

"No, I'm not," Joel snapped. "And she's not my girlfriend."

"Sweetie," Alison said, looking at Taylor, "we agreed not to talk about that, remember?"

"I know," Taylor pouted. "I'm just tired of him being down all the time. It's really starting to bum me out."

"Just be patient with him, please."

Covering his ears, Joel dashed into his room. He had requested silence from his family on the subject of Felicity, not only because talking about her made him sad but also because he didn't want to get pulled too deeply into a line of inquiries regarding her whereabouts. He had explained to everyone—including Felicity's older sister, Victoria—that she had decided to move to a remote island nation to do some volunteer work assisting the native population there. That was a true statement; Spectraland *was* a remote island (since it was in another galaxy, dimension, or what have you), and as a Wavemaker (a person with the ability to create magic with music), Felicity *was* volunteering to perform deeds that would help the people of said island. But then more questions came, about passports and vaccinations and which island nation this was, exactly, and Joel basically had to feign ignorance, which, given his general distaste for lying, made him feel very uncomfortable.

I don't know how much longer I can do this, he thought, closing the door and flopping down on his unmade bed. *I guess if I cheer up, they might stop asking me about her...but how the heck am I supposed do that, after everything that happened?*

A chime rang out. It was Joel's wavebow, the magical musical instrument from Spectraland that he kept hidden under his bed, telling him that he had a message.

Now what?

Joel rolled off the bed, sat on the floor, and pulled the wavebow out. It really was a beautiful piece of work when you stopped to admire it. A mandolin-like instrument with a mother-of-pearl finish, its silky strings were pulsing with a soft glow that lit up the room with a warm incandescence. The pulse reminded him of a silent heartbeat, or, less poetically, the blinking of an answering machine.

You've got mail.

He plucked the instrument's high *E* string.

"Hey, Joel," Felicity's voice said. "This is, like, the fourth message I've left for you now. How come you're not calling me back? I'm gonna assume it's because you're busy."

Yeah, busy trying to forget.

"Anyway, I think it's, what, Thanksgiving over there now, right? So yeah, just wanted to remind you that the wedding's next week over here, so that means you have to leave by tomorrow, your time, otherwise you're gonna miss it."

Oh, right—the wedding. Ugh.

"Or wait, was it today? I dunno. Leave tonight, after dinner or something, just to be safe. You'd better make it. All right, see you soon."

Joel sighed as the strings on his wavebow dimmed. Not only had Felicity moved to Spectraland permanently, she was also now marrying one of its native inhabitants—a fellow Wavemaker named Thornleaf, who was kind of the typical tall, gruff, alpha-male type of guy that Joel resented and admired at the same time. He really didn't want to attend their wedding, but he figured that he should, at least out of courtesy.

I guess I should get ready to go, before it gets too—

Someone knocked on the door. "Joel?" It was Art.

"Yes?" Joel replied, sliding the wavebow back under his bed.

"Can I come in?"

Joel hesitated, not in the mood for one of Art's consoling talks, but he decided it would probably be better just to get it over with now before he left for Spectraland. "Sure."

The door creaked open. "Wow, it's pretty dark in here," Art noted. "Mind if I turn on the light?"

"Yeah. I mean, no. I mean—go ahead."

Art flipped the light switch. "So...how's it going?"

"Good."

"Cool. Wanna play some *Halo 4*?"

"No."

"Okay," Art said, sitting down across from Joel. "Still miss her, huh?"

"Who?"

"Felicity."

"Oh—uh, yeah. I guess." Joel did miss her, but there was a lot more to his melancholy than that.

"I miss her too," Art said, nodding. "She's a really great person. Not to mention an awesome guitar player."

"Yeah."

"So I don't blame you for feeling this way. Thing is, though, it's starting to make your mom a little worried."

"Did you tell her that worrying is a waste of time?"

Art chuckled. "Well, she hasn't really come out and said that she's worried, exactly, but I can tell. I think you can too."

Joel hung his head. It was true—he knew that his constantly dark mood had been putting stress on his whole family ever since he got back from Spectraland a little over three weeks ago. On top of that, it was also causing him problems at school, affecting his grades as well as his relationships with his teachers. He had to do something about it, and soon.

"Do you remember what you told me?" he said, looking back up at Art.

"About what?"

"Happiness...being a state of mind."

"Oh yeah, of course. That's one of my favorites."

"Well, if that's true, then how come I'm having such a hard time being happy?"

Art flashed a gentle smile. "Hey, I hear ya, bud. And, you know, I think I owe you an apology."

"You do? For what?"

"I may have given you some advice that was...how should I put it?"

"Wrong?"

"Incomplete." Art chuckled. "You see, happiness *is* a state of mind, but it's not something you can just flick on, like a light switch. It's more like playing music—it takes practice. And you have to do it every day, on a regular basis, in order to get really good at it."

"So...it's like your brain is practicing a happy song."

"Exactly. You're training it to have a positive outlook, basically. And there will be times when it's easier to do, and times when it's harder."

"Like now."

"Yup. I think this is the first real test you've experienced since I gave you that particular piece of advice. Life has been pretty good these past few months, you gotta admit."

Art was right, life *had* been pretty good. After Joel had met Felicity earlier this year, they'd formed an awesome rock band, gotten signed, and, oh yeah, they'd helped save Spectraland not once, not twice, but three times from the evil schemes of Joel's ex-idol turned archenemy, Marshall Byle.

But then things had gone south. Near the end of their third round of foiling Byle's plans, when they were also helping to liberate the Mono Realm—a.k.a. the Six States beneath the Shroud (Spectraland's continental neighbor)—from its oppressive ruler, Marshall had killed Auravine, the young Wavemaker healer who had professed her affection for Joel. He felt an enormous amount of grief and guilt over her death, as she had basically sacrificed herself to save him.

Then, on top of that, after he had returned home and informed everyone that Felicity wasn't coming back, his band had lost its spot opening for the multiplatinum rock act Sugarblood at an arena show in December. Apparently, Joel's group had been selected mostly because of the novelty of having both a boy and a girl on the autism spectrum in the same lineup, and Sugarblood's management didn't want to wait for them to find a suitable replacement. Since then, they hadn't even gotten together to practice, much less perform, and their very future as a band was in doubt.

"So yeah, you just have to keep at it," Art continued. "Always be reminding yourself about everything you have to be thankful for."

Like Marshall, that jerk, finally being dead, Joel thought.

"Also, maybe if you think about how Felicity is doing all those good things for the people on that island, that'll help too."

"Yeah, maybe."

Art stroked his goatee. "You know, when I was about your age, I went through something kind of similar. This girl I was dating in high school graduated and went away to college in another state. We tried the long-distance thing for a little while, but it didn't work out."

"She broke up with you?"

"No, I broke up with her."

"Why?"

"We just sort of grew apart." Art smiled. "Also, I found out she was seeing someone else behind my back."

"Oh."

"Yeah, I remember being pretty upset about it at the time."

"Is that when you started learning about happiness?"

Art chuckled. "Oh, no. I didn't do that until much, much later in life. I was a stubborn, angry young man for many years, for all kinds of silly reasons. People tried to help me, but I was very resistant to changing things, especially myself."

Joel glanced at Art, finding it hard to imagine him as anything other than a mellow, laid-back guy who constantly spouted cryptic philosophical sayings like some kind of mountaintop guru.

"Which is why I give you a lot of credit," Art went on. "You're open to personal growth."

"What does that mean?"

"You're receptive to new ideas that can help you improve your life and yourself. It's a very mature outlook to have, especially at your age."

"Um, okay."

"Anyway, is it all right if I tell your mom that you're gonna be fine?"

"Sure."

"Cool. I think she'll be—"

A soft melody sounded from under Joel's bed. It was the signal that someone from Spectraland—Felicity, probably—was trying to contact him.

Uh oh.

"What was that?" Art asked.

"What was what?"

The melody sounded again.

"That. It's like a...a ringtone, or something," Art said.

"Oh, uh, that. Yeah, um, it's my phone."

"You keep your phone under your bed?"

"No, I just...I dropped it, and then I accidentally kicked it under there. I was trying to find it when you knocked."

"Oh, gotcha. Do you need help?" Art bent over and squinted at the space underneath Joel's bed.

"No, no thanks," Joel replied, leaning over to block Art's view. "I got it. It's, uh, it's really messy under there. You know, dirty clothes, old food, that kind of stuff. Pretty embarrassing. I need to clean it up."

"Okay, well, I'll leave you to it," Art said, getting to his feet. "Join me for some video games later?"

"Yeah. Totally."

"Sweet." Art smiled as he left the room and closed the door.

After a moment, Joel exhaled and pulled his wavebow out. The strings were pulsing again. Another message. Joel plucked the high *E* string.

"Dude," Felicity's voice said, "are you still on Earth? If you are, you gotta leave *right now*. Fireflower just told me that if you don't, you're not only gonna miss the wedding, but you're gonna skip ahead, like, two or three or ten years or something. So hurry up and get over here!"

Aw man, I hate time pressure.

Joel got up, grabbed his backpack, and stuffed his wavebow into it. He was just about to run out when he remembered something.

Oh yeah—my loudstone. Can't leave without that.

He opened his desk drawer. His loudstone, a little yellow fragment that stored the power of the Aura (the energy that could be found not only within oneself, but also everywhere else in the known universe), was lying there next to a couple of quarters and a stick of peppermint gum. It was this artifact that allowed his wavebow to function continuously here on Earth, and it would also come in handy when he performed the particular wavecast—a melody that created magical effects—that would send him back to Spectraland. He picked it up and stuck it in his pocket.

Let's see...where am I gonna do this?

Joel opened his door and headed back toward the dining room, which blended with the living room in his family's little downtown Seattle apartment.

"I'm, uh, I'm going for a walk," he announced.

"Now?" Alison said, washing dishes.

"Yeah. You know, to clear my head, or whatever."

"Why do you have your backpack?"

"It, um, it makes me feel more comfortable," Joel improvised.

"Must be an autism thing," Taylor said, playing *Halo 4* with Art.

"Taylor!" Alison hissed.

"No, no, yeah, she's right," Joel said. "Totally an autism thing. I'll, uh, I'll be right back. I promise."

"Did you find your phone?" Art asked.

"Yeah."

"All right, well, be safe."

"I will."

Joel went out into the hall, which smelled strongly of burning turkey.

I'll just do it in the elevator, he decided.

He jogged over to the elevator door and looked up at the indicator. It showed that the elevator, already moving, was nearing his floor, the nineteenth.

Cool, he thought, pressing the "down" button.

A few moments passed.

Sixteen, seventeen...man, this thing is slow...

A few more moments went by. Then—*ding* went the elevator.

The door opened. Joel took a step forward.

"Oh, excuse me!" Mrs. Park—Joel's seventy-nine-year-old neighbor from three doors down—exclaimed, having almost walked right into him.

"Oh—uh, no, I'm sorry," Joel said. "My fault."

Mrs. Park and Joel did the awkward same-side-stepping dance for a couple of seconds before they finally maneuvered around each other. "Happy Thanksgiving," she said, laughing.

"Um, yeah—happy Thanksgiving," Joel replied as he held the elevator door open.

"Where are you going? Did you have dinner yet?"

Joel took a moment to process the double question. "I did, yes," he replied, choosing to ignore the first question.

"With your family?"

"Yes. My family."

"That's good. Oh—speaking of which, I have something for your mom."

"Um, okay."

"Hold on just one second...I have it in my purse here somewhere..."

As Mrs. Park rummaged through her unusually large purse, Joel heard a high *E* note from inside his backpack, followed by Felicity's muffled voice.

"Hello?" she said. "Joel, I know you're there. I didn't want to do it, but I had Blackspore look for you."

Mrs. Park glanced up from her purse. "Do you need to get that, dear?"

"Uh, no, it's fine."

"Dude," Felicity's voice said, "you have literally thirty seconds left, or I'm gonna be a great-grandma when you get here."

The elevator's nudge mode alarm started up.

"I'm sorry, dear, hold on," Mrs. Park said, "If I don't give it to her now, I'm sure I'll forget."

"She's, um, she's actually home right now," Joel said, thinking fast. "You can just go over there and give it to her."

"Oh! So...you're going somewhere by yourself?"

"Yeah. Bye!" Joel said, letting the door close.

"Fifteen seconds," Felicity said.

Trying to stay calm, Joel took his wavebow out of his backpack. As soon as he started playing, the elevator stopped on the eighteenth floor.

Dangit!

"Five seconds."

The doors began to open.

No, no, no, don't come in, Joel thought, pressing the "close" button with his nose while he continued playing.

"Four...three..."

C'mon, c'mon, c'mon...

"Two...one..."

Darkness.

CHAPTER 2: SHOWERS

Joel blinked several times. Everything was blurry, making him concerned that he had accidentally wound up somewhere else (*I forgot to use my loudstone!* he realized), but then, after a few moments, he saw that he was standing atop the offshore islet of Crownrock, where the Rift—the main gateway between Earth and Spectraland—was located. It was the middle of the day, and the sun was out, but a light rain was falling; "liquid sunshine," they called it back in Hawai'i.

Shielding his eyes, Joel scanned the shore. According to one of Felicity's previous messages, the wedding was supposed to take place here, on the beach, but he didn't see anyone for miles in either direction.

Uh oh—did I miss it?

He played a lick on his wavebow. Seven seconds passed, and there was no response, not even Felicity's "leave a message" message. He tried again. Another seven seconds ticked by. Still nothing. He tried once more. Then, finally—

"Hello?" Felicity's voice said through his instrument. She sounded...old. "Who is this?"

"Hey, um, Felicity, it's me."

"Me who?"

"Me—Joel. I'm here. Where is everybody?"

"Joel...oh, Joel! Yes, I remember now." She coughed. "We used to play in a band together, right?"

"Right."

"Boy, I haven't seen you in ages. What are you doing in Spectraland?"

"I'm...I'm here for your wedding."

"My what?"

"Your wedding."

"I'm sorry, you'll have to speak up. My hearing isn't what it used to be."

"*Your wedding*. I'm here for your wedding."

"Oh!" She laugh-coughed. "You're a bit late for that, I'm afraid."

The liquid sunshine turned heavier. "I am? How late?"

"Eh...a bit. Why don't you come over to the Wavemaker Temple and I'll tell you all about it."

"Um, okay."

The strings on Joel's wavebow dimmed. He put up the hood on his hooded sweatshirt, but just as he did so, the precipitation abated.

Okay, just a passing shower. Good. I wasn't looking forward to flying through the rain.

He performed the flying wavecast and took off, shooting through Crownrock's golden dome of protective Aura and up into the sky. Despite the fact that the flying cast required a good deal of focus and concentration, he found his thoughts wandering as he soared over the tropical landscape.

I wonder just how many years have gone by. Felicity was nineteen, so if she's a great-grandma now, she'd probably be around, what, Mrs. Park's age? Seventy-nine? So that would be sixty years...yikes.

As Joel tried to come up with an acceptable way to explain and apologize for his extreme tardiness, the Wavemaker Temple, surrounded by a protective Aura dome of its own, came into view. It didn't look much different from when he'd last left it.

Wait a minute, he thought, flying through the dome (it was made so that Wavemakers could pass right through). *What if she's pranking me? I bet she is.*

He landed at the top of the stairs right in front of the main entrance. Putting on his best approximation of a smirk, he knocked on the large wooden double doors. Twelve seconds passed. Then, just as he was about to knock again, the doors creaked open.

"Okay, good one," he said. "You really had me going there for a—"

Someone, a woman, peeked out from between the doors. She had short white hair and her pale face was lined with wrinkles.

"Joel?" she croaked.

Joel's eyes grew wide. "Um...Felicity?"

"Wow, I can't believe you're here," she said, pulling the giant doors all the way open with extreme effort. "I tried calling you for years, but there was no answer, not even the message tone. I guess you were in transit."

"Uh, yeah, I, well..." he stammered.

"C'mon in."

Joel walked in. The temple's main hall was as beautiful as ever, with multicolored waves of Aura swirling around everywhere he looked.

"Nice, huh?" Felicity said. "My grandkids do a pretty good job with the upkeep."

"Your grandkids?"

"That's what I just"—she paused to hack and cough—"said. Or is it? I dunno, sometimes I forget."

"Look, I'm really sorry I missed the window," Joel said, launching into his preplanned apology. "I was sure I was going to make it, but then I ran into my neighbor in the elevator, and she said she had something for my mom, so then I had to—"

"Well, maybe if you had returned some of my calls, we could've prevented all of that last-second business!" Felicity snapped, abruptly angry. "At the time, I gave you the benefit of the doubt, but after thinking about it for a few decades, I realized that you were just avoiding me. And now look what happened—you missed my entire life!"

Joel gulped. She was right—he *had* been avoiding her, and now he felt very guilty about that. "I'm—I'm really, really sorry. I just—"

"Oh, stop apologizing already," she said with a dismissive wave. "That's not gonna do any good. Remember what you told me once, all those years ago? 'You can't change the past, no matter how much you regret things you have or haven't done.'"

"Um, yeah. I guess I did say that."

"Anyway," Felicity chuckled, "why don't you come out back? You can meet everyone."

Confused but relieved by Felicity's suddenly brightened demeanor, Joel followed her as she slowly walked toward an open doorway at the far end of the hall. "So, um, is Thornleaf still alive?" he asked. "And Redstem? What about Riverhand and Windblade?"

Felicity turned and grinned at him. "You'll see."

They passed through the doorway and into the arboretum-like courtyard area where Auravine once performed a healing incantation on Joel, seemingly—and now, in reality, he realized—so long ago. The golden grass felt like lush carpet beneath his feet, and spouts of water from the courtyard fountain twirled and spiraled around each other in midair, just like he remembered them doing way back when. No one else was around, although he could see faint outlines of what looked like people standing in front of the trees that bordered the area.

"What's...what's going on here?" he asked, squinting. "Are they..."

Before Joel could finish his question, the air around him shimmered and the outlines filled themselves in, revealing a group of seven familiar individuals.

"Surprise!" they yelled in unison.

"Whoa!" Joel exclaimed. "What the—?" He scanned everyone's faces. His fellow Wavemakers—Thornleaf, Redstem, Riverhand, Windblade, and even Fireflower—were all there, along with Thinker and Keeper, his gray-skinned, alien-looking friends from the Six States. None of them appeared to be any older than they had been when he last saw them.

"Gotcha!" Felicity chortled, slapping Joel on the back. "Oh, dude, you should have seen your face. It was classic."

"But I—you—if they're—then why are you..."

"Old?" She turned to Fireflower. "Show him, boss."

Fireflower, the diminutive Wavemaker leader, stepped forward and played a melody on her wavebow. As she did so, Felicity's features gradually changed; her wrinkles disappeared, and her locks grew out to the middle of her back, resuming their normal golden hue.

"Oh," Joel said, realizing what was going on, "you used a...a..."

"Shapeshifting cast," Felicity finished his sentence as she shook out her hair. "Which, I found out, is technically forbidden, just like invisibility. But I managed to talk Fireflower into letting us do both, just for the sake of punking you."

Fireflower flashed a mischievous smile. "Welcome back, Joel."

"So then I'm not too late?"

"You are actually a little early," Fireflower answered. "We are conducting a prewedding celebration ritual for Thornleaf and Miss Felicity. She wanted to make sure you attended."

"I guess it's sorta like a minireception, or a bridal shower," Felicity explained to Joel. "But don't worry about a present. Your expression when you saw me is more than enough."

"The ritual is taking place in the dining hall," Fireflower said. "Shall we?"

Together, the group headed up a series of celery-stalk ramps and thick, vinelike walkways that led toward the upper middle section of the structure (technically, they could have just flown up, but in a nonemergency situation like this, doing so was considered gratuitous and excessive, kind of like lighting a candle with a flamethrower). Along the way, Joel learned that only seven Spectraland months had passed since he was last here but quite a lot had happened during that relatively short period of time. Thinker—with his knowledge of Six States technology and his skills as an inventor—had introduced the concept of the wheel, which quickly led to the development of not only slimeback-drawn wagons but also a rudimentary prototype of a self-propelled vehicle that sort of resembled a quadracycle, which the natives had appropriately dubbed a fourwheel. Also, the

Silencers—a group of villagers who were once opposed to the existence of the Wavemaker Order—had finally resolved their differences with the Wavemakers and signed a treaty of peace and cooperation that was aptly named the Auravine Accord. And on a smaller but no less significant note, Starpollen—Auravine's younger brother, who could barely talk but possessed some unique Aura-manipulating abilities—had made his first friend: a girl his age (around eleven, the same age as Taylor) from the village of Spearwind.

They arrived at the dining hall—a large rectangular hut resting on a lily pad–like platform—and entered. Inside, Joel saw two more familiar faces: Blackspore, the master Wavemaker who had assisted with the liberation of the Six States, seated by himself at the end of a long surfboard-shaped table, and Yellowpetal, Fireflower's mother, cutting up what appeared to be a giant blue cake.

"Joel! Hello!" Yellowpetal waved with her free hand.

Joel waved back. "Hello."

Blackspore looked up from a set of parchments that were spread out on the table in front of him. "Ah, Joel, good to see you again."

"Um, good to see you too."

"Ye old master shaman here didn't want to take part in our little prank," Felicity scoffed good-naturedly as she sat down on a wooden stool at the opposite end of the table. "Said it was too mean, or something."

Blackspore smiled. "I did my part by locating him for you."

"Sure, yeah, whatever."

Everyone else, including Joel, took a seat as well. Yellowpetal began distributing pieces of the cake-looking foodstuff on small wooden plates.

"What is this?" Joel asked.

"It is...ah..." Yellowpetal looked at Felicity. "What did you call this again?"

"Lifepod cake," Felicity answered. She turned back to Joel. "I figured out a recipe. Turns out you can make flour from those cattails at the Groaning Geyser."

"Oh—um, cool."

"So," Blackspore said to Joel as other conversations buzzed around them, "how have you been?"

"All right, I guess," Joel responded. It wasn't a total lie.

"Glad to hear." Blackspore leaned forward. He had a strange expression on his face, one that Joel couldn't quite decipher. "After this, I would like you to come with me down to the archives. I have something to share with you."

"Um, okay."

"Cake!" someone screamed from behind, causing Joel to whirl around. It was Starpollen, with Sammy the silvertail—a native Spectraland animal that resembled a cross between a squirrel and a monkey—perched on his shoulder. Behind the young boy was a girl of a similar age that Joel didn't recognize, although she did look a bit like Taylor, with a button-shaped nose and shoulder-length black hair.

"Yes, it is time for cake." Yellowpetal smiled. "Did you two have fun playing with the slimebacks?"

"Fun!" Starpollen exclaimed.

"Joel," Fireflower said, gesturing toward Starpollen's companion, "this is Seaberry, Starpollen's friend from Spearwind."

Joel waved. "Hello."

"Hi," Seaberry said, returning his wave.

The two children sat at the table as Yellowpetal served them pieces of cake. As Joel looked around for a fork or some other kind of utensil, he noticed that everyone was eating with their hands. He decided not to follow suit.

"So, uh, what did you want to share with me?" he asked Blackspore.

"Not now," the middle-aged shaman replied, his mouth full. "I will show you later."

The so-called minireception/bridal shower continued on, with Joel sitting mostly in silence while the other attendees made short speeches about their favorite Thornleaf-and-Felicity moments—most of which seemed to have happened during the time when Joel wasn't around—before presenting the couple with little gifts that were wrapped in leaves and/or parchment. Then, after all the gifts were opened, the group encouraged Thornleaf and Felicity to kiss. Joel wanted to look away, but for whatever reason, his gaze remained fixed in their general direction, as if he were gawking at a car accident. He was prepared to cringe, but when Thornleaf leaned in toward his soon-to-be-bride, she held up her hand and ducked away.

"Ew, not now, I told you," she said, sounding irritated. An awkward moment of silence ensued.

Joel narrowed his eyes. *Wait, what just happened?* he wondered. *Is she just kidding around? I know she doesn't really like physical contact, especially in public...or is she mad at Thornleaf about something? Hard to tell.*

"Well, that concludes the ritual," Fireflower said, standing and clapping her hands together. "As you all know, the wedding ceremony will take place tomorrow morning, so I would like everyone—the happy couple excluded, of course—to please spend the remainder of the day seeing to the tasks I assigned each of you earlier. Thank you."

As everyone began filing out of the hut, Felicity walked up to Joel. "Hey, dude. You don't have any jobs to do, so you should come hang out with me and Thornleaf in the backyard. We're gonna practice wavebow dueling. It'll be fun."

"Oh—well, I, uh, I have to, um—"

"I will be borrowing Joel for a while," Blackspore intervened. "Unlike the rest of you, I have not had the chance to catch up with him yet."

Felicity rolled her eyes. "Fine." She turned to leave, and Fireflower stepped up into her spot.

"You are going to show him your findings now, I assume?" The Wavemaker leader addressed Blackspore with a serious look.

"Yes, I am," Blackspore responded.

"Good." Fireflower nodded. "Remember, I am trusting you to do this in an appropriate manner while I oversee the wedding preparations."

"Fireflower, relax," Blackspore said. "I was a master Wavemaker long before you even knew how to tune your instrument."

"An exaggeration that you never tire of repeating," Fireflower said. Neither she nor Blackspore were smiling, so Joel deduced that this was probably not friendly banter. "Just be careful," she said. And with that, she exited the hut.

"I will, Mother," Blackspore sighed.

"Wait, Fireflower's your mother?" Joel asked. It was a fair question; chronologically, Blackspore was older than Fireflower by at least a decade, but when the magic of wavecasts and the Aura was involved, anything could be possible, he reasoned.

"No, of course not," Blackspore replied. "Now, come with me."

Joel followed Blackspore down a twisting series of vine walkways. Neither of them spoke until they arrived at a small pyramid-shaped hut on the ground level.

"While you were away," the master shaman said, unsealing the hut's door by pressing his forearm to it, "I managed to discover and decipher some information that I think you will find most interesting." He pulled the door open and motioned for Joel to enter.

"Okay," Joel said, walking into the hut, "but I don't understand why you couldn't have just—"

"Hello, legendary—*hic*—offworlder," a voice said.

Darkeye!

CHAPTER 3: THE VIRTUOSO VISION

Blackspore!" Joel exclaimed, pulling his wavebow into playing position. "Darkeye—he's here! In the temple! We need to—"

"Calm down, Joel," Blackspore said, grabbing Joel's arm. "I know he is here. He is allowed to be here."

"What? Why?"

"Remember that deal you struck with him? At the Town below the Mountain?"

"Oh, yeah...right," Joel mumbled, recalling the details of said deal: in exchange for information about Marshall Byle's location, Darkeye was to be granted full access to the Wavemaker archives, among other things.

"As it turns out," Blackspore said, "having him here has proven quite beneficial, actually. With his assistance, I have been able to translate many old writings that no one has ever been able to figure out before."

"But...is he in here alone? Unsupervised?"

"He is."

"Isn't that a little, I dunno, risky?"

Darkeye made a sound that was like a cross between choking and chuckling. "If you recall, a—*hic*—condition of our deal was that if I did anything—*hic*—illegal under

Spectraland law, then the whole agreement would become—*hic*—null and void," the wizened old native said, his lips forming a toothless smile. "I certainly would not want to jeopardize my—*hic*—freedom by doing anything foolish."

"Well, I guess that makes sense," Joel said, mostly to himself.

"Besides," Blackspore said, "we have him under an alarm cast that will trigger if he wanders into any areas he should not be in. Which is basically anywhere but here."

"Okay," Joel said, still a little wary. "So...anyway, are you going to tell me now? About the thing—whatever it is?"

Blackspore took a deep breath. "Do you recall what I told you in the limbo plane, about all the visions that master Wavemakers have had about you over the years?"

Joel hated it when people answered a question with a question, but he assumed that Blackspore was trying to get to the point. "Um, yeah."

"I thought all the records of those visions had been destroyed, but I was wrong," the master shaman said. "As it turns out, one of them survived."

He stepped forward. Joel followed. The interior of the hut was dim and musty. Sheets of parchment were strewn about everywhere, and the walls were lined with wooden shelves filled with stacks of scrolls. In the middle of the hut stood something that looked like a folding music stand made out of tree branches.

"Darkeye," Blackspore said, stopping in front of the stand, "the document, please."

"I do not believe being your—*hic*—assistant was part of the deal."

"I only ask because you had it last."

Darkeye grabbed a parchment from one of the shelves and handed it over to Blackspore, who placed it on the stand like a piece of sheet music. The master Wavemaker then took out his wavebow and proceeded to play a complex tune that reminded Joel of the concert band song "Incantation and Dance" by John Barnes Chance. After a few seconds, a white stream of Aura snaked out of the instrument's headstock, flowed through the parchment, and formed a large swirling globe in the middle of the space.

"I, uh, I still don't get it," Joel said.

"Patience." Blackspore sniffed.

The Aura-globe turned into something resembling a giant crystal ball, and an image of a native Spectraland woman appeared inside it. Her close-cropped gray hair framed an elegant, handsome face, and she wore what appeared to be a dress made entirely out of feathers (which Joel found odd, seeing as how there were no birds to speak of in Spectraland). In her hands was a gold-tinted wavebow, which she started to play. As the seconds ticked by, her song gradually grew louder, as if someone were turning up the volume.

"Is this, like, a video or something?" Joel asked.

"Shh," Blackspore shushed.

Then, to Joel's surprise, the woman began to sing.

A master shaman from another world
His gift of sight becomes unfurled
Of time and distance, he is aware
A special sense beyond compare

The woman stopped singing but continued to play her instrument.

"I assume you know she is talking about you," Blackspore said, looking at Joel.

"Oh—she is? Um, okay."

The woman started singing again.

From long exile, one will return
To guide this master and help him learn
With proper training and practice long
His talents grow, as does his song

Another instrumental passage ensued.

"That particular verse refers to me, and my role in helping you," Blackspore said.

Joel just nodded. He was busy marveling at how these lyrics, when translated from the Spectraland language, were rhyming perfectly in English.

Until one day his skills will sum
And the Virtuoso he shall become
Able to travel through time and space
Without a limit for him to face

"Wait, what?" Joel said. "What did she say?"

"Just keep listening," Blackspore replied.

But all are warned to take great care
To keep him safe from temptation's snare
For with these powers, he is ordained
To save existence from evil's reign

The woman continued playing for a few seconds, and then both the image and the music slowly faded out. The Aura-globe dissipated in a shower of sparks.

"So," Blackspore said, "what are your thoughts?"

Joel wasn't sure. "Um, I dunno. What does this all mean, exactly?"

"It means that you are the one destined to become...the Virtuoso."

"The what?"

"The Virtuoso. The most powerful Wavemaker ever to live. And as such, it will be your duty to save the entire universe from destruction."

"Whoa," Joel said. "Seriously?"

"Yes. I realize that sounds like a rather monumental task. Even a burden, perhaps."

"Well, a little, yeah."

"That is why, even though this destiny was foretold in a vision, ultimately, it is up to you. You can choose to either accept or refuse this responsibility."

Joel gulped. After all of his previous adventures in Spectraland and the Six States, he felt that he had amassed a fair amount of experience with saving the day. But this whole Virtuoso business sounded like an entirely new level altogether. Was he ready for this?

"If you decide to accept, know that I will be here to guide you at every step along the way," Blackspore said. "The vision you just heard assures us that as long as you have my help, you can and will succeed."

That gave Joel a measure of comfort. After all, Blackspore *was* the last true master shaman (Fireflower having been largely self-taught after Marshall wiped out the rest of the Wavemaker Order), and he had a vast store of knowledge and experience that Joel was sure would come in handy.

And didn't the vision say something about being able to travel through both time and space? Man, how sweet would *that* be? Joel started to feel excited. If it was true, he would be able to do all sorts of awesome stuff, like preventing wars, visiting different worlds, and maybe even...*saving Auravine.*

"Think it over," Blackspore said, putting a hand on Joel's shoulder. "You do not have to decide right—"

"I'll do it."

Blackspore blinked. "Are you certain?"

"Yeah. Because, well, you know...sometimes, you just gotta say, what the heck. And go with it."

"Very well, then." Blackspore smiled. "In that case, we can get started now, if you wish."

"What are we gonna do?"

"To begin with, I have two wavecasts to teach you. One allows you to travel through space. The other allows you to travel through time. We will go slowly at first to determine exactly where your present skill level lies."

Joel glanced at Darkeye, still feeling a bit uneasy about the old potion-maker's presence; it seemed like this was a lot of sensitive information to be talking about in front of him. Darkeye just grinned in response.

"Okay," Joel said, figuring that if Blackspore was cool with Darkeye being here, then he shouldn't be concerned. "Are we doing it in here?"

"No, in the training chamber." Blackspore turned to Darkeye. "Darkeye, fetch me the appropriate parchments."

"Now that time, it really—*hic*—did sound like you consider me your—*hic*—assistant. Or servant, even."

Blackspore sighed. "Do we have to go over this again?"

"Um, it's okay," Joel said. "I don't need sheet music. I can just follow whatever you play."

"Very well," Blackspore said. "Darkeye, you remain here."

"Naturally," Darkeye purred.

Joel followed Blackspore out of the hut. As they strode across a wooden walkway, the master shaman began to speak. "The space-travel cast that I will show you is actually just short-range teleportation," he said. "Limited in distance, but much more flexible than the transfer or portal casts. It is the one I used to get past the Forbidden Tides. As you may recall me saying, I developed it by observing the movements of swordcats."

"Yeah, I remember that."

"The time-travel cast, which I started composing a long time ago but only recently completed, is also limited. When I have performed it, I have only been able to go backward in time a few minutes at most. But I think that with practice, your limits for both of these casts will eventually stretch out much farther than mine."

Blackspore opened the door to another hut, this one a large, dome-shaped structure with a high ceiling. It was mostly empty, save for a few straw-dummies scattered about. The master shaman walked in, stopped, and moved his wavebow into playing position.

"We will start with space travel. Are you ready?"

"Um, sure." Joel raised his wavebow as well.

Blackspore proceeded to play a complicated, almost neoclassical-sounding run that he repeated over and over again. While doing so he said, "As with most wavecasts, you simply have to envision your desired outcome. For this demonstration, I am going to picture myself teleporting to the opposite end of the chamber." A cloud of silvery-gold Aura emerged from his instrument's headstock and engulfed him. Then, in a flash, he disappeared and reappeared next to the far wall of the hut.

"Your turn," he said.

Joel picked out a spot some nineteen feet away, next to one of the straw-dummies. He played the run, producing a cloud of Aura energy similar to Blackspore's. The moment the cloud finished surrounding him, he felt a slight tugging sensation—similar to what he felt while riding a teleporting swordcat—after which he realized that he was now standing in the exact spot he had been looking at, nineteen feet from his original position.

"Very good," Blackspore said, walking up. "I figured you would not have much trouble with that one. Now, for time travel." He began playing a pattern of licks that Joel could have sworn came straight out of Marty McFly's guitar solo in *Back to the Future*. A multicolored stream of Aura flowed out and wrapped itself around the master shaman. Then, a moment later, he abruptly vanished.

Joel waited a few seconds. When nothing happened, he said, "Blackspore? Are you there?"

As if in response, the door to the hut opened and Blackspore came walking in. "I just traveled back ten minutes," he announced. "Did I miss anything?"

Joel grinned. "Cool."

"All right, now you try it. Do not go too far back. Just a few minutes will be fine."

Joel played the pattern of licks and imagined himself going back ten minutes as well. His wavebow generated the appropriate polychromatic Aura stream, which then coiled around him like a snake. It stayed in place for a few seconds before fading away. Joel looked around.

"Did it...did it work?"

"Hmm," Blackspore said. "I do not think so. Try again."

Joel tried again. Same result.

"What are you envisioning?" Blackspore asked.

"Going back ten minutes, just like you."

"All right, once more."

Joel tried a third time. And a fourth. And a fifth. Still, nothing. He bent over to catch his breath.

"I do not understand," Blackspore muttered, sounding disappointed. "Perhaps you are not fated to become the Virtuoso after all."

"No," Joel said in between gasps, "don't—don't worry. I've got this. I have an idea."

"Oh?"

"I can use this." Joel pulled his loudstone out of his pants pocket.

Blackspore nodded. "Yes...yes, that just might work. Go ahead, try it."

Joel pressed the loudstone against his temple. A surge of energy shot through his body, so intense that his knees nearly buckled. Then, after putting the loudstone back into his pocket, he closed his eyes and played the time-travel cast.

Go back ten minutes...ten minutes...ten minutes...

He began to feel a bit queasy, but it was nothing like when he traveled from Earth to Spectraland; if anything, the sensation was more similar to anxiety than nausea. A ringing noise started up in his ears as the sound of his own wavebow became distorted. As he continued to play, the noise morphed into a loud, constant *whoosh* that resembled the roar of a rushing river. He wanted to stop, but it was like something had taken control of his fingers, forcing him to keep going.

Then, after what felt like a very long time (but was actually only twelve seconds), the noise abruptly ceased. Joel's eyes snapped open. The hut was gone. Blackspore was gone. There were seaweed-palm trees everywhere, along with a narrow river.

Did it...did it work?

Just then, he spotted something: about twenty feet away, an animal that resembled a cross between a tiger and a ram was standing among the trees, drinking from the river. It looked similar to Nineteen, the powerful and mysterious creature that had helped Joel during some of his previous adventures, except that its horns had a slightly different curvature.

Wait, Joel thought, *weren't all of those guys supposed to be extinct, except for Nineteen, who now lives in an alternate plane? Maybe I should try talking to it...*

"Um—hello?" Joel called.

The creature looked up. Joel expected it to communicate telepathically with him, just as Nineteen had done before, but nothing happened.

"Hello?" Joel repeated.

The creature turned and started to run.

"Wait!" Joel said. "Come back! I won't hurt you, I promise!"

But the creature didn't listen. As Joel watched it disappear into the distance, he suddenly felt a warm gust of wind at his back. The gust was followed by a low, guttural growl.

Uh oh.

Joel slowly turned around. There was another creature standing there behind him, but this one was much, much larger and resembled a brontosaurus with glowing eyes and luminescent scales.

"Um...hello," Joel said. "I'm hoping you're a vegetarian?"

Screeeeeeeeech! the creature roared, revealing rows of sharp, serrated teeth—three deep on both the top and bottom.

"Okay, maybe not." Joel raised his wavebow and fired a stunning cast that hit the creature right between the eyes. It blinked a couple of times, but it didn't go down; instead, it reared its head and roared again.

Screeeeeeeeech!

Joel took a couple of steps back. The creature took a step forward, growling and stretching out its neck as it did so. Joel took a step to the left. The creature's head followed him with surprising swiftness. Joel took a step to the right. Same result. He thought about flying, but he figured that the creature would probably gulp him up like a lizard swallowing a moth. He thought about trying short-range teleportation, but he wasn't fully confident in his ability just yet (materializing inside of the creature was a distinct possibility, one he wanted to avoid). That left running, but even that wasn't a good option; the creature was blocking the space in front of him, while the river was to his back. He looked over his shoulder in an effort to gauge if he could possibly jump over the river, seeing as how he certainly couldn't swim across it (he still didn't know how to swim).

Well, it's narrow, but it's not that narrow...it's about fifteen feet wide—there's no way I can jump that far. But wait a minute...fifteen feet...and I recognize the shape. This is the river in the clearing in front of the Wavemaker Temple. I must be close to the same spot I was in, I just went too far back in time. Like, way too far back. Maybe if I...

Joel raised his wavebow again and started playing the time-travel cast.

Screeeeeeeeech! the creature roared once more.

Joel continued playing, trying very hard to imagine himself back in the training chamber with Blackspore.

C'mon, c'mon, c'mon...

The queasy feeling started to set in. While he played, Joel kept slowly backing up until he was standing at the edge of the river. The creature kept pace with him and was now right in front of him. There was nowhere left to go.

C'mon, c'mon, c'mon...

Joel heard the ringing sound, which only turned into the rushing river noise after what felt like a dangerously long period of time. The creature opened its toothy maw, its jaw unhinging like a snake's. Joel squeezed his eyes shut. He was certain he was going to be eaten when suddenly—

"Joel?"

Joel opened his eyes. He was back.

"Did something happen?" Blackspore said. "You seemed to shimmer there for a moment, but I was not sure if..."

"Oh yeah," Joel exhaled, "something happened, all right."

CHAPTER 4: HAVING DOUBTS

Alone in the temple's guest hut, Joel tossed and turned as he lay on his raised sleeping mat. The events of the afternoon had left him exhausted but excited, unable to sleep.

Time travel—I really did it!

After they'd finished practicing for the day, Blackspore told Joel that, at the moment, no one else knew about the Virtuoso Vision besides the two of them, Fireflower, and Darkeye, the latter of whom had been sworn to secrecy. The reasoning was that Joel needed to accept the responsibility first, otherwise it would be a moot point, and there was no sense in unnecessarily distracting the others from Thornleaf and Felicity's impending big day. If Joel did accept, then after the wedding, Blackspore and Fireflower would request an audience with the Chieftain Council (which now included Chief Sandthroat of the Roughrock Tribe) to obtain the proper approvals, a process that would admittedly take some time. Then, assuming the chiefs gave their blessing, Joel would remain in Spectraland for as long as it took for him to master his new skills, even past the window allowing him to return home on Thanksgiving night; after all, once he became a bona fide time traveler, such windows would no longer be relevant to him.

Still too excited, Joel got up off the mat, figuring he would go for a walk while reviewing his mental list of all the awesome time/space travelers he could follow in the footsteps of.

Just think, he thought, strolling out into the double-moonlight, *I can be just like the Doctor, or Hermione Granger, or Kyle Reese, or the Enterprise crew in* Star Trek IV: The Voyage Home...*but for real!*

And after I save Auravine, maybe I'll even get a second chance at love. Especially now that Felicity won't be single anymore...or will she? What if I went back in time and made it so that she and Thornleaf never...?

Giddy, Joel did a little skip step as he headed for the dining hall to see if there was any lifepod cake left. As he approached the base of one of the celery-stalk ramps, he heard voices coming from the courtyard.

"...must tread very carefully," one of the voices was saying. It was Fireflower.

"Yes, yes, I know," the other voice—Blackspore's—responded. "With my guidance, he will be fine. Trust me."

"Trusting you is something I am still working on."

"Fair enough. But what about him? You trust him, do you not?"

"Of course, it is just..."

"Just what?"

"Too much power can corrupt even the best of us. You know that. It happened to Graymold. It can happen to anyone. And Joel has shown signs of having a dark side. You told me that yourself."

"All right, I admit, there was that incident in the Six States..."

"When he tapped into the Aura of anger?"

"Yes. But that is why having me as his mentor is so important. I understand his pain, more than anyone else. I can help him. I *will* help him."

"Like how you helped your village win the Fourfoot War by summoning Marshall Byle to our island?"

"That is something completely different, and you know it."

"I am not so sure," Fireflower muttered.

"This needs to be done. It has been foretold."

"I understand that. But even if he does not stray...what about the potential for timeline damage?"

"You worry too much."

Fireflower sighed. "The energy is telling me that this is the correct path. Still, though, I cannot help but feel great concern."

"And this is where your inexperience shows," Black-spore said.

"Believe me, I have much more experience than you know," Fireflower retorted, her voice turning steely. "While you were busy languishing in self-exile, I—"

"Fireflower?" a third voice interrupted, that of a young girl.

"Seaberry? Why are you awake, my dear? We all have a big day tomorrow."

"I could not sleep," Seaberry replied. "It is...I am having the feelings again."

"Oh—I am sorry to hear that," Fireflower said sympathetically. "Did the mantra I taught you not help?"

"Mm-mm."

"All right, well, I will prepare some warm tea for you in a moment."

"Okay."

"Blackspore, we will continue this discussion after the wedding."

"Very well."

Not wanting Blackspore or Fireflower to know that he had eavesdropped on their conversation, Joel turned and slunk away from the courtyard, hoping they wouldn't notice him through the trees. Now feeling unsettled instead of excited, he returned to the guest hut and slept in fits and starts until the morning finally arrived.

♪♪♪

The wedding ceremony turned out to be a much larger event than Joel had anticipated. With an hour still to go before the actual proceedings, over two hundred villagers from all over the island had already gathered on the beach near Crownrock, with more arriving every minute. After meeting and attempting to make small talk with many familiar faces, Joel retreated to the safety and seclusion of a temporary hut reserved for special guests, where he found Blackspore sitting at a round stone table nursing a distinctly alcoholic-smelling beverage.

"Care to join me?" the master Wavemaker said, holding up his cup.

"Join you? I'm already here."

"I meant for a drink."

"Oh—uh, no thanks," Joel said, sitting down on a small stool next to the table. "I'm only seventeen."

"Ah, yes, I forgot. Your homeland observes a slightly different custom."

"So...why aren't you outside?" Joel changed the subject, feeling uncomfortable for some reason. "You know, mingling, or whatever."

Blackspore smiled. "Despite my official pardon from the chiefs, I am still, shall we say, a bit unpopular with certain members of the population. As I am sure you can imagine."

"Oh—right. Because of the whole bringing-Marshall-to-Spectraland thing."

"Indeed." Blackspore refilled his cup from a tall wooden pitcher. "Joel, there is something I must tell you."

"Um, okay."

"As the Virtuoso, you will have the power to set a great many things right. You will be able to change history for the better."

"Assuming I stay out of—what did the vision say?—'temptation's snare'."

"I am not concerned about that at all, for I know you to be a man of the highest character."

"Um, yeah, you know, about that...I'm not really sure if I am."

"Ah, right, still only seventeen. Not quite a man yet, at least not in your world."

"No, no, I mean I'm not of the highest character."

Blackspore raised an eyebrow. "Now, why would you say that?"

"Well...I get angry," Joel replied. "I get jealous. I hold grudges. And sometimes I have bad thoughts. Selfish thoughts." *Like about using my new powers to make sure Felicity and Thornleaf never meet*, he added silently.

"That is only natural. All of us feel like that from time to time. It does not make you a bad person."

"I guess, but shouldn't the Virtuoso be someone who's, like, even less bad? I mean, it's easy for us to say now that I won't abuse these powers, but who knows what'll happen once I actually master them? What if I turn into a bad guy? A villain?"

"Joel, listen to me," Blackspore said. "I have faith in you. All of us do. You have already proven yourself worthy time and time again. And with my guidance, you will be able to handle this challenge as well." He paused to take a sip. "That is my promise to you. As long as I am here, you will have nothing to worry about."

"I still don't know..."

Blackspore set his cup down hard, causing a few drops to fly out. "Are you trying to tell me that you are having second thoughts?" he snapped.

"Um, no," Joel answered, startled by Blackspore's sudden mood swing. It reminded him a lot of his dad. "Or maybe—maybe I am. I thought you said I had a choice?"

"And I thought you had the courage to take this on! Are you letting fear control you now? Is the burden too much for you?"

"What? No, I just think that if I—"

Blackspore drained the remainder of his cup in one gulp and stood up. "If you will excuse me, I believe I will do some mingling after all." And with that, he stumbled out of the hut.

Joel remained in his seat, flustered and confused.

Why did he get so mad? I was only trying to make sure this whole thing is a good idea. I mean, if Fireflower was worried about it, then—

"There you are!" Redstem peeked into the hut. "We are starting the fanfare in a few minutes. Did Windblade not tell you?"

"Um, no. I mean, yes. I mean—what fanfare?"

"I am going to kill that boy," Redstem groaned. "We—you, me, Windblade, and Riverhand—are performing the music for the ceremony. First, we will open with a short fanfare, and then that is to be followed by the processional march. Come with me. I will go over it with you along the way."

Joel walked with Redstem through the crowd of assembled guests, trying his best to pay attention to her as she described the chords and hummed the melodies that they were going to play. After a minute (fifty-two seconds, actually), they arrived at the spot where the ceremony was to take place. There, a small round stage supporting an arch and a lattice backdrop stood about twenty feet away from the shoreline. It was surrounded by exotic, elaborate floral arrangements, and rows of wooden chairs arranged in front of the stage in semicircles went back ten deep. Windblade and Riverhand were standing by the first row, wavebows in hand.

"Windblade!" Redstem exclaimed. "You were supposed to tell Master Joel about the music!"

"Oh—I apologize," Windblade said, looking chagrined. "He was busy with Master Blackspore all afternoon yesterday, and then I got occupied and then...well, I guess it slipped my mind."

"Excuses, excuses," Redstem muttered.

"It's okay," Joel said. "I got it. I'm ready."

"Yes, relax, Redstem," Riverhand said. "You have been uptight all morning."

"You would be too, if you were the one in charge of these proceedings." Redstem shook her head. "And now we are a minute late. Let us get started."

The four of them took up spots in front of the stage, raised their wavebows, and began to play. The fanfare was a simple but dramatic-sounding tune, and it had the added effect of creating a sparkling rainbow-hued halo of Aura over the immediate area. Aware of their cue, all of the attendees began to gravitate toward the stage. The first two rows of chairs were taken up by the chiefs and other favored guests—including Thinker, Keeper, and even Thornleaf's father Stoneroot, who had been granted a one-day parole from prison so that he could attend his son's wedding—while the rest of the chairs were occupied on a first-come, first-served basis. Once they were all filled up, the remainder of the guests gathered around in standing-room-only fashion. There was just one noticeable absence: Blackspore.

Maybe he passed out or something, Joel figured.

At that point, he and the others switched to the processional music, which was a repeating motif bearing an uncanny resemblance to the verse melody from R.E.M.'s "The One I Love."

I wonder if Felicity suggested that, Joel thought, *or if it's just a coincidence. Probably a little bit of both.*

As he continued to play, the wedding party started to emerge from a nearby temporary hut. First came Thornleaf's friend Whitenose, performing the role of what Joel assumed was the "best man," albeit while carrying a rather dangerous-looking spear. Thornleaf himself followed shortly thereafter, decked out in the Spectraland equivalent of male formal wear: a vest covered in gleaming seashells, cut-off leggings layered with animal fur and scales, and a necklace made from what Joel figured was probably stripeclaw teeth. The four who came after were, in order, Ringneck (the Four Villages' minister of justice, who apparently moonlighted as a wedding officiant), Starpollen (the ring bearer), Seaberry (the flower girl), and Fireflower (in some role that Joel wasn't sure of what the Earth equivalent was—emcee, perhaps).

Wait, he thought, *since Thornleaf has a best man, shouldn't Felicity have one too? I mean,* I *could've been her best man. Oh, but I guess brides have maids of honor, or something like that. So if the bride's best friend is a guy, I wonder how that works...what would you call them, a man of honor? Or still a maid? So confusing...*

Everyone's heads turned. Joel had imagined this moment as being like one of those in a movie where the bride, beautiful and resplendent in a flowing white gown, emerges under a shining spotlight to the strains of an angelic choir—at least in the eyes of the boy harboring an unrequited crush on her, his suddenly unattainable goddess.

As it turned out, this moment was a little bit like that, but a little different as well. Wearing a simple sea-green tunic and a crown of flowers, Felicity was beautiful, all right, but not any more than usual, not any more than she always was. As she strode through the crowd toward the stage with an awkward little smirk on her face, Joel realized that whether she was playing a sweaty rock show in a smelly nightclub, beating up queen Lightsnakes in an alternate plane, or being the glowing bride at her own wedding, it didn't matter; to him, she was something special, regardless.

Stupid Thornleaf, Joel thought, pursing his lips. *Why is* he *so lucky? 'Cause he's a jerk, that's why. A bad boy. Maybe there is something to that, after all. What did Felicity tell me that one time? 'You don't have to be a jerk or a bad guy. You just have to be confident.' But then look at who she's marrying.*

Once Felicity took her place on the stage with the rest of the wedding party, Redstem and the others gradually ended the song, so Joel followed suit. After he sat down in the front row, Fireflower strummed her wavebow and took a step forward.

"Thank you all for coming," the Wavemaker leader said, her voice amplified. "We are very happy that you could join us today for this special and joyous occasion. As you know, this ceremony will make official the union of..."

Joel tuned Fireflower out as his gaze darted furtively back and forth across the stage. It would be easy to simply stare at Felicity as she stood there looking radiant (if a bit uncomfortable), but he had learned the hard way a few years ago that doing something like that was considered...what was the word? Oh yeah: "creepy."

Maybe it's okay if I turn into a bad guy. Or an antihero. Maybe it's good to be selfish. Thornleaf is, and look how well things have turned out for him.

Fireflower finished up her little speech, performed a blessing incantation, and then was replaced by Ringneck, who started to drone on and on about Spectraland tradition, the legality of marriage, and other such boring topics (none of which, Joel noticed, included the opportunity to object to the pending union).

I can't, though. I just can't. I'm a good guy. That's who I am, and that's who I'll always be. I don't want to be anything else, especially if I'm supposed to become the most powerful Wavemaker who ever lived.

Starpollen dropped the bride's wedding ring, which was a polished wooden band with Felicity's loudstone set into it. The boy started to cry, causing the surrounding Aura to shift a little. Fireflower quickly moved to console him while Whitenose picked the ring up off the stage floor.

So I'll do it. I'll train with Blackspore, and he'll make sure I stay on the right path. I'll embrace my destiny and become the Virtuoso.

"Do you, Thornleaf of Headsmouth," Ringneck said once Starpollen had settled down, "accept Felicity Smith of the Bluerock as your mate and life partner, now and forever?"

"I do."

"And do you, Felicity Smith of the Bluerock, accept Thornleaf of Headsmouth as your mate and life partner, now and forever?"

Felicity paused. Joel's breath caught in his throat. He wondered if this might be like one of those scenes where either the bride changes her mind, someone decides not to forever hold their peace, or something else drastic happens to disrupt the proceedings. But then—

"I...I do."

Joel's face fell.

"Then I pronounce you officially wed."

Oh well. What did I expect? I mean, it's not like—

His train of thought was interrupted by a piercing scream.

CHAPTER 5: UNEXPECTED GUESTS

Everything seemed to freeze at that moment. Startled, Joel turned and saw that the source of the scream was Keeper, her hands held up to where her ears would be if people from the Six States actually had ears.

"Keeper!" Fireflower exclaimed from the stage. "Are you all right?"

Keeper didn't reply. Instead she stood up, turned toward Thinker, and unexpectedly gave her countryman a vicious left hook to the jaw.

"What are you doing?" someone—Joel couldn't really tell with all of the confused babbling now going on—yelled. Keeper took another swing, this one a swift right uppercut that knocked Thinker out of his chair and onto the sandy surface.

Joel stood up and whirled around, wondering what to do. Several guards who were posted off to the side started to charge in as Chief Raintree grabbed Keeper's arms, attempting to restrain the out-of-control Six States citizen. While he struggled, Redstem took aim with her wavebow and fired out a precise stunning cast that barely missed the Spearwind chief and struck Keeper right in the back of her head. Fireflower jumped off the stage, followed by the rest of the wedding party.

"Everyone, make way!" Thornleaf barked. "White-nose, fetch our wavebows from the hut!"

As Whitenose dashed off, Chief Raintree laid the now-unconscious Keeper on the ground.

"Stand down," Chief Twotrunk ordered the nearby guards, holding up his hand.

"Clear some space for Fireflower," Chief Sandthroat added.

The guards moved the chairs away as a circle formed around Keeper and Thinker, the latter of whom was writhing and moaning as he clutched at his face. Fire-flower knelt down and looked him over, like a football team's doctor inspecting an injured player.

"Thinker," she said, "can you speak?"

Thinker just groaned in response.

Fireflower played a few chords on her wavebow. Thinker's head lit up with a faint golden glow. After about six seconds, the glow faded and Thinker exhaled.

"Thank you," he said.

"Your friend there is much stronger than she ap-pears," Fireflower remarked. "Your jaw was fractured in three places."

"Yes, that was rather surprising," Thinker said, rub-bing his face as he sat up. "In more ways than one."

"Fireflower," Thornleaf, who was kneeling next to Keeper, said. "You must see this."

The Wavemaker leader moved over to them. Joel, standing between Riverhand and Chief Scarskin, craned his neck to get a better look. He noticed little wisps of dark-blue Aura energy coming off of Keeper's still form.

Thornleaf shot Fireflower a concerned look. "Could this be...?"

"Mind control," Fireflower answered her second-in-command's unfinished question. "But how?"

Thornleaf stood up and turned to his father, who was standing near the fringes of the circle. "This is your doing, is it not?" he said.

"What? No!" Stoneroot responded, sounding aghast and defiant at the same time. "How could you even think to accuse me?"

"I never really did forgive you," Thornleaf growled, taking a step forward. "I always knew that you would somehow return to your old ways."

"Thornleaf, stop," Fireflower said.

"I have been in prison for the last seven months!" Stoneroot asserted. "There is no way I could have—"

"And we should have left you there!" Thornleaf shouted. "I knew this was a mistake, letting you come here today!"

"Thornleaf!" Fireflower snapped.

"All right, all right, everyone just chill," Felicity said, stepping in between her newly minted spouse and his father like an experienced boxing referee. "Okay, now, let's all take a deep breath and..." She trailed off as a sudden rumbling sound—almost like thunder but not quite—started up somewhere in the distance. "Is that what I think it is?"

"The Forbidden Tides," Fireflower breathed.

Joel looked toward the horizon. Sure enough, a giant wave was rising up out of the ocean about nine miles away.

"What could have triggered them?" Chief Silverfern wondered aloud.

Chief Scarskin turned to Chief Sandthroat. "One of your fishermen, perhaps?"

"They know better than that," Sandthroat scoffed.

A moment later, Joel spotted ten—no, make that twelve—small round shapes in the sky above the cresting wave. They all appeared to be heading toward the island. "I see something," he announced. "They're, like, UFOs—flying saucers."

"Could they be from the Six States?" Windblade said.

"Can't be," Felicity said. "If they had developed flying vehicles, I'm sure Guider would have mentioned it."

"You've been talking to Guider?" Joel asked. Guider was short for Guider of the Worthy, the former leader of the rebellion against the Mono Realm and now the governor of one of its six liberated states.

"Of course. We invited her and her lieutenants to the wedding—Blackspore offered to teleport them over—but they said no thanks."

"Maybe they wanted to surprise you."

"Maybe."

"They should have said something," Redstem grumbled. "Now we need to clear the beach before the waves arrive."

"The stage and the guest huts should be fine where they are," Fireflower said. "Just move the chairs and everything else to higher ground." She turned to Riverhand. "While she is doing that, you and Windblade escort the chiefs and the other guests to Headsmouth village. We can hold the reception there instead. Oh, and"—she lowered her voice and aimed a sidelong glance in Stoneroot's general direction—"see if you can figure out what happened to Keeper, please."

"Yes, Fireflower," Riverhand said.

"What about us?" Felicity asked.

"No need to work on your big day." Fireflower smiled. "You, Thornleaf, and Joel can just help me greet our visitors."

"And inform them that we have only a few minutes before we need to head inland," Thornleaf added, sounding perturbed.

"I would also like to remain here," Thinker said. "If that is all right."

"Of course," Fireflower said.

The vehicles continued to approach. They weren't extraordinarily fast, but they were at least swift enough to outpace the incoming waves. At this point, Joel could see that they did indeed look like classic flying saucers, bubble-tops and all. As they got closer, he noticed that the bubble-tops were slightly tinted, obscuring the view of whoever was inside.

"Hey," Felicity said, slapping him on the arm, "can you tell me which one of those things Guider is in? I have an idea for a prank."

"Hard to tell." Joel squinted. "Can't really see inside the cockpits."

"Um, hello—the Sight?"

"Oh—right." The Sight was Joel's ability to notice small details that seemingly no one else could. Back on Earth it wasn't good for much, but here in the world of Spectraland and the Six States, it had not only helped save the day numerous times, it also allowed him to see into the recent past—and it was, he just now realized, probably a prerequisite of sorts for becoming the Virtuoso.

And now I'm going to use it for a prank, he sighed to himself. *Okay, well, here goes.* He cleared his mind, stared at the flying saucers, and proceeded to think of a random list.

How about...Generation II Pokémon in National Pokédex order: Chikorita, Bayleef, Meganium, Cyndaquil—

The tint on the saucers' bubble-tops appeared to lighten, and the figures within them became a bit more visible. The first two figures that he saw weren't familiar at all. The third one, however, was indeed Guider of the Worthy, her feathery silver hair tied up in a severe bun.

"I found her. She's in that one," Joel said, pointing.

"In the middle?" Felicity asked.

"Yeah."

"Cool. All right, so here's what we're gonna do..."

As Felicity explained the details of her prank, Joel noticed something alarming: faint wisps of dark-blue Aura energy rising up out of Guider's hair bun.

"...and after they land, we'll be, like—"

"Uh oh," Joel said.

Felicity turned. "What?"

"I think Guider's under mind control too. Just like Keeper."

"You see the blue Aura around her?"

"Yup."

"But how can that be?" Fireflower said.

"The two of them were among those that Byle placed under his mind-control cast back in the Six States," Thornleaf recalled. "After he died, the effects went away. The only way they could have returned automatically like that, without a new cast being performed, is if..."

"Marshall came back to life," Joel said. "Again."

Felicity clicked her tongue. "Man, I *knew* we should've checked around for his body."

"But if that is the case," Thinker said, rubbing his jaw, "why would Keeper of the Light fall back under his control only now?"

"The victims have to be within a certain range of the caster," Fireflower explained. "Which must mean that Byle is on one of those ships."

Feeling waves of anger and nausea coming on, Joel quickly scanned the other vehicles. After seeing three more unfamiliar Six States citizens, he spotted one of Guider's lieutenants seated next to someone wearing a dark hooded cloak. That person didn't have any blue Aura coming off of them, but they did have a surrounding field of personal energy that Joel instantly recognized.

"Yup, it's him. It's Marshall. He's with them."

"They must be coming to attack us," Thornleaf declared.

"Why does this kind of thing always happen at weddings?" Felicity grumbled.

The saucers were now within a hundred yards of the shore.

"I think he wanted to trick us," Joel surmised. "He probably learned about the wedding from Guider. He figured they could land and catch us off guard. I'm sure they have countercoms." Countercoms were the handheld smartphone/self-defense devices from the Six States that could take control of multiple people's bodies at the same time. If Marshall or any of the mind-controlled citizens were to get on the ground within range and use one of them, then everyone here would be in very, very big trouble.

"I'm sure you're right," Felicity said.

"What should we do?" Thinker asked.

"I say we catch *them* off guard first," Thornleaf said, raising his wavebow.

"No, wait—" Fireflower said, but it was too late. Thornleaf shot out several exploding casts that the saucers easily maneuvered around.

"Welp, now they know we're on to them," Felicity muttered. "I think we should—"

She was interrupted by bursts of laser and flame that came shooting out of the first few saucers, striking the sand just about ten feet in front of her and the others.

"Whoa!" she exclaimed, jumping back.

"Those vehicles are armed!" Thinker shouted.

"Yeah, no kidding!"

More shots were fired. A few of them hit the wedding stage, reducing it to a pile of broken, burning wood. Fireflower and Joel started up shield casts while Felicity and Thornleaf fired back at the saucers, all of which were now circling over the water right off the shoreline like a kettle of high-tech vultures.

"What is happening?" Redstem shouted, running over toward them.

"What's it look like?" Felicity shouted back.

"Redstem!" Fireflower turned as shots continued to be exchanged. "Contact Riverhand and Windblade and tell them to protect the villages!"

Redstem hesitated, looking up at the saucers and holding her wavebow as if she wanted to join the fight instead.

"I don't think they want to attack the villages," Felicity said in between shots. "If they did, some of 'em would be headed that way already. I think they want to establish a beachhead first."

"Like in that old 1983 game for the Commodore 64?" Joel said.

"I was thinking the 2000 version, but yeah."

"Good," Thornleaf grunted. "Then we can just end this here." He motioned for Redstem to come over and join them, which she eagerly did.

"Surely you are not planning on killing them, are you?" Thinker, hunkered down behind Fireflower's Aura-shield, asked.

"Just one of them in particular," Thornleaf answered as he launched off another exploding cast. "If we can take out Byle, then the rest of them will be freed from his spell."

"No," Fireflower said. "No killing. We will not violate our code under any circumstances."

"But then how else will we—"

Just then, someone came charging out of the nearby trees. It was Blackspore, screaming at the top of his lungs and holding his wavebow high over his head.

"Begone, invaders!" he shouted. As he ran, he took aim with his wavebow and began firing haphazardly into the air.

"Blackspore, no!" Joel cried. "Don't—"

Then horror struck. A couple of saucers strafed the master shaman with laser blasts, and he crumpled to the ground.

"Blackspore!"

Raising his shield-cast like an umbrella, Joel dashed over to his fallen would-be mentor with Fireflower right behind him. Once they arrived at Blackspore's side, Joel expanded his shield-umbrella into a small dome that surrounded the three of them.

"How is he?" Joel asked, struggling to remain calm.

"Alive—but just barely," Fireflower replied. "I will take him back to the temple and attempt to heal him. Inform the others."

"Okay." Joel kept his shield-dome going while Fireflower conjured up a flying cast that surrounded both her and Blackspore. As soon as they were away, Joel changed his shield-dome back into an umbrella form and ran over to Thinker, Redstem, Felicity, and Thornleaf, the latter two of whom were apparently arguing even as they continued to fire at the attacking saucers.

"Killing degrades your own Aura!" Felicity was saying. "You told me that yourself!"

"Under most circumstances, yes!" Thornleaf said. "But this is different!"

"Look, I hate him too, but there's gotta be another way!" Felicity retorted.

"If you have an idea, then share it with us!"

"Hey, uh, guys?" Joel said.

"What?" the couple snapped at the same time as they turned to him.

Joel pointed out toward the ocean. The remains of the Forbidden Tides, smaller but still formidable, were churning their way toward the shore. "I think we need to get out of here."

"I was just trying to tell them that," Redstem said. "How is Master Blackspore?"

"He's alive, but barely," Joel replied. "Fireflower's taking him back to the temple."

"Then we should all head there as well. I will take Thinker."

"The two of you go with them," Thornleaf said to Joel and Felicity. "I will hold off the attackers."

"No, you're gonna try to kill Marshall," Felicity said. "I won't let you do that. *I'll* hold them off."

"Why don't we all just go at the same time?" Joel suggested. "We can run into the trees and then take off from there. That'll give us some cover."

Thornleaf and Felicity both glanced at him, and then at each other.

"Makes sense to me," Felicity said.

"Very well," Thornleaf sighed.

Under the safety of their shield-casts, the four Wavemakers and Thinker darted into the trees, conjured up some flying casts, and took off into the air just as the giant waves arrived. As they flew, several laser blasts streaked by. Joel glanced over his shoulder and saw that three of the saucers were giving chase.

"Take evasive action!" he shouted.

Heeding his warning, the other Wavemakers swerved and looped around as more laser blasts were fired their way. Fortunately, the saucers were no faster than they were at top speed, so they were able to maintain their distance.

Just a little farther...

A few minutes later the Wavemaker Temple came into view, its large surrounding dome of shield-Aura a welcome sight. The saucers continued firing—one shot missed Thornleaf by inches—until the party flew through the shield-dome and landed at the base of the temple's front stairway. The saucers fired off a few more blasts, all of which deflected harmlessly off the shield, before they turned and flew back in the direction of Crownrock.

"That was close," Redstem exhaled.

"Indeed," Thinker said, dusting himself off.

Felicity looked at Joel. "What do you suppose he's up to?"

"Who—Marshall?"

"No, Elvis Presley."

"Huh?"

Felicity rolled her eyes. "Yes. Marshall."

"I dunno. Revenge?"

"If that's all he wanted, I don't think he'd just park at the beach. And how'd he come back to life?"

"Um—"

The sound of swelling music could be heard nearby.

"That must be Fireflower," Thornleaf said.

The group jogged up the temple's stairs and into the main hall. Fireflower was on the dais, crouched over

Blackspore's supine figure, her eyes screwed shut with intense concentration. As she played a steady progression of chords on her wavebow, a thick, constant stream of rainbow-colored Aura flowed out of the dais's basin, through her and her instrument, and onto the injured master shaman.

"I hope he's gonna be okay," Joel said.

"She looks like she could use some help," Felicity noted, looking up at the dais. "Too bad Auravine isn't"—she glanced in Joel's direction—"oh...whoops. Sorry, dude. Didn't mean to bring her up."

"No problem," Joel replied, even though his stomach did twist a little at the mention of Auravine's name. Trying to keep his mind in the moment, he looked up at the dais. Felicity was right—Fireflower did appear to be under a considerable amount of strain. Beads of sweat ran down the Wavemaker leader's face, and she was visibly shaking. An additional healer, especially one as skilled as Auravine was, would certainly be welcome here.

Maybe I should go back in time now, he thought, *and try to save—*

"Hold on, I got it," Felicity said, snapping her fingers. "The swordcats. Doc, especially."

"Oh—uh, yeah. Good idea." Joel nodded. Admittedly, that did seem like a more practical alternative at the moment, seeing as how he didn't quite have the time travel cast completely mastered yet.

"We should be able to locate them rather easily using a tracking cast," Thornleaf said.

Felicity threw up her hands. "Then what are we waiting for?"

CHAPTER 6: THE CONTRADICTION

While Redstem and Thinker stayed with Fireflower and Blackspore at the temple, Joel, Felicity, and Thornleaf made the long flight up to Sunpeak Mountain, using their loudstones to give them an additional burst of speed. Sunpeak, the highest point on the island, was home to a rare species of animals known as swordcats—lion-sized feline creatures with spiky horns who possessed the powers of healing and short-range teleportation. Previously thought to be wild and dangerous, three of them—whom Joel and Felicity had affectionately named Platinum, Goldie, and Doc—had actually played an important role in helping the Wavemakers foil one of Marshall Byle's previous schemes.

The trio landed near the area where they had first met the swordcats, which was a copse of goldenorb trees a little ways down from the burial ground known as the Sacred Site. Thornleaf started up a tracking cast on his wavebow as Joel took a look around.

"I, uh, I don't see them anywhere," Joel said, shading his eyes.

"Well, what'd you expect?" Felicity said. "Thought they would just be waiting here for us?"

Joel's initial impulse was to reply with a simple no, but then he shifted gears at the last moment and said instead, with as much sarcasm as he could muster, "Sure, because everything in Spectraland is always easy, all of the time."

Felicity gave him the response he was looking for: a smirk. "Of course it is."

"In fact, it's so easy, we, uh...we..."

"Yeah, better just quit while you're ahead."

"I picked up their signal," Thornleaf announced, his instrument's headstock turning a faint shade of green as he aimed it toward the mountain's summit. "They are not very far away."

"All right, so maybe it was just a *little* easy," Felicity said.

Following the tracking cast, the three shamans hiked their way up a rocky trail that zigzagged around the slope. While they did so, Joel decided to call Redstem to check up on Blackspore's condition.

"Nothing seems to have changed, for better or for worse," Redstem's voice came through Joel's wavebow. The sounds of Fireflower's healing cast droned on in the background. "Still, I am not sure how much longer she can keep this up."

"Okay," Joel said. "We located the swordcats, so we should be back soon."

"Did you hear from anyone else?" Felicity asked.

"I contacted Riverhand and Windblade and informed them about everything that had transpired," Redstem replied. "They have not seen the flying vehicles anywhere, but they are setting up Aura-shields around all the villages and settlements, just in case."

"Cool," Joel said. "How are the wedding guests?"

"All are fine and accounted for. They are a bit worried, though, as you might imagine."

"As soon as we get Blackspore taken care of, we can come up with a plan for dealing with Marshall," Joel said.

"One that *doesn't* involve killing," Felicity added.

"I heard that," Thornleaf said as he walked ahead, his attention on the tracking cast.

"Very well," Redstem said. "I will inform Fireflower and contact you if anything changes over here."

"Sounds good," Joel said. "Suzuki out." The strings on his wavebow dimmed.

"'Suzuki out'?" Felicity chuckled. "Seriously?"

"I've always wanted to say something like that."

"Yeah, me too, actually."

"You've always wanted to say 'Suzuki out?'"

"No, I—you know what I mean."

"I do." Joel grinned. "So what do you think Marshall's plan is this time?"

"Hey, *I* already asked *you* that question."

"But you were the one who said the thing about the beachhead."

"True, but that doesn't mean I know what he has in mind after that."

The buzzing of the tracking cast suddenly grew much louder. Joel looked at Thornleaf's wavebow and saw that the green glow surrounding its headstock had turned a few shades brighter.

"They must be just up ahead," Thornleaf said.

"Where?" Felicity said, craning her neck. "I don't see anything. Joel, do you?"

Joel stared in the direction Thornleaf's wavebow was aimed. At first glance, he saw nothing there but the sheer cliffside and some bushes, but then he noticed what looked like an opening behind some of the vegetation.

"Over there," he said, pointing.

They jogged up and pushed through the bushes. Sure enough, in the face of the cliff was a tunnel just large enough for a swordcat to fit through. Thornleaf's tracking cast was buzzing loudly.

"This must be their den," the tall shaman said.

"Platinum?" Joel bent down and called. "Are you in there? Goldie? Doc?"

For a few moments, there was no response. But then, without warning, the swordcat named Doc suddenly appeared in the mouth of the tunnel.

"Whoa!" Joel exclaimed, recoiling. "You scared me there."

"Typical sneaky cat behavior." Felicity sniffed.

Doc gave a little growl of greeting.

"Hey, bud," Joel said. "We were wondering if—"

He was interrupted by another growl, this one coming from deeper within the tunnel.

"That must be Platinum or Goldie," Joel said. He looked back down at Doc. "Anyway, we—"

Before Joel could finish, Doc turned around and trotted away.

"Well, that's rude," Felicity remarked.

"We should follow it," Thornleaf said.

The three Wavemakers got down on their hands and knees and crawled into the tunnel. It continued on in a straight line for about twenty feet before it opened up into a small cave area. There, nestled up in one corner amidst a pile of straw and leaves, was Goldie—along with a litter of sword-kittens, five of them in all, mewling and nursing at her belly. Doc padded up to them.

"I see you guys have been busy!" Felicity chuckled.

"It appears that the two of them are mates," Thornleaf said.

"Yeah, no kidding."

"Appropriate, since the female one was your companion, while the male was mine."

"If you're suggesting that we're gonna have five kids, you can forget it."

"I wonder where Platinum is?" Joel said, trying to change the subject.

"Who knows?" Felicity said. "Just ask Doc if he'll come back with us to the temple."

Doc tilted his head, as if to say, *What for*?

"Yeah, um, Blackspore—one of the Wavemakers—is hurt," Joel said to the swordcat. "Fireflower's trying to heal him, but she needs help. Can you come to the Wavemaker Temple with us?"

Doc glanced at Goldie, then back at Joel.

"Oh—hmm." Joel turned to Felicity. "I don't think he wants to leave his family here alone."

"I guess I can understand that. Well, we can always look for Platinum."

"Yeah, that's what I was gonna—"

Interrupted by a muffled growl, Joel turned to see Platinum standing at the den's entrance with a six-legged, three-tailed fish in his jaws.

"Perfect timing," Felicity remarked.

Platinum trotted over, dropped his catch, and then rubbed his cheek against Joel's leg.

"Nice to see you too," Joel said, petting the swordcat.

"We should hurry," Thornleaf said.

"Do we ever do anything else around here *but* hurry?" Felicity quipped.

Joel knelt down next to Platinum and explained the situation. The three swordcats then exchanged looks and growls for a few long seconds before Doc finally stepped forward.

"Oh—I think Doc's coming with us after all," Joel said.

"Well, good," Felicity said, "He's the strongest healer, anyway."

"Naturally," Thornleaf said.

"Are you trying to make a point there?" Felicity said. "'Cause, you know, if you are, I don't get it."

"Thanks, Doc," Joel said to the swordcat. "Hopefully this won't take too long."

To speed up the journey, the three Wavemakers shared the duty of carrying Doc with their flying casts. One cross-island flight later, they arrived back at the temple and rushed into the main hall. Fireflower was still on the dais, playing her wavebow. Redstem and Thinker were standing next to one the pillars as if they hadn't moved an inch since Joel and the others had left.

"We have returned," Thornleaf announced.

"I think they can see that," Felicity said.

Doc bounded up onto the dais. Fireflower seemed to barely take notice as the swordcat licked Blackspore's wounds a few times before starting up a loud purr that sounded like an idling V8 engine.

"Just in time," Redstem said. "I have already lent all my energy to her, and the communal basin is almost empty."

For a moment, Joel considered lending his energy to Fireflower as well. But after the long flight to Sunpeak and back, he himself was quite low, even with his loudstone, and he figured that it wouldn't be a good idea for everyone to be drained at the same time, especially with Marshall lurking about.

"Any news on Byle?" Thornleaf asked Redstem.

"Nothing so far." Redstem shook her head. "Riverhand set up an island-wide tracking cast to follow his movements, but it appears he is content to simply remain at the beach for now."

"Perhaps it is a trap," Thinker theorized. "He wants to lure some of you down there so he can use a countercom and gain possession of your musical instruments."

"Maybe," Felicity said. "But I'm sure he knows that we know that he might do that."

"Could you devise a way to reverse the effects of the countercom?" Thornleaf asked Thinker.

"Possibly. I would need your help, though."

"Of course."

Minutes ticked by, slow as molasses. Fireflower's healing cast and Doc's purring seemed to merge together into a single harmonious symphony, one that caused the floor itself to vibrate while filling up the entire hall with warmth and light. They continued this way for what felt like a very long time until, finally, the music faded away, Doc stopped purring, and Fireflower let out a long, heavy sigh. This was followed by a moment during which there was nothing but absolute silence.

Thornleaf was the first to speak up. "So?"

"He is still alive," Fireflower said. "But he does not have much time left, I am afraid."

"How long?" Redstem asked.

"Three days, perhaps four. At most."

Joel's stomach turned cold. "Wait, what?" he said, stepping up toward the dais. "Are you serious?"

Fireflower stood up and wiped her brow. "We did all we could. His injuries were much too severe."

"But—but he can't die!" Joel exclaimed. "I need him! The vision says that—" He cut himself off, remembering that only a few were supposed to know about the Virtuoso prophecy. But it was too late.

"What vision?" Redstem asked.

"Yeah, what are you talking about, dude?" Felicity said.

Joel glanced up at Fireflower. The Wavemaker leader wore an expression that seemed to convey resignation, disappointment, or both.

"There is an old vision that tells of the most powerful Wavemaker ever to live," she said, addressing everyone in the hall. "According to this vision, this individual will have the ability to travel anywhere in time and space, without limitation. And with this power, he is supposedly fated to save all of existence from an evil force."

There was a long pause during which it seemed like everyone was letting this information sink in. Finally Thornleaf said, "So then...this Wavemaker is Blackspore?"

"No." Fireflower shook her head. "It is Joel."

Everyone turned to look at Joel, making him feel very uncomfortable. Almost involuntarily, his face formed sort of a sheepish half grin. "Yeah, um...it's me."

"Wait," Felicity said, "so you mean you're like Valerian? Or Hiro Nakamura?"

"Yup." Joel nodded. "Well, sort of—not yet, exactly. I mean, I just started practicing yesterday, so I'm not all that good at it yet, but—"

"Dude, that's amazing! And it totally makes sense too, when you think about it. I mean, you know, since you were already good at estimating time and distance and stuff."

"This is incredible!" Redstem said. "Just imagine all the possibilities...all the good deeds Master Joel could perform!"

"Now hold on a moment," Thornleaf said, raising his hand. "Why did we all not know about this?"

Fireflower stepped off the dais. "I myself did not know until just a few days ago, when Blackspore and Darkeye finished translating the records," she replied. "We decided to hold off on informing the rest of you until after the wedding."

"So the chiefs are not aware either?" Thornleaf asked.

"They are not. We were going to request a hearing with them later."

"A single Wavemaker possessing those kinds of abilities is a very serious development," Thornleaf said. "One that the Silencers will not be pleased to learn about. It could threaten the stability of the Auravine Accord."

"Since when did you care about the opinion of the Silencers, Thornleaf?" Redstem scoffed.

"Have you forgotten that I was our order's representative in those negotiations?" Thornleaf snapped. "I will not have my efforts undone by an offworld amateur who can barely control whatever power he has now!"

"Um, you know I'm standing right here, right?" Joel said.

"Thornleaf, be respectful," Fireflower said. "Now, I understand your concerns. I share them as well."

"What is there to be concerned about?" Redstem said. "Master Joel is the nicest young man I have ever known. And on top of that, he has built up quite the track record. Surely if anyone can be trusted with this power, it is him."

"And didn't you say that he's destined to save all of existence?" Felicity asked Fireflower. "I figure the Silencers would appreciate that a little, at least."

"Just whose side are you on?" Thornleaf said.

"The side of logic?"

"It is true, the vision does say that is what he is meant to do," Fireflower said, sidestepping the couple's budding argument. "However, it is assuming that he is able to stay away from temptation."

"That sounds like a rather ominous caveat to me," Thornleaf muttered.

"But that's why Blackspore can't die," Joel insisted. "According to the vision, he was supposed to guide me. Be my mentor. If he did that, then everything was gonna turn out okay."

"Is that true, Fireflower?" Redstem asked.

Fireflower nodded. "That seemed to be the most likely interpretation of that particular passage, yes."

All right, Joel thought, *this must be the sign. The sign that I have to go back in time to save Auravine. That way, she'll be alive, and then she can heal Blackspore, and then everything will be fine. I don't care if I haven't fully mastered the cast yet, all I have to do is—*

"Well then, I have the answer," Felicity declared. She turned to Joel. "Since you can travel through time, just go back and fix it."

"Yeah, actually, I was about to say that I—"

"You mean, change history?" Thornleaf interrupted. "What if he alters something that he should not?"

"He doesn't have to go too far back or anything crazy like that." Felicity shrugged. "Just far enough—like, say, to the wedding—so he can make sure that Blackspore stays away from those flying saucers. Clean and simple."

"But if Joel sees himself in the past," Thinker said, "would that not create some sort of a...a paradox?"

"Easy solution—invisibility cast." Felicity snapped her fingers. "Bam. You guys are thinking about this way too much."

"Invisibility casts are forbidden," Thornleaf pointed out.

"Dude, we just used one yesterday for my prank on Joel." She turned to Fireflower. "It's cool with you, right?"

"An invisibility cast among ourselves is one thing," Fireflower said around a thoughtful frown. "But outside the temple grounds...and with time travel on top of that? If the chiefs found out, there would be some serious repercussions."

"Ugh," Felicity groaned. "Those guys are *so* not fun."

"The harmony of the island is their primary concern," Thornleaf said.

"And saving the universe is ours, apparently," Felicity retorted. She turned to Fireflower. "C'mon, boss—you heard Joel. He needs Blackspore. *We* need Blackspore. I'm sure Joel can handle the job, quick and easy. If we have to, we can go to the chiefs later. There's a famous saying on Earth: 'It's always easier to beg for forgiveness than ask for permission.'"

"I suppose if he is only going back a few hours..." Fireflower paused for a long moment before continuing. "Very well." She looked at Joel. "But please try not to do anything beyond protecting Blackspore."

Joel nodded. He was disappointed that he wouldn't get a chance to save Auravine, but he understood the plan's rationale.

I can always try to save her later.

"I'll be careful," he said out loud.

"Let it be known that I object to this course of action," Thornleaf grumbled.

"Too bad, hon." Felicity smirked. "You've been outvoted."

"What should we do about Byle in the meantime?" Redstem asked.

"We need to find out what he might be up to," Fireflower said, folding her arms. "Without Blackspore's far-vision cast, however, that will be rather difficult. Any suggestions?"

"Wait," Joel said, "I thought you could do that too?"

"Do what?"

"Look at stuff far away. Like when you were stalking—um, I mean, watching—Sting on Earth."

"Oddly enough, my ability to do so is restricted to your world. If I could observe events in this world, I would have been following your activities in the Mono Realm."

"Naturally," Felicity muttered.

"Well, then I have an idea," Joel said. "I'll go back to the beach first. That way, I'll time travel from the right spot, which lowers the chance of me messing something up along the way, and then, while I'm there, I can check out what Marshall is doing."

"If you fly there, they will see you coming from miles away," Thornleaf warned.

"Then I'll go by slimeback."

"I am sure they will have soldiers posted at the entrances to Stonelight Tunnel."

"Then I'll go through the Jungle of Darkness," Joel said, quietly pleased to have ready responses to all of Thornleaf's objections. "The short-range space-travel cast Blackspore taught me will make it faster and safer."

"Sounds like a plan to me." Felicity shrugged.

"All right." Fireflower nodded. "But someone should go with you, just in case."

Joel glanced at Felicity, expecting her to volunteer. Just as it seemed as if she were about to do so, however, Thornleaf spoke up.

"Redstem should go," the tall shaman said. "Her surveillance and combat skills make her the perfect choice for such a mission. The rest of us will stay here and work on a way to negate the countercom's effects."

"Ooh, like a counter-countercom," Felicity said. "Sounds cool. Yeah, okay, I'll help with that."

Joel opened his mouth to protest, but he couldn't come up with anything to say.

"It is settled, then," Fireflower declared. "In the meantime, the swordcat and I will continue to do what we can for Blackspore. May the Aura guide us all."

CHAPTER 7: THE BEACH

Joel and Redstem rode tandem on Destiny, Joel's faithful mount, back out toward Crownrock. They went as fast as the slimeback's legs would allow, only slowing to a trot after several miles, when she finally required a break.

"I have not traveled this way in quite some time," Redstem said, their reduced pace allowing for conversation. She was seated behind Joel with her hands affixed to Destiny's sticky sides.

"You mean, in this direction?" Joel asked.

"No, I mean via slimeback."

"Oh."

"Fortunately, your mount provides a rather smooth ride, I must say."

"Yeah, she's always been good like that. I don't even really have to do anything."

A pause. Then: "So, have you given much thought as to how you will apply your new abilities?" Redstem asked. "Besides preventing Master Blackspore's death?"

"Um, a little."

"I would imagine a great many lives could be preserved by such powers."

"I guess."

"Perhaps even Auravine's."

"Yeah, I, um...I thought about that."

"I assumed you would have. The two of you really seemed to bond during our mission in the Mono Realm."

Joel wasn't quite sure how to respond to that, so he decided to—using a tip that he had picked up in his social communications class—redirect the conversation's subject back to Redstem. "So, uh, what about you?"

"What about me?"

"Is there anyone that you...you know...have bonded with?"

"If I understand what you are saying correctly, then no, not at the moment."

"What about Riverhand, maybe? Or Windblade?"

Redstem laughed. "Oh, no, definitely not them."

"Why? Because they're, like, coworkers?"

"Well, that, and also..."

"Also what?"

Redstem cleared her throat. "If I tell you, will you promise not to repeat what I say to anyone?"

"Um, sure," Joel said. "I promise."

"I have not bonded with Riverhand or Windblade in that fashion because...because they are men. Or boys, really."

Joel took a couple of seconds to process what Redstem had just said. "Wait, so you mean..."

"I am attracted to those of my own gender."

"Oh."

"Is that surprising?" Redstem asked, her tone seeming to suggest that she thought perhaps she had said too much. "Are there not people in your world with those kinds of preferences?"

"Oh, um...no, it's not surprising, and yes, there are. Kind of a lot, actually."

"That is good to know," Redstem said, sounding relieved. "There are not many of us here in Spectraland, and we try to keep our identities a secret, which limits the possibilities for bonding."

"I, uh, I can imagine."

"How are those like me treated in your world? If there are a lot, as you say, they must be quite readily accepted."

Joel wasn't quite sure how to respond to that. As a member of two minority communities himself, he was well aware of the existence of prejudice and intolerance back on Earth, but the whole thing was such a complex sociopolitical debate that he didn't really know where to start. He decided to go with a line he had learned from Felicity, one that seemed to have limitless applications.

"It's complicated."

"As it is here, as well," Redstem sighed. "From what I have been told, we used to be, if not accepted, at least tolerated by our culture, until a terrible incident occurred a number of years ago."

"What was it?"

"The stories are vague, so I am not exactly sure. It is as if people want to bury that part of Spectraland history for some reason. All I know is that, at one point, someone with preferences similar to mine committed a deplorable act, and ever since then we have been associated with evil and destruction."

"But...that's dumb," Joel said. "Just because one person is bad doesn't mean that everyone who is like them is bad as well."

"I agree."

"I mean, you're a Wavemaker. How can anyone think that you're bad just because of who you want to, you know, bond with?"

"That is an interesting question. I wish I knew the answer."

"Well, don't worry, Redstem. I know you're a good person."

"I appreciate that. If your homeworld has even one more individual who thinks like you do, it must be a wonderful place indeed."

Joel found himself once again at a loss for words. "I guess it's okay," he finally said. "We're working on it."

They rode in silence for a few moments before Redstem spoke up.

"I have an idea," she said. "Perhaps one day you could take me to your world so that I might have an opportunity to meet someone. You know, like you and Auravine, or Thornleaf and Felicity."

"Sure, yeah," Joel said even as he wondered how, exactly, they would accomplish such a thing. Sign her up for online dating, maybe?

"Really?"

"Really."

"How exciting! Thank you so much."

"You're, uh, you're welcome."

"I am happy we had this talk, Master Joel."

"Me too," Joel auto-replied.

"Now I will be depending on you for more than just saving the universe," Redstem added with a chuckle.

At that, Destiny turned her head and gave a little croak, as if to say that she was ready to resume a full gallop.

"Okay," Joel said.

The slimeback took off. Eventually, they made their way to the Jungle of Darkness, which—thanks to Joel's new short-range space-travel wavecast—they were able to navigate all the way through relatively quickly and without incident. Once they were about a mile from the beach, Destiny slowed down once more.

"How close should we get?" Redstem asked.

"As long as we stay hidden in the trees, I think we can go all the way to the spot that Blackspore came running out from before he got shot," Joel replied.

They headed in the direction of said spot. Along the way, Joel scanned the skies for any evidence of flying saucer activity, but there was none. Once they reached their destination, though, he did see, through a dense copse of seaweed palm trees, all twelve ships parked on the sand near Crownrock, arranged in a rough semicircle. A number—fifteen, to be exact—of Six States soldiers were standing around, keeping watch or talking to one another. There was no sign of either Guider or Marshall.

"While you do your part, I will attempt to hear what the soldiers are saying," Redstem whispered.

"You mean, like, eavesdropping?" Joel said. "How are you gonna do that?"

"There is a wavecast designed specifically for that purpose," Redstem answered with a slight grin. "It too is forbidden, but since we are breaking a number of rules anyway..."

"Might as well, I guess."

"Exactly."

"All right, so then I'll do the time travel now. If everything works out the way it should, I'll be back before you even finish casting."

"Good luck."

Joel engaged the Sight and rewound the scene a few hours. Then he touched his loudstone to his temple, played the time travel melody, and waited. One queasy sensation later, Redstem and Destiny had vanished, leaving him alone amidst the trees. Looking out, he could see Riverhand and Windblade helping to evacuate the crowd of wedding guests as the sound of the approaching waves rumbled in the distance.

Okay, here goes.

He raised his wavebow and prepared to play the invisibility cast. Just as his fingers touched the strings, however—

"Joel!"

Joel whirled around. Blackspore was there, having emerged from behind a large bush.

"Have you been lurking for me?" the master shaman asked, obviously intoxicated.

"What? Lurking?"

"Yes, lurking. I mean, looking. Loo-king."

"Oh—um, yeah. Pretty much."

"Ah, well...the last thing I remember, I wandered in here to relieve myself, but then I must have passed out. Did I miss the wedding?"

Joel nodded. "You did."

"That is too bad," Blackspore said, stumbling. "I hope they will forgive me." He bent over and threw up.

Joel grimaced. "Yeah, um, you know, you seem kind of sick. You should probably go back to sleep, or something."

"Nonsense, my boy! I feel fine. I need to get out there and apologize."

"No, really, it's okay. I'm sure Felicity and Thornleaf are cool with it. Just stay here."

"Why, are you ash-maim—ashamed of me? Your mentor?"

"No, no, it's not that, it's—"

Joel was interrupted by the sound of wavecasts, followed by shots from the flying saucers.

"What is that?" Blackspore said.

"Uh...nothing! Just, um, fireworks. You know, for the wedding celebration."

"I was not aware that such a demonstration was planned."

"It, um...it was a surprise."

An explosion rang out—the saucers had blown up the wedding stage.

"Was that part of it as well?" Blackspore said.

"Um, sure, yeah."

Voices could now be heard shouting: Redstem's, Felicity's, and Fireflower's.

"That all sounds rather exuberant." Blackspore smiled. "I must go and see."

"No!" Joel protested, grabbing Blackspore's arm.

"Why not?"

"Because—because—"

Blackspore wrenched his arm free. "Let me go, Joel. I have already missed too much."

"Please, just—"

"I must—*what* are *those*?"

Joel turned. The saucers, firing at the Wavemakers, were now clearly visible through the trees.

"That is no celebration," Blackspore said. "We are under attack!"

"I know, but just let Fireflower and the others—"

"Come, Joel! We must help them!"

"Wait!"

Joel tried to grab Blackspore again, but he was too late. With a blood-curdling cry, the master shaman rushed out of the trees and toward the melee. Joel started to run after him, but then he stopped at the edge of the copse when he realized that the other Wavemakers—his past self included—would spot him, Present Joel, thus potentially creating a time-damaging paradox.

"Begone, invaders!" Blackspore shouted, raising his wavebow.

Joel wasn't sure what to do. As he struggled to come up with an idea in the heat of the moment, Blackspore began firing into the air.

"Blackspore, no!" Past Joel cried. "Don't—"

A couple of saucers shot out lines of laser blasts, striking Blackspore. It was done.

Dangit.

Frustrated, Joel decided not to hang around any longer. He closed his eyes, pictured himself back with Redstem and Destiny in the present time, and played the time travel cast. He heard a *whoosh*, and then—

"Oh—Joel?"

Joel opened his eyes. Redstem was there, giving him a quizzical look.

"Did it work?" she asked. "You started to play, but then you shifted positions a little, so I assumed..."

"Well, the cast worked," Joel said, frowning. "But I wasn't able to stop Blackspore from getting killed."

"What happened?"

"I just—I wasn't really ready, that's all. I'll try again."

Joel rewound the scene a little further and then went back again. This time, he was able to perform the invisibility cast before Blackspore staggered out from behind the nearby bush.

"Wha...hoozair?" the master shaman slurred.

Joel froze, silently scolding himself for not coming up with a plan beforehand.

"I heard you playing," Blackspore said, straining to enunciate his words. "Come out, wherever you are."

"I...I am the wraith of Crownrock," Joel said, using his best Batman voice. It was the only thing he could come up with at the moment.

Blackspore snorted. "There is no wraith of Crownrock."

"You have been gone from Spectraland a long time, Master Blackspore. I evolved during your absence."

"But how could you—"

"Silence!"

Startled, Blackspore stopped in his tracks.

"Now, listen to me very carefully," Joel went on. "In approximately forty-two seconds, you are going to hear some noises."

"Noises? What kind of noises?"

"Like...wavecasts. Laser blasts. Explosions."

"Why are there—"

"You are to ignore these noises. Ignore them and remain here, hidden in the trees. Or, um, better yet, return to the Wavemaker Temple. Yes, yes, do that instead. Do that right now. Do you understand?"

"Joel?" Blackspore squinted. "Is that you?"

"No!" Joel tried to remain as still as possible. "I told you, I am the wraith of Crownrock. Now, heed my warning!"

Blackspore glanced around, looking confused. Joel held his breath, hoping that the master shaman's drunken condition was bad enough that this little—and yes, poorly executed—ruse would work. For a moment, he thought it just might, but then Blackspore raised his wavebow and said in a rather coherent fashion, "I do not know whether this is a harmless prank or some malicious trick, but either way, I know when I am being deceived."

"I swear"—Joel started to say in his normal voice before he caught himself and switched back to Batman—"I swear, I am not trying to deceive you. I am trying to help you."

At that moment, the sound of wavecasts could be heard, with the shots from the flying saucers coming soon after.

"This *is* a trick!" Blackspore declared. "You are trying to distract me!"

"No, I just don't want you to get hurt!"

"Show yourself, coward!" Blackspore growled, waving his instrument around.

The wedding stage exploded. Blackspore fired a stunning cast that missed Joel by about a foot.

"Okay, okay, stop, it's me," Joel said, dispelling the invisibility cast.

"Joel! Why are you—?"

"I'll explain later, just, please, don't go out there."

"What is happening?" Redstem could be heard shouting. Blackspore turned toward the sound of her voice.

"What's it look like?" Felicity responded.

"Redstem!" Fireflower cried as shamans and saucers exchanged fire. "Contact Riverhand and Windblade and tell them to protect the villages!"

Blackspore turned back to Joel. "They need our help," he insisted.

"I know. But trust me, they're gonna be okay. It's you that..."

"What?"

Joel forced himself to look Blackspore straight in the eye. "If you go out there, you're gonna die."

"How do you..." Blackspore trailed off as he returned Joel's stare. Several long seconds ticked by. It seemed as if either a million thoughts were running through the master shaman's head or he was preparing to vomit; Joel couldn't tell exactly which, so he took a step backward just in case.

"I understand now," Blackspore finally said.

"Good," Joel exhaled. "So, yeah, just stay here and—"

All at once, before Joel knew what was happening, Blackspore let out a ferocious scream, raised his wavebow above his head, and charged out of the trees.

"Wait!" Joel exclaimed. "Stop!"

"Begone, invaders!" Blackspore shouted.

"Blackspore, no!" Past Joel cried from his spot further away on the beach. "Don't—"

Present Joel didn't even bother to look. Instead, as the sounds of saucer fire rang out, he growled to himself, envisioned being back in his own time, and played the time travel riff once again. He heard a *whoosh*, and then—

"Oh—Joel!" Redstem said, whirling around with her wavebow in playing position.

"Whoa," Joel said, "Yeah, it's me."

"I apologize, you startled me. Did it work this time?"

"No, I—wait, what do you mean, 'this time'?"

"You failed once, and then you disappeared for several minutes before returning again just now."

"Oh...I must've overshot the return point, or something. But, um, no, it didn't work the second time either."

"What happened?"

Joel was about to launch into a play-by-play recap before he remembered what Felicity would always tell him: summarize. "The first time, I didn't do the invisibility cast fast enough, and then he ran out of the trees before I could stop him. The second time, I tried to pretend I was a wraith, but then he..."

"What?"

"I dunno, it was weird. I told him if he went out there, he was gonna die. But then he did it anyway."

"That is unfortunate. Do you have enough energy for another attempt?"

Joel glanced at his loudstone. It was already running low, probably a result of all the space- and time-travel casts he had just performed. "No, I'll need to go back to the temple and reload. Were you able to find out anything?"

"As a matter of fact, I was. Something quite alarming."

"What is it?"

"Remember when we were in the Mono Realm—in the hills of The Vast Wasteland?"

"Yeah."

"And the Redivision forces used a very loud countercom signal to subdue the soldiers who were pursuing us?"

"Yeah. And us too."

"Well, apparently the soldiers here are assembling a large device that will have a similar effect, only way more powerful. They expect its range to include the entire island."

"Um...uh oh. That's not good."

"Indeed. And what is worse, I overheard one of the soldiers saying that it will be ready in four days."

At that moment, Joel spotted a couple of the soldiers on the beach starting to head toward the spot where he, Redstem, and Destiny were hiding.

"Okay," he said, "we'd better get out of here for now. Once we're back at the temple we can tell Fireflower everything and then come up with a plan."

"Agreed."

CHAPTER 8: THE FATEWAVE

When Joel and Redstem arrived back at the Wavemaker Temple, they found Fireflower and Doc still in the main hall, on the dais. The Wavemaker leader was sitting next to Blackspore's body like a cat keeping vigil for a fallen littermate, while the actual feline creature was curled up next to her, apparently sound asleep.

"I wasn't able to save him," Joel said as he walked to the front of the hall.

"I assumed as much," Fireflower responded. "What about Byle? Were you able to discover anything about his intentions?"

Redstem relayed what she had learned about the giant countercom.

"Well, that is unfortunate," Fireflower said.

"No, you think?" Joel said.

Redstem turned and gave him a quizzical look.

"You know—sarcasm?" he said. "Sorry, just trying to fill in for Felicity."

"She has taught me about the sarcasm. I am not sure that your particular tone of voice accurately conveyed your—" Redstem cut short as two people entered the main hall from the back left doorway. One of them was Riverhand, the other, Keeper.

"I see that it worked," Fireflower said to them from her perch.

"Yes, thank you," Keeper responded. "I feel much better now."

"Wait," Joel said, "so—she's not mind-controlled anymore?"

Keeper smiled. "I am not."

"How did you...?"

"The mind-control antidote that you secured from Darkeye months ago," Riverhand explained.

"I had a feeling it would come in handy one day," Fireflower said.

"Oh yeah." Joel grinned. "I remember you saying that."

"Anyway, the situation has now become much more urgent," the Wavemaker leader said, standing and addressing everyone in the hall. "We need to formulate a new strategy. Riverhand—please contact Windblade and ask him to return to the temple at once."

"As you wish."

"While he's doing that," Joel said, "I'll recharge my loudstone."

"I am afraid there is still not enough energy in the communal basin," Fireflower said. "The restorative process will take a while, especially with my continual efforts to keep Blackspore alive. You should probably just get some sleep."

"I think some rest might be good for all of us," Redstem said. "We can afford one night. Their giant countercom will not be ready for another four days."

"Yes, that is a good idea," Fireflower concurred. "We will convene in the morning."

♪♪♪

Joel lay down on his sleeping mat in the guest hut, hoping—expecting, even—that a good night's sleep would not only replenish his Aura energy, it would also provide him with a vision proving what he suspected: that saving Auravine would be the best course of action to take. After his recent failure at the beach, he was convinced that bringing her back from the dead to heal Blackspore was, simply, destiny.

C'mon, clairvoyance, don't fail me now.

It didn't take long. In what seemed like an instant after he closed his eyes, Joel found himself not in the guest hut, but in the middle of a swirling cloud of mist. He got to his feet.

All right, once this clears up, I'll be in the Mono Realm, probably at the coliseum. Auravine will be there, and I'll find out what I have to do.

The mist cleared and, as expected, Joel found himself in the Mono Realm, back in the stadium-like structure where Marshall had killed Auravine. He was standing about ten feet away from a group of people that he recognized as his fellow Wavemakers, along with Thinker, Keeper, and Guider. They were all gathered near a body on the ground that had a blanket draped over it. He took a few steps closer.

"What of the mind-control effect?" Keeper was saying. "That was such a terrible feeling...like the energy control, only much worse."

Wait a minute, Joel thought, *this is a flashback of the end of our last adventure, not a vision of a possible future. My time-travel training must be messing things up.*

"If you wish, we could return with our leader, Fireflower," Riverhand said. "She should be able to adjust your energy signatures so that you will be permanently protected, without having to use the soulshifter salve."

"Should we be concerned that one of you may attempt something like that again?" Guider asked.

"Well, no, but—"

"Then I do not see that as a priority."

Yeah, you probably should've taken him up on that, Joel thought ruefully. *All right, maybe I need to wake myself up and then try to—*

The body under the blanket began to rise.

What the—

Joel, a voice echoed all around.

"Um...Auravine?"

The body was now sitting up fully, although it was still covered by the blanket. Oddly, no one around it seemed to notice.

Joel...please...

"Auravine! It's me—I'm here. Please what?"

The body stood up. Still covered by the blanket, it looked like it was wearing one of those homemade Halloween ghost costumes, only without the eyeholes. It would have been funny if it wasn't so eerie.

Please...forgive...

"What? Forgive?"

Forgive...m—

At that moment, the scene shifted. In the blink of an eye, Joel went from the confines of the coliseum to a dense jungle filled with seaweed-palm trees and other assorted flora.

"Whoa—Auravine? What happened?"

Joel, a different voice—a man's—said.

"Wait—Blackspore?"

"Yes," Blackspore said, walking out of the trees. He looked no worse for wear. "I apologize for intruding on your vision, but I have an urgent message for you."

"How did you—are you all right?"

"I am dying, as you know. I am using what little energy I have left to communicate with you."

"Well, okay, but..."

"Joel, listen to me," Blackspore said, stepping forward. "I know what your mission is now."

"Yeah, it's to save Auravine. Then she can heal you, and then—"

"No. It is to stop me from bringing Marshall Byle over to Spectraland."

"To stop me—I mean, you—from...what did you say?"

"Stop me from bringing Byle over. During the Fourfoot War, twenty years ago. If you do that, then all will be set right."

"Um..."

"If you are successful, you will save many lives, including Auravine's. You will even solve your current problem with the Six States soldiers and their giant device."

"I get that, but Thinker and Thornleaf are working on a counter-countercom, and we have the mind-control antidote, and—"

"You must do this, Joel," Blackspore said, adamant. "You must travel back to the time of the Fourfoot War and stop me."

"Well..." Joel was about to say okay, but then he realized something. Something important. "If I do that, won't that mean I'll never come to Spectraland either? Since Marshall was the one who brought me over?"

"That could very well be the case, yes."

"But then if that happens, who will be the Virtuoso? What about the prophecy?"

"My feeling is that the prophecy is being fulfilled at this very moment."

"What do you mean?"

"First of all, by informing you of this mission, I am giving you the guidance that you need. Then, using your new powers, you will prevent Byle from coming to Spectraland, thereby saving existence from evil's reign."

"So...Marshall is the evil that the vision talked about?"

"I now believe that, yes."

"Okay, but my time-travel skills aren't even that good yet."

"They will suffice."

"And also..." Joel paused. He had another, more personal concern.

"Also what?"

"If I never come to Spectraland, I'll never meet Felicity. And I won't have any of the cool adventures I've had here. I'll just be stuck in my old life, with no friends."

"Are you telling me that you would sacrifice hundreds of lives, including Auravine's, for the sake of your own selfish purposes?"

Joel frowned. Obviously, he didn't want all those people to die at Marshall's hands, but at the same time, the thought of him never coming over to Spectraland made him feel very sad. It would be like losing a family, something he had already experienced when his father left.

"Please, Joel," Blackspore said. "Please promise me you will do this."

"I—"

"*Please.*"

"Um—"

At that moment, something jumped out of the trees, and Blackspore abruptly vanished. Joel turned. The thing—a large humanoid, as it turned out—kicked Joel in the stomach, sending him sprawling to the ground. Wincing in pain, Joel looked up at his assailant and saw that it was a tall, muscular man dressed in a flowing green robe made out of vines. A wooden helmet adorned with what looked like giant deer antlers covered the man's face, concealing his identity.

Wait, Joel thought, clutching at his midsection, *that's Chief Fourfoot! The fake one that Marshall made up to scare me and Felicity way back when, anyway.*

The mysterious figure produced a long spear, seemingly out of nowhere. He brought it down on Joel, who rolled to the side just in time to avoid the strike. The figure tried again. Joel barely managed to dodge the blow once more. After a third attempt, which grazed Joel's arm, the tip of the spear became lodged in the ground, giving Joel a chance to scramble to his feet. He felt for his wavebow, but it wasn't there.

"Stop!" he yelled. "I'm not here to fight you!"

The figure pulled the spear free. Joel glanced down at his arm. It was bleeding.

Okay, that's not good. What kind of vision is this?

The figure aimed the spear at Joel and took a menacing step forward. Deciding not to stick around any longer, Joel turned and took off running.

C'mon, Suzuki, wake up.

Joel could hear his attacker behind him, giving chase. He kept running. The air turned cold. His chest started to burn.

Wake up, wake up, wake up—

And then he did, sitting bolt upright on his sleeping mat as rivulets of sweat ran down his face. He looked at his arm. It was unscathed.

♪♪♪

Joel tried to go back to sleep but, unnerved, he gave up and decided to go walking around the temple instead. He headed for the main hall to check on Blackspore, thinking that maybe the master shaman was now conscious. When he got to the hall, however, nothing much had changed; Blackspore was still in a coma, and Fireflower was still sitting next to him, apparently deep in trance. That only difference was that Doc was no longer there.

Hmm. Wonder where he went.

Looking around, Joel noticed that the front doors were ajar. Since the temple was protected by the surrounding Aura-shield, keeping the doors closed wasn't a real necessity, but to find them open, especially at night, was still unusual. He was about to take a peek outside when he remembered that his Sight power might show him who had passed through here in the last few hours.

Random list...how about...Mega Man original series games and their year of release: Mega Man, 1987; Mega Man 2, 1988 in Japan, 1989 in the U.S.; Mega Man 3, 1990...

Sight engaged, Joel saw a ghostly image of Doc heading out the doors accompanied by a young girl. At first he thought the girl was his sister Taylor, but then he realized it was Seaberry. Curious, he followed the image through the doors and down the stairs. Once he set foot in the clearing in front of the temple, he realized that he didn't need to keep the image going; Seaberry and Doc were there, in real time, sitting by the edge of the river some thirty feet away. He waved. Seaberry waved back. He walked up to them.

"What are you guys doing out here?" he asked.

"I could not sleep," Seaberry replied, stroking Doc's fur.

"Oh—yeah, me too."

"Do you have the feelings, as well?"

"Um...I have feelings all the time," Joel said, sitting down. "What kind of feelings are you talking about?"

"They are hard to describe. I suppose they are like fear, even when there is nothing to be afraid of. They build up inside of me, like the winds of a storm, until I feel as if I might explode. Sometimes I scream. Sometimes I shake uncontrollably. And sometimes I have a hard time breathing."

"Is it like...a panic attack? Anxiety?"

Seaberry gave Joel a quizzical look. "If the translation cast is working correctly, then yes, I believe what you have just said is quite accurate."

"Okay, yeah, then I know what you mean. That used to happen to my mom sometimes after my dad, um...never mind."

"I also feel sad a lot, even when perhaps I should not be."

"So, like, depression?"

"I suppose."

"That's tough."

"It is. But I am glad you brought One Thousand and Twelve here, so that I had a chance to meet him. Just being around him makes me feel so much better."

"You're welcome. Um—wait, One Thousand and Twelve? Who's that?"

"Him." Seaberry nodded at Doc, who was gently purring. "You call him Doc, but One Thousand and Twelve is his real name."

"It is? How do you know?"

"He told me."

"He...told you?"

"Yes. He has told me many things. We have been talking all night."

Joel looked at Doc. He knew that swordcats were highly intelligent, and that he shared a bond with them that allowed for some general communication, but if Seaberry could actually converse with them, that was something else altogether.

"Did you know that his ancestors were among the original inhabitants of Spectraland?" the young girl continued.

"Oh—um, yeah, I did. I actually met one of them."

"I know. His name is Nineteen, correct?"

"Yeah."

"One Thousand and Twelve has told me about him. He sounds very wise."

"He is."

"One Thousand and Twelve is very wise as well. He has given me good advice about dealing with my feelings."

That gave Joel an idea. "Hey, could you do me a favor?"

"What is it?"

"I have some questions for Doc—um, I mean, One Thousand and Twelve. Could you translate his answers for me?"

"Can you not understand him yourself? With the translation cast?"

"It, uh, doesn't seem to work on animals."

"I see. Very well."

Joel looked at the swordcat. "Okay, so, there's something I have to do. Something that Blackspore wants me to do. I have to go back in time and prevent him from bringing Marshall Byle over to Spectraland."

Doc nodded, apparently understanding.

"If I'm successful," Joel continued, "then it'll save the lives of everyone who Marshall has killed, and it'll solve the problem of the giant countercom."

Doc just blinked.

"But if I do that, I'll never come over to Spectraland either, which makes me feel...well, like Seaberry does when she has a panic attack. And more importantly, if I make such a drastic change to history, who knows what other kinds of problems it might create?

"So, my question is: what should I do?"

Doc tilted his head and then, after a few moments, responded with a series of growls, purrs, and throaty meow-like sounds.

"What is he saying?" Joel asked Seaberry.

"He says that...you must ride the fatewave."

"The what?"

"The Aura is like water, flowing like a river, like the tides of the ocean."

"Um...are you sure you're translating this correctly?"

"Things happen as they will happen, when the time is right," Seaberry continued, ignoring Joel's question. "No sooner, no later."

Joel's brow furrowed. *What kind of answer is this?*

"It is the wave of fate that you must follow in order to succeed," Seaberry said, looking at Doc. "If you think about it, the answer will make itself clear to you." She turned back to Joel.

"So, wait—that's it?"

"Yes."

I suppose I shouldn't have expected anything else, Joel thought, pursing his lips. *Nineteen always gave cryptic advice as well.*

"Oh, and one more thing," Seaberry said.

"Yeah?"

"One Thousand and Twelve says that he is not the mate of One Thousand and Four—Goldie, I believe you call her. He is her brother. The other one, One Thousand and Seven—he is her mate."

"Platinum?"

"Yes."

For some reason that Joel didn't quite understand, this news perked his mood up a little.

CHAPTER 9: DECISIONS

A loud chiming melody—the Wavemaker Temple's version of a wake-up call—rang out, heralding the advent of morning. Not having slept a wink since his vision ended, Joel stood up, performed an antifatigue cast on himself, and walked out of the guest hut.

It is the wave of fate that you must follow, he repeated to himself, trying to parse out the meaning of Doc's advice. *It is the wave of fate—*

"Good morning!" someone chirped, interrupting Joel's train of thought. It was Windblade, his usual cheery self.

"Good morning," Joel muttered.

"Did you have a good night's rest?"

"Um...no, not really."

"Oh—did you have a vision?"

"Yeah."

"What was it about?"

"I'll, uh, I'll tell everyone at the meeting."

"Understood."

"Is everyone at the other villages okay?"

"When I left them, they were."

"Cool."

Windblade asked Joel about his vision a few more times as they headed up the celery-stalk ramps, but Joel just put him off until they arrived at the meeting hut, a large pyramid-shaped structure in the middle of a lily-pad platform on one of the upper levels. Inside, Fire-flower, Riverhand, Redstem, Thinker, and Keeper were seated on wooden stools that were arranged around a cylindrical stone table resembling an oversized hockey puck. Joel sat down next to pair of empty stools that he assumed were being saved for Felicity and Thornleaf.

"Are you feeling refreshed?" Fireflower asked.

"He did not sleep very well," Windblade answered for Joel in a tone of voice that sounded like he was either making a statement of great importance or being very sarcastic; Joel couldn't quite tell which, but knowing Windblade, it was probably the former. "*He had a vision.*"

"I see." Fireflower raised an eyebrow. "What did it show you, Joel?"

"A bunch of stuff."

"Such as?"

"Um..."

"All right, all right, we're here," Felicity announced as she and Thornleaf entered the hut. They both looked like they hadn't gotten much sleep either; Felicity's hair was tousled, and her eyes were bloodshot. "What's this all about? And where's Blackspore?"

"The mission at the beach was unsuccessful," Red-stem responded. "Master Blackspore is still dying, unfortunately."

"What?" Felicity said. She turned to Joel. "What happened?"

"Well, first, we went down to the beach, and then we—"

"Never mind, forget it," Felicity interrupted, holding up her hands. "Did you find out what Marshall and his mind-controlled minions are up to?"

"They are constructing a giant countercom," Redstem replied. "Like the one the Redivision used in The Vast Wasteland, only much stronger. They expect to have it completed in four—well, no, three days, now. Their exact words yesterday, according to the translation cast, were 'the dawn of four days hence.'"

"Oh." Felicity's face fell. "Awesome."

"Since I was not in the Mono Realm with all of you," Fireflower said, "please remind me how, exactly, that device worked."

"It was super loud and annoying," Felicity muttered.

"I can elaborate," Thinker said. "It was similar to the handheld countercoms in that, with a single brief tone, it allowed the user to take control of the bodies—below the neck, anyway—of those affected. The larger device simply had greater range and power."

"And now this one will be able to reach the whole island," Redstem said.

"I can try to identify some locations that might be shielded from its effects," Thinker said, "but there is no guarantee at this point."

Fireflower looked around the table. "Any other ideas?"

"What about the nullifier?" Keeper asked.

"The what?" Joel asked.

"The counter-countercom," Felicity said. "I insisted on a shorter name."

"It is ready," Thinker said. "But it will only work on the small handheld units, and one at a time, at that. We were not expecting the large variety."

"Can it be modified?" Fireflower asked.

"Possibly. But I will need more than a few days."

"How long?"

"A full week, perhaps. Probably longer."

Fireflower shook her head. "Then that will not work, I am afraid."

"We do have the mind-control antidote," Riverhand said. "We could use it on the Six States soldiers."

"Yes," Redstem said, "and using the nullifier as well, a group of us could infiltrate their camp and shut them down."

"But if we missed just one of them and they were able to deliver a wavebow to Byle, all would be lost," Fireflower said. "That possibility makes such a mission far too risky."

"I have started working on something that might mitigate the risk," Thinker said. "A variation on soulshifter salve that masks your energy signature altogether. It could make you virtually invisible to the eyes of Six States citizens."

"I don't like the words *might* and *could* there," Felicity said.

"Well, it has performed at eighty-three percent efficacy in my early tests."

"Great. A seventeen percent chance of total failure."

"This whole discussion is a waste of time," Thornleaf said. "All we have to do is eliminate Byle himself, and the threat will be over."

"No," Fireflower and Felicity said in unison.

"I still do not understand your objection to that idea," Thornleaf said to Felicity, his voice rising. "We have been breaking rule after rule, mostly at your insistence! But the one rule that is preventing us from saving our island, you want to obey?"

"Yup, that's right."

"Why?"

"Because."

"Because what?"

Felicity paused and sighed. Then she said, "Because, dummy, I don't want to be married to a murderer! Okay? There, I said it."

"Is that really what this is all about?"

"What the—of course it is! What else would it be?"

Thornleaf got to his feet. "Sometimes I wonder." He stormed out of the hut.

Felicity propped her elbows on the table and buried her face in her hands. "Whatever," she groaned.

An awkward silence ensued. Joel looked around the table. Everyone appeared rather uncomfortable. Finally, after what seemed like a very long time (but was, in reality, only five seconds), Thinker spoke up.

"If all of you feel that killing Byle is the best solution, then—as a former soldier with blood on his hands—I can volunteer for that task," he offered. "I am neither bound by your moral code nor am I married to Miss Felicity here."

"Even so," Fireflower said, "there are practical concerns about such a plan. A failed attempt could prove disastrous. And for reasons I do not quite understand, Byle seems unusually resistant to dying."

"Or staying dead, anyway," Felicity added, hands still on her face.

"Besides, the giant countercom is only one of our problems," Redstem reminded everyone. "We still have Master Blackspore to be concerned about."

"There must be something else we can try," Windblade said.

There was, Joel knew. He didn't necessarily like it, but it seemed as if everything was pointing in that direction. Is this what Doc meant by following the wave of fate? "I, uh, I think there is," he said.

"Is this about your vision?" Windblade asked.

"Yeah."

"Tell us, please," Fireflower said.

"Blackspore...he appeared to me," Joel said, ignoring the Auravine and Fourfoot parts. "He had a request. He wanted me to go back to the time of the Fourfoot War and stop him from bringing Marshall over to Spectraland."

Everyone glanced at each other.

"I suppose that...could work," Windblade finally said.

"It would negate all of our current problems," Riverhand noted.

"As well as save many lives," Redstem added.

"I have some serious reservations about that idea, however," Fireflower said, folding her arms. "To go back to that time period would be an extremely dangerous undertaking."

"I'll be careful not to change too much stuff," Joel said.

"I am not even talking about that," Fireflower said. "The Fourfoot War was a brutal, ruthless conflict. Even if you manage to avoid a confrontation with Byle, there is still a great chance you could be hurt in any one of its more conventional battles."

"Blackspore really wanted me to, though. It was like his dying wish."

"Why not just try to stop the war from ever happening in the first place?" Windblade asked.

"I guess, but...that's not what he asked for," Joel replied. "He was really specific about what he wanted."

"Perhaps he knows that preventing the war altogether would lead to even greater problems," Riverhand postulated. "After all, his Aura sensitivity is stronger than any of ours."

Fireflower frowned, as if she were reluctant to acknowledge that fact. She turned to Joel. "If you were to attempt such a feat, are you confident that you could succeed, after what happened at the beach?"

"Yeah," Joel said. "I mean, I know that plan didn't work, but I think that's because it wasn't *meant* to work. This just feels like the right thing to do, for some reason."

"Dude," Felicity said, peeking through her fingers. "You realize if you do that, we might not ever come to Spectraland either, right?"

Murmurs broke out around the table.

"I know." Joel nodded.

"Are you both willing to take that chance?" Fireflower asked.

"If it means saving all those lives, then, well...yeah, I am," Joel said, trying to hide his reluctance.

"Felicity, what about you?"

Felicity didn't answer. She just continued to sit there with her hands on her face.

"I know you'd be giving up a lot more than I would," Joel said.

"Do you want some time to think about it?" Fireflower asked.

Felicity lowered her hands and looked around the table. Then, for a few long moments, her gaze lingered on the stool that Thornleaf had vacated. Finally, she said, "No...no, I'm good. Like Joel said, it's worth it."

"Then perhaps this is the Virtuoso Vision being fulfilled much sooner than we expected," Fireflower said.

"Yeah, that's what Blackspore thought too," Joel said.

Fireflower nodded. "Very well, we shall put it to a vote. What say all of you?"

"I admit that on one hand it sounds favorable," Windblade said, his voice shaking, "but to lose the two of you..."

"You'll be fine," Joel said, "because if Marshall never comes over, there'll be no need for anyone to stop him."

"It is not only that, though," Redstem said, her eyes tearing up. "You are our friends. We will miss you. If you are gone, we will have to live with that pain forever."

"No, you won't," Felicity said, "because you'll never even have known us."

"That is a good point," Riverhand said.

Redstem slammed her hands on the table. "You impassive, unfeeling—"

"I was only trying to—"

"Look," Joel said, "this is a hard decision for me too. But I don't think we have any other choice. I feel like the Aura is leading us down this path."

"And who knows," Felicity said, "maybe something cool will happen and we'll end up back here anyway. You never know."

Redstem took a deep breath and wiped her eyes. "All right," she exhaled. "I...I vote in favor."

"As do I," Windblade said, sniffling.

"I also vote in favor," Riverhand said.

"Now wait a minute," Keeper said, "I am not sure if I get to vote, but I have an objection nonetheless. Without Joel and Felicity, the Uniter would never have been toppled and the Mono Realm would still be in existence."

"Actually," Thinker said, "I have something to confess. If Master Blackspore had not contacted me during his search for someone to assist with his war effort, the Uniter would probably never have come to power in the first place."

"What? How so?"

A pained expression crossed Thinker's face. "The Uniter and I...we used to work in the same military division. I was in line for a powerful leadership position until I met Master Blackspore and tried to inform my superiors about the existence of this island and its people."

Keeper's already-wide eyes widened even more, as if she were having a terrible realization. "After which you were dismissed and discredited as part of the government's cover-up."

"Indeed. So, since I was no longer a candidate, the Uniter was given the position instead. It was from there that he was able to expand and consolidate his influence, eventually leading to...well, you know what it led to."

"Why have you never said anything about this?"

"You think I wanted to admit something like that? I felt a tremendous amount of guilt for years. It was something I wanted dearly to forget about."

Keeper stood up. "I am no longer under mind control, but I am of a mind to break your jaw once again!"

"It—it wasn't his fault," Joel said. "Please, everyone, just calm down. This is all the more reason why I need to honor Blackspore's request. If I can stop him from opening that portal altogether, then maybe I can save all those lives in the Six States as well. So it's settled. I'm doing this."

Felicity took a deep breath and straightened herself up. "And I'm going with you," she declared. "One last adventure." She managed a little smirk. "Besides, someone has to make sure you stay out of trouble."

♪♪♪

Forty-five minutes later

Standing in the clearing outside the temple, Fireflower exhaled as she finished up the shapeshifting cast. Joel glanced down at himself. His skin was a light shade of green, and he had little leaves sprouting out of his arms and legs. It was like the Halloween costumes he and Felicity had made a month prior (Earth time), only more authentic; the plant-like protrusions on his body felt almost like additional limbs that he could wiggle around if he tried hard enough. He looked at Felicity. She was also now green and leafy, and aside from her hair, which she had wanted to keep blond, the rest of her features were barely recognizable.

"Dude," she said, returning his stare. "Now you look more like Ichiro Suzuki than Joel Suzuki."

"What?"

"Facial hair," Felicity said, rubbing her chin.

"Oh—right." Joel felt his face. Sure enough, Fireflower had given him a thin layer of stubble in order to make him appear older than he was. Even at seventeen years of age, he still couldn't manage to grow more than just a little peach fuzz on his own. "I don't know why I've never asked this before," he said, turning to the Wavemaker leader, "but how come you're the only one who can do this shapeshifting wavecast?"

"It is actually a variation on healing," Fireflower explained.

"She rearranges the cells in your body," Felicity added, pulling her hair into a ponytail. "You know, like Mystique from the X-Men."

"So...does that mean Auravine could shapeshift too?"

"I never taught it to her, since it is a forbidden cast," Fireflower replied. "Another law that we are breaking."

"Well, if everything goes as planned, none of that will matter," Felicity said.

A chill hit the pit of Joel's stomach. *I know we're doing the right thing*, he told himself.

"So when you go back," Fireflower said, "there is a chance you may meet my sister."

"Oh—yeah," Joel said. Fireflower's sister, Greenseed, had been killed in the Fourfoot War. "Do you want me to try to...you know...save her?"

Fireflower paused for a long moment before replying, a pained look on her face. "There is nothing I would like more," she finally said. "But I believe that fulfilling Blackspore's request is the only change to history you should attempt to make. Doing anything else could possibly lead to disastrous consequences."

"Okay."

"If you could, though, please just tell her that...I love her very much."

"Won't that be confusing, though?" Felicity said. "I mean, you were around during that time. Wouldn't she wonder why you weren't just telling her yourself?"

"Our relationship was rather—what is the term you use?"

"Complicated?"

"Yes."

"All right, fine, we'll let her know if we see her."

"Thank you."

"Okay, we're off."

"Are you sure you do not want to say goodbye to Thornleaf first?"

"Yeah, I'm sure," Felicity replied. "It's better if he doesn't know what's happening."

"Very well." Fireflower nodded. "Good luck to both of you. And in case we never meet again, I want to tell you that—"

"Please," Felicity interrupted, holding up her hand, "just—stop. Like I told everyone else, if we start doing any sappy farewells, there's a chance I might change my mind."

Fireflower smiled. "Understood."

With that, Joel and Felicity played the flying cast melody and headed toward Nightshore, which is where Fireflower said Blackspore would most likely be found (during the war, only the Wavemaker Elders remained at the temple). Once the village came into view, Joel flew over closer to Felicity and shouted through the wind: "We shouldn't get too close!"

"Yeah, yeah, I know the drill," Felicity responded. She pointed to a copse of seaweed-palm trees down below. "Let's land over there."

Joel followed her down to the spot she had indicated.

"All right," Felicity said once her flying Aura had faded away, "so how does this work?"

"How does what work?"

"Taking me along with you into the past. We don't have to hold hands or anything, do we?"

"Um, actually...I'm not sure."

"What?"

"I'm not sure. I haven't taken anyone along yet."

"Wait, are you serious? I thought Redstem went with you."

"She came with me to the beach, but not back in time."

"Why not?"

"Well, she wanted to—"

"Never mind, it doesn't matter. Let's just try it. If it doesn't work, then it doesn't work."

"Okay, well—wait, why don't you want to hold my hand? You've done it before."

"It would just seem weird, now that I'm married."

"But if we succeed, then you probably won't be anymore."

"We haven't succeeded yet, have we?"

"True. All right, then, um, stand close, I guess."

"How about back-to-back."

"Sure."

Felicity walked around Joel and stood with her back touching his. Aside from maybe a high five or a fist bump, it was about as platonic a form of physical contact as you could get; still, though, Joel felt a small swarm of butterflies erupt in his stomach.

"You all right there?" Felicity asked over her shoulder.

"What? Oh, uh—yeah. Hold on."

Joel engaged the Sight and imagined going back twenty Spectraland years, to the time of the Fourfoot War. Once he had the picture clear in his mind, he touched his loudstone to his temple and played the time-travel melody. There was a queasy sensation, followed by a *whoosh*, and then—

"Whoa," Felicity exhaled. "That was different."

"I'm pretty used to it now," Joel said, stuffing his wavebow into his supply pack.

"I'm sure. So, I guess it worked?"

"Let's go find out."

The pair walked toward the village, which, Joel noticed once they were within a hundred yards or so, looked less like the Nightshore of the present and more like the one he had seen during his first visit to Spectraland, only more intact.

"Okay, yeah, I think it worked," he said.

"Cool," Felicity said. "Oh, hey—check it out. Seems like something big is going on."

Joel looked past the huts lining the village's perimeter. Sure enough, quite the commotion was taking place; a large group of natives was congregating in the central courtyard area, and as he and Felicity got closer, Joel could hear a lot of excited chatter.

"Wonder what they're doing?" he said.

"Maybe a war rally, or something."

The pair entered the village proper. At the far end of the courtyard was a tall stage that supported a wood-panel backdrop and a tall-legged chair. A shorter stage, upon which five young women all probably around Joel and Felicity's age stood, was set up near the middle of the area. Each woman was dressed in a silky white tunic and assorted floral accessories. A sweet smell, like perfume, lingered in the air.

Joel glanced at Felicity. "Do you think they're...sacrificing them, or something? Like, for luck?"

"I don't think human sacrifice is a thing here." Felicity shook her head. "Besides, those girls all look way too happy for that."

Joel scanned the five women. Sure enough, each of them—if he was reading their body language correctly—seemed genuinely pleased and excited to be where she was. They were smiling and glancing at each other, as if sizing one another up.

Felicity tapped a spectator on the shoulder. "Hey," she said when he turned around, "my friend and I here are vagabond travelers, just passing through. What's all this about?"

"This is the betrothal ritual for Chief Fourfoot," the spectator replied. "He has just turned seventeen years of age, so he gets to select a mate."

"Oh, so kind of like *The Bachelor*."

The spectator gave Felicity a quizzical look. "I am not sure what you just said."

"Never mind."

A drumbeat started up. A few seconds later, a trio of guards emerged from behind the taller stage's backdrop, followed by a short and skinny male native wearing a furry cloak and a large horned headdress that threatened to tip over with every step he took.

"That's Chief Fourfoot," Joel whispered into Felicity's ear. "The real one."

"Yeah, duh."

Following behind Fourfoot were three more guards, a middle-aged female native with a beehive hairdo, and a male native with a wavebow strapped around his shoulder.

"Is that Blackspore?" Felicity asked, craning her neck.

Joel squinted, examining the native. "No," he said, "his facial features don't match up."

Each member of the chieftain's procession made their way up onto the stage. Fourfoot seated himself on the tall-legged chair (his feet didn't reach the stage floor), and everyone else gathered around him. Once they were all in place, Fourfoot made a gesture, halting the drumbeat. The female native with the beehive hairdo then stepped forward, unrolled a parchment, and began reading from it.

"Today, the brave and honorable Chief Fourfoot of Nightshore will bestow the privilege of being his life partner on one fortunate member of our village," she said. "The chosen one will become our chieftess and will be granted all the rights and benefits that come with that title."

"Kind of weird to be doing this in the middle of a war, no?" Felicity said to no one in particular as the well-coiffed woman continued reading aloud.

The spectator Felicity had talked to earlier turned around again. "A war? What war?"

"The, uh...forget it."

"And so," the woman said, "without further ado, I present to you our leader, Chief Fourfoot."

The crowd applauded. Fourfoot hopped off the chair. "Greetings, my people," he said. "Thank you all for being here today on this very special occasion."

Felicity turned to Joel. "Dude, I think you may have overshot it," she said under her breath.

"Overshot what?"

"The time period. I don't think the war's even started yet."

"Oh...um, oops."

"We should probably get out of here and try again."

"Now?"

"In a minute. I just want to see how this turns out."

"Okay."

"And with that," Fourfoot said, "I will now make my decision."

Some of the girls on the smaller stage giggled. Fourfoot stepped forward and stared in their direction. He looked back and forth, back and forth, as if he were watching a tennis tournament.

"Would you just pick someone already?" Felicity muttered.

Fourfoot gave his chin a thoughtful scratch. His gaze extended beyond the stage to the crowd gathered around it on either side. Finally, after what seemed like a very long time, he raised his arm, pointed, and announced: "I choose...that one."

Gasps erupted from the audience. At first, Joel didn't know why, but then he realized that Fourfoot was pointing not at the smaller stage, but in his and Felicity's direction. Everyone turned to look at them.

"Oh, uh," Felicity said, "no...no, no. I can't—I'm not available. I mean, I'm already married. See?" She held up her left hand, showing everyone her wood-and-loudstone ring.

"Not you, you ignoramus," Fourfoot said. "*That* one."

Joel looked at Fourfoot's outstretched finger. Upon closer examination, it was, indeed, aimed directly at him.

CHAPTER 10: THE COURTSHIP

"Who—me?" Joel said as confused murmurs rippled through the crowd.

"Yes, you," Fourfoot replied, still pointing.

"Forgive me, my chief," the beehive-haired lady said, "but...are you sure?"

"Of course I am sure!"

"What about us?" one of the young women on the small stage asked.

"Hah!" Fourfoot scoffed. "You are all fairly attractive, but none of you come even close to matching the radiance of this exquisite stranger."

Felicity snorted. Joel glanced at her.

"Sorry, dude," she said, trying—without much success—to suppress a grin. "Couldn't help it."

"Ah—everyone, please give us a moment," the beehive-haired lady addressed the crowd. "Do not go anywhere. The selection ritual will continue shortly."

"What are you talking about?" Fourfoot said to her. "It is over. I have made my decision."

Mumbling something, the beehive-haired lady took Fourfoot by the arm and pulled him away.

"What are you doing?" the young chief protested as he was led off the stage.

Felicity looked at Joel. "Okay," she said, having regained her composure, "now's our chance."

"For what?"

"To make a break for it."

"Oh—right."

The two of them turned to leave, but no one parted to let them through.

"Ahem," Felicity said, "'scuse us, please."

"Where are you going?" one of the members of the crowd asked, still not moving aside.

"We, uh...we're late for our next stop," Joel improvised.

"But you have been chosen by Chief Fourfoot," another villager said. "It is a great honor."

"I'm sure it is," Felicity said, "but we really have to leave."

"I am afraid we cannot let you," the villager said. "If the chief finds out that we did..."

"Then what?" Joel asked.

He was greeted by silence. Then he felt a tap on his shoulder. He turned around to see the unnamed Wavemaker standing there, wavebow in hand.

"Your presence is required."

"Um..."

The Wavemaker moved his instrument into playing position.

"Okay," Joel said.

"Proceed to the area behind the main stage. Both of you."

Joel and Felicity began walking, and the crowd parted for them.

"Oh, sure, *now* they move," Felicity grumbled.

The pair followed the Wavemaker behind the stage. There, Fourfoot, the beehive-haired lady, and several guards were standing around.

"Take a good look, my chief," the lady said, gesturing at Joel.

Fourfoot looked Joel up and down. "I am. So?"

"You do realize that the one you have chosen is...a male?"

"I know that!" Fourfoot snapped. "I am not stupid!"

"But what about the five lovely girls we assembled for you?"

"I do not want them. I want *him*!"

"My chief, I think that—"

"I am seventeen now," Fourfoot said, his tone shifting from whiny to menacing. "And as such, your authority as my advisor has expired. If you try to stop me from marrying this newcomer, I *will* have you exiled."

The lady pursed her lips, inhaled, and turned to Joel. "What is your name?" she asked.

"I'm, uh...um..." Joel stammered, realizing that he and Felicity had forgotten to come up with fake Spectraland-appropriate names for themselves.

"He's Sightguy," Felicity said, stepping in. "And I'm Goldilocks."

"Very unusual names," the lady said, narrowing her eyes. "Where are you from?"

"Nowhere, really," Felicity answered. "We're vagabonds, just passing through."

"And you are married, you say. To him?"

Felicity paused, glanced at Joel, and then said, "Yeah. Yeah, I am. To him."

Even though he knew it wasn't true, Joel felt a little spark of happiness at hearing her say that.

"So that's why neither of us can marry your chief," Felicity continued. "End of story. Can we go now?"

The beehive-haired lady nodded. "Yes, I suppose that—"

"She is lying!" Fourfoot said. He turned to the Wavemaker. "Tealfinger, confirm that she is lying."

The Wavemaker—apparently named Tealfinger—glanced at the beehive-haired lady.

"Do it!" Fourfoot said. "I command you!"

"As you wish." Tealfinger raised his wavebow and began playing a soft, eerie melody that Joel recognized as a lie-detection wavecast. He felt a twinge of panic, realizing that the cast would not only confirm that he and Felicity weren't married, it might also confirm that they weren't vagabonds but were, instead, something a lot harder to explain.

"Whoa, whoa," Felicity said, putting a hand on the neck of Tealfinger's instrument. "No need for that. Okay, I'll confess: we're not married."

"I knew it!" Fourfoot exclaimed.

"Why did you attempt to deceive us?" Tealfinger asked, sounding genuinely curious.

"Because...I didn't want to be separated from him," Felicity said. "We're traveling together, and I didn't want to be left alone. I mean, you know how dangerous this island can be sometimes."

"I am sympathetic to your plight," Fourfoot said.

"Cool. So yeah, if you don't mind, we'll just be on—"

"As such, I will allow you to remain here in Nightshore," Fourfoot interrupted. It seemed as if he hadn't even heard what Felicity had been trying to say. "I am sure we can find some use for you. As a servant, perhaps."

"But—"

"It is settled!" Fourfoot clapped his hands together. He turned to the beehive-haired lady. "Now, dismiss the crowd, so that we may adjourn to the residence."

The beehive-haired lady, Tealfinger, and several of the guards all exchanged glances. No one seemed really sure of what to do.

"I said *now*!" Fourfoot snapped.

♪♪♪

A few minutes later, Joel found himself being escorted, along with Felicity, to the far end of the village where the chieftain's residence was located. It was an awkward procession; Joel kept looking around, wondering if he and Felicity should try to simply run away, while the guards seemed torn between allowing them to escape and not wanting to incur the wrath of their chief.

"Okay," Felicity said out of the corner of her mouth as they walked, "so what's the an-play?"

"The what?" Joel said.

"You know...the an-play. Pig Latin? Ig-pay atin-lay?"

"Oh! Um...ing-way it-yay?"

"Ate-gray," Felicity muttered.

Eventually, they arrived at the residence. It was an opulent structure, even more so than its counterpart in Headsmouth village, Spectraland's de facto capital. With a number of interconnecting huts, platforms, and tree houses all built around a single giant banyan, it looked almost like a smaller version of the Wavemaker Temple.

"This is a lot bigger than I remember it," Joel mumbled to Felicity. "You know, when Darkeye was holding us prisoner?"

"Most of it probably got burned down, or whatever. I told you, we're early."

"Oh—right."

Once inside the chieftain's residence, the group made their way up a flight of wooden stairs, along several sloping walkways built on massive branches, and across some large lily-pad platforms until they finally arrived at a small rectangular hut that was covered, top to bottom, in leaves and flowers. There Fourfoot stopped and turned to Joel.

"Now," the young chief said, "it is time for the courtship phase."

"Um...the what?" Joel said.

"It is when you and I will spend some time alone together, to become better acquainted," Fourfoot explained, like a boy talking to his new pet. "It is mostly a formality, of course. While we are doing that, my advisor will take your companion to the servant's quarters."

Joel and Felicity glanced at each other.

"The rest of you, carry on with your normal duties," Fourfoot said to the others. "Oh, but first"—he turned to one of the guards—"take their supply packs and dispose of their contents, which I am sure are disgusting. Vagabonds and their rotten lifepods..." He shuddered.

"Hey, yeah, that's okay," Felicity said hastily, "we'll throw away our own stuff. 'Cause, you know, you don't want to be touching—"

"I will take care of their supply packs, my chief." Tealfinger stepped forward, an odd look on his face.

"You will?" Fourfoot chuckled. "Such a task is not beneath your status as a shaman?"

"No, my chief. It is not."

"Very well."

Tealfinger took Felicity's supply pack, and then Joel's. As he did so, he nodded at Joel ever so slightly.

Is he trying to tell me something? Joel wondered.

With that, everyone departed save for Fourfoot and a lone guard, who opened the door to the leaf-and-flower-covered hut.

"Come now!" Fourfoot said, grabbing Joel's arm.

"Uh—"

Fourfoot pulled Joel into the hut. The guard closed the door behind them. Inside, it was dark, save for a few dim patches of glowmoss on the walls and ceiling. Once Joel's eyes adjusted, he saw a round stone table and two wooden stools in the middle of the space and a doorway with a vine-rope curtain on the opposite wall.

"Please, have a seat," Fourfoot said.

Joel sat down on one of the stools.

"I will be back in a minute," Fourfoot said, heading for the doorway.

Joel glanced at the entrance, wondering if he should make a break for it.

There's probably just the one guard out there, he thought. *If I run fast enough...*

Before he could work up the courage for an attempt, however, Fourfoot returned. The Nightshore chief had exchanged his cloak and horned headdress for a simple sleeveless tunic and a floral crown.

"I love formal wear," he said, "but it can get rather uncomfortable in this heat." He sat down on the stool opposite Joel and leaned his elbows on the table. "So, tell me...Sightguy, was it?"

"Um, yeah."

"Tell me, Sightguy, how do you feel?"

"Nervous, I guess."

Fourfoot nodded. "I suppose that is to be expected. After all, it is not every day that one receives the honor of becoming a village chieftain's mate."

"Okay."

"Anyway, tell me more about yourself. You are a vagabond...does that mean you are originally from that nomadic tribe that lives near the Coast of Fang?"

Despite his distaste for lying, Joel saw no alternative at this point. He figured that at least Tealfinger wasn't here to verify whether he was telling the truth or not. "Yes. I am."

"I have encountered some of your people before. Rather disgusting bunch, I must say. Among them, you must have stood out like a shining beacon."

"Sure. Yeah."

There was an awkward pause. Then Fourfoot said, "You certainly are a quiet one."

Joel just sat there, unsure of how to respond.

"Well, that will not be an issue," Fourfoot said, smiling, "as I can be rather verbose. So I will do all the talking, and you will do all the listening. A perfect arrangement."

There was a knock on the door.

"Enter!" Fourfoot said.

The door opened. Joel turned to see Felicity walking in, holding a tray with two large stone flagons on it.

"Your drinks, my...chiefs," she said.

"Ah, put to work already, I see!" Fourfoot said. "Yes, yes, just set those down right over here."

Felicity placed one of the flagons in front of Fourfoot, and the other in front of Joel. As she did so, she flashed Joel a look that seemed to say something along the lines of *we really need to get out of here soon*. Her task complete, she turned and exited the hut.

"I think she will work out just fine," Fourfoot said, raising his flagon. "A toast! To our impending union."

Joel, feeling more and more uncomfortable by the second, raised his flagon and gingerly tapped it against

Fourfoot's, who then took a long sip. As he did so, Joel sniffed at his own flagon's contents. It smelled a lot like the beer his dad used to drink on a daily basis. He put the flagon down.

"You are of sufficient age to consume fermented beverages, are you not?" Fourfoot asked, apparently noticing Joel's reluctance.

"No," Joel said, before remembering that the legal drinking age in Spectraland was, in fact, seventeen. "I mean, yes. I am."

"Good," Fourfoot said. "I assumed you were, given your facial hair." He shook his head. "It is bad enough that my advisor questions the gender of my mate. I would not have her questioning his age as well. If she did, I would need to have her exiled for sure, and she does still come in handy from time to time."

Joel sensed that there was some kind of opportunity in what Fourfoot had just told him, although he wasn't exactly sure what it was. He decided to follow the plan he had suggested to Felicity earlier: wing it. "So, uh...why is she questioning the gender of your mate, anyway?"

"Honestly, Sightguy, I do not know." Fourfoot shook his head. "She has been like that ever since my parents died and I took over as chief. Never letting me make my own decisions. Not taking me seriously. Always objecting, never accepting."

Another knock on the door.

"Enter!" Fourfoot said.

The door opened, and Felicity walked in, carrying a tray with two plates on it.

"The...appetizers, my chiefs," she said, wrinkling her nose.

"Excellent," Fourfoot said.

Felicity set one of the plates down in front of Fourfoot, and the other in front of Joel. What was on them didn't look appetizing at all: small rat-like animals that had been burnt, skewered, and drizzled in a thin red sauce that may or may not have been blood.

"I will return shortly with the first course," she said, monotone, before making a hasty exit.

Fourfoot picked up the appetizer by the sticks protruding from its mouth and rear end and took a healthy bite. As he chewed, he said, "You may eat."

"No thanks," Joel said. "I, uh, I'm not hungry. You know, 'cause I'm still all nervous, and stuff."

"I see. Well, I certainly hope that are you not quite as nervous at next week's wedding ceremony."

Joel gulped. At first, the mention of a wedding ceremony made him even more nervous, but then he realized something. *If I have a whole week, then that should give me and Felicity enough time to figure out a way to get our wavebows back and get out of this situation before...well, before who knows what will happen.*

"I will talk some more," Fourfoot said after another bite. "Hopefully that will help you relax."

"Okay."

"So where was I...oh yes, my advisor. She probably means well, but still, she treats me like a child. I am so glad that I am now officially a man. You do not know how frustrating it is sometimes, being a chief and not being able to—"

Another knock.

"That was fast," Fourfoot said. "Enter!"

This time, instead of Felicity, it was the beehive-haired lady.

"What are *you* doing here?" Fourfoot said, nearly choking.

"Forgive me, my chief," the lady said, "but I felt this to be so important that it could not wait."

"What is it? Did the cook ruin the main course?"

"No, no, it—the food is fine. I just wanted to say that...well, before we proceeded any further with the courtship process, I wanted to voice my strong objection to your selection of this...this man."

Fourfoot slowly put his skewered rat back down on his plate. "Did I not say that I would have you exiled?" he said through clenched teeth. "Or perhaps you did not hear me clearly?"

"No, I did hear you," the lady said, a hint of resolve creeping into her voice. "But know that I am not alone in my opinion. Even if you have me exiled, others will try to stop this wedding from happening. They may even resort to drastic measures."

"Then I will not give them the chance," Fourfoot said. "Instead of next week, the wedding will take place today!"

Joel's eyes grew wide. Right at that moment, there was yet another knock on the door.

"To-today?" the beehive-haired lady stammered. "But...but, my chief..."

"But what?"

The beehive-haired lady looked around, as if an acceptable answer was written somewhere on the walls of the hut. Finally, she said, "But...the closest officiant is in Spearwind. It will take her days to get here."

"Ringneck can do it!" Fourfoot spat. "He is a minister of the law, is he not?"

"Still merely an apprentice," the lady said.

"That will suffice." Fourfoot stood up. "The wedding will take place in the throne room in one hour. I expect everything to be ready."

With that, the young chief walked over to the door, flung it open, and stormed out. Felicity was standing there, holding a large tray of steaming lifepods and other assorted fruit.

"Did I miss something?" she said.

CHAPTER 11: THE CATALYST

A little over an hour (actually sixty-two minutes, by Joel's count) later, a small crowd had gathered in a spacious hut on the ground level of the chieftain's residence: Fourfoot, the beehive-haired lady, Tealfinger, Joel, Felicity (along with two other servants, one male and one female), a half dozen guards, and a distinctly younger-looking—he couldn't have been any older than Joel or Felicity—Ringneck. The official reason they were all here was for Joel and Fourfoot's wedding ceremony, but there was nothing even slightly ceremonious about the setting; there were no decorations, no musicians playing, no food or drinks being served. No one had even changed their clothes from an hour ago.

"This is all highly irregular," Ringneck said, finally plucking up the courage to protest. He seemed fidgety and skittish, not at all like the self-assured, indifferent future version of himself, the one who had presided over Felicity and Thornleaf's wedding in the manner of one who was simply going through the motions.

"I agree," the beehive-haired lady said, sounding relieved. She turned to Fourfoot. "My chief, may I suggest that—"

"No, you may not suggest anything!" Fourfoot cut her off. "This wedding will happen, and it will happen *now*!"

Ringneck mumbled something to himself as he leafed through a stack of parchments.

"What was that?" Fourfoot demanded.

"Nothing, Fourfoot—uh, I mean, my chief. I am simply checking for—"

"Just get on it with it!" Fourfoot exclaimed. The young Nightshore chief slapped at the parchments, knocking them out of Ringneck's hands and sending them flying around the hut. "I swear, if you were not my cousin, I would have you exiled the moment this was over."

Oh, so Ringneck is Fourfoot's cousin, Joel thought. That bit of information wasn't very helpful as far as his current predicament was concerned, but it was interesting nonetheless.

"Understood, my chief," Ringneck said, crouching down to pick up his fallen papers.

"You do not need any of that," Fourfoot said, sweeping away several pieces of parchment with his foot. "Just skip all the preliminary nonsense and get to the part where you ask us if we do."

"Very—very well," Ringneck said. He stood up, a single parchment in hand, and looked around. "We do seem to have the requisite number of witnesses here, so I suppose that—"

"Stop talking and proceed!" Fourfoot snapped.

Ringneck looked down at his parchment and began reading. "Do you, Chief Fourfoot of Nightshore, accept..."—he looked up at Joel—"what was your name, again?"

"Um...Sightguy."

"Do you, Chief Fourfoot of Nightshore, accept Sightguy of the Roughrock vagabond tribe as your mate and life partner, now and forever?"

"Yes, yes, I do."

"And do you, Sightguy of the Roughrock vagabond tribe, accept Chief Fourfoot of Nightshore as your mate and life partner, now and forever?"

Everyone glanced at Joel. His face turned hot. He could feel beads of sweat forming everywhere. Was this really happening?

"I..."

Joel looked at Felicity. She gave him a sheepish, barely perceptible shrug in response. Her words from a couple of adventures ago echoed in his mind: *Don't be afraid to say what's on your mind, or to say how you feel about stuff*.

"I..."

Then, his own words: *Sometimes, you just gotta say, what the heck*.

"I...I don't."

There was an audible gasp. Joel wasn't really sure who it came from.

"Forgive me," Ringneck asked, blinking hard, "but...what did you just say?"

Joel straightened his posture, trying to strike what he thought was a confident, almost defiant pose. "I said I don't," he answered. "I do not."

A long, tense pause ensued, during which Joel turned his eyes to Fourfoot. The young chief's lips were creased into a grimace, and his light-green complexion had turned a few shades darker. If this were an old-fashioned cartoon, Joel thought, steam would probably be leaking out of his ears.

Then, finally: "How *dare* you reject me!" Fourfoot exploded. "How *dare* you refuse such an honor? Do you know who I am? Do you?"

"Um, you're...Fourfoot?" Joel responded, trying to give a sincere answer.

"I am the *Chief of Nightshore!* And as such, you have no choice in the matter—you cannot reject me, even if you wanted to!"

"Actually, my chief," the beehive-haired lady interjected, "I believe he can. Is that not correct, Ringneck?"

"What?" Ringneck said, still looking shocked. "Oh, uh, well...yes. I mean no, you are correct."

"She is?" Fourfoot said.

"Indeed." Ringneck nodded, his brow furrowed. "According to Spectraland law, if a chief selects a potential mate that is not from his or her own village, that person has the right to refuse," he said, sounding like he was reciting a line that he had just recently memorized.

"What—that—that cannot be!" Fourfoot sputtered.

"I am afraid it is, my chief," Ringneck said.

"Then I will break that law!"

"If you do so, your title will become forfeit," Ringneck said, his demeanor a bit more confident. "You would no longer be a chief."

"Then—then I will *change* the law! Chiefs can do that. I know they can!"

"Not by themselves," Ringneck said, sounding more and more like his future self by the moment. "Laws can only be changed via unanimous vote of the Chieftain Council. All four members must be in agreement."

"The *council?*" Fourfoot shrieked. "Those imbeciles never listen to *anything* I have to say. Trying to get them to agree with me would be futile!"

"I am sorry, my chief," Ringneck said. "I truly am. But I do not know what else to tell you."

Fourfoot glanced around the room. He was breathing hard and his fists were clenched; he looked as if he wanted to hit someone. Anyone there would have made an easy target, as they were all standing perfectly still.

The beehive-haired lady was the first to break the silence. "Well, with that, I believe we can resume the selection ritual," she said, cheerily, to no one in particular. "I will reconvene the prospects and the villagers at once." She started to head for the door. As she passed by Fourfoot, he reached out—suddenly, like a striking snake—and grabbed the lady's arm.

"No," the young chief growled, whirling her around. "You will do no such thing."

"Forgive me, my chief, but I—"

"*You,*" he said, "are hereby exiled. You will leave this village now, never to return."

The lady's face fell. "But..."

"You are lucky that *Spectraland law*"—Fourfoot spat out those last two words with undisguised contempt—"prevents me from having you executed instead."

"My chief, I..."

"Guards! Escort this traitor out. I never want to see her hideous visage again."

The guards all glanced at each other.

"*Do it!*"

Two of the guards stepped forward, seized the lady by her arms, and began dragging her out.

"You are making a huge mistake, you spoiled little brat!" the lady called over her shoulder, all pretense of respect now gone. "You will regret this, I swear!"

Fourfoot turned around and clapped his hands together. "Now then, where were we?" he said through a sinister, tight-lipped smile. "Ah yes, the Chieftain Council. Ringneck?"

"Y-yes, my chief?" Ringneck answered, nervous once again.

"If the council were to consist of, say, just one member instead of four, and that member voted to change a particular law, would that be considered unanimous?"

"I...I suppose so. But if one of the chiefs is no longer able to serve on the council for whatever reason, be it death or debilitation, he or she is immediately replaced by a successor. Just as you replaced your mother and father."

"Fair enough." Fourfoot scratched his chin, seemingly in thought. "All right then, what if one of the chiefs had more power than the others? Like, perhaps, a High Chief, in charge of the entire island?"

"To my knowledge, there has never been precedent for such a thing."

"That being the case, this High Chief could make or break any rule that he so desired, could he not?"

"I...I suppose."

Fourfoot turned to one of the guards, nodding. "Assemble the army at once."

"Army?" the guard said, puzzled. "My chief, we do not have..."

"An army? Of course we do. You, along with the rest of my elite guards, will gather up every able-bodied villager and arm them with a weapon. You will give them a quick training session on how to fight. Then we will take over the other villages and install me as the High Chief and sole ruler of Spectraland!"

Uh oh, Joel thought, exchanging a knowing glance with Felicity.

"Chief Fourfoot," Tealfinger said, "with all due respect, I think that these actions may be a bit drastic. If you would, please, just take a moment to calm down and—"

"You are lucky that I cannot exile *you*, shaman," Fourfoot said. "That said, your Elders have granted me some measure of authority over you, have they not?"

"You know they have, my chief."

"Then my command to you is this: either support me, or stay out of my way. Understood?"

Tealfinger nodded. "Understood."

"Good. Now, while I make war plans with my guards, take my *betrothed*"—he shot Joel an angry glance—"and place him under house arrest. There he will remain until I am High Chief and can legally force him to be my mate."

"Yes, my chief."

"Take his vagabond companion as well. Otherwise, I suspect that she will try to help him escape."

Felicity shook her head. "No clue what gave you that idea," she muttered under her breath.

♪♪♪

Tealfinger and a pair of guards escorted Joel and Felicity to a small hut that was perched on one of the residence's highest branches. The guards then shoved the pair of offworlders inside and shut the door. A moment later, the sounds of Tealfinger performing a locking wavecast could be heard.

"Well, good job, dude," Felicity said, her sarcasm level set to medium-high.

"What are you talking about?" Joel said.

"You just started the Fourfoot War."

"I didn't start it, Fourfoot did." *That must have been the terrible incident that Redstem was talking about*, Joel realized.

"Yeah, but you rejected him."

"What else was I supposed to do? I can't marry him. We're only supposed to be finding Blackspore, not doing anything else. Otherwise we might change history for the worse. Remember?"

"Not to mention, you're only into girls."

Joel felt himself blush. "Well...yeah, that too."

"All right, all right, I know, I was just giving you a hard time. So how are we going to get out of here?"

Joel looked around the hut. Other than a single sleeping mat on the floor, it was completely empty and devoid of anything they could possibly use to facilitate an escape attempt.

"Hmm...not sure."

"Great. Okay, I'll try something." Felicity walked up to the door. "Hey," she called to the guard who was standing outside. "If you let us out of here, we'll make it worth your while."

"I cannot," the guard grunted in response. "I do not wish to be exiled."

"No, I suppose you don't," Felicity muttered. She walked back over to Joel. "All right, so that didn't work."

"If they're gonna be keeping us in here for the entire length of the war, we should have plenty of opportunities," Joel said, trying to stay optimistic. "Like, maybe when they open the door to give us food and stuff, you could do some karate on them."

"Oh, sure, like it's that simple. Don't you think they'll be expecting something like that?"

Joel thought hard, trying to remember a similar situation from a movie or television show he had seen where the captives had managed to escape. Or even something from his own life; after all, hadn't they managed to get out of plenty of jams like this before?

"Maybe Sammy will come and scratch out a hole in the wall of the hut," he said, recalling the time that Sammy had busted him, Felicity, and Fireflower out of a prison hut in this very same village.

"Yeah, no. Any other ideas?"

"Um...some Lightsnakes will pull us out?" That one was from the time he and Felicity were saved from burning to death at the Wavemaker Temple, after Stoneroot had set it on fire.

"This isn't funny, you know."

"Sorry."

"Don't apologize," she sighed. "Look, I know what you're trying to say, but I don't think there's any deus ex machina coming to save us."

"Any what?"

"Deus ex machina."

Joel furrowed his brow. "You mean the central interface of the Machine City in *The Matrix*?"

"What? No, I mean like the giant eagles that flew out of the sky to save the hobbits."

"Oh—okay, I get it."

"Yeah, so I think this time, we're gonna have to rely on our own wits."

"Then we might be in trouble."

Despite the gravity of their situation, Felicity smirked. "Good one," she said.

"Thanks." Joel grinned.

"You know what the cool thing about you is?"

"What?"

"You're always growing."

"I've been the same height since I was fifteen."

"No, I don't mean that. I mean you're...how do I say this...you learn stuff, and you change. You adapt. Not, like, to please people or anything like that, but to improve yourself. People—like me or Art or Blackspore or whoever—will give you advice and then you take the parts that you like and blend them into your personality, in a way that you're comfortable with. I've noticed that about you. It's pretty awesome."

Based on Felicity's tone of voice, Joel estimated that her sarcasm level was currently set to zero. "Oh—um, yeah. Art said something similar."

"Figures," Felicity chuckled. "Anyway, keep it up. I know some people who don't do that—they're all stubborn and inflexible and whatever, and I gotta say, it can get pretty annoying."

"Like who?"

"Well, like..."

She trailed off as voices came from outside the hut. One of them was the guard, and another sounded like Tealfinger. Joel and Felicity glanced at each other before moving up to the door in an effort to eavesdrop.

"...need to speak with the vagabonds," Tealfinger was saying. "In private, please."

"Very well," the guard said. "Out of curiosity, may I ask why?"

"They had some very unusual items in their supply packs. I want to interrogate them about it."

"Will you be safe in there, alone?"

"Of course. But I will call for you, if necessary."

"Understood. Proceed."

Joel and Felicity backed away from the door as the sounds of Tealfinger dispelling the locking cast reverberated outside. A moment later, the door opened, and the native shaman entered. He didn't say anything; instead, he just shot curious glances at the two offworlders, regarding them as if they were exotic zoo animals.

"Hey," Felicity said.

Tealfinger shut the door behind him. His wavebow hung at his hip, and he had both Joel's and Felicity's supply packs slung around his shoulders. "So," he said, "do you want to tell me who you really are?"

"We told you already," Felicity said. "He's Sightguy, and I'm Goldilocks. We're vagabond travelers."

"I do not need a truth cast to know that you are lying," Tealfinger responded. "Vagabond travelers do not carry wavebows with them. I believe that you are, in fact, Wavemakers."

"Well, uh, maybe we stole them from some actual Wavemakers," Joel said.

"Yeah, that's probably not the best story to go with," Felicity mumbled.

"I am familiar with every single instrument carried by each current member of the order," Tealfinger said. "And I would have felt it in the Aura if the Luthier had, for whatever reason, created new ones."

Everyone glanced at each other for a few seconds.

"I can help you," Tealfinger finally continued.

"How?" Felicity said.

"I can get you out of here."

"Why would you want to help us?" Felicity asked.

"I would like to prevent Chief Fourfoot from committing a huge mistake."

"You mean, marrying me?" Joel asked.

"No, his advisor was the one who was opposed to the marriage. I, personally, do not care about that—in fact, my preferences in a mate are similar to the chief's."

"Oh."

"What I do care about is his declaration of war. That is why I want to help you. I think that if you were to return to where I suspect you came from, then perhaps this conflict can still be avoided."

"And where, exactly, do you suspect we came from?" Felicity asked.

"The future."

Felicity turned to Joel. "Hey, this guy is pretty good," she said, aiming a thumb at Tealfinger.

"One of my colleagues—a master shaman—has been researching how to travel through time. It would not be unreasonable to assume that he will eventually perfect such an ability."

"Are you talking about Blackspore?" Joel asked.

"Yes."

"Where is he, anyway?" Felicity asked.

"At the Wavemaker Temple. He spends most of his time there, in the archives, while I and my sister, who is also a shaman, tend to the village."

"That makes sense," Joel said. "Because, you know, in the future, he—"

Tealfinger held up his hand. "Do not tell me anything about the future," he said. "I do not want to know."

"Oh—okay."

"I presume that the two of you were sent back here to stop Chief Fourfoot from starting this war. If I release you and you return to your own time, then I believe that your mission will have been accomplished."

Joel and Felicity exchanged glances. That wasn't their mission. But then again, they couldn't just stay stuck in here. And even though preventing the war itself wasn't what Blackspore had requested, it *would* accomplish their two main goals: Marshall would never come over to Spectraland, and the Uniter would never rise to power in the Six States. True, it was possible that history could be altered for the worse, but at this point, Joel figured that it was a chance they had to take. Maybe this was their fatewave—the way things were meant to happen. And if that was the case, he figured, then he was sure everything would all work out fine in the end, somehow.

"All right, sounds good," he said.

"But how are you going to bust us out?" Felicity asked Tealfinger. "It wouldn't really be cool for that guard out there to get exiled. He's just doing his job."

"I will take care of that," Tealfinger said. He handed over the supply packs and turned around. "One of you, place me in a hold."

Felicity placed Tealfinger in a chokehold. "Like this?"

"Yes," Tealfinger croaked, "but...not that tight, please."

"Oh, okay," Felicity said, loosening the hold. "Good thing you said something. Normally I can knock someone out in a few seconds with one of those."

"That is not my intent here."

"Gotcha. I think I know what you're doing."

Joel looked at her. "I don't. What is he—?"

"Guard!" Tealfinger cried. "Help!"

The door swung open and the guard charged in, spear at the ready. "Release him at once!" he barked.

Tealfinger broke out of Felicity's hold and shot out a few short stunning casts. Most of them struck the wall of the hut, but the final one hit the guard, who immediately slumped down onto the ground.

"An error on my part," the shaman said.

"It was?" Joel asked.

"Dude, this is his cover story," Felicity said.

"Oh."

"Now you overpower me, finish what you started by rendering me unconscious, and then escape to your own time," Tealfinger said. "Good luck." And with that, he fired a stunning cast at himself.

"Well then," Felicity said, fishing her own wavebow out of her supply pack, "I guess that worked out after all."

"Yup," Joel agreed, also retrieving his instrument. He looked it over. It didn't seem to have been touched.

"What is happening down there?" a voice called from outside.

"Uh oh," Felicity said. "We'd better bail."

"Okay. So, back to the future?"

"You've just been waiting to say that, haven't you?"

Joel grinned. "Yeah."

CHAPTER 12: PARENTAL GUIDANCE

Even though he wasn't sure it was going to work, Joel envisioned himself and Felicity returning to the exact time and place they had left from. He played the time-travel cast, heard the now-familiar *whoosh* sound, and then—

"Ugh, a little rougher trip that time," Felicity said, rubbing her temples. "But I think it worked—this is the same spot, right?"

Joel blinked. When his eyesight cleared, he saw that they were indeed standing in a copse of seaweed-palm trees a hundred or so feet away from Nightshore village, which looked like its normal, "modern" self. Everything else also appeared to be unchanged, except that it had been daytime when they left and now it was night.

"Mostly, I guess," he said. "I think I just overshot it by a few hours."

"Close enough," Felicity said. "But wait—if we're still in Spectraland, doesn't that mean the war still happened?"

"Maybe," Joel said. "Or...maybe we prevented the war but somehow came over anyway?" His hopes started to rise. "It'd be like we ate our own cake."

"That's not exactly how that saying goes," Felicity said. "But I know what you mean."

Joel tingled with excitement. Could this be one of those time-travel scenarios where everything turned out even better than expected? Could they have created an ideal future, one in which they saved a bunch of lives while retaining their connection to Spectraland? Felicity would probably still be married to Thornleaf, but at least Auravine would be alive...

"Hey, someone's coming," Felicity said.

Joel turned. Sure enough, a native riding a slimeback was approaching, having veered off from a nearby trail to enter the copse of trees. It took Joel a second to recognize who it was.

"It's Whitenose."

"Oh, cool," Felicity said. "We can ask him how things are."

"Hello, travelers!" Whitenose called out once he was within earshot. "Are you in need of assistance?"

"Whitenose, it's us," Joel said, stepping forward. "Joel and Felicity."

"Joel and Felicity?" Whitenose raised his spear.

"Yeah, you know, the legendary offworlders?" Joel said, wondering if perhaps this was now actually their first appearance in Spectraland.

"But you do not look like them." Whitenose squinted. "Well, perhaps a little."

"Oh," Joel said, remembering that they had been shapeshifted. "Yeah, no, we're just in disguise."

"Disguise? Again? Why are you—?"

"Long story," Felicity said. "Anyway, got a few questions for you. First of all, did the Fourfoot War ever happen?"

"Of course it did," Whitenose answered, looking befuddled. "Why would you even ask that?"

Hmm, Joel thought.

"Second question," Felicity said, "did someone named Marshall Byle ever come over to Spectraland?"

"Do you mean during the Fourfoot War, or the attack on your wedding ceremony?"

"Uh oh," Felicity said, exchanging glances with Joel.

"And why did you refer to him as someone I might not be familiar with?"

"We'll explain later," Felicity replied. "Last question. How many days has it been since the wedding?"

"Two."

Felicity turned to Joel. "That means we lost, like, a day and a half."

"And the giant countercom will be ready the morning after tomorrow," Joel said. "If nothing's changed, that is."

"Yeah, I don't think anything has," Felicity said, grabbing her wavebow. "We'd better go."

"Back to the temple?" Joel asked as he too prepared to play his instrument.

"Yup."

"Wait," Whitenose said, "you should come with me to Nightshore. I could use some help rounding up the rest of—"

Not waiting for Whitenose to finish, Joel and Felicity fired up some flying casts and zoomed off.

"I wonder why nothing changed!" Joel called out through the wind.

"Who knows? That's not the priority right now!"

It was probably inevitable, Joel figured. *Again, which is why Blackspore specifically wanted me to stop him from bringing Marshall over, not prevent the war itself.* As soon as he finished that thought, he spotted something down below.

"Hey, look!"

"At what?"

"It's Thornleaf!"

"What? Where?"

Joel pointed to an area on the ground roughly a hundred yards ahead. There, on a narrow trail, a hooded figure was riding a slimeback, galloping in Joel and Felicity's general direction at full speed. To any other observer, the rider's identity would not have been obvious, but Joel could tell who it was. Felicity, most definitely aware of this, didn't stop to question—she merely cursed and then went into a nosedive.

Why is she upset? Joel wondered before following her down.

The rider—Thornleaf—seemed to take note of their approach. Instead of slowing down, however, he veered off into some nearby trees, adding to Joel's confusion.

What is he doing?

Felicity made a sharp course correction and abruptly dropped down into a copse. Joel followed suit. They landed right in front of Thornleaf and his slimeback, who had to pull up at the last second to avoid crashing into them.

"Out of my way!" Thornleaf barked.

"Well, hello to you too," Felicity sneered. "Not even happy to see me back, huh?"

"Once I heard about your foolish plan, I knew it would not work and that you would return."

"And just in time, it looks like. You need to stop what you're doing."

"What is he doing?" Joel asked.

"He's going to the beach to kill Marshall."

"We are running out of time," Thornleaf said. "Someone has to save our island."

"Did Fireflower give you permission to do this?"

"It is always easier to beg for forgiveness than to ask for permission."

"Using my own lines against me. Cute."

"Now step aside."

"Where's Thinker? Why didn't you bring him along?"

"I would not ask anyone else to take this risk."

"Oh, but it's fine for you?"

"If someone does not stop Byle right now, all of our people will become enslaved. Is that what you want?"

"Yes, dear, it'd be my dream come true," Felicity said, sarcasm level set to maximum overload. "Look, I know he has to be stopped. Just give Joel's plan another chance."

"It is too late."

"No it's not. Nothing's too late when you can time travel."

"If you are so confident in his abilities, then why are you trying to stop me? If he succeeds, then none of this will happen anyway. We will not even know each other."

"I know, but—"

"Killing Byle now, in the present, is the best solution," Thornleaf said. "He is the evil force that the Virtuoso is supposed to stop, I am sure of it. So if he is eliminated, then there will be no need for Blackspore to guide anyone. There will be no need for a single powerful shaman that the Silencers will fear. Spectraland will be saved without having to tamper with history or disrupt the harmony of the island. We will not have to gamble our future on an unproven ability that, so far, seems quite unreliable."

"Yeah, but—"

"Are you on my side or not?" Thornleaf demanded.

"I..." Felicity paused and took a deep breath. Then: "Fine. But I'm going with you."

"What?" Joel and Thornleaf said at the same time.

"You heard me. I'm going with you. To the beach. You're gonna need help. You can't do this alone."

"No. It is too dangerous."

"I don't care what you say. You can't stop me."

"But—"

"Joel." Felicity turned and moved up close. "Go back to the temple, recharge, and then try the plan again," she said in a lowered voice. "Hopefully you'll succeed this time and none of this will be necessary."

"You mean...by myself?"

"Sure, yeah."

"I thought someone needed to make sure I stay out of trouble."

"I was just kidding about that. You went back the first time by yourself, right?"

"That was just a few hours, though."

"Believe me, you'll be fine."

"Um, okay."

♪♪♪

Joel arrived back at the Wavemaker Temple and entered the main hall. To his surprise, there was no one there—not even Blackspore.

Did Fireflower heal him?

Curious, Joel exited the hall and walked into the courtyard. No one was there either. Everything seemed eerily quiet. Even the fountain was dry, as if someone had turned it off.

Weird. I wonder where everyone—

"Master Joel?" a voice said from behind.

Joel whirled around. Riverhand was standing there, holding a couple of supply packs. "Oh—Riverhand. You startled me."

"Apologies."

"No problem."

"I almost did not recognize you."

"What? Oh, right—this is what Fireflower shapeshifted me into," Joel said, rubbing the stubble on his chin. "You know, so people in the past wouldn't ask too many questions."

"I see. What are you doing here, may I ask?"

"Um, well, the plan...it didn't work. I mean, obviously. So I came back here to recharge, and then I'm gonna try again."

"Where is Miss Felicity?"

"She's..." Joel trailed off, unsure of how much he wanted to say. "It's complicated. Where is everyone else?"

"Fireflower decided that, while we were waiting for your plan to work, we would evacuate as many villagers as possible to the Thirsty Tunnels."

"The what?"

"Thirsty Tunnels. An underground area near the northwest coast that, according to Thinker, should be shielded from the effects of the giant countercom."

Joel couldn't believe there was a place in Spectraland that he wasn't yet familiar with. "I've never been there before."

"It is not a very hospitable locale. As such, it will not be a long-term solution, but it should buy us some time. I only returned here to pick up some remaining items."

"Is Blackspore there too?"

"No. He and several others were relocated to the swordcat den that you found up near the Sacred Site. It is smaller but safer there, and the swordcats can keep him alive for as long as possible."

"Oh. Cool."

"Why did your plan not work?"

"We—I just overshot the time period, basically. I'm sure I'll get it right this time."

"I am sure you will. Best of luck." Riverhand turned to leave.

"Hey, uh, Riverhand?"

Riverhand stopped and looked over his shoulder. "Yes?"

"Do...do you want to come with me?"

"You mean, to the past?'

"Yeah. I could use the help."

Riverhand reacted with an odd, unreadable expression. "Do you think that is really a good idea?"

"I don't see why not." Joel shrugged. "You weren't alive at the time, right? So you won't run into yourself, or anything."

"No, I suppose not," Riverhand said. He glanced at the supply packs in his hands. "Fireflower is expecting these, however."

"If we're successful, she won't need them. You'll just reappear back here and live on in a much more peaceful timeline."

"Are you sure?"

"Yeah," Joel said, even though he wasn't all that sure. It was just that, after his harrowing experience with Fourfoot, he really didn't want to go back in time again by himself.

"Very well, I will accompany you," Riverhand said. "I would like to ask for one small favor, however."

"Okay."

"Could we add an additional task to our mission? It should not take long."

"You mean, like a side quest?"

"If I understand what you are saying correctly—yes."

Can't hurt, Joel figured. *He said it shouldn't take long. And even if it does, it won't matter, because of time travel. At least, I hope so, anyway*. "All right, yeah, no problem."

♪♪♪

After recharging in the main hall, Joel and Riverhand flew most of the way to Headsmouth village before they landed in a nearby jungle, where Joel performed the time-travel cast. From there, they began walking.

"So, um, what were your parents' names, again?" Joel asked.

"Watertongue and Rosewort," Riverhand replied.

"And what am I supposed to tell them?"

"To accept their future child exactly the way he is."

"Because of your hand?"

"Yes. They were not pleased that I was born...unwhole," Riverhand said, holding up his clawlike right hand. "We had a very contentious relationship because of that. I was so happy to leave them when I was young and train with Fireflower as a Wavemaker."

"You know, that reminds me of something I've wanted to ask you."

"What is that?"

"Couldn't Auravine"—it hurt a little to say her name—"couldn't she have given you, you know, extra fingers? Like how she regrew mine after they were cut off?"

Riverhand looked as if he were about to give an angry retort, but then his expression softened. "She offered, but I never accepted," he said. "I was always happy with myself the way I was. I wanted to prove to my parents, to everyone, that not only could I function normally with my so-called disfigurement, but that I could thrive. I could not only be a Wavemaker and play a wavebow, but I could do everything that anyone else could, just as well, or even better."

"Oh—um, and yeah, you totally can."

"I know."

"Sorry if I offended you."

"No offense was taken."

"Cool."

They arrived at the village outskirts.

"I will wait here for you," Riverhand said, drawing up the hood of his traveling cloak. "It would not do for me to be seen by my parents. Or anyone else, really."

"Good point," Joel said. "Oh—and, uh, while I'm in there, I'm gonna try to find out what stage the war is in. If I timed it right, it should be near the end, when Blackspore is about to bring Marshall over."

"Understood." Riverhand nodded.

Joel headed in and looked around. It certainly appeared as if there had been a war going on; most of the village's huts had spears sticking out of them, several trees had been uprooted, and even a few of the surrounding rock formations had been toppled over. It seemed as if he had arrived just after an attack, as a number of natives were busy working to assess and repair the damage. Joel recognized one of the natives as Suntooth, the good-natured older villager that Marshall had unceremoniously used—first as a servant and then as a talking puppet—before ultimately killing him as part of an evil scheme to obtain a powerful artifact known as the Songshell. Joel felt a little pang of sadness as he approached. Then, suddenly, Suntooth turned toward him.

"Greetings!" the villager said.

Joel stopped in his tracks. *Wait—does he recognize me? How would he—?*

"Suntooth, what are you doing?" one of the other villagers, a stocky male, hissed. "He could be a spy for Fourfoot."

"I know everyone from Nightshore personally," Suntooth insisted. "This traveler is certainly not one of them." He turned back to Joel. "What is your name, young man?"

Okay, good, he doesn't know who I am.

"I'm, uh, I'm Sightguy," Joel said.

"An odd name," the other villager said. "What village are you from?"

"I'm from none village," Joel replied. "I mean, I'm not from any village. I'm a vagabond. A neutral, unarmed vagabond."

"What are you doing here?"

"I'm just passing through."

"Well, Sightguy, your timing is excellent," Suntooth said, chuckling. "You just missed all of the action."

"I can tell." Joel nodded.

"Anyway, forgive my lack of manners," Suntooth said. "Welcome to Headsmouth. I am Suntooth, the prime advisor to our chief. And this"—he gestured at the other villager—"is Watertongue."

"Oh! You're Riverhand's—" Joel started to say, momentarily thrown off track by the lucky chance meeting. Fortunately, he caught himself before he was able to give anything more away. "Um, I mean, nice to meet you."

Watertongue gave Joel a quizzical look. "What did you just say?"

"I said, 'nice to meet you.'"

"No, no, before that."

"Uh, nothing. So...there's a war going on, right?"

"I am afraid so," Suntooth replied.

"Good. Um, I mean, not good. I mean—what started this war, anyway?"

"I am not completely sure, to be honest. All I know is that Chief Fourfoot of Nightshore desired additional power."

"How long has it been going on for?"

"Nearly six months now."

"Oh, so there's still a ways to go."

"What do you mean by that?" Watertongue asked.

"Er, I—"

"Watertongue!" a female villager called out as she approached. "Greenseed needs you over at the chieftain's"—she stopped and looked at Joel—"well, hello," she said, smiling. "Who are you?"

"This is a vagabond named Sightguy," Watertongue answered before Joel had a chance to say anything. "Sightguy, this is Rosewort. My spouse."

Joel wasn't sure, but it seemed as if, for some reason, Watertongue had placed an unusual amount of emphasis on the word *spouse*. "Um, hello."

"What brings you to Headsmouth village?" Rosewort asked.

"He is just passing through," Watertongue said. "He will be leaving shortly."

"Nonsense," Rosewort said, still smiling. "I am sure he is weary from a long journey. We should show him some hospitality."

"I, uh, that's okay," Joel said. "I actually have to get going."

Rosewort's smile morphed into sort of a half-pout, half-smirk. "How unfortunate."

"Before I leave, though," Joel said, "I have something to tell you."

Rosewort raised an eyebrow. "Oh?"

"Yes, both of you," Joel said, turning to Watertongue. He cleared his throat. "If you ever have children," he intoned, launching into his preplanned speech, "be sure to cherish and accept them just the way they are. Do not reject them simply because they do not conform to some arbitrary standard of what is considered to be normal."

Watertongue furrowed his brow. Rosewort bit her lower lip. A long moment passed.

"Those are wise words," Suntooth finally said, breaking the awkward silence.

"Yeah, they are," Joel said. "You see, I'm a wise vagabond. You know, like a traveling guru—I go around giving advice to people."

"A noble pursuit, especially in these troubled times," Suntooth said.

"I know. It's, like, my calling, and stuff."

Rosewort took a step closer, making Joel feel very uncomfortable. "Are you sure you cannot stay longer?" she asked. "I have many questions I would like to ask someone as...intelligent as yourself."

"He needs to be on his way," Watertongue grunted. "We would not want to deprive the other villages of his knowledge."

"Yeah," Joel agreed. "What he said."

Rosewort sighed. "Very well."

With that, Joel turned and began walking.

"Farewell, Sightguy!" Rosewort called after him. "Feel free to return anytime!"

Joel kept walking. He didn't look back.

CHAPTER 13: STEALTH MISSION

"I still say we should've flown to Headsmouth first and then taken slimebacks from there," Felicity complained, riding tandem with Thornleaf.

"And I already told you," Thornleaf said, "if Byle and his forces saw us in the sky, they would be able to deduce what we were up to."

"But Joel and I flew to Nightshore. Headsmouth is on the way there. So, same thing."

"Maybe so, but this way, we maximize our chances of success."

"Along with maximizing the pain in my butt."

"You have grown spoiled. I used to travel all around the island via slimeback when I was young."

"Been there, done that. Which is why I want to avoid doing it now."

"Let us just go over the plan once more."

"Fine," Felicity sighed. "We get to the beach, stun everyone, save the day. The end."

"That is not how it goes."

"Oh, that's right, I left out the part where you want to kill Marshall. Whoops."

"The nullifier has only been tested on a single device—Thinker's," Thornleaf said, sounding more and more agitated with every word. "If we find ourselves overwhelmed, then killing Byle will be our only alternative. It is the only way to stop the mind control all at once."

"We won't get overwhelmed," Felicity insisted. "It'll be dark, and we'll be invisible. Like, double invisible, with both the salve *and* the wavecast. No one will see us coming."

"I thought you were the one who was skeptical about the invisibility salve."

"Hey, an eighty-three percent chance of it working isn't bad."

"We must be prepared for the other seventeen percent. If I have to kill Byle, then I will kill him."

"No. No way. If we need to retreat, then we retreat. But no killing."

"It almost sounds to me as if you want to save Byle's life."

"I want to save *your* life, dummy!" Felicity snapped.

"I appreciate the sentiment," Thornleaf responded, "but I will do what I must to save our island."

"See, that's the problem. I don't think you'd be doing it to save Spectraland. You'd be doing it out of hate and anger. Which is a great way to turn yourself into the next Graymold."

"Graymold was seduced by the power of the Songshell. I have no such artifact at my disposal."

"Yeah, you're totally missing the point there."

"How many times do I have to reassure you about my motivations?"

"Hey, I thought that maybe you *had* changed. But then after that scene at our wedding, I wasn't so sure anymore."

"What scene?"

"You know, when you almost attacked your dad?"

"He cannot be trusted! You, of all people, should know that!"

"That doesn't mean you should be jumping to conclusions. As it turned out, it wasn't him doing the mind control after all, right?"

"This discussion is over," Thornleaf growled, urging his mount into a faster gait.

♪♪♪

While they continued to argue about a variety of subjects, Felicity and Thornleaf made it through the Jungle of Darkness relatively unscathed—a minor skirmish with a rabid pack of elephant-sharks was all—and arrived at the beach near Crownrock under the cover of nightfall. Once there, they rode through the trees until they got to about fifty yards from where the Six States vehicles were parked.

"So how many soldiers are there?" Felicity asked, eyeing up the perimeter of the beachhead.

"A few," Thornleaf replied. "Can you not see them yourself?"

"Right, right. I'm just used to getting an accurate count. Do you have the thing?"

"What thing?"

"The nullifier."

Thornleaf reached into a pouch on his belt and pulled out a device, if you could call it that. It was basically a wooden half shell with some circuitry inside of it, as if someone had packed random pieces of broken computer hardware into a small coconut. A single blinking red light, indicating where its toggle switch was located, gave it the unnerving appearance of a grenade. "Here you go," he said, handing it over.

"Cool. Now do the salve and stuff."

"I still say I should be the bait."

"No, you're better with a blowgun."

"I suppose that is true." Thornleaf applied some soulshifter salve—the one that Thinker had modified to completely mask one's energy signature—to Felicity's cheeks and forehead. Then he performed an invisibility cast on her, followed by a muting cast. When that was done, he said, "Just be careful."

"Nah, I like being reckless instead," Felicity said, although because of the muting cast, no sound actually came out of her mouth. She then stalked her way through the trees, hugging the line where the vegetation met the sand, until she arrived right in front of Marshall's camp. From there she could see that there were seven soldiers standing around, positioned at ten-foot intervals around the twelve ships. The ships themselves were arranged in a semicircle that surrounded two structures: one of them large, metallic, and boxy, like a shipping container, the other a familiar, small hut.

That scumbag is using one of the guest huts from my wedding! she realized.

Shaking off the distraction, she looked closer at the soldiers. They were each carrying a standard-issue Six States rifle, and a handheld countercom hung from each of their belts.

All right, here goes nothing.

She picked up a nearby rock and hurled it at one of the soldiers. It missed, but that wasn't really the point.

"Hey," the soldier said, turning, "did you see that?"

"See what?" one of his colleagues replied.

The soldier pointed the tip of his rifle at the rock on the ground. "That. I think it came flying out of the trees."

"They have flying rocks on this island?" the other soldier said, her antennae twitching.

"They are not supposed to have flying anything, according to the Orchestrator. Except for the shamans, of course."

"Then how did it get out here?"

These guys are dumber than Stormtroopers, Felicity thought. *Must be because of the mind control.*

"I understand the shamans can levitate objects with their instruments."

"If one of them did that, we would have heard it."

"Should we wake the Governor? Or the Orchestrator?"

Wait, the Governor is Guider, but who is the...oh, right. "The Orchestrator" is the lame Mono Realm name that Marshall picked for himself. Man, he's such a poseur.

"No. Definitely do not wake either of them. Have you already forgotten what happened last time?"

With an impatient groan (inaudible, of course), Felicity picked up another rock and, this time, hit the first soldier square in the head.

"Hey!" he exclaimed. "All right, something strange is going on."

"I saw it this time," the other soldier said, aiming her rifle in Felicity's general direction. "It came from over there."

"Could it be the local wildlife?"

"Possibly. But best not to take any chances. We should investigate."

"Agreed."

The second soldier grabbed her countercom and spoke a few words into it. A third soldier, stationed about twenty feet away, looked over at her and nodded.

Perfect, Felicity thought.

The first two soldiers began walking into the trees. Felicity threw another rock in their direction before she began slowly making her way back toward Thornleaf's position.

"Do you see anything?" the first soldier asked.

"No. Nor do I hear anything," the second soldier replied.

Cool, Felicity thought. *Thank you, Thinker's salve.*

"Very odd," the first soldier said.

"Could this be a trap set by the shamans?"

"Possibly."

"If it is, I do not see what the purpose would be. Even if they captured us, I am sure we would be released once the Ultracom has been activated."

The Ultracom? Felicity instinctively suppressed a snort. *Is that what they're calling it?*

"True. We shall keep going, then."

Keeping her eye on the soldiers, Felicity began purposely ruffling some of the nearby bushes as she walked.

"Did you see that?" the second soldier said, antennae twitching.

"See what?" the first soldier answered.

"Movement...right over there." The soldier raised her countercom and pointed it in Felicity's direction.

This thing had better work. Felicity raised the nullifier, aimed it back at the soldier, and pressed one of its buttons. A heartbeat later, the soldier pressed a button on her device. It emitted a high, squealing noise, but it was very faint. Felicity grimaced for a second, but then, to her relief, she realized that her defensive measure had worked—all of her limbs were still mobile. She took a few steps back.

"Did you get it?" the first soldier hissed.

"How should I know? I cannot even see it!" The second soldier pushed the button again, and, although it still made the squealing sound, her countercom had already been neutralized without her knowing it.

Chumps. Felicity chuckled to herself as she kicked up a little dirt and sand.

"You missed," the first soldier said. "Let me try." He aimed his device and pressed a button on it while Felicity did the same with hers. Another favorable result: faint squealing noise, no frozen limbs.

All right, let's get this party started.

Felicity started walking faster, rustling bushes and kicking up ground as she went.

"It is still moving!" the first soldier exclaimed. "After it!"

Felicity broke into a jog, glancing over her shoulder to make sure the soldiers were following closely, but not too closely. After a few seconds, she neared the spot where Thornleaf was hiding behind a seaweed-palm tree.

Just don't hit me, she thought.

The soldiers got within range. Thornleaf peeked out from behind the tree, blowgun to his lips. Before the soldiers knew what was happening, two quick darts flew out, one striking the first soldier in his arm, the other hitting the second soldier in her stomach area. They both pulled up.

"Did you feel that?" the first soldier said, looking around. "Some kind of stinging sensation—"

"Yes, you idiot," the second soldier said, pulling the dart out. "We have been shot. Look at your arm."

"Oh. I...wait, where are we?"

"I...I have no idea."

"You're in Spectraland," Felicity said, forgetting that no one would be able to hear her.

Thornleaf stepped out. "You have been under mind control. I have remedied that. Now, come with me."

♪♪♪

"No, seriously," Felicity said, her muting cast dispelled, "you don't know *anything* about Marshall's plans?"

"I swear, I do not," the male soldier, named Catcher of the Clouds, asserted.

"Neither do I," the female soldier, named Seeker of the Sun, said. "How is he still alive, anyway? I thought he fell into the cryoriver at the coliseum. No one could have survived that."

"Yeah, we don't really understand it either," Felicity muttered.

"But you *do* know about the giant countercom," Thornleaf said.

"The Ultracom? We know of its existence," Catcher of the Clouds—or just Catcher, since Felicity insisted on shortening the soldiers' names—said. "But nothing about how it works or how it will be used." He turned to his colleague. "Do you recall anything?"

"The only thing I am sure of is that, once it is ready, it can be used one time per day," Seeker of the Sun—or just Seeker—said. "I cannot remember anything else."

"Unfortunately," Thornleaf said to Felicity, "memories formed while one is under the mind-control cast are not always retainable."

"Great," Felicity huffed.

"No matter." Thornleaf looked back at the soldiers. "If you can just capture Byle for us, then all of his plans will become irrelevant."

The two soldiers exchanged glances before Seeker responded. "Our colleagues will prevent us from entering his hut," she said.

"We can make you invisible," Thornleaf said.

"But we are expected back at our posts," Catcher said. "If we do not return soon, it will raise suspicion."

"That's a good point," Felicity grumbled. She turned to Thornleaf. "You know, this plan wasn't very well thought out."

"Because my other idea is superior," the tall shaman said.

"Shush," Felicity said. She turned back to the soldiers. "All right, just tell me—is Marshall currently asleep?"

"He is supposed to be, yes," Seeker said.

"Okay, then *I'll* sneak into the hut and capture him," Felicity declared.

"Too risky," Thornleaf said, shaking his head.

"No, it's not," Felicity responded. "He doesn't have a wavebow, so he can't put up any kind of protections. And I'll be silent and invisible, remember?"

"I still do not think it is a good idea."

"Why?"

"Because...well, because you are my wife."

"Whoa. If you think I need to be coddled or sheltered because I'm a woman, then you've got some serious problems, buddy."

"No, I am only saying that because I care for you."

Felicity threw up her hands. "What, and you didn't care for me before we were married?" she said. "I seem to recall charging headfirst into all kinds of dangerous situations, and you didn't object then!"

"Well, what about your objections to my original plan?" Thornleaf shot back.

"Killing Marshall, you mean?"

"Yes. You said that you were against it because you were concerned about my Aura. How is that any different?"

"That is a totally different thing. Don't try to turn this around on me."

"You have not answered my question."

"It doesn't deserve an answer."

Seeker's countercom crackled to life. "Seeker of the Sun," a voice said through it. "Report. Are you and Catcher of the Clouds all right?"

"Oh—er, yes. Yes, we are," Seeker replied. "We tracked down the source of the disturbance."

"What was it?"

"Just a—a native creature. We took care of it."

"Very good. Well, return to the camp immediately. I have received word that phase two will begin shortly."

"Ah...excellent." Seeker glanced around, shrugging. "We will be right there. Seeker of the Sun out."

"What is phase two?" Thornleaf asked.

"No idea," Seeker replied.

"Whatever it is, it doesn't sound good," Felicity said. "So I'm going. Don't try to stop me."

"We will do it together," Thornleaf said.

"You promise you won't do anything stupid?"

Thornleaf smirked. It had been a while since he did that. "Only if you promise the same thing."

"Fine."

CHAPTER 14: LIGHTSPROUT

"Thank you again for delivering my message," Riverhand said.

"Um, no problem," Joel replied.

"So, are you sure you do not want to try the time-travel cast again?"

"Yeah. Since I keep missing the mark, I don't want to take that chance. We're close enough, at least, that I figure we can just try to talk Blackspore out of bringing Marshall over now."

"As you wish."

Using the space-travel wavecast, Joel and Riverhand made their way from Headsmouth over to Nightshore village. There they traded places, with Joel waiting outside the village (to avoid possibly being seen by Fourfoot, Tealfinger, or anyone else who might recognize him) while Riverhand went in to inquire about Blackspore's whereabouts. After a few minutes, Riverhand returned.

"That was fast," Joel said.

"Yes," Riverhand agreed.

"So is he here?"

"No, he is not. No one is here. The village appears to be deserted."

"That seems weird. Shouldn't there be at least someone hanging around to defend it?"

"From what I was taught, the war did not hinge on occupying the other villages. The goal was to force the other chiefs to surrender their authority. So everyone is probably all out fighting somewhere."

"Oh."

"Shall I try a tracking cast?"

"Sure."

Riverhand started up a tracking cast. He waved his instrument around for a few moments. Nothing happened. "That is odd," he said.

"Maybe it doesn't recognize a past version of someone as being someone it knows," Joel theorized.

"Possibly. Perhaps we should—"

"You there!" someone shouted. "Both of you!"

Joel turned. A long-haired female native riding a slimeback was approaching. She appeared relatively young, in her early twenties, and she was dressed in a pale-yellow tunic. Her features were unfamiliar, yet Joel felt a sudden flash of recognition.

Wait, that's the woman that Blackspore...

"What are you doing here?" she demanded. As she drew closer, Joel noticed that a wavebow hung at her side. "Are you spies from another village?"

"No, we're just vagabonds," Joel said, going with the now-standard alibi.

"We stopped by Nightshore to trade for fresh supplies," Riverhand elaborated, "but we found the village empty."

"Did you steal anything?"

"Of course not."

The woman raised her wavebow. "I am not sure if you know this, but I can confirm whether or not you are telling the truth."

"We are familiar with the Wavemakers and what you can do," Riverhand said. "In fact, my companion here is a friend of Blackspore's."

Joel nodded. "That's right, I am."

"A friend?" the woman said. "Of Blackspore's? You must be joking."

"I am not," Riverhand said. "That is why we decided to come to Nightshore. Do you know where he is?"

The woman didn't answer. She just looked back and forth between Joel and Riverhand with a suspicious scowl on her face.

"Is he fighting in the war?" Joel asked.

"No. The Wavemakers are remaining neutral in this conflict, by order of our Elders."

"Then is he at the temple, perhaps?" Riverhand asked.

"I do not know." The woman moved her wavebow into playing position. Joel felt a twinge of panic, thinking that maybe she was going to stun him and Riverhand. "If you are truly his friend, then you can ask him yourself." She played a short lick, and, a moment later, a familiar voice—Blackspore's—sounded through her instrument.

"Lightsprout?" he said. "Are you at the village?"

"I am," the woman, apparently named Lightsprout, replied.

"Did you find Tealfinger?"

"Not yet."

"Is he still not responding to you? I am concerned he might have gotten himself involved in the war."

"I keep telling you, he knows better than that," Lightsprout said dismissively. "There must be some other reason he is presently unaccounted for."

"All right, so why did you contact me?"

"I have encountered someone claiming to be your friend."

"Who?"

Lightsprout looked at Joel. "What is your name?"

"Um—Sightguy. It's Sightguy."

Lightsprout's brow furrowed. "Hold on—did you say...Sightguy?"

"Yeah."

"You were the one chosen by Chief Fourfoot to be his mate!"

Whoops.

"That means..."

"Stay with them," Blackspore said, "I will be there shortly."

"Hurry," Lightsprout said. The strings on her wavebow dimmed. "Blackspore's friend," she scoffed, giving Joel the stink eye. "I knew you were lying. Now, into the village—both of you."

Joel began walking, Riverhand right next to him. Despite the awkwardness of the situation, Joel figured that at least he was going to be able to speak with Blackspore, which was his main goal. With Lightsprout riding her slimeback behind the two future-time shamans as if she were a mounted farmer herding livestock, they entered the village.

"Third hut on the right," she said.

"Um...what about it?" Joel asked.

"Go there."

"Oh."

Joel walked up to the hut, which had an entrance covered in vine-ropes. He and Riverhand stopped there while Lightsprout dismounted.

"Inside," she said.

Everyone entered. Like most Spectraland huts, this one was sparsely furnished, with just a sleeping mat, one wooden stool, and a few boxes.

"Sit," Lightsprout ordered.

Joel started for the stool.

"On the ground," Lightsprout clarified.

Joel and Riverhand sat on the ground. Lightsprout took the stool for herself.

"You used to have another companion," she said to Joel. "A yellow-haired girl. Goldilocks, I believe she was called."

"Um, yeah."

"Where is she?"

"I, uh, I don't know."

Lightsprout aimed her wavebow at Joel and played a soft, eerie melody. A dark-blue stream of Aura seeped out of the instrument and circled around Joel's head like a halo.

"At least you telling the truth about that," Lightsprout said.

Joel remained tight-lipped, unsure of how to respond. No one said a word until finally, thirty-two minutes later, the vine-ropes parted and Blackspore entered the hut. Naturally, he looked much younger, with a jet-black head of hair and a smooth light-green complexion that hadn't yet been ravaged by almost two decades of non-Aura-mitigated sun exposure. He was carrying a dark-blue wavebow that seemed to be actively humming with Aura energy.

"So, this is the infamous Sightguy," the master shaman said. He turned to Riverhand. "And who might you be?"

"A mere vagabond, sir," Riverhand replied. "My name is unimportant."

"How true," Blackspore snorted. "I hope you realize that after what happened at Chief Fourfoot's failed wedding, your people have even less status than before."

"Understood," Riverhand said.

Blackspore turned back to Joel. "But at last we have the original perpetrator in our grasp. The one who refused our chief's proposal, thereby bringing this terrible, destructive war upon us."

Seeing as how it was really Fourfoot's idea to start this war, Joel wanted to object, but he decided against doing so.

"I do not know how you managed to elude us these past few months," Blackspore continued, "but no matter. The Aura has seen fit to deliver you into our hands."

Wait, Joel thought, *he doesn't know where I was...which must mean that Tealfinger never told him that I'm a Wavemaker from the future. And why is he acting all...what's the word...grandiose?*

"What should we do with them?" Lightsprout asked.

"Treat them as the war criminals they are, of course," Blackspore replied. "Since the vagabond tribes have no authority, we will"—he paused and sniffed the air, as if some delectable scent had suddenly come wafting through the hut—"I sense something. Do you sense it?"

Lightsprout replied with a sideways head motion that was the Spectraland equivalent of a shrug.

"Your supply packs..." Blackspore turned to Joel and Riverhand. "Open them."

Joel glanced at Riverhand, who merely sat motionless.

"I said, *open them!*" Blackspore snapped, raising his wavebow.

Slowly, Riverhand began to comply, so Joel did the same. Once their packs were fully open, Blackspore leaned over for a closer look. His eyes widened and his jaw dropped.

"How did you get those?" he asked.

"Those...what?" Joel said.

"Those wavebows!"

"We, um...well, you see, we..." Joel stammered.

"You are Wavemakers!" Blackspore exclaimed.

"How can that be?" Lightsprout asked, standing to look at Joel and Riverhand's instruments. "These do not seem familiar at all."

"There can only be one possibility," Blackspore said. "My research...you must be from the future!"

"That is correct," Riverhand admitted.

"So the time-travel cast was perfected?" Lightsprout said, incredulous.

"Um, sort of," Joel replied.

"Why are you here?" Blackspore asked. "Who sent you? Why were you at Chief Fourfoot's betrothal ritual?"

The multiple questions made Joel's mind swim. After shaking his head to clear it, he decided to cut to the chase. "We're here to stop you from making a big mistake."

"A mistake?" Blackspore said. "What kind of mistake?"

"Blackspore, are you sure this is a good idea?" Lightsprout said. "Changing history could have some serious consequences. Remember, Mistress Moonear only allowed you to continue with your research because—"

"I know, I know," Blackspore cut her off. "But history has already been altered. By refusing the chief's proposal, they started this war."

"Actually," Joel said, "the war kinda happened anyway."

"So did you come back to try to prevent it?" Blackspore asked.

"Um..."

"Was *I* the one originally responsible for starting it? Is that the mistake you are talking about?"

"No." Joel shook his head. "There's a bigger mistake that happens later on."

"Blackspore, I am not comfortable with this," Lightsprout said, hands over her ears. "Before you have them say another word, I think we should consult with Mistress Moonear."

"But she was probably the one who sent them back here in the first place," Blackspore said.

"Actually," Joel said, "it was you. You're the one who wanted me to come back."

"Then I am *definitely* telling Mistress Moonear about this," Lightsprout said. She looked at Joel and Riverhand. "You two—come with me."

"Wait, no, I"—Blackspore started to protest, but then as Lightsprout pushed past him, he heaved a heavy sigh—"oh, very well." He turned back to Joel. "As she said—come with us."

"Okay."

♪♪♪

Joel squirmed as he sat behind Lightsprout and Riverhand on the former's slimeback, right on top of its hump. Lightsprout had insisted that both he and Riverhand ride with her in order to keep them from telling Blackspore anything about their mission or the future. Her slime-back's hump was a bit flatter than most, but still, to be seated on top of it was very uncomfortable, especially when they rode over rougher terrain. It was so distracting that Joel wasn't able to give much thought to Lightsprout's identity other than the fact that she was, without a doubt, the woman that Blackspore was, or would be, in love with. After about an hour of riding (fifty-seven minutes, to be precise), Joel was sorely tempted to suggest a flying cast, but he knew that doing so would be unwise, so he just suffered in silence until he spotted a large group of armed natives about a hundred yards off in the distance.

"Um, do we want to be avoiding that?" he asked.

"Avoiding what?" Lightsprout replied, not turning around.

"There's, like, a fight or something happening. Past those trees on the left."

"Oh—yes, I see it." Now she turned around. "Blackspore."

"Yes?"

"There might be a battle going on up ahead, near the Singing Swamp. We should change our path."

"All right," Blackspore agreed. "We can reach the temple via the"—his wavebow chimed as it suddenly lit up with a bright-green glow—"Tealfinger."

"You have located him?" Lightsprout asked.

"Yes," Blackspore said, waving his instrument around. "He is...at that battle."

"What? Are you sure?"

"Positive."

"That cannot be! He knows he is not to get involved!"

"Nevertheless, we should investigate."

"Agreed."

Lightsprout urged her slimeback into a faster gait, making matters even more painful as far as Joel's backside was concerned. As they approached the scene, he saw that the armed natives were divided into two factions that were not yet fighting but simply facing each other as if in some sort of standoff. One of the factions consisted mostly of natives Joel had seen during Fourfoot's betrothal ritual, while the other was made up of villagers that had been working on the Headsmouth repairs, Watertongue included. Tealfinger was standing in the middle of the two groups.

"Riverhand," Joel whispered, his eyes on Watertongue. "That's your dad."

"I know," Riverhand replied, drawing his hood even tighter over his head.

"Tealfinger!" Lightsprout exclaimed.

Tealfinger turned. Joel shrunk down in his seat, trying his best to hide behind Riverhand. Lightsprout rode up and pulled her mount to a stop.

"What are you doing here?" she said.

"I am attempting to broker a peace," Tealfinger responded.

"The Elders gave us strict instructions to remain neutral," Blackspore said.

"I *am* remaining neutral," Tealfinger said. "I am not fighting on anyone's side. I am negotiating a truce."

"How can you be negotiating a truce if none of the chiefs are here?" Lightsprout said.

"If I can convince enough villagers to change their mind about this war, then I am sure Chief Fourfoot will reconsider."

"Reconsider what?" a villager from the Headsmouth group asked.

"That is a good question," Watertongue said. "Why did Fourfoot even start this war in the first place?"

"He started it because he wanted to change the island's law," one of the natives standing opposite Watertongue replied. "So he could marry a man."

"Not exactly," Tealfinger said. "You see, he—"

"Wait," Watertongue interrupted. "We are killing each other because of your chief's unnatural preferences?"

"There is nothing unnatural about it," Tealfinger said. "But that is not the true reason why this war began."

"Then what is the reason?"

"The person that Chief Fourfoot selected refused the proposal. That was his right, under Spectraland law. So the chief wanted to—"

"That is him!" One of the villagers on the Nightshore side pointed at Joel, looking and sounding as if he had just recognized a celebrity in his midst. "The vagabond who turned down the chief!"

Everyone turned. Joel tried to shrink down even more. Tealfinger's eyes met his, but the Nightshore shaman didn't say anything.

"Sightguy?" Watertongue said.

"Um, hello," Joel said, his voice small.

Watertongue turned to face his fellow Headsmouth villagers. "That is the vagabond who tried to seduce my wife!"

"What? No, I wasn't trying to—"

"I knew he was a Nightshore spy," Watertongue seethed. "He is working with their shamans, who have come here to destroy us!"

"Hold on, Watertongue," Blackspore said. "We are not here to 'destroy' anyone."

"He told us to accept that which is not normal, trying to convince us that Fourfoot is justified in what he is doing," Watertongue went on as the other Headsmouth villagers were becoming visibly agitated. "This is all just a convoluted conspiracy to help Fourfoot and Nightshore take over the island!"

"Everyone, please, calm down," Tealfinger said. "Try to be rational about this."

"And you"—Watertongue pointed his spear at Tealfinger—"you were trying to deceive us!" he spat. "With your talk of peace. You were merely stalling us until your sister and her lover arrived!"

"We did not even know Tealfinger was here," Lightsprout protested. "We were on our way to the Wavemaker Temple when—"

"But we will not go down that easily!" Watertongue yelled, now virtually foaming at the mouth. Some of his fellow villagers raised their weapons and shouted in agreement. "You can break our huts and our homes, but you will never break our spirit!"

"Watertongue," Tealfinger said. "Listen to me. If you would just—"

With a piercing cry, Watertongue plunged his spear through Tealfinger's chest. The Nightshore shaman's eyes widened in shock before he fell to his knees, and then onto his side, dead.

CHAPTER 15: KILLING IS MY BUSINESS

"Resume your posts," one of the still-mind-controlled Six States soldiers ordered.

"Yes, ma'am," Catcher and Seeker said in unison.

As the two returned to their positions in front of the ships, Felicity and Thornleaf—invisible to both light-seeing eyes as well as energy-sensing ones—followed closely behind them. The hope was that once they got beyond the line of ships, none of the soldiers—all of whom were facing outward—would notice their footsteps in the sand as they stalked their way to the guest hut. Neither shaman was under a muting cast, as their plan called for the use of their wavebows and, most likely, verbal communication, so they tried to move as silently as possible.

So far, so good, Felicity thought once they were past the ships.

The entrance to this particular guest hut didn't have a door, only a set of vine-ropes. Felicity recalled how she had argued for a full door, saying that the guests might want more privacy, but Fireflower had assured her that Spectraland natives were quite used to the vines, and in fact preferred them. She took a moment to thank the Aura or whatever that she had lost that particular argument.

Once she arrived at the entrance, she stopped and turned to make sure that Thornleaf was still right behind her. His footprints confirmed that he was. After he stopped as well, she turned back to the hut and peeked through the vines. Guider and two of her lieutenants were inside, standing up against the walls. Felicity panicked for a moment, thinking that they were awake, but then she remembered that the denizens of the Six States slept standing up. Then she spotted Marshall, lying supine on a blanket that had been spread out over the sand (the hut didn't have an actual floor). His arms were crossed over his chest, and he had a faint, smug smile on his face as he slept, as if he were having the most pleasant dream. Felicity felt a hot surge of anger flare up within her gut.

Man, it really would *be easy to just finish him off right now, wouldn't it?* she mused. *After everything he's done...who could blame us?* She took a deep breath. *But no. No. No matter how tempting it might be, we're going to do this the right way.*

The right way, they had decided, was for Thornleaf to first administer the mind-control antidote to Guider. Then Felicity would stun Marshall and any others who might be in the hut. The mind-controlled soldiers who were outside would hear the sound of the stunning cast and come to investigate. By then, though, they would have several options: Felicity could stun them as they approached, or, if the soldiers decided to use their countercoms from a distance (the single nullifier probably wouldn't be enough to hold them all off), Guider could issue an order to have them released. The timing was a little tricky, and there were more moving parts than Felicity would have liked, but overall, it was a solid plan, she felt.

She reached behind, feeling for Thornleaf to give him the signal that she was going in. She brushed his arm, and then his hand, which grasped hers in response. Satisfied, she tried to let go, but he didn't relinquish his grip; instead, he tightened it and pulled her closer to him.

What are you doing? she screamed silently in her mind.

Thornleaf wrapped his invisible arms around her. Before she had a chance to react, she felt his hot breath on her face followed by his lips, first clumsily planted on her right cheek, and then squarely on her lips.

Not now, you idiot! She squirmed out of his embrace and pushed him away. *Of all the stupid...*

She took another deep breath to compose herself. Then she turned and slipped through the vine-ropes, trying as hard as she could not to move them too much. Once inside, she walked over to where Marshall lay, wiped the soulshifter salve off her face with a freecloth (unfortunately, Thinker had proven unable to modify the salve's wavecast-negating properties), and took aim. With her wavebow trained on Marshall, she looked up at Guider, waiting for Thornleaf to administer the antidote. Her hands formed the proper chord for a maximum-strength stunning cast.

All right, she thought, *let's do this.*

Two seconds ticked by. Then two more. Guider remained asleep; there was no sign that anything was being done to her.

What the heck is taking him so long? We're gonna—

A loud bell rang out, kind of like the ones you hear in schools at the end of the day. Felicity froze for a moment, her eyes darting around. In that moment, Marshall leaped to his feet with a rising handspring, knocking the wavebow out of Felicity's hands.

"Who's there?" Marshall barked.

"A shaman!" Guider cried, able to clearly perceive Felicity due to the lack of salve on the offworlder's face.

Felicity's head spun. Where was Thornleaf? The soldiers outside were undoubtedly closing in fast. And even worse, her wavebow was lying on the ground near Marshall, fully visible to him since she was no longer holding it.

"Aha!" Marshall exclaimed.

"No!" Felicity said. She lunged for her instrument, but she was too late; Marshall had beaten her to it. She grabbed its neck and tried to wrestle it from his grasp. "Let go!"

"Let go?" Marshall laughed. "You lose all sense of irony when you're desperate, my dear."

He was right—she *was* desperate. Even if she were somehow able to regain control of her wavebow and stun Marshall, the mind-controlled soldiers would still be able to overwhelm her and Thornleaf—wherever he was—with their countercoms. The plan had been a total failure. She had only one hope left.

C'mon, Joel, bail us out of this.

As soon as she finished that thought, Marshall's grin vanished. Open-mouthed, he loosened his grip on the wavebow, and Felicity yanked it away.

"Wow, that actually worked," she muttered out loud, waiting for her adversary to shimmer and vanish, the expected result of him never coming over to Spectraland in the first place. That didn't happen, however. Instead,

Marshall remained whole and present, with one difference that became glaringly obvious upon closer inspection: the bloody tip of a blade poking its way out of his chest. "What the—?" She stepped out of the way as Marshall's lifeless body fell forward.

"What is happening?" Guider said, sounding disoriented.

"Where are we?" one of her lieutenants asked. "Is that the Orchestrator?"

"Felicity? Thornleaf?" the other lieutenant said.

"Thornleaf?" Felicity echoed. "He's not—"

She was interrupted by the sound of a wavebow, and suddenly, Thornleaf appeared in front of her.

"You are welcome," he said.

"What—what did you do?" she sputtered.

"That alarm went off before I was able to give Guider the antidote," Thornleaf explained. "So, at that point, there was only one alternative left."

"To...to kill Marshall?"

"Correct. Now, none of the soldiers are under mind control, and the threat is over."

Felicity looked down at Marshall's body. The handle of Thornleaf's knife was sticking out of its back. "You...I told you not to do that!"

"What other choice did I have?" Thornleaf bent over and pulled his knife out. "He was about to possess your wavebow."

"Would someone *please* tell me what is going on here?" Guider said.

"You have been under mind control," Thornleaf responded. "Byle—the Orchestrator—brought you and some of your soldiers here, to Spectraland."

"How did he—I thought he perished in the coliseum?"

"He did."

"But then...he came back to life?"

"Yes. It is possible that his heart simply stopped beating for a while before resuming shortly thereafter. Now, though, there is no chance of that happening."

Catcher peeked into the hut. "Is everything all right here?" he asked.

"It is," Thornleaf replied.

"Seeker of the Sun and I noticed the others breaking out of their trance, so we briefed them on what was going on."

"Good." Thornleaf nodded. "We appreciate your assistance. If you wish, you can join us for a victory meal before you return home."

Catcher nodded. "That sounds good." He turned and left.

"I can't believe you did that!" Felicity exclaimed, still upset.

"Did what? Save Spectraland? And possibly all of existence?"

Felicity could feel tears welling up in her eyes. "You *promised* you wouldn't do that."

"I promised not to do anything stupid. What I did was incredibly smart."

"Fireflower is going to expel you from the order!"

"I doubt that. Once I tell her exactly what happened, she will understand."

There was a noise outside that sounded like the Forbidden Tides, along with more Six States ships, approaching.

"That must be the second phase," Thornleaf observed. "Which justifies what I did even more."

"No, it doesn't," Felicity said. "You just needed to be faster with the antidote!"

"I am done with this argument," Thornleaf said. He started to make his way outside. "We will talk again once you have calmed down."

"Geez, you are *such* a jerk."

As he walked past, Thornleaf stopped, turned, and gave Felicity a smirk. "That is why you married me."

Felicity pursed her lips. *Is it?*

♪♪♪

Some thirty minutes or so later, after the latest onslaught of seawater from the Forbidden Tides had subsided, Felicity was standing by herself on the beach, staring up at the twin moons. Indeed, more Six States ships—fifteen of them in all—had arrived. According to the nearby chatter she was overhearing, the ships' troops had flown to Spectraland under Guider's orders, but none of them remembered the part of their journey where they would have crossed the Forbidden Tides. The explanation was that they had been out of range of Marshall's mind control up until that point, then went back under, and then snapped out of it the moment Marshall was dead once again and they were already close to landing.

Felicity didn't really care about any of that right now, though. Her thoughts were focused on Thornleaf: what he had just done, what effects it would have, and, most of all, why she felt what she did for him.

Have I made a mistake? she wondered, not for the first time.

The subject of her thoughts was standing about ten feet away, talking to Guider and a couple of other Six States soldiers. He seemed to be completely nonchalant about the fact that he had just killed someone in cold blood—by stabbing them in the back, no less. Looking at him, Felicity felt confused and conflicted; even though she found his demeanor to be repulsive and upsetting on one level, it was strangely attractive on another. In a way, she realized, that was one thing she had liked about him all along: the fact that he said and did whatever he wanted, without apology or remorse.

But what does that make me? Am I just one of those stereotypical girls that falls for the bad boy? I can't be...can I?

She thought about her mom and dad. They were both very passionate and assertive people who, now that she paused to consider it, reminded her a bit of herself and Thornleaf. They had argued constantly, and their whole family would probably have been better off, in Felicity's opinion, if they had split up. In fact, it was one of their arguments that led directly to the car accident that had claimed their lives. If that was the kind of path she and Thornleaf were headed down, then maybe this whole marriage was, indeed, a mistake. She glanced down at the scorpion tattoos on her arms, the ones that honored her parents (whose astrological signs were both, appropriate to their personalities, Scorpio).

What do you guys think?

"Felicity?"

Felicity turned. It was Seeker. "What?"

"Are you all right?"

"Huh? Yeah, no—I mean, yeah, I am."

"Good. You appeared unsettled about something."

"No, I'm fine. What's up?"

"I just wanted to thank you for freeing me and my colleagues from that horrible mind-control effect. It is frightening to know that someone could have forced me to perform actions according to their will. It was even worse than a countercom."

"Yeah...no problem."

"The Orchestrator was quite the evil person, was he not?"

"Oh, you have no idea."

"Such a relief that the world is now rid of him. I must thank your spouse for his heroic deed."

"Right. Heroic."

"In fact, I will do that right now. Thank you, once again."

Felicity didn't reply as Seeker turned and walked away. The soldier's last few words had triggered something in her mind; something that bothered her even more than Thornleaf's so-called "heroic deed."

I'd better go check on Marshall's body.

She jogged back over to the guest hut, chastising herself along the way.

Stupid, stupid, stupid. I should've taken care of this first. But instead, I let myself get distracted by my thoughts about Thornleaf.

She stopped in front of the hut and readied her wavebow. Then, ever so carefully, she parted the vines covering the entrance and peeked inside. She was alarmed, but not surprised, by what she saw: where Marshall's body had been lying, there was nothing but sand.

All right, Smith, don't panic. Just 'cause his body's not there doesn't mean he came back to life again. Maybe someone just moved it while I wasn't paying attention. Maybe—

A hand grabbed the neck of her wavebow. Felicity shrieked. Another hand joined the first, and together they tugged on the instrument, dragging her into the hut.

"What took you so long, my dear?" the owner of the hands—Marshall—sneered.

"Help!" she cried, not so much out of concern for her own safety as for the fact that she wanted to alert people as to what was going on.

"That won't work," Marshall said. "Now that I'm alive again, everyone will go right back under my control. You can't win."

Thinking fast, Felicity stopped pulling quite so hard on her wavebow, allowing Marshall to reel it—and her—closer to him. Once there, she gave him a well-placed knee to a sensitive area between his legs. With a grunt of pain, Marshall let go of the wavebow and crumpled to the ground. Felicity followed that up with a quick stunning cast to his head.

"We'll see about that," she spat.

"Felicity!" someone called from outside the hut. It sounded like Seeker. "Where are you? Something terrible is happening!"

Felicity knew what it was. Even though Marshall was now stunned, his mind-control cast would still have been automatically reactivated when he came back to life, influencing any susceptible Six States soldiers who were within range. Having been exposed to the antidote, Seeker and Catcher would be the only ones not affected.

"Felicity!" Seeker called again. It sounded like she was nearby.

Felicity peeked out of the hut. Indeed, Seeker was standing only about five feet away. The other soldiers—the ones she could see, anyway—were all gathered in a group, standing right about where she had last seen Thornleaf.

"Seeker!" Felicity hissed.

Seeker turned. "There you are! You need to—"

"Shh," Felicity shushed her. "Quick, in here."

Seeker looked over her shoulder twice before she turned and dashed into the hut. She seemed frantic. "Something terrible—my colleagues—Catcher of the Clouds, and—and your spouse, they—"

"Just calm down," Felicity said. "I know what's happening. It's okay, we'll figure something out."

"But they have your spouse!"

"What? What do you mean?"

"One moment, they were all talking to each other, making celebration plans, but then they stopped and, without warning, they used their countercoms on him! Catcher of the Clouds tried to intervene, but then when he did, they froze him as well. I pretended to be under mind control and slipped away. What are we going to do?"

That was a good question. What *were* they going to do? It was the same pickle as before, except now there were even more mind-controlled soldiers to contend with. There seemed to be only one good option at this point.

"All right, I have an idea," Felicity said. "Think you can carry that bozo over there?" She nodded at Marshall's unconscious form.

"The—the Orchestrator?" Seeker said, just now noticing him. "But—I thought he was alive?"

"He is, but now he's stunned," Felicity replied. "I know, it's complicated. Just pick him up and stand close."

While Seeker complied, Felicity fired up a flying cast. Within seconds, a cloud of green Aura had expanded to envelop all three of them.

"What are you doing?" Seeker asked.

"I'm gonna airlift us out of here. I figure by the time they notice us, we'll be out of range of their countercoms."

"But what about your spouse? And Catcher of the Clouds?"

"We'll come back for them. We'll have Marshall as a hostage, so maybe we can bargain or something. I dunno, we'll figure it out later."

"All right."

"Hang on."

They flew through the vines of the hut and up into the air. Not looking down, Felicity heard shouts, followed by the squeals of many individual countercoms. She grimaced.

Please be out of range, please be out of range...

Her prayers were answered; she felt a small tingling sensation in her legs, but to her relief, they didn't seize up. Several laser shots zipped by, but thanks to a combination of evasive maneuvers and dumb luck, none of them hit their mark. Still, it wasn't until they were about half a mile away from the beach that Felicity finally exhaled.

CHAPTER 16: SINGING SWAMP

Time seemed to freeze for a moment, at least in the little area where Joel had just witnessed the brutal murder of a fellow Wavemaker. Then Lightsprout, with a ferocious scream, fired out a stunning cast so powerful it sent Watertongue flying some twenty feet through the air.

"You will pay for what you have done!" she shouted. "All of you will pay!"

"Lightsprout!" Blackspore said. "You must not—"

Chaos erupted. Roaring in unison, the Headsmouth villagers charged forth, thrusting their spears and firing blowdarts at their Nightshore counterparts. Lightsprout strummed her wavebow, creating an Aura-shield that deflected most of the projectiles. As she did so, her slimeback bellowed and reared back, causing both Joel and Riverhand to fall off. Joel was relieved to not be seated on the animal's hump anymore, but at the same time, he wasn't sure his new position—sprawled out on the ground in the middle of a skirmish—was preferable. He scrambled to his feet.

"Are you all right?" Riverhand, who had also managed to stand, asked.

"Yeah, I think so. But Riverhand...your dad—he—"

"I know. Apparently your message of acceptance did not change his attitudes."

"Sorry."

"It is not your fault. You tried."

"But now you still won't get along."

"I suppose that is just the way it is meant to be. Never mind that now, though—what should we do?"

"I, um, I don't know," Joel replied. He considered taking his own wavebow out of his supply pack, but he wasn't sure if he should get any more involved than he already was. He glanced around at the scene. As the villagers were engaging each other in battle, Lightsprout was performing a number of quick wavecasts, alternating between shields and stunning. Blackspore was standing near the edge of the fray, dismounted but motionless.

"Blackspore!" Lightsprout called. "Help me!"

Joel read Blackspore's expression as being one of acute indecision. Then—

"Die, vagabond!"

Joel whirled. A Headsmouth villager wielding a club-like weapon was standing right behind him, but she wasn't addressing Joel—Riverhand was her target. Before either future-time shaman had a chance to react, the villager swung the club. With a sickening crunch, it connected with Riverhand's head and sent him sprawling to the ground.

"No!" Joel cried.

"Your turn!" the villager shouted.

Joel fumbled with his supply pack as the villager wound up for another swing. Before he could get it open, though, a red bolt of Aura whizzed past him and struck the villager square in the chest. Joel turned. The bolt had come from Blackspore.

"Get out of here!" the master shaman yelled as he ran up. "Return to your own era!"

Joel looked down at Riverhand, who had a huge bloody gash on the side of his head, and then back up at Blackspore. "But—"

"No healer of this time will help you. You must go back. That is his only chance."

"But—"

"Save him first, and then come back for me later. Although I fear I may have already made the mistake you said I was destined to make."

"Blackspore!" Lightsprout shouted once more. "Please!"

Blackspore looked Joel in the eye. "Go."

Joel nodded. Then, steeling his jaw, he bent down and picked Riverhand up, draping his fallen friend's arm over his shoulders. He started walking, dragging Riverhand along as quickly as he could. He had put about fifteen feet of distance between them and the melee when he felt a stinging sensation in the back of his neck.

What the—

Joel touched his neck, expecting to feel some sort of insect bite. What he felt instead, however, was something much worse: a tiny blowdart.

Dangit.

He pulled the dart out, tossed it aside, and resumed walking. Fervently hoping that he wouldn't pass out, he headed straight for the Singing Swamp, away from the sounds of fighting and wavecasting. Once he reached his destination, he placed Riverhand on the ground next to a tree, sat down, and took out his wavebow. Feelings of dizziness and nausea began to set in even before his fingers got into position.

Must be from the dart, he figured.

Mustering up every last ounce of strength he had, Joel played the time-travel melody. There was a loud *whoosh*, and then—

All at once, the swamp's surrounding trees were replaced by dancing people: Earthlings, Spectraland natives, Six States citizens...none of them familiar. Loud music—some strange blend of metal and classical—was blaring. Lights were flashing, and there was sweet-smelling smoke everywhere. Joel looked around for Riverhand. He wasn't there.

Did—did I mess up the time-travel cast?

One of the dancing Earth people, a girl wearing a Sugarblood tank top, extended a hand to Joel. "Hey, why are you sitting down?" she shouted through the din.

"Um..."

"C'mon, man, get up and dance!"

Joel took her hand. She pulled him up. There was nothing but dancing people as far as the eye could see.

"What's your name?" she asked.

"Um, Joel."

"What?"

"Joel. Joel Suzuki."

"Nice to meet you, Joe! I'm Tricia."

"Where—where are we?"

"Some place called Specter...Septra...you know, I'm not really sure. But who cares, right? Woo!"

"What year is this? Why are all these Earth people here?"

"Whoa!" Tricia laughed. "Someone's had too much to drink."

"No, I—" Joel looked down at himself. He was no longer shapeshifted; instead, he was back in his normal, Earthly form.

I must be having a vision, he realized. *I must've passed out. Oh no—Riverhand.*

"Hey, uh, Tricia?"

"Yeah?"

"I need you to slap me. Like, really hard."

"Why?" Tricia smiled. "You haven't tried anything yet."

"What? No—my friend...he's hurt, and I have to get back to him."

"Okay, but how is slapping you going to help?"

"I'm asleep, and I have to wake up."

Tricia's smile disappeared. "All right, now you're starting to creep me out."

"I'm serious. Please, just—just slap me."

"If I do, will you promise to go away?"

"Yes, yes, I promise."

Tricia reared back. Bracing himself, Joel closed his eyes. A second later, he felt the quick sting of Tricia's hand on his cheek, and his eyes shot open. Now, the music, lights, and everything else were gone, replaced by overhanging fronds and a slight breeze. The twin moons loomed large in the night sky. As Joel realized that he was lying down, a shot of panic rushed through him.

Riverhand.

He turned and sat up. Riverhand was lying next to him. Joel placed his hand (which was green once again) on his fellow shaman's chest and felt a heartbeat.

Whew. He exhaled. *Okay, we made it, and Riverhand's still alive.*

Joel's relief was short-lived, however. As his senses settled in, he noticed something alarming: faint purple streaks were running up and down both of his arms, and his leafy protrusions were wilted. The feelings of dizziness and nausea returned, and the spot on his neck where the dart had hit him began to pulse with pain. He turned his head and dry-heaved.

Have...have I been poisoned?

He picked up his wavebow and played a lick. A few seconds passed. Then a voice sounded from his instrument.

"Hi, this is Felicity."

"Hey Felicity, it's me. I—"

"I can't answer the wavebow right now. I'm either busy saving the day or I'm just ignoring you. So yeah, leave a message after the tone."

Dangit. "Felicity, it's me—Joel. The second attempt failed. Riverhand is hurt badly, and I think I've been poisoned. It's"—Joel looked at the sky and noted the pattern of the stars in relation to the moons—"still the same night as when you left with Thornleaf for the beach. So, I hope you guys are okay. If you are, please come and get us. Thanks."

The strings on Joel's wavebow dimmed. Just as they did, he realized something.

Aw man, I forgot to tell her where we were!

Joel replayed the lick, but, to his dismay, nothing happened. Apparently the time-travel cast, coupled with his poisoned state, had sapped most of his personal Aura energy, leaving him unable to perform any more wavecasts for a while—possibly ever, unless he could find some help soon.

Well, Riverhand did say that most of the villagers are hiding out in the Thirsty Tunnels, so I could try heading there. Problem is, I don't know where that is, other than somewhere near the northwest coast. And on top of that, I can't fly or even short-range teleport. I suppose I could try walking. It's a long shot, but it's better than just sitting here, waiting to be eaten by wild creatures or, worse, caught by Six States soldiers. I can't risk them finding me out in the open and then giving my wavebow to Marshall. Hopefully, if I'm lucky, I can last long enough to recover some Aura energy.

Grimacing, Joel got to his feet. Then, with supreme effort, he picked Riverhand up and started walking. Each step sent a jolt of pain throughout his entire body. He decided to distract himself by thinking about how his experience with time travel had, so far, not really lived up to his expectations.

Okay, let's see, I went back twice to try to save Blackspore on the beach. Neither of those tries worked—he always ended up getting hurt no matter what.

Then Tealfinger thought that by releasing us, the Fourfoot War would have been prevented, but for some reason, it happened anyway.

And then when we finally found Blackspore, instead of talking him out of bringing Marshall over, we ended up in a battle that became the reason he and Lightsprout got involved in the war in the first place.

It's like no matter what I do, I can't change the past. And if that's the case, then what good is being the Virtuoso, anyway?

Blackspore of the present, if you can hear me, I could really use some guidance right about now.

Joel continued to take step after excruciating step. As the breeze blew through the trees of the Singing Swamp, it created a melody that sounded uncannily similar to "The Dream Is Over" by Dave Derby.

Okay, Joel thought, *that's not helping at all.*

♪♪♪

After flying away from the beach at top speed, Felicity, Seeker and the unconscious Marshall Byle arrived at the Wavemaker Temple, which they found deserted. Confused, Felicity contacted Fireflower via wavebow.

"Felicity?" the Wavemaker leader said, sounding surprised. "You are still here, in the present!"

"Yeah. Actually, Joel and I did go to the past, but then we came back."

"What happened?"

"The plan didn't work, obviously," Felicity replied. "But he's trying again. Where are you guys?"

"As a contingency, we decided to evacuate most of the villagers to the Thirsty Tunnels."

"What? Why there?"

"It is large enough to house everyone, and Thinker said that it would be insulated from the effects of the giant countercom."

"Okay, but hello, it's always underwater," Felicity said, recalling her one previous visit to the locale in question.

"We are doing what we can to keep the water at bay. It was only meant to be a temporary solution."

"All right, well, sit tight. I'll head over there now. I have a couple of surprise guests with me."

"Who?"

"A non-mind-controlled Six States soldier and...Marshall."

"What?"

"Yeah, don't worry, he's stunned. I'll explain everything along the way."

"While you are flying?"

"I'm not gonna fly. I don't want to leave an Aura trail in the air leading to the hiding spot."

"Ah, yes, good thinking."

"Did you guys leave any slimebacks or wagons here at the temple?"

"We took all of them. The fourwheel should still be there, however."

"That'll work. See you in a bit." The strings on Felicity's wavebow dimmed.

"What is a 'fourwheel'?" Seeker asked.

"Something that Thinker whipped up. It's like a—"

Felicity's wavebow emitted a chime.

"Huh. That's weird," she said. "Someone left me a message. Hold that thought." She plucked her instrument's high *E* string.

"Felicity, it's me—Joel," Joel's voice croaked. "The second attempt failed. Riverhand is hurt badly, and I think I've been poisoned. It's...still the same night as when you left with Thornleaf for the beach. So, I hope you guys are okay. If you are, please come and get us. Thanks."

"Wait—is that it?" Felicity snapped. "Why didn't you tell me where you are? And why is Riverhand"—she rolled her eyes in frustration—"ugh, forget it. I'm talking to an answering machine."

"What is happening?" Seeker asked.

"We have a little job to do. Grab Marshall and follow me."

Seeker picked Marshall up and draped his unconscious body around her shoulders. Then Felicity led the way to the temple's stables, which reeked badly of slimeback droppings. Apparently, no one had bothered to clean out the place before they had evacuated.

"What is that unusual aroma?" Seeker asked. "It smells like that mind-control antidote your spouse administered to me and Catcher of the Clouds."

"Trust me, you don't want to know." Felicity walked over to the corner of the main stable, where a large tarp was covering an object the size of a small car. She pulled the tarp off, revealing a four-wheeled, four-seater vehicle that was constructed mainly out of wood slabs and tree branches. It had one steering wheel and two sets of pedals. "Voila," she said. "The fourwheel."

"That...looks like a very inefficient method of transportation," Seeker said.

"It is," Felicity responded, "but I have a way of speeding it up. Toss that scumbag into one of the back seats and then sit up front next to me."

"All right."

As they got situated, Felicity performed a tracking cast. "Okay, Joel, where are you?" she muttered. It took a whole minute, but she finally got a signal, albeit a faint one. "Looks like he's about halfway between here and the Thirsty Tunnels, so that'll work out well. Grab the steering wheel and start pedaling."

"Start what?"

"Pedaling. Just do what I do."

Felicity placed her feet on the set of pedals below her seat and began pumping her legs, causing the fourwheel to move forward. Seeker followed suit.

"Okay," Felicity said, "now keep doing that while steering. I'll play a levitation wavecast that'll make this thing a lot lighter, so it'll go faster with less effort."

"Which direction should I go in?"

"Just go straight for now. I'll tell you when and where to turn."

And so they headed out. As they went, Felicity alternated between levitation, tracking, and communication casts—the latter of which she used to inform Fireflower of what had been going on. After a couple of hours of nonstop pedaling, she and Seeker finally decided to take a break.

"Man, I really need to learn that short-range teleportation cast," Felicity grumbled, massaging her calves.

"I beg your pardon?" Seeker said.

"Forget it." Felicity shook her head. "Hey, can I ask you something?"

"Of course."

"Do you have, like, a boyfriend, or a husband, or whatever?"

Seeker's antennae twitched. "I used to."

"Used to? What happened?"

"He...well..."

"Died? Got caught with someone else?"

Seeker shot Felicity a perturbed look.

"Oh—yeah, sorry," Felicity mumbled. "That was kind of unfiltered."

"Let us just say that he and I were never a good fit to begin with and leave it at that."

"Hmm. Fair enough."

"Why do you ask?"

"Just curious."

"Does this have something to do with your spouse?"

"No, I think it has more to do with me." Felicity let out a humorless chuckle. "But look at us—sitting here, talking about guys. Alison Bechdel would be ashamed."

"Who?"

"Never mind." Felicity restarted her tracking cast. "Let's get going. Even though we're getting closer, Joel's signal is getting weaker instead of stronger. That makes me a little bit worried."

"So rather than discussing men, we should be rescuing them instead?"

"You're a quick learner."

They set off again, eventually arriving at the Singing Swamp, which, according to the tracking cast, was where Joel was—hopefully, at least. It was hard to be completely sure, as his signal was beginning to fade in and out.

"Will it be all right to take the vehicle into this area?" Seeker asked. "The surface seems rather unstable."

"It'll be fine. Thinker built this thing with some surprisingly good suspension."

"You keep mentioning this 'Thinker'. Are you, by any chance, referring to Thinker of Deep Thoughts?"

"Yeah, I am. He moved here after the Six States were liberated. Didn't you know that?"

"No, I did not. But I am familiar with him. He is a very talented inventor."

"I know, he came up with—wait, *he's* not your ex, is he?"

"Oh no, not at all. We were simply colleagues, years ago, at Outpost Eight."

"Okay, good, 'cause that would've been just a little too coincidental."

"I am not sure what you mean by that."

"Just keep pedaling."

♪♪♪

Joel couldn't take it anymore. The pain and the nausea were simply too much. And to make matters even worse, if he had recovered any Aura energy at all during his long slog through the Singing Swamp, he couldn't tell because of the intense pounding in his head. The breeze had stopped producing actual melodies a while ago; now it only created a low monotone sound that resembled the chanting of a monk. Completely drained of stamina, Joel laid Riverhand on the ground and crumpled down next to him.

Hang in there, Riverhand. Maybe someone will find you after I'm dead.

Time ticked by. Normally, Joel would've been able to tell how much of it, exactly, but in his current state, minutes seemed like hours, or even millennia. He could feel small creatures starting to nip at his arms and legs.

Don't eat me, he thought. *If you do, you might get poisoned too.*

He felt his eyelids getting heavy. He tried to resist, but it was much too difficult. Whatever strength he had left, both physical and mental, was quickly disappearing. Accepting his fate, he closed his eyes.

I guess this is it. Sorry, everyone.

"There they are!"

Wha...Felicity?

A few long seconds—or years? No, definitely seconds—passed. Then Joel felt a pair of warm fingers on his neck.

"Okay, he's still alive," the voice that sounded a lot like Felicity's said. "Dude? Joel? Can you hear me?"

Despite his condition, Joel managed to muster up the tiniest of grins. "No."

Someone laughed. It was Felicity, all right.

"Good one," she said.

CHAPTER 17: CULTURE CLASH

Exhausted, Felicity and Seeker—with their three unconscious passengers (Joel had passed out along the way)—finally pulled up at the seaside cave entrance to the Thirsty Tunnels. They had ridden the fourwheel all night and well into the following day, and the sun was beating down on them mercilessly. A cool, salty breeze was blowing in from the ocean, providing some relief. Felicity leaned forward and rested her head on the fourwheel's front rail.

"So, this is the place?" Seeker said.

"Yep," Felicity replied, too tired for sarcasm.

"I believe someone is approaching."

"Thank goodness." Felicity looked up to see Fireflower running out of the cave and through a small fleet of parked wagons.

"You made it," the Wavemaker leader said. "How are they?"

"Still alive, but barely."

Fireflower inspected Joel, and then Riverhand. "You arrived just in time," she said. "Their conditions are serious, but I will be able to help them."

"Great."

"You should go inside and rest."

"Way ahead of ya," Felicity said, climbing out of the fourwheel. "Oh, by the way, this is Seeker. Seeker, this is my boss, Fireflower."

Fireflower nodded. "I am pleased to make your acquaintance."

"Likewise," Seeker replied.

"The two of you go on ahead," Fireflower said, starting up a healing cast. "I will work on them out here and then join you in a few minutes once they are stabilized."

"Sounds good," Felicity said. She led the way into the entrance and onto a downward-sloping path. The last time she was here—with Thornleaf on one of their so-called "dates"—there was nothing but a huge, deep pool of seawater. Now, though, her eyes beheld an enormous cavern with several smaller grottos and tunnels branching off from it. The whole area, packed wall-to-wall with people and animals, was abuzz with conversation.

"This is the entire population of the island?" Seeker asked.

"Mostly, yeah," Felicity replied.

"An average town in the Six States has way more individuals than this."

"It's a small island."

"Felicity!" a voice called out.

Felicity looked in the direction of the voice.

"Over here!"

Over where? She thought, squinting. *I'm not Joel Suzuki, you know.* Scanning the crowd, she spotted a number of familiar faces—Whitenose, Ringneck, even Sixhair and Rocktoe, the elderly caretakers of Red Gulch's bloodseed orchard—until finally she noticed a lone non-Spectraland native standing near the left edge of the cavern, waving his arms: Thinker.

"Over here!" he repeated.

"All right, all right, I'm coming," Felicity muttered. With Seeker following, she made her way through the dense throng, tersely acknowledging greetings and belated congratulations on her wedding along the way, until she reached the spot where Thinker was waiting.

"Fireflower filled me in on what had happened," he said. "Are Joel and Riverhand all right?"

"They'll make it."

"Thinker of Deep Thoughts," Seeker said. "I never guessed that we would meet again."

"Good to see you, Seeker of the Sun." Thinker nodded. "Although I wish it were under happier circumstances."

"So where's Keeper?" Felicity asked.

"She is providing support to Windblade and Redstem in keeping the seawater out of the area."

Now that he had said that, Felicity could make out, over the crowd noise, the strains of wavecasts emanating from the tunnels. "Gotcha."

"Why could they not just collapse the tunnels from where the water originates?" Seeker asked.

"It's against Spectraland culture to harm the land like that," Felicity replied.

"Not to mention," Thinker added, "it would cause the entire space to cave in."

Seeker nodded. "Ah."

There was a sudden commotion. Felicity turned to see Fireflower walking down the sloped path. As the Wavemaker leader held a sustained *G* chord on her wavebow, a trio of unconscious bodies floated in the air behind her, following along in a single file line as if they were rats to her Pied Piper. Some of the villagers expressed surprise and concern at seeing Joel and Riverhand in their injured states, but most of the crowd's reactions were reserved for the person at the tail end of the procession.

"That is Chief Byle!"

"Miss Felicity must have captured him!"

The entire gathering erupted into cheers. Before they could go on too long, however, Fireflower played a loud, brief note on her wavebow, and all fell silent.

"Everyone," the Wavemaker leader said, her voice amplified. "We do indeed have Marshall Byle in our custody once again. However, the threat remains. There are still mind-controlled soldiers from the Six States preparing their giant countercom device, which we expect they will have ready by dawn tomorrow. And now they have also taken Thornleaf prisoner."

"What about the mind-control antidote you are rumored to have?" someone yelled.

"Unfortunately, the remaining supply was in Thornleaf's possession," Fireflower answered.

"Then just kill Chief Byle!" another native—Stoneroot—exclaimed. "That will end the mind control, will it not?"

Like father, like son, Felicity thought.

"As you know, Stoneroot," Fireflower said, her voice steady, "killing is against both the Wavemaker moral code and the laws of the island."

"But this is an emergency!" Stoneroot protested. "My son is in danger from those gray-skinned freaks!"

"Wait, who are you calling a freak?" Seeker said.

Felicity pursed her lips. Not wanting to get Thornleaf into trouble, she hadn't yet told Fireflower that he had already killed Marshall, to no avail.

"I understand your concern," Fireflower said. "I too am worried about Thornleaf. But I am afraid that—"

"Fireflower!" Chief Silverfern said, emerging from one of the side grottos along with the other members of the Chieftain Council. "What is going on here? Did I hear you say that you have..." She trailed off, apparently noticing Fireflower's floating prisoner.

"Marshall Byle, yes, my chief," the Wavemaker leader said. "Felicity captured him when she infiltrated the Six States' encampment."

"But they have Thornleaf!" Stoneroot yelled, facing the members of the council. "My chiefs, you *must* give us permission to kill Byle. Then we can end this entire nightmare right here and now!"

Chief Silverfern straightened her pose. "Killing is against—"

"The laws. The moral code. Yes, yes, I know," Stoneroot said. There were a few scattered gasps; interrupting a chief was not exactly considered good etiquette, especially for a convicted criminal. "But this is Byle we are talking about. One of the worst, if not *the* worst, villain in all of Spectraland's history."

"Killing him will only drag us down to his level," Chief Sandthroat said.

"And besides," Chief Raintree said, "we all know that taking a life—whoever's it is—does irreparable harm to the taker himself. I would not ask anyone to make such a sacrifice."

"You do not have to ask anyone," Stoneroot said. "I volunteer myself for the task."

"Come now, Stoneroot." Chief Twotrunk shook his head. "Think about what you are saying."

"I know very well what I am saying. I am already a criminal. After this crisis is over, I know that I will be immediately returned to prison. So I am offering to do this as a service to the island—a penance of sorts—and also...to save my son."

"Perhaps we should consider his offer," Chief Scarskin said to his fellow village heads.

"My chiefs," Fireflower said, "with all due respect, I must strongly object to this. Allowing any kind of exception to the law, even under these extraordinary circumstances, will set us down a slippery slope. I am sure of it."

At that moment, Keeper came running out of one of the connecting tunnels. "Fireflower," she said, "pardon the interruption, but I have something important to tell you."

"What is it?"

"The pressure from the water is much stronger than we anticipated—Redstem and Windblade will not be able to hold it back much longer."

"How long do we have?"

"A day, perhaps, at most."

Mutters rippled throughout the crowd.

"That is unfortunate," Fireflower sighed.

"You said we would be safe here for several weeks, at least!" someone shouted.

Felicity raised her hand. "I can help once I'm recharged," she offered.

"Thank you," Fireflower said. "That should buy us a little more time."

"Once we are forced to evacuate," Chief Silverfern said, "we will be at the mercy of the mind-controlled soldiers and their device."

"Yes, my chief, I know," Fireflower said, "But before that happens, I—"

"My chief," Whitenose interrupted, "If you do not mind me saying, I would much rather drown down here than become a slave to those outlanders."

"I understand, Whitenose," Chief Silverfern said, "but I cannot force that fate upon those who feel otherwise."

"Besides," Fireflower said, "after Joel recovers in an hour or so, he can try his plan once again. There is still hope."

"Hope?" Stoneroot scoffed. "We cannot rely on hope, especially when our supposed savior has already failed twice. And why should we have to, when an actual, easy solution is right here at our fingertips?"

"Because—"

"And on top of that, this whole time-travel business was never formally approved in the first place, correct? Permission was only granted after the fact!"

"That is true," Chief Scarskin said.

"Roundbark," Stoneroot said, turning to the villager who had replaced him as the head of the Silencers, "how do you and your people feel about that?"

Roundbark glanced in the chiefs' direction before answering. "We do harbor some concerns, I must admit. The unilateral actions of the Wavemaker Order..."

"Violate the terms of the Auravine Accord, do they not?" Stoneroot pointed at Ringneck.

"Well...technically, yes. They do," the island's justice minister replied.

"We only did that because we were trying to save everyone's skins," Felicity protested.

"An attempt that was obviously unsuccessful," Stoneroot said. "My chiefs, I implore you," he went on, sounding and posturing like a skilled lawyer wrapping up his closing arguments, "you have already granted numerous pardons to the Wavemakers for their rule-breaking. Now please, grant me mine. Let me kill Byle."

The entire cavern was quiet for a few seconds. Then someone in the crowd spoke.

"Let Stoneroot do it."

"Yes," someone else agreed. "Stoneroot, go ahead. Kill him."

"Yes, kill him!" another shouted.

"Kill him!"

"Kill him!"

The crowd took up the call, chanting *kill him, kill him* as if that was the name of some death-metal band they were beseeching for an encore.

"Silence!" Chief Silverfern cried. Fireflower tried to aid her by playing a loud, piercing tone on her wavebow, but the crowd was undeterred. They continued their chant, even louder than before.

Seeker turned to Felicity. "Should we be doing something?" she asked.

"Maybe..."

With Stoneroot leading them, the crowd started to move toward the sloped path. Fireflower gripped her wavebow, seemingly unsure if she wanted to stun her own fellow citizens.

"I could freeze eight, maybe ten people with my countercom," Seeker said.

"As could I," Thinker said. "And Keeper of the Light also has—"

"No, that might set them off even more," Felicity interrupted. "I know what to do." She took a few steps forward. "Hey!" she shouted. It was like tossing a pebble into a tidal wave; the chants of *kill him, kill him* went on unabated. She performed a voice-amplification cast and tried again.

"Hey! Listen up!"

It worked this time. The chants slowly faded away, and everyone turned.

"Killing Marshall," she said, pausing for effect, "will not work."

"Why not?" Stoneroot shouted.

"Calm down, I was just getting to that. It won't work because I already did it. *I* killed Marshall. But then he came back to life."

"In the Six States?" someone asked.

"No—I mean, yes—I mean, yeah, he came back to life there, but also here. Again. I dunno, I stabbed him when we were at the beach. He was dead for a few minutes, but then he came back, so I stunned him. Don't ask me how he does it."

"What if we kill him and then burn his body?" Seeker said.

"In this culture, that's only for honorable people." Felicity shook her head. "Besides, if we do that, we might just end up with the Human Torch, which could be even worse."

"I could decapitate him for you," Thinker suggested nonchalantly, eliciting various expressions of shock from the crowd. "Or dismember him. Would that work?"

"Geez, remind me never to die in the Six States," Felicity muttered. "But again, no. We don't do that kind of thing here. Plain old killing might be immoral and illegal, but something like that goes even deeper, from what I've been told. I don't think even Stoneroot would go that far. Right, dear old Dad-in-Law?"

Stoneroot just grimaced and folded his arms.

"I'll take that as a yes," Felicity said.

"Very well." Thinker shrugged.

"Look," Felicity continued, "I know everyone might be nervous about relying on Joel again, but we have this saying back on Earth: 'third time's the charm.' So just give him a chance to rest, and then—"

"Actually," Chief Silverfern interrupted, "I am afraid we must rescind our permission of the time-travel cast."

"Excuse me?"

"Yes," Chief Twotrunk said, "in order to preserve the harmony of the island and maintain the integrity of the Auravine Accord, that particular wavecast must never be performed again."

Incredulous, Felicity scanned the chiefs' faces. From what she could gather by reading their expressions, it seemed as if they were reluctant to be making this particular decision, but even more reluctant to risk creating a potentially disastrous flashpoint right here in the cavern, which—she had to admit—was a distinct possibility, given just how packed-in, tired, and scared everyone was. "All right, fine," she sighed. "In that case, everyone just chill and give us a few minutes to figure out something else, okay?"

There were some uncertain murmurs, but the crowd complied.

"Okay, cool." Felicity ended the amplification cast and turned to Seeker and Thinker. "Let's go talk to Fireflower."

"So you did attempt the deed, after all," Thinker said. "Fireflower did not mention that."

"Yeah, that's 'cause I didn't tell her."

"Wait," Seeker said, "I thought your spouse was the one who killed the Orchestrator?"

"Did you actually see what happened?"

"Well, no, but the Governor told me—"

"Yeah, I think Guider was kinda loopy from all the mind control back-and-forth. No, it was me."

"Oh."

"C'mon."

Felicity, Thinker, and Seeker walked through the crowd and up the sloped path. There Fireflower was gently laying Joel, Riverhand, and Marshall down on the ground via a slow dissolution of her levitation cast.

"Okay," Felicity said, "we need to come up with a plan. Something that everyone will be satisfied with."

Fireflower turned. She had a grim expression on her face. "I cannot believe you did that."

"Did what? Get everyone to shut up?"

"You broke our code. Our law. You, of all people!"

"I had to, all right? I had no choice," Felicity said. She wasn't particularly happy about lying, but she didn't want Thornleaf to get into trouble.

"There is *always* a choice," Fireflower seethed, getting up into Felicity's face. "Especially when you are a Wavemaker. With our abilities, there is never a need to take anyone's life. Never! Do you understand?"

"Sure, yeah, but I didn't take it, right? I mean, look, he's here, alive and well. Sort of, anyway."

"That is beside the point. Your intent was to kill. And here I thought we were of the same mind on this."

Felicity shrugged. "Well, you know, sometimes you just gotta do what you gotta do."

"What you have done, offworlder, is irreparable damage to your own Aura. You realize that, do you not?"

"You realize that by standing around here arguing, we're wasting valuable time?"

Fireflower took a step back, her face creasing into a humorless smile. "You are starting to sound more and more like Thornleaf." She nodded and crossed her arms. "Do you want to know why Spectraland has no death penalty? Why Wavemakers are prohibited from killing? Because we used to. Oh, how we used to. Anyone suspected of any kind of crime would be tortured, killed, made an example out of. But then we realized that our hatred and our anger was consuming us. Poisoning us. It would have been the end of us, eventually. So we had to make a choice. Continue down that path, or stop.

"Those cultural customs you just talked about—there are reasons for them. Cremation is now reserved for special individuals because it did not used to be. A teenage boy once set fire to the Forest of Light. You know what we did to him? Burned him alive, in front of his whole village. Mutilation of a dead body is now considered blasphemous because of Graymold's punishment. It is way too horrific for me to describe, but suffice it to say that what is buried up there at the Sacred Site is something less than an intact corpse."

"Okay, you're really starting to gross me out. Do you want to help me make a plan or not?"

"Very well. I will work with you one last time. But assuming we are successful, after that you will be expelled from the Wavemaker Order and exiled from Spectraland forever. I am sorry, Felicity, but I have no choice. You will never see your husband or anyone here ever again."

Felicity rolled her eyes. "Wasn't that sort of the original plan anyway?" she muttered.

"Hello," a soft voice said. It was Joel, now awake. "What are you guys talking about?"

"Nothing," Felicity said. "Just rest."

"I'm feeling a lot—*cough*—better now."

"Yeah, right. You sound terrible."

"The poison needs time to fully work its way out of your system," Fireflower said.

"But I need to go back in time and try again," Joel insisted.

"You do not have enough strength for wavecasting yet."

"And besides," Felicity added, "we kinda just used up all of our get-out-of-jail-free cards with the chiefs."

"But then what about Blackspore? And Thornleaf? And—*cough*—the giant countercom?"

"Give me a second to think." After a pause, Felicity turned to Fireflower. "None of the mind-controlled soldiers know we're here, right?"

"Correct. Unless they managed to follow you on the ground."

"Nah." Felicity shook her head. "We didn't see anyone for miles around."

"I do not believe the Governor would have sent out any search parties," Seeker said. "She is probably just waiting until tomorrow morning, when the Ultracom can be activated."

"That is a reasonable assumption," Thinker said.

"And you said it can be used once a day, right?" Felicity asked Seeker.

"That is the one detail I recall for sure, yes."

Felicity frowned. "So even if we're safe here tomorrow morning, by the next day we'll be hosed."

"I regret that this location turned out to be less safe than expected," Fireflower said.

"I must apologize for that," Thinker said. "I identified this place as being a good hiding spot."

"It is not your fault. I thought we would be able to hold the water back longer."

"So really," Seeker said, "the only thing that being here was good for was to bring everyone together."

Felicity sniffed. "I wouldn't exactly call that a good thing, since it basically stopped us from being able to try the time-travel plan again," she said, folding her arms.

"That does give me an idea, though. It won't fix everything, but it's a start." She reactivated her voice amplification. "Hey!" she shouted to the gathering. "Everyone be quiet. I'm gonna try to call Thornleaf on his wavebow and get him to put Guider on."

"What are you planning to do?" Fireflower asked.

"Wing it." Felicity played a brief lick on her instrument. A few seconds passed. Then—

"You should not have contacted me," Thornleaf's voice said. "They are—"

"Greetings, offworlder," a female voice interrupted. It was Guider. In the background, it sounded like someone was muffling Thornleaf.

"Hey, Guv'nor," Felicity said. "You'd better not be hurting my husband, there."

"He will survive. What can I do for you?"

"You know we have Marshall, right?"

"The Orchestrator? Yes, I am aware of that."

"I want to make a deal. We'll swap him for Thornleaf. And all of Thornleaf's stuff."

Guider chuckled. "I have no reason to accept such a proposal. When the Ultracom is ready, we can simply force you to return the Orchestrator to us."

"Yeah, maybe. But if you don't take this deal, what you'll be getting back is a dead body. Or, more specifically, tiny little charred pieces of one."

"I think not," Guider scoffed. "The Orchestrator has told me about your people's ways. You will not kill him."

"I guess that means you can't remember what went down when I was in your camp. I stabbed Marshall. Then he came back to life. I won't let that happen again."

"Lies. Your island's laws and customs prevent you from—"

"Okay, let me stop you right there. In case you didn't know, I'm not originally from this island. I'm from a place like yours, where people kill and mutilate each other all the time. So I'll do it, I swear."

"You are bluffing," Guider said.

"As they say in the movies—try me."

Guider paused before responding. "What do you have to gain by murdering him?" she finally said. "You will all be our slaves in the end, regardless."

"Yeah, I know that. But Thornleaf's village wants him back with them when it happens. Togetherness—it's a cultural thing."

No response.

"Look," Felicity continued, "if you refuse, you'll still win, like you said, but you'll have a dead Orchestrator. If you accept, you'll win, *and* you'll have him back, safe. I don't see why this is so hard."

"Very well. I accept. Bring the Orchestrator to our camp by sundown."

"Okay. We'll be there."

"And no tricks."

"Right back at ya."

The strings on Felicity's wavebow dimmed.

"Other than getting Thornleaf back," Fireflower said, "I do not see how this plan benefits us."

"He had the mind-control antidote, remember?" Felicity said. "Once we have that, we can use it to free Guider and then she can issue an order to stop everything."

"That sounds risky."

"It's the best shot we have."

"What if," Seeker said, "instead of going through with this deal, you simply take the Orchestrator down to the beach and then kill him again? Even though he appears to be able to return from the dead, doing so might give you an opportunity to retrieve the antidote. If I recall correctly, he was incapacitated for at least thirty minutes or so the last time."

"No," Fireflower said, exasperated. "Absolutely not."

"I can do it," Thinker volunteered.

"Despite your past, Thinker of Deep Thoughts," Fireflower said, "I cannot permit you to perform such a deed while you are living among us on this island. Or do you wish to be exiled as well?"

"No, I suppose I do not."

"It's okay," Felicity said. "This is gonna work. Trust me. I'll start heading down there now."

"Alone?" Fireflower said.

"Sure, yeah. You need to stay here and fix up Riverhand. And if I take these guys with me"—she gestured at Thinker and Seeker—"I think it'll look too suspicious."

"I want to go with you," Joel said. "If I can't try the time-travel plan again, it's the—*cough*—least I can do."

"Dude, you still need time to recover."

"I'll be fine by the time we get down to the beach," Joel insisted. He managed a little smirk. "Besides, someone has to make sure you stay out of trouble."

"Now *you're* using my own lines against me," Felicity said, rolling her eyes. "Must be contagious."

CHAPTER 18: ANYTHING FOR LOVE

With both of them too drained to perform a flying cast, Joel and Felicity rode a small uncovered wagon drawn by Destiny down to the beach, taking turns in the "driver's seat" (atop the slimeback) while the other napped in the wagon in an effort to regain as much energy as possible. Joel didn't care much for the idea of sleeping next to Marshall's unconscious body, but it wasn't that much different from what he had been doing in the fourwheel on the way to the Thirsty Tunnels, so he did his best to remain unperturbed.

Eventually, while Joel was taking point, they arrived at the beach. He noticed that there were a lot more soldiers here now than before, along with a bunch of large crates that looked like shipping containers. The giant countercom appeared to be almost ready; various lights around its surface were flashing, and it was giving off a steady humming sound. He parked the wagon near the outskirts of the encampment and dismounted.

"Felicity," he said, turning to his sleeping companion. "We're here."

"Mmm...five more minutes," she mumbled.

"Okay."

"I'm kidding." Felicity sat up, rubbed her eyes, and hopped out of the wagon. "Help me carry this guy out, will ya?"

"Um, sure."

The two of them lifted Marshall out of the wagon.

"All right," Felicity said, "you drag him along, and I'll keep my wavebow aimed at him. You know, to make it look threatening."

"Sounds good. Hey, um—did you really try killing him already?"

"No. That was Thornleaf."

"Oh," Joel said, feeling a sense of relief. "Then why did you say—"

"I was just covering for him, that's all. Now grab Marshall and let's go."

"Okay."

Joel picked Marshall up. With all of the recent experience he had gained carrying Riverhand around, it was a lot easier than he had expected. They walked through the trees and toward the Six States camp. As they got closer, a few soldiers noticed them approaching.

"Intruders!" one of them exclaimed.

"Relax," Felicity said. "We're here with the Orchestrator. Guider is expecting us."

The soldier reached for his handheld countercom, which was hanging from his belt.

"Eh-eh," Felicity snapped, sticking the headstock of her wavebow into Marshall's chest. "We had a deal. No funny stuff."

"Relax," the soldier responded in what sounded vaguely like a mocking tone of voice. "I am not going to freeze you. I am simply contacting the Governor to notify her of your arrival."

"All right, but I know how those things work. Move your finger slowly. If I see it heading for the wrong button, this guy is toast."

The soldier lifted the countercom off of his belt and slowly pressed one of the buttons on it.

"Yes?" Guider's voice came crackling through.

"Governor—your guests are here."

"We will be right out."

The soldier replaced the device on his belt. "Stay there," he said.

Felicity shrugged. "We're not going anywhere."

A few moments later, one of the large crates opened up and Guider emerged from it, followed by four soldiers. Two of them were carrying a roughed-up-looking Thornleaf, while one of the others was holding his wavebow and supply pack.

"What is happening?" the tall shaman demanded. "Where are you taking me?"

"See for yourself," Guider said, pointing in Joel and Felicity's direction.

Thornleaf looked up. "What—no!" he barked. "What are you doing?"

"We're taking you home," Felicity replied.

"Are you mad? Destroy Byle! That is the only way to—"

One of the soldiers punched Thornleaf in the gut. "Be quiet," she ordered.

"All right, is that really necessary?" Felicity said.

Guider and her party strode up. "I must admit," she said, "I am still not sure exactly why you want your spouse returned to you. He is a particularly bellicose individual."

"Yeah, but he's our...whatever word you just said," Felicity replied. "Besides, does it really matter why? We actually have all the leverage here, when you think about it."

"I suppose." Guider smiled. "In the sense that you have nothing more to lose." She nodded at Marshall. "When will he wake up?"

"Soon enough."

"Can you revive him?"

"He's under a maximum-strength stunning cast. Only our healer can snap him out of it, and she's not here. Best thing is for you to wait. Should just be a few hours, give or take."

"Very well."

"Okay," Felicity said to Joel, "let him go."

Joel set Marshall down on the ground.

Felicity turned back to Guider. "Now give us Thornleaf and his stuff."

The soldiers that were holding Thornleaf pushed him forward and onto the sand. The soldier carrying his wavebow and supply pack tossed both items down next to him.

"Joel, can you help him up?" Felicity said.

"Sure." Joel helped Thornleaf to his feet and then grabbed the tall shaman's belongings.

"All right, I'm gonna keep my wavebow trained on Marshall while we slowly back away," Felicity warned Guider and the soldiers. "One wrong move, and I swear I'll disintegrate him and anyone else who's unlucky enough to be too close."

"Such savagery," Guider said. "I suppose I underestimated you."

"You sure did."

"Do not worry, we will allow you to leave. You will be back here, under our control, soon enough."

"I can't wait."

While continuing to face Guider and the soldiers, Felicity, Joel, and Thornleaf backed away one step at a time until they reached the wagon.

"Okay, open the pack," Felicity whispered to Joel.

"Right." Joel opened the pack and held it out in front of him.

"Are you not even going to inquire about my well-being?" Thornleaf rasped, leaning against the wagon.

"You're alive, that's what matters," Felicity said as she rummaged through the supply pack. "Now where's that stupid antidote? I swear, your pack is worse than Vicky's purse."

"The mind-control antidote?"

"No, the"—Felicity clicked her tongue and rolled her eyes—"yes, the mind-control antidote."

"They confiscated it."

"They—wait, what?"

"They took it. Along with the invisibility salve and the nullifier."

"Why did they even care what it was? I mean, it basically smells like raw sewage."

"That is actually what made them curious. So they tortured me until I admitted its true purpose."

"Why the heck did you do that?"

"I just told you—they tortured me."

"But...ugh," Felicity groaned. "This whole plan was dependent on it!"

"What plan?"

"After we traded Marshall for you and your stuff, I was gonna use the antidote to snap Guider out of her mind control. Like the plan we were *supposed* to follow the last time."

"And you trusted them to return it to you?" Thornleaf scoffed. "A rather foolish plan. I will give Byle one thing—at least his schemes are well thought out."

"Yeah, I'm gonna pretend you didn't just say that."

"They probably expected such a plan, so they tricked you by releasing me with my instrument and supply pack, minus the thing that you truly wanted. You did not even ask them to open the pack first to verify its contents. A careless mistake, but I suppose anyone could have made it."

"I feel like there's some kind of passive-aggressive jab in that statement, but I can't quite place my finger on it."

"Since we have our wavebows, we can just go back down there and try to stun them," Joel suggested, wanting mostly to defuse Felicity and Thornleaf's argument.

"Dude," Felicity sighed, "if something like that had even a remote chance of working, we would've tried that first. In case you haven't noticed, they have even more soldiers than before, all of them with rifles and handheld countercoms."

"Oh. So...what happened to your box idea?"

"What box idea?"

"You know, the one where you put distracting thoughts into a box in your head. So you won't make mistakes."

"Why are you asking me about that now? I haven't been distracted."

"I thought you were."

"What gave you that idea?"

"Because...well, because this plan didn't work, and you've been fighting with Thornleaf a lot."

Felicity exchanged glances with Thornleaf. Then she turned back to Joel and said, "Okay, maybe I *have* been a little distracted. But that whole box technique...it's cool, and it works most of the time, but I've been tired, and stressed out, and...it takes practice. And discipline. I can't be Miss Mental Strength all the time, you know."

"Oh, okay, like with Art's 'happiness is a state of mind' thing. I get it."

Thornleaf gave his throat a conspicuous clearing. "I suggest we stop talking about irrelevant subjects and begin working on—"

He was interrupted by a low whining sound that started up in the near distance. Destiny gave a little croak of alarm.

"They are turning on the Ultracom!" Thornleaf said.

"What?" Joel said. "It's not supposed to be ready until tomorrow morning!"

"More Six States trickery, I guess," Felicity muttered. "We have to get out of here, now."

"Its reach extends to the whole island," Thornleaf said. "They told me that the only safe spot is within twenty feet of its control panel. We have nowhere to run."

Joel glanced at his wavebow.

I know I'm not supposed to do this, but I don't think I have a choice.

"I have an idea," he said out loud. He picked up his instrument and played. There was a *whoosh*, and then—

The whining sound, the wagon, and Destiny were all gone. The surrounding trees were still there, but now they were on fire. Smoke was everywhere, projectiles were flying through the air, and shouts could be heard all around.

"What did you do?" Thornleaf demanded.

"I time-traveled us out of there," Joel answered.

"Back to the Fourfoot War?" Felicity asked.

"Seems like it."

Joel heard the sounds of wavecasts as the shouting continued. He engaged the Sight and scanned his surroundings. Through the dense clouds of smoke, he saw some Wavemakers off in the distance, but none of them were Blackspore or anyone else familiar.

"Could you not have taken us to a slightly more peaceful moment?" Thornleaf said.

"I—I'm still not totally in control of the cast yet," Joel said.

Thornleaf looked around. "Based on what I have learned, this appears to be the Siege of Crownrock. Not a very wise choice."

"Is that near the end of the war?" Joel asked.

"It is the second-to-last major campaign, right before the Battle of Red Gulch," Thornleaf replied.

"Then I have a feeling we're supposed to be here," Joel said." It's like we're riding the fatewave."

"Riding the what-what?" Felicity said.

A large explosion went off nearby. Everyone cowered.

"I'll explain later," Joel said. "Right now, we should find some cover."

"Yeah, you think?" Felicity said.

Joel and Felicity helped Thornleaf to his feet, and together the three of them scrambled as quickly as they could away from the scene. Once the sounds of fighting seemed to be a safe distance away, they stopped to rest.

"All right," Felicity said, "so what was that about a wave or something?"

"The fatewave," Joel said. "Doc told me about it. Or, well, he told Seaberry, and then she translated."

"Seaberry can talk to swordcats?" Thornleaf said.

"Yeah."

“Never mind that right now,” Felicity said. “What is the fatewave? Is it like the Forbidden Tides?”

“No, it’s an expression about the way the Aura flows, and how things will happen when they’re meant to happen, no sooner, no later. It’s similar to what Nineteen told me before, when we were in Prism Valley. I guess it’s kinda like destiny, or whatever.”

“I recall Fireflower mentioning that term when I was a child just starting my Wavemaker training,” Thornleaf said. “I dismissed it as a way for her to justify making me do extra repetitions.”

“So you’re saying the fatewave guided us to this particular point in time?” Felicity asked.

“I’m pretty sure.” Joel nodded. “Because if we’re near the end of the war, then that means Blackspore will be bringing Marshall over soon, and now is our chance to stop him.”

“In other words, this is where we were trying to go in the first place.”

“Yeah.”

“Well then, let’s get to it.”

♪♪♪

Using the short-range teleportation cast, Joel, Felicity, and Thornleaf went in search of Blackspore. Since the master shaman wasn’t at Crownrock, Joel figured they would try Nightshore once more; after all, if anyone could open a gateway to Earth without using the Rift at Crownrock, it was Blackspore, and Joel assumed he would be most comfortable doing it in the privacy of his own home.

When the trio got to the village, the place was in shambles. Huts were toppled, tree houses lay on the ground, and piles of smoldering wood were everywhere. Even the chieftain's residence, which Joel could see from the outskirts of the settlement, had been decimated. There appeared to be only one hut still relatively intact, on the far side of the courtyard area. There were lights—multicolored and flashing, like those found on a Christmas tree—coming from inside the hut, and the sounds of wavecasting could be heard.

"Looks like we got lucky," Felicity said. "Maybe there is something to this fatewave business after all."

"If I recall correctly, your first several attempts at this mission were complete failures," Thornleaf noted. He sounded like he felt much better.

Ignoring the tall shaman's remark, Joel headed for the hut. The door was closed, and it had the Wavemaker locking seal on it.

"Hey, uh, Thornleaf," Joel said. "Can you open this?"

"That reminds me," Felicity said, "I never got my forearm tattoo."

"The need never arose," Thornleaf said. "And, if this is successful, it never will."

"Let's not start talking about that right now, okay?"

"This seems as good a time as any to talk about it."

The wavecasting sounds intensified.

"C'mon, we *have* to do this," Joel pleaded. "We have to stop Blackspore. It's gonna be tough for me too, going back to my old pre-Spectraland life, but it's the only way."

"Very well," Thornleaf sighed. He pressed his right forearm against the door and, with a *whoomp* sound, it creaked open. "After you."

Joel peeked inside. Blackspore was standing on the left side of the hut, furiously playing his wavebow as if he were auditioning to become Ozzy Osbourne's next lead guitarist. He was looking at a piece of parchment that was set on a tree-branch music stand in front of him. A sphere of Aura, about six feet in diameter, swirled like a miniature hurricane opposite where the master shaman stood. An image was materializing within the sphere—it was very faint, but Joel could tell who it was: Marshall Byle, clad in torn jeans and a Biledriver T-shirt.

That means we're too late to save the Six States, since Blackspore would've already contacted Thinker by now, Joel realized. *But at least we can do this—the only thing we were meant to do, probably*.

"Blackspore?" he said.

Blackspore either didn't hear Joel, or he did and was choosing to ignore him, as he just continued playing. Joel opened the door wider and walked in.

"Blackspore," he said again, louder this time, as Felicity and Thornleaf filed in behind him.

Blackspore gave Joel a sidelong glance. "Sightguy," he said, sweat dripping down his face. "Finally back from the future, I see. And with different companions this time."

"I know what you're doing," Joel said, "and you need to stop. This is the mistake I was telling you about."

"It is too late," Blackspore said as he continued playing.

"No, it's not."

"Did you see my village? It lies in ruins! Warriors from the other villages have killed nearly everyone, including Lightsprout's entire family. Even my former friends in the Wavemaker order have turned against us. I am desperate, Sightguy. You must let me continue."

"I can't do that."

"Then help me. Join me in the war and help me defeat the other villages before it is too late."

"I can't do that either. Look, Blackspore, *you* were the one who sent me back here. You did that because you're about to bring over someone who will eventually wipe out almost all of the Wavemakers and take over Spectraland."

"Not to mention a whole bunch of other bad stuff too," Felicity added.

The image of Marshall within the sphere was growing stronger.

"*Almost* all of the Wavemakers?" Blackspore said, his left eye twitching. "Who survived?"

"You," Joel said, "and..."

"And Lightsprout?"

"No."

"So are you saying that Lightsprout dies because of what I am doing right now?"

"Pretty much, yeah."

Blackspore stopped playing his instrument. The sphere continued to swirl on, but Marshall's image began to fade, just a little.

"If I stop," Blackspore said, turning to Joel, "what will happen?"

"I can't say for sure," Joel admitted. "But my guess is that without the extra help, Fourfoot will be forced to surrender and the war will end."

"Then the Elders will punish me and Lightsprout for getting the Wavemaker Order involved in the first place."

"Maybe, but at least she'll be alive, and you can still be together. Isn't that worth it?"

Blackspore lowered his instrument, a thoughtful look on his face. "Perhaps you are right."

Joel felt a flutter of mixed emotions. His mission was about to be a success. Marshall Byle would never come to Spectraland, and many lives would be saved. For Joel and Felicity personally, it would be a bittersweet victory, but a victory nonetheless. The flutter turned into a more concrete sensation. Joel glanced down at himself and noticed that he was beginning to fade and flicker. He looked at Felicity. The same thing was happening to her.

"Sightguy?" Blackspore said. "What is—?"

"It's, uh, it's complicated. But thank you for making the right choice."

"Bye, babe," Felicity said. She was talking to Thornleaf. "It was fun while it lasted." She turned to Joel. "And, well, nice knowing you, dude. Maybe we'll run into each other eventually."

"Yeah," Joel said. As he continued to fade, the interior of the hut started to change; it was gradually looking more and more like his room back in his family's Seattle apartment. Judging from the room's contents and how they were arranged, he was sure that it was from a year ago, before he met Marshall Byle on the street outside of Art's guitar store. In a few moments, he would lose all memory of Spectraland and Felicity, because they would have never existed in his life.

I'm doing the right thing, he reminded himself, even as a lump formed in his throat. *I know I am.*

"No," Thornleaf growled. "I will not lose you." He raised his wavebow, aimed it at the sphere, and began playing the same melody that Blackspore had been playing.

"What are you doing?" Blackspore said. He moved to stop Thornleaf, but the tall shaman elbowed him aside. "No!" Blackspore got up and tried again, so Thornleaf turned his wavebow on him and fired out a brief stunning cast.

"I will not lose her!" Thornleaf returned his attention to the sphere, playing louder and faster. The sphere resumed swirling. Joel looked around. The image of his room faded, and both he and Felicity were becoming solid once more.

"Thornleaf, stop!" Felicity cried. She tried to grab her husband, but her hands passed right through him.

"We will find another way!" Thornleaf exclaimed.

Marshall's image reappeared, and by the time Joel and Felicity were solid enough to stop Thornleaf, Marshall was solid as well. He stepped out of the sphere, looking dazed and confused.

"Blimey," he said. "Where...where am I?"

"Welcome to Spectraland," Thornleaf replied.

Joel just stood there, mouth agape, unsure of what to do. He glanced at Felicity, who flashed him a look that by now he understood to mean she felt the same way.

"Septra...what?" Marshall said.

"Spectraland," Thornleaf repeated.

"What in blazes is a 'Spectraland'?" Marshall said. "Is that some sort of an amusement park? Is that why you're green? And why don't your mouth movements match your words? How are you doing that?"

"Relax," Thornleaf said. "Everything will be explained in time. For now, you just need to rest."

"I *am* rather dizzy," Marshall said, holding a hand to his forehead. He glanced over at Blackspore's unconscious form. "That bloke seems to have the right idea." He stumbled over to where Blackspore was, sat down, and passed out.

"What the heck are you thinking?" Felicity shrieked at Thornleaf. "Wait—scratch that. I know what you were thinking. I heard you say it. But man, seriously, what a dumb move. I'm really not worth this, trust me."

"If you keep talking, I might be inclined to agree," Thornleaf said, albeit with a smirk.

"So, uh, what are we gonna do now?" Joel asked.

"Simple," Thornleaf said. "We stay here and make sure that history unfolds exactly as it is supposed to."

Felicity put her hands on her hips. "So you're gonna let all those people die, just so we can stay married."

"Who is to say that all those people will not die anyway?" Thornleaf countered. "Is that not how the fatewave works?"

"I hate it when you turn things around like that," Felicity muttered.

"At least this way, we will be sure of the outcome, which includes the two of us being together. And you will also get to keep your little friend here, as well."

"Um, Blackspore's not really that little," Joel said.

"He's talking about you," Felicity replied.

"Oh."

"Speaking of Blackspore...he is the only variable," Thornleaf continued, rubbing his chin. "Since now he knows what is going to happen, we will need to remove him from the picture somehow."

"Whoa, whoa," Felicity said. "You are *not* going to kill Blackspore."

"What? Of course not," Thornleaf scoffed. "We will just send him out to the atoll where we will find him twenty years later."

Felicity shook her head. "I can't believe this is happening."

"Look," Thornleaf said, placing his hands on his wife's shoulders. "I am not happy about it either, trust me. You know how outraged I get at the very mention of Byle's name."

"Which is why this is so weird. I have a headache now."

"It is just that, at the moment when you were nearly gone, I realized that things have to happen this way. The past cannot, and should not, be changed. Terrible things happen, but beautiful things happen as well. And we need both, for that is what makes life a complete experience. If you really think about it, you will realize that we are of the same mind on this."

Joel thought it over. Was Thornleaf right? After all, like he had reminded himself earlier, there had already been multiple instances where his time-travel efforts were for naught. Maybe the past really couldn't be changed.

"And say we did change history," Thornleaf went on. "What if things end up turning out even worse?"

"That's a good question," Felicity said, backing up a few steps. "But I'd rather take my chances."

She grabbed her wavebow and aimed it at the tall shaman. A heartbeat before she was able to play it, however, Thornleaf raised his own instrument and stunned her.

"Forgive me, my love," he said. "In time, I know you will understand."

Shocked, Joel froze, even as every synapse in his brain was screaming at him to grab his wavebow.

"Perhaps you should have practiced dueling with us after all," Thornleaf said before he turned his instrument on Joel and fired out another stunning cast.

CHAPTER 19: THE TIMES THEY ARE A-CHANGING

Joel opened his eyes. He was no longer in Black-spore's hut. Instead, he was floating in the middle of teal-colored nothingness.

What the–did Thornleaf send me to the limbo plane?

Just as he had the last time he was here, Joel saw spectral versions of familiar objects hovering in the air around him: guitars, video game consoles, ham sand-wiches, and so forth. Waves of Aura were here too, but he didn't have his wavebow with him, so he had no idea how he was going to escape.

"Felicity?" he called out. No response.

I can't believe Thornleaf turned on us like that, he thought. *Well, actually, I guess I can. In a way, I sup-pose, I've been expecting him to do that for a long time now.*

Not knowing what else to do, Joel began flapping his arms. He air-swam around aimlessly until he spotted the ghostly figure of a Spectraland native some thirty feet away.

That looks like Fireflower, he thought. *This version of her probably can't talk, but maybe she can point me in the right direction.*

Joel maneuvered himself over to her. Aside from the shadowy appearance, she looked like the "future" version of herself.

"Hey, uh, Fireflower," Joel said. "Do you know—"

"Joel?" the apparition said, her image suddenly gaining a lot more color.

"Whoa!" Joel flinched. "Um, you scared me. I mean—Fireflower? Is that you? The real you?"

"Yes, it is. I sense that you have returned to the past."

"Yeah, I have. Sorry about that."

"No, do not be. We heard the initial activation of the giant countercom and feared that you and Felicity may have been captured."

"We weren't. The plan to get the antidote back didn't work, so I time-traveled the two of us and Thornleaf out of there to escape. But how did you find me here, in the limbo plane?"

"You are not in the limbo plane. You are having a vision. By communing with the Aura, I was able to connect with you."

"Oh," Joel said, relieved to learn that he was, in fact, not trapped here.

"I need to give you a warning," Fireflower continued.

"About what?"

"Do not return to the future. Remain in the past. A day after you and Felicity left for the beach, we had to evacuate the Thirsty Tunnels. We tried to find another suitable hiding spot, but the giant countercom was activated a second time and now we are all under energy control."

"Even you?"

"Yes, even me. We are being forced to travel, via our own wagons and slimebacks, to the Six States encampment. For what reason, I do not know. But soon, Byle will have our wavebows in his possession."

"That's, um, that's not good."

"Indeed. So please, remain there and try to finish your original mission. Stop Blackspore from bringing Marshall Byle over to Spectraland. That is our only hope now."

"Okay, but...well, there's a little problem with that."

"A problem? What is it?"

Joel grimaced. "Marshall's already here."

"Already there? Did you arrive too late?"

"No, actually, we got here at the perfect time—finally. And I even managed to talk Blackspore out of it. But then..."

"What?"

"Well, then Thornleaf brought Marshall over instead."

Fireflower's face fell. "Thornleaf? Why?"

"When Blackspore stopped playing the portal cast, Felicity and I...we started to disappear. Thornleaf didn't want to lose her, so he stunned Blackspore and finished up the incantation."

"I cannot believe this," Fireflower said, shaking her head.

"Yeah, so then Marshall passed out, and Felicity tried to stop Thornleaf, but then he stunned both of us. Which means I'm still unconscious, which I guess is why I'm having this vision."

"So now Thornleaf will try to make sure that history unfolds as it did," Fireflower said, almost to herself. She looked up at Joel. "Do you think you can stop him? And send Marshall back to your world?"

"I can try."

"Please do. I am afraid that something terrible is going to happen otherwise."

"I'm on it."

"Thank you. You truly are a good person."

"Um, okay."

"Who are you?"

Joel blinked. The scene had abruptly shifted; instead of the limbo plane, he was now back in Blackspore's hut. Fireflower was still in front of him, but instead of her older, "future" self, she was now the nineteen-year-old version from the time of the Fourfoot War.

"I'm, uh...Sightguy," Joel answered.

"The vagabond?" Fireflower said. "What are you doing here? What has happened?"

Joel looked around. He realized that he was sitting on the ground in the corner of the hut, wrapped in a tight binding cast. Felicity was next to him, also bound but still unconscious. Both of their wavebows and supply packs were gone.

"Um...something bad," he said, ignoring Fireflower's first two questions.

The Wavemaker leader-to-be walked over to the tree-branch music stand. The parchment that had the portal incantation inscribed on it was also gone. "Was someone performing a wavecast? Was it Blackspore?"

"Sort of."

"What do you mean?"

"It's—it's complicated." He nodded at Felicity. "She can probably explain better."

Fireflower raised an eyebrow. "Who is she? Is she a vagabond as well?"

"Her name is, um, Goldilocks," Joel replied, wondering why Fireflower had to keep asking him multiple-part questions. "And actually...she's not a vagabond. And neither am I. We're both Wavemakers. From the future."

Fireflower narrowed her eyes and aimed her wavebow at Joel.

"Wait," Joel said, "what are you—"

Fireflower played a short, soft melody, and a cloud of dark-blue Aura popped into existence around Joel's head.

"How interesting," she said. "You are telling the truth." She aimed her wavebow at Felicity and played a short riff.

"Stop, you jerk!" Felicity blurted out, snapping awake. "I—whoa. Wait"—she blinked rapidly—"Fireflower?"

"I would ask how you know who I am, but I think I already know the answer to that question."

Felicity looked over at Joel. "You told her that we're from the future?"

"Yeah."

"So, future shamans," Fireflower said, "tell me what happened here."

"Well," Felicity said, "an offworld Wavemaker named Marshall Byle just came over to Spectraland. In a little while, he's gonna kill lots of people and take over the island."

"Offworld?" Fireflower blanched. "So the incantation that Blackspore stole from the archives was a...a portal cast?"

"Yep," Felicity said. "He wanted to find someone to help Nightshore win the war."

Fireflower grimaced. "That treacherous, treasonous—"

"But then he stopped," Joel interrupted. "I talked him out of it."

"Then who—?"

Joel glanced at Felicity. "Do you want to tell her?"

Felicity sighed. "We had a third Wavemaker from the future with us—let's call him Jerkface. We all came back here to try to prevent this whole deal. But just when Blackspore was going to close the portal, Jerkface decided that he didn't want to change history after all, so he ended up finishing the cast."

"I see." Fireflower frowned. "Then what happened?"

"Marshall passed out, and Jerkface stunned the rest of us. Not necessarily in that exact order."

"So where are they all now?"

"Not sure."

"All right, I will find out." Fireflower started up a tracking cast. "I have located Blackspore. He appears to be alone," she said, moving her wavebow around, "and rather far from here. Possibly out on the ocean."

"Uh oh," Joel said.

"Jerkface must be trying to send him to that atoll," Felicity said.

"Atoll?" Fireflower asked.

"Yeah, it's a long story," Felicity said.

"We need to save him," Joel said. "I don't think he knows the short-range teleport cast yet."

"The what?" Fireflower said.

"You're probably right," Felicity said. She looked at Fireflower. "Think you can unbind us?"

"Even if we manage to procure a vessel," Fireflower said, releasing the binding casts on Joel and Felicity with a quick strum, "there is no way we will be able to catch up with him before he reaches the Forbidden Tides."

Felicity smirked. "Oh yes, there is."

♪♪♪

"This is incredible!" Fireflower shouted as she, Joel, and Felicity zoomed through the air out over the ocean. The two offworlders were being carried along by the flying cast that they had just taught Fireflower how to perform.

"Yeah, but stay focused!" Felicity shouted back. "You're still a newbie at this."

They continued flying, this time in silence. Then, once they got near the spot where Blackspore was supposed to be, Joel spotted something: a distinct trail in the ocean made of both residual Aura and the natural disturbance in the water caused by a floating object, like a fast-moving boat.

"Look at that!" he shouted, pointing.

"I see it," Felicity replied. "That must be him."

They followed the trail until they saw what was creating it—a large, flat plank of wood that seemed to be propelling itself. Lying atop the plank was a prone figure.

"Yup, it's him," Joel said.

They flew down for a closer look. Sure enough, it was Blackspore, secured to the plank with vine-ropes. The plank itself had a swirling cloud of Aura attached to its aft end that appeared to be acting as a sort of motor.

Marshall must've given Thornleaf that idea, Joel thought.

"My Aura energy is starting to wane," Fireflower warned. "I will not be able to carry much more weight."

"Then just get Blackspore and leave the plank," Joel said.

"Swoop down!" Felicity exclaimed.

They swooped down.

"Fireflower!" Blackspore exclaimed. "How are you—?"

"Never mind that now," Felicity said. "Just hold still!"

Once they got near enough, Felicity severed the vine-ropes with Fireflower's knife. Then Fireflower expanded the flying cast to envelop Blackspore, and they turned around just as the plank crossed the Far Edge.

"This is gonna be close!" Joel said.

The rumbling of the Forbidden Tides started up. Fireflower pressed her arms to her side and pushed forward, obviously straining. A few seconds later, Joel could hear the giant wave rising up behind them, but he didn't turn to look. The four shamans sped along, barely out-pacing the tsunami, until they were about a mile from the shore; at that point, Fireflower's cast began to flicker. Felicity shouted something, but Joel couldn't hear what it was. They began to slow down. Joel could almost feel the wave right behind them. They started to lose altitude.

"You can do it!" Joel shouted at Fireflower, even though he knew that she probably couldn't hear him.

Then, right as they reached the shore, the flying cast vanished. Instead of falling, however, the foursome was engulfed by the giant wave as it crashed onto the sand. It carried them along for a while until, finally, they were deposited in a soaking heap among a group of trees.

"I am *so* sick of that wave," Felicity remarked, coughing.

"Me too," Joel responded. He turned his head, blew saltwater out of his nose, and gingerly got to his feet.

"Is everyone all right?" Fireflower asked.

"I think so," Joel said.

"Never been better," Felicity quipped, squeezing out her hair.

"Thank you all for rescuing me," Blackspore said. "But what—"

Fireflower slapped the master shaman across his face. "You *fool*!" she snapped. "How could you do that?"

"Do what?"

"You know very well what. You have put our island in mortal danger!"

"First of all, an apprentice should never strike a master like that," Blackspore said, rubbing his cheek with one hand and jabbing a finger at Fireflower with the other. "Secondly, I realize that I what I did was wrong."

"That does not change anything."

"It is not too late to stop them. The future shaman still needs to train the offworlder some more. We have time."

"But three of us don't have our wavebows," Felicity said. "And trust me, even if Marshall isn't fully trained yet, we're still gonna need all the firepower we can get."

"Where are the other Wavemakers?" Joel asked.

"A few are at their home villages, guarding the war prisoners and tending to those who cannot fight," Fireflower replied. "The rest are currently escorting the united three armies toward Red Gulch, where the remainder of the Nightshore forces have holed up." She shot Blackspore a dirty look. "Including Lightsprout, as you know."

"She is only doing what she feels is right."

"Can you talk her out of fighting?" Joel asked. "Before Marshall and Th—um, I mean, the other future shaman reach her?"

"Without my wavebow, there is no way to contact her." Blackspore shook his head. "Since Nightshore is at war with the other villages, she will not answer a summons from any shaman's instrument besides mine."

"What if we get the rest of the Wavemakers together and track the delinquent duo down first?" Felicity asked.

"If we pull the other shamans out of their positions," Fireflower said, "I am sure Chief Fourfoot will take advantage of the situation and attack."

"What if we tell him that he's gonna get killed too?" Joel said.

"I am afraid the chief is beyond reason at this point," Blackspore said. "The only way he will stop fighting is if he is forced to surrender."

"Great," Felicity muttered. "Any other ideas?"

"I know," Fireflower said. "We should consult with the Elders. I need to report back to them anyway."

"In person?" Felicity asked.

"That would be preferable, if we are going to request their assistance."

"Well, you're out of energy," Felicity said, "and I'm not walking all the way to the temple from here." She turned to Blackspore. "Do you remember how to play the portal cast? Without the scroll?"

"Yes."

"So can you just teleport us over there?"

"Unfortunately, I do not know how to create an intra-island portal as of yet."

"Ugh," Felicity said. "Future-you does."

"I beg your pardon?"

"Forget it."

Fireflower offered her wavebow to Felicity. "I trust you enough now to lend you my instrument," she said. "You can handle the—what did you call it, again?"

"Flying."

Blackspore gave Felicity a quizzical look. "Is that a wavecast from the future?"

"No, it's a type of squirrel."

"Yes, it's a wavecast," Joel said.

"Did I develop it?" Blackspore asked.

"Actually," Felicity said, nodding at Fireflower, "she did."

Fireflower flashed a smug expression at Blackspore that Joel could have sworn was a smirk.

♪♪♪

With Felicity handling the flying cast, the four shamans zoomed over to the Wavemaker Temple, the appearance of which was a bit different from what Joel was used to. The tall stone statues were still there, but the structure itself was smaller, and there was no protective Aura-dome surrounding it. Joel's mind flashed back to his first adventure in Spectraland, when he had visited the temple in the aftermath of the war; at that time, it had appeared largely the same as it did right now, except that it was damaged, abandoned, and had a cloud of dark Aura hanging over it. He felt a small chill at the memory.

They landed in the clearing out in front and walked up to the double doors, which Blackspore opened with his forearm tattoo. The main hall looked a bit more familiar, with the usual streams of colored Aura floating around the glowing pillars. No one was inside except for a small spinedog sitting near the edge of the dais. It barked out a short greeting. Blackspore paused to pet the animal before he led the way out of the hall, past the old library, and toward a large dome-shaped hut nestled in between a few trees. Once there, he stepped forward and played a couple of notes on Fireflower's wavebow.

"Master Blackspore," a smooth female voice said. She didn't sound very elderly. "Using an apprentice's instrument. Very odd. Have you lost yours?"

"Yes."

"How irresponsible."

Blackspore sighed. "I would like to request an audience with the Elders."

"I am sorry, but they are rather busy at the moment."

Felicity turned to Joel. "Wow, they even have secretaries to screen their visitors."

"She is not actual person," Fireflower said. "She is a wraith. An Aura-spirit."

"Oh, a virtual assistant. Like Siri."

"Who?"

"Never mind."

"It is very important that we see them," Blackspore insisted.

"Why is that?"

"We have guests."

"Guests? What kind of guests?"

"Wavemakers...from the future."

Five long, silent seconds passed by. Then, finally: "You may enter."

The interior of the dome-shaped hut was rather dark, the only source of light being a single glowmoss-covered stone attached to the ceiling near the entrance. It was roomy for a hut—about 185 square feet, Joel estimated—but, of course, sparsely furnished; there were just four stone stools arranged around a flat, two-inch-thick circular wooden platform in the middle of the floor. Upon each of the stools sat a native: a female with long gray hair and a sallow complexion, a bald male with a bushy beard, a female sporting a pixie cut, and a male with a hairdo like a Troll doll. None of them looked very busy; in fact, Joel thought, they looked almost bored.

"Greetings, Elders," Blackspore said with a deferential nod.

"Greetings, Master Blackspore," the gray-haired Elder replied in a deep, masculine voice. Joel noticed that despite having predominantly female physical features, she also had an Adam's apple. His first instinct was to say, *Wait, I thought you were a woman*, but he managed to suppress the urge. "And greetings to you as well, Fireflower," the Elder continued.

"Greetings, Mistress Moonear," Fireflower replied.

Mistress Moonear stood up. She was fairly tall for a Spectraland native—about five feet ten, Joel figured, almost as tall as Thornleaf. "So, these are our guests, I presume?"

"Indeed," Blackspore said.

"Wavemakers from the future...it appears your research will eventually bear fruit."

"Yes, but they are not the primary reason we are here."

"Oh? Then what is?"

Blackspore bowed his head. "I am afraid I have committed a grave error. I have allowed a powerful shaman from another world to enter our beloved land."

"You were searching for a way to win the war for Nightshore, were you not?" the bald, bearded Elder asked.

"Yes, Master Snowlip," Blackspore replied. "But these shamans from the future"—he gestured at Joel and Felicity—"warned me of the consequences."

"And yet, you still continued?" the pixie-cut Elder asked.

"No, Mistress Pinkwood. One of their own turned on them. At the last moment, he decided that history should not be altered."

"He sounds rather wise," the Troll-doll Elder said. There was something strangely familiar about him, but Joel couldn't quite place it.

"Wise?" Felicity said. "No, he's being a complete idiot."

"Is he now?"

"Yeah, he is. If history isn't changed, then after the war, this offworld dude—Marshall Byle is his name—will destroy the Wavemaker Order and take over Spectraland. So he needs to be stopped."

"If you and your companion are Wavemakers from the future, then things must turn out all right, eventually."

Felicity clicked her tongue. "I guess you could say that," she admitted. ""But things will get a lot worse before they get better."

"So we're trying to prevent that," Joel added.

"All right." The Troll-doll Elder nodded. "Let us assume you will be successful. Who is to say that by doing so you will not just be creating another disaster? Possibly one of even greater magnitude?"

"Forgive me, Master Boneshoot, but I do not see how that could be possible," Blackspore said.

Mistress Moonear chuckled. "We granted you the rank of master, Blackspore, but I see you still have much to learn."

"What do you mean?"

"Is it not obvious? Say the four of you save the Wavemaker Order from this offworld shaman. Well, what if one of those whom you save—even me, perhaps—goes on to become an even bigger threat?"

"Mistress, with all due respect, I do not believe something like that could ever happen."

"We're going in circles here," Felicity said. "Look, the bottom line is that we can't take this dude on by ourselves, especially without wavebows. We need help from someone powerful, like you guys."

Mistress Moonear sighed. "Blackspore, Fireflower—please wait outside. There are things I need to discuss with the future Wavemakers."

"But Mistress," Blackspore protested, "I—"

"Please," Mistress Moonear repeated, "wait outside." This time, it sounded more like a command than a request. Without another word, Blackspore and Fireflower turned and exited the hut. Once they were gone, the gray-haired Elder looked at Joel. "Quiet one—you are destined to become the Virtuoso, are you not?"

"Oh, um—what?"

"The Virtuoso. The one who is fated to save all of existence."

"I, uh, I guess so. How...how did you know that?"

"When you get to be my age, some things are just obvious."

"Oh."

"So as the Virtuoso, you are blessed with the Sight. Can you not see what I am trying to tell you?"

"I, uh, I don't think the Sight works like that."

"Indeed." Mistress Moonear smiled. "What I am trying to say is that even now, at this early stage in your evolution, you are already more powerful than all four of us here combined. Because, thanks to your ability, you should already know that what you want to do should not be done. Therefore, you do not need our assistance."

"But if we don't do this, lots of people will die. Maybe now, and in our time as well."

"I understand."

"And you'll die too."

Mistress Moonear gave Joel a Spectraland shrug. "If that is the will of the Aura, then so be it."

"What good is being the Virtuoso if I can't fix stuff like this?"

"Being the Virtuoso is not about altering timelines. It is about knowledge. Wisdom. Growth."

"I still don't understand. Even if it's risky, don't we have to try?"

"The Aura is like water flowing in a river. It goes where it wants to go. We can place rocks in its path, maybe even change its course, but eventually it ends up in the same place."

"But—"

"You cannot change the past, Joel Dylan Suzuki," Master Snowlip said.

"Um—how do you know my real name?"

"You cannot change the past, nor should you want to," Mistress Pinkwood said. "You can only accept it."

"But—"

"You cannot change the past, but you *can* shape the future," Master Boneshoot said. "By taking what you have learned and applying it to the present. It is not too late."

"This really isn't like the movies, is it?" Felicity grumbled.

"I sense that you will do what you want to do, however," Mistress Moonear conceded with a sigh. "So we will help you."

"Oh, cool," Joel said, relieved. "Thanks. You know, I—"

"By lending you our wavebows." Mistress Moonear nodded at the other Elders. Each of them stood up and handed their instruments over to Joel and Felicity.

"But..."

"Best of luck to you," Mistress Moonear said. With that, she and the other three Elders suddenly disappeared from sight.

"Whoa," Joel said. "Where'd they go?"

"Not really sure I want to know," Felicity said. "Anyway, it looks like we're on our own."

"Yeah," Joel muttered.

"Wait," Felicity said, turning, "your middle name is Dylan?"

CHAPTER 20: DESTINY FULFILLED

Joel and Felicity explained the situation to Blackspore and Fireflower, leaving out the specifics about the Virtuoso Vision. Then, on their way out, the four Wavemakers took a few minutes to recharge their Aura energies in the temple's main hall. After that, they exited the temple and gathered in the front clearing next to the river, where Felicity started up a tracking cast on her borrowed instrument.

"Uh oh," she muttered.

"What's wrong?" Joel asked.

"If this thing is accurate, Marshall and Jerkface are already somewhere in the vicinity of Red Gulch."

"Who is Jerkface?" Blackspore asked.

"The other future shaman."

"He introduced himself to me as Iceheart."

Felicity snorted. "You've gotta be kidding me."

"I will alert Lakereed," Fireflower said.

"All right." Blackspore nodded. "And we ourselves should get over to Red Gulch as quickly as possible. This will be our chance to send the offworlder back."

"Sounds good," Joel said.

"Wanna learn the flying cast?" Felicity offered.

"As much as I would love to, time and energy are at a premium right now," Blackspore replied. "If we make it through this, Fireflower can teach it to me later."

"Perhaps," Fireflower said with a mischievous grin, "if I feel like it." She turned and played a short note on her wavebow.

"Fireflower?" a male voice sounded.

"Hello, Lakereed."

"Did you capture Blackspore?"

"In a manner of speaking, yes."

"Good. Make sure he is secure and then rejoin us as soon as possible. We are about to finish this war once and for all."

"Yes, about that...you may want to be careful."

"Why?"

"There are two new shamans who are about to join Fourfoot's army. One of them in particular is extremely dangerous."

"Fireflower, I think your communication cast is faulty, because I thought I heard you say 'two new shamans.'"

"That is exactly what I said. I will explain everything when I arrive. For now, please refrain from advancing."

"Very well. But if this is another one of your jokes, know that I do not find it very amusing."

The strings on Fireflower's wavebow dimmed. She turned back to the others. "Shall we?"

♪♪♪

The foursome flew to an area of Spectraland that was relatively arid compared to the rest of the island. There weren't many trees or bushes, and the ground was more dirt and rocks than grass. Running through the middle of the area was a deep but narrow ravine that Joel recognized as Red Gulch; he noted, near the midpoint of the ravine, the spot where Sixhair and Rocktoe maintained their bloodseed orchard. The ravine ran for roughly twelve miles before it terminated in a small mountain range. A big cone made up of golden Aura energy—an Aura-tent, Joel realized—stood near the edge of the ravine, about two miles away from the mountain. The tent was surrounded by dozens of slimebacks—one of whom Joel recognized as Destiny, the other as Dreamer, Felicity's former (future?) mount.

"Over there!" Fireflower shouted, pointing.

The four shamans landed in front of the Aura-tent. Joel glanced in Destiny's direction but avoided stopping or making direct eye contact. Instead, he followed Fireflower as she walked up to the tent's front "door"—a spot that was a different color (sort of a pale yellow) than the rest of the energy-based structure.

"Lakereed!" Fireflower called. "I am here."

A few seconds later, a head popped out of the tent. It was round, male, and topped off with a mop of bluish hair. "Fireflower? How did you get here so quickly?"

"That is not important right now," Fireflower replied. "May we come in?"

"Who is—?" the native apparently named Lakereed said, looking past Fireflower. "Blackspore! What are you doing here?"

"Greetings, Lakereed," Blackspore said.

"Fireflower, what is happening?" Lakereed said, sounding alarmed.

"Everything is all right, I promise," Fireflower replied. "Please, let us enter."

Lakereed's head disappeared for a moment, but then his hand emerged and parted an opening in the Aura-tent. The four shamans entered. The tent appeared much larger on the inside; there were over a hundred (one hundred and five, to be exact) natives gathered within, some sitting, some standing, some holding weapons, others poring over parchments. Joel instantly recognized four of them: Chief Raintree of Spearwind, Chief Twotrunk of Bluecrest, Stoneroot, and Greenseed. Fortunately, none of the villagers from the initial battle where Tealfinger was killed—Watertongue included—were present. A number of heads turned.

"Everyone!" Fireflower said before anyone had a chance to react. "This is Sightguy, Goldilocks, and, of course, you all know Blackspore. We bring important news."

"Has Fourfoot finally decided to surrender?" Chief Twotrunk asked.

"I am afraid not," Fireflower replied. "In fact, he is about to get reinforcements."

"Yes, Lakereed gave us your message about two new shamans," Chief Raintree said. "Are these the two you were talking about?'

"No," Fireflower said. "These two are on our side."

"Where are they from?" someone else asked.

"The future."

Gasps and murmurs broke out.

"Everyone, settle down," another native said, stepping forward. With a head of short white hair (topped off with a floral crown) and a wrinkle-lined face, she appeared as old as the Wavemaker Elders, but her mannerisms gave the impression of someone spry and fit. "Fireflower, it sounds like you and your guests have some very interesting stories to tell us."

"Indeed, Chief Stormfruit," Fireflower said.

A space was cleared out, and the foursome sat down in a circle with the three chiefs, Lakereed, and five other natives carrying wavebows.

"Sightguy and Goldilocks," Fireflower said, "these are—"

"Yeah, don't bother with introductions," Felicity interrupted. "I'll never remember all your names. And besides, if everything goes as planned, we won't be around here much longer anyway."

"Very well," Fireflower said. "In that case, you may go straight to the explanations."

"Me?"

"You know the story better than I."

"Fine." Felicity proceeded to outline the situation for the gathered audience, who listened with rapt attention to her every word.

"So," one of the unintroduced Wavemakers said when Felicity was done, "this offworld shaman—Byle, you called him—he can...kill?"

"'Fraid so."

"Did the other future shaman teach him that cast?"

"No"—Felicity paused and furrowed her brow—"at least, I don't think so."

Lakereed turned to Chief Stormfruit. "My chief, what should we do?"

Chief Stormfruit crossed her arms and took a deep breath. "We should continue with our original strategy," she declared. "Fourfoot may have new shamans on his side, but so do we." She looked at Blackspore. "Including the one who can banish the offworlder."

"I concur," Chief Twotrunk said.

"As do I," Chief Raintree said.

"It is settled, then," Chief Stormfruit said. "We will depart immediately." She stood up, and everyone followed suit. Just then, Greenseed came walking over.

"I have a request, my chief," she said.

"Oh? What is it?"

"I would like to accompany the war party."

"Definitely not," Fireflower said before Chief Stormfruit was able to reply.

"Why do you always treat me like this?" Greenseed snapped. "Just because I am not a Wavemaker like you does not mean I am helpless, you know."

"But you are also not a warrior, or even a guard," Fireflower retorted. "You are merely a servant."

"Oh, I assure you, she is quite more than that," Chief Stormfruit said with an air of pride. "In fact, I consider her, along with Suntooth, to be among my most trusted and capable advisors. If she wishes to join the war party, I see no reason to decline her request."

"But, my chief, it is just that I..."

"You what?"

An awkward silence ensued. Joel decided to fill it with a message that he had been asked to pass on.

"She loves you," he said to Greenseed. "Very much."

The two sisters turned to him, both of them wearing expressions that seemed to scream, *What did you just say?*

"Um, so...yeah," Joel went on. "I think she just wants you to be safe, that's all."

"We will talk about this later," Fireflower said with a sigh. "Right now, we have a battle to prepare for."

♪♪♪

With the three chiefs leading the way, the combined forces of Headsmouth, Spearwind, and Bluecrest villages headed up toward the mountain on slimeback. Joel, Felicity, Fireflower, and Blackspore did so as well, not wanting to expose too many people to the phenomenon of flying. They weren't riding Destiny and Dreamer, though; their future mounts were serving some of the other Wavemakers.

So we ended up inheriting them after their original riders died, Joel realized.

When they arrived at their destination, Joel saw, in the face of the mountain, a cave whose entrance was covered by a dense, humming shield of Aura energy.

"Shall we get to work breaking down the shield?" Lakereed asked Chief Stormfruit.

"Wait," Blackspore said before the chief could reply. He dismounted and stepped toward the cave. "Lightsprout! I want to speak with you!"

No response.

"Lightsprout!"

"Hello, Blackspore," an amplified voice responded, echoing throughout the air. But it wasn't Lightsprout. It was Thornleaf. Felicity cursed and jumped off of the slimeback she was riding.

"Where is Lightsprout?" Blackspore demanded.

"She is...indisposed," Thornleaf replied.

"What have you done with her?"

"Do not worry, she is perfectly fine...for now. I must say, you are very lucky that the one you love is so loyal to you. If only I were as fortunate."

Felicity stepped forward. "Hey!" she shouted.

"Speaking of which..."

"You know you almost killed Blackspore, right?"

"He would have made it through. Somehow."

"I still can't believe you're doing this. If you help us now, maybe someday I'll consider forgiving you."

"There is nothing to be forgiven. I am simply doing what is right. For both of us."

"This isn't right for *anybody*, you jerk! Why can't you see that?"

"You are the one who is not seeing. But in time, I know everything will become clear, and all will return to normal."

"Not if I can help it."

"Do not try to stop us. I do not want you to get hurt."

"I already am."

Joel glanced at Felicity. Tears were streaming down her face. She quickly wiped them away and turned around.

"Let's do this," she said.

Several of the Wavemakers dismounted and jogged up to the cave. As they did so, Blackspore played a melody on his borrowed instrument, creating a sphere of Aura in front of him.

"What are you doing?" Joel asked.

"I need to make sure Lightsprout is all right."

An image formed within the sphere: Marshall, holding Blackspore's original wavebow and standing next to a tall native wearing a face-covering antler-helmet and a long, green robe made out of vines.

"Wait," Joel said, "is that...?"

He was about to say "Fourfoot," but then the image panned out, revealing the short and frail Nightshore chief skulking about the back of the cave, a manic grin on his face. Behind him, on the ground, was Lightsprout, tied up in a binding cast and apparently unconscious.

"They will pay for this," Blackspore growled.

"Keep the cast going," Joel said.

Blackspore complied. The image panned out even further, showing that Marshall and the tall native were positioned in front of a small group of warriors who were holding spears, clubs, and other assorted weaponry.

"Nightshore!" the tall native addressed the gathering.

"Whoa," Joel breathed. "That's Thornleaf."

"Who?" Blackspore said.

"Um, I mean—"

"Now is the time to fulfill your destiny!" Thornleaf shouted. "Despite being vastly outnumbered, you *will* emerge victorious! As a shaman from the future, I know this to be true!"

The Nightshore warriors—there couldn't have been more than fourteen or fifteen of them, but it was hard to tell for sure through Blackspore's far-vision cast—cheered.

"Sightguy! Blackspore!" Felicity called, firing a constant stream of light at the shield covering the cave entrance. "Help us!"

"Oh, uh, okay." Joel nodded. He turned to Chief Stormfruit. "Get everyone ready," he said. "The battle's about to begin."

"We were born ready!" the chief cried, raising her spear. Everyone else behind her cheered and hollered.

Joel and Blackspore ran up to the cave entrance. Felicity, Lakereed, and the other Wavemakers were making some progress in breaking down the Aura-shield, though there was still a way to go.

"Once the shield is down," Felicity said over the din, "everyone play a stunning cast. Hopefully we can end this before it begins!"

With Joel and Blackspore (especially Blackspore) adding their Aura-streams to the mix, portions of the shield began to flicker. Moments passed, each one longer than the last.

"Almost there!" Lakereed shouted.

The shield faded. Joel could now see the outlines of everyone within the cave.

Just a little more...

Then, all at once, the shield disappeared. But in the split second before the Wavemakers could do anything else, a huge blast of sonic energy knocked them all backward and off their feet.

"Charge!" Thornleaf bellowed.

Joel scrambled to get up. Streaks of Aura flew in his direction. Warriors dashed out of the cave, yelling and brandishing their weapons. And in between it all, he could hear Marshall cackling with glee.

All right, it's on.

Ignoring the conventional warriors running past him (who, fortunately, were ignoring him as well), Joel scanned the scene for Marshall and Thornleaf. Within two seconds, he spotted them waiting inside the cave, standing next to Chief Fourfoot. Thornleaf was maintaining a shield cast out in front of the three of them while Marshall fired out blasts of dark-purple energy. Fortunately, Marshall's aim wasn't that good yet, so none of the blasts were connecting with a target, but Joel knew that wouldn't last long. He shot a couple of stunning casts at them. Both deflected harmlessly off of Thornleaf's shield.

"We'll take them down together!" Felicity shouted as she cast a shield of her own.

Joel formed up with her and the other Wavemakers, creating a shoulder-to-shoulder horizontal line. Half of the shamans produced a shield, while the other half fired out streams of red stunning energy at their two adversaries.

"Focus your fire on a single spot!" Blackspore ordered.

They did so, and for a moment Joel thought he saw Thornleaf's shield flicker. But then the tall shaman simply strummed his instrument again and his shield was restored, stronger than before.

"Just keep going!" Felicity said.

They continued firing. A few of Marshall's shots hit their shields, creating a loud, dissonant sound with every strike.

"He is not that powerful!" Lakereed chortled. "Victory will be ours!"

"Don't say stuff like that!" Felicity yelled.

Sure enough, a moment later a terrible—if predictable—thing happened. One of Marshall's shots hit Lakereed's shield with such force that it not only knocked the blue-haired shaman's shield out, it sent him flying nearly fifty feet through the air and down into the nearby ravine.

"Lakereed!" someone cried.

"Ha-*ha*!" Marshall exulted. "Now I've got it!"

The Biledriver singer fired another shot. It hit one of the other shamans, and this time, instead of propelling her away, it caused her to explode into a million tiny bits. A few of the Wavemakers, Fireflower included, cried out in horror.

"Brilliant!" Marshall exclaimed.

"Remember which ones are off-limits," Thornleaf's voice, still amplified, said.

Marshall rolled his eyes before he fired yet another shot that barely missed.

"We need to retreat!" someone said.

"No!" Blackspore responded. "I will get rid of him. Cover me!"

Blackspore took a few steps forward with his shield-mate at his side. He started up the portal cast, but before the energy sphere got any bigger than a basketball, Marshall fired out two quick shots in succession; the first blew away the shield-caster, and the second—a bolt of red light—hit Blackspore square in the chest. The master shaman collapsed.

"Well done," Thornleaf said.

Joel heard shouts coming from behind him. While still firing, he glanced over his shoulder and saw that the conventional battle was all but finished; the meager Nightshore contingent had been, despite Thornleaf's exhortations, no match for the combined three-village forces. As prisoners were being rounded up, Chief Stormfruit led a number of natives up to where Joel and the other Wavemakers were standing.

"We will help you!" she declared. "They cannot repel all of us at once!"

"No, my chief!" Fireflower responded. "Please, do not—"

With a blood-curdling war cry, Chief Stormfruit charged ahead, surrounded by dozens of her fellow villagers, including Greenseed. For a moment, Joel thought that maybe she was right, that perhaps Marshall, even with his incredible power, would be overwhelmed by their sheer numbers.

But that hope was quickly dashed. Marshall began spraying out wide swaths of dark-purple energy that mowed down the onrushing villagers in an easy and indiscriminate fashion, disintegrating them upon contact. Aghast and powerless to stop the slaughter, Joel saw that

Chief Stormfruit was the first to go, followed shortly thereafter by Greenseed.

"No!" Fireflower screamed. She rushed forward, maintaining her shield cast as she went. Before she could protect anyone, however, one of Marshall's blasts hit her shield, knocking it out, destroying her wavebow, and sending her flying even farther than Lakereed had. Joel looked back and saw that, based on her trajectory, she would land in the ravine, possibly near the bloodseed orchard.

A few more villagers were killed before one of the Wavemakers stopped firing, dropped his instrument, and raised his hands.

"Stop!" he shouted. "We surrender!"

The other shamans followed suit. Joel did as well, and finally, so did Felicity. Marshall ceased firing, and Fourfoot stepped forth.

"The war is over," he declared, "and Nightshore is victorious. Thus, I hereby anoint myself...High Chief of Spectraland!"

CHAPTER 21: DEUS EX MACHINA

With the remainder of the defeated forces wrapped up in binding casts, Fourfoot led the long, slimeback-mounted march over to Headsmouth village. Before they had left the Red Gulch area, Joel had offered to change his mind about marrying Fourfoot, but the new High Chief simply scoffed, saying that he did not care about that anymore.

"But I suppose I should thank you," he added. "For your rejection was what inspired me to new heights of achievement. Without you, none of this would have happened."

That unsettling thought stuck in the back of Joel's mind like a splinter, filling him with enough guilt and anxiety for a month's worth of sleepless nights. Still, though, he was so exhausted from all the recent flying and fighting that he found himself nodding off every so often as he rode. After a couple of hours of resisting the urge to close his eyes, the scenery around him finally shifted.

"Whoa," he said aloud, realizing he was back in what looked like the limbo plane. *Guess I fell asleep after all.*

"Joel," a voice whispered behind him.

Joel turned around to see the spectral form of Fireflower floating in the air a couple of feet away. “Oh—hey, Fireflower.”

“How is your mission progressing?”

“Um...not good.”

Fireflower sighed. “I assumed as much,” she said. “Things are not well here, either. Byle now has our wavebows, and all of us are being forced to build a structure on the beach.”

“A structure?”

“Yes. I do not yet know what it is or what purpose it will serve, but it will apparently be very large.”

“Whatever it is, I’m sure it’ll be for something bad.”

“Indeed. Where are you now in the timeline?”

“We just finished the Battle of Red Gulch. Marshall killed a bunch of people and Fourfoot declared himself High Chief.”

“I see. And Greenseed...?”

“She’s gone. I’m sorry.”

Fireflower nodded, her face grim.

“I, uh, I passed on your message, though,” Joel continued.

“I know. Thank you.”

“You’re welcome.”

Fireflower’s head turned, as if she had been startled by something in her peripheral vision. “I must go now. But there is still hope. Please keep trying.”

“I will.”

Joel snapped awake. Even though his conversation with Fireflower had been short, he saw, to his surprise, that the procession had already made it almost all the way to Headsmouth; its surrounding rock formations were clearly in view about 150 yards in the distance.

Good thing slimebacks can mostly steer themselves, he thought.

They marched into the village proper. Gasps and mutters quickly turned into louder cries of alarm before Thornleaf—still wearing the antler-helmet and green vine robes—silenced them all with a single note on his wavebow.

"Headsmouth!" Fourfoot shouted. "The war is over. Come and meet your new ruler!"

A number of villagers—including one carrying a wavebow and two others that Joel recognized as Suntooth and Yellowpetal—emerged from nearby huts. The villager with the wavebow raised his instrument, but before he could play it, Thornleaf felled him with a quick stunning cast.

"Satisfactory," Fourfoot said, nodding at Thornleaf. "But be sure to kill him later."

"Where is Chief Stormfruit?" Suntooth demanded.

"She is dead," Fourfoot replied. "And Raintree and Twotrunk are here as my prisoners. I am now the High Chief of Spectraland, and all will bow to me!"

"We will never bow to you!" one of the villagers shouted.

Fourfoot turned to Marshall. "Will you show our forces the proper way to handle someone like that, please?"

Marshall grinned. "With pleasure." He aimed his wavebow and shot out a dark-purple bolt that reduced the defiant native to a smoking pile of ashes. Expressions of shock rippled all throughout the village.

"Anyone else dare to challenge me?" Fourfoot said.

No one did.

"As you can see," Fourfoot continued, "I am now served by the two most powerful Wavemakers this island has ever known—more powerful than Blackspore, the Elders, or any shaman of legend, for that matter. They are completely at my command, and they will not hesitate to quell any signs of dissent. Is that understood?"

There were scattered murmurs of grudging agreement.

"Good," Fourfoot said. "Now, I shall inspect my new residence and begin planning for my official coronation ceremony. Master Byle"—he turned to Marshall—"you will escort me while Master Iceheart"—he turned to Thornleaf—"processes the prisoners. And, in the meantime, if anyone tries to resist"—he swept his gaze over the village—"deal with them accordingly."

"Yes, my chief," Thornleaf said.

Fourfoot and Marshall turned and directed their mounts toward the chieftain's residence. Once they were gone, Thornleaf addressed one of the Nightshore warriors.

"I will take the shamans to the prison hut," he said. "Watch over the others until I return."

"Yes, Master Iceheart."

Thornleaf directed his slimeback through the village and toward the prison hut. The slimebacks carrying Joel, Felicity, Blackspore, Lightsprout, and the other surviving Wavemakers all followed behind. When they arrived, Thornleaf levitated each bound shaman off of their mounts one at a time and moved them into the hut.

"Iceheart? Seriously?" Felicity sneered when it was her turn.

"It is an appropriate alias."

"Nice outfit, by the way. Where'd you get it, Jerk's Warehouse?"

"We will speak more later."

"Whatever."

Once everyone was inside the hut, Thornleaf closed the door and sealed it with a locking cast.

"Lightsprout," Blackspore said, "are you all right? Did they harm you?"

"I cannot believe you did what you did," Lightsprout said. "If I was not bound, I would strike you."

"You know why I did it."

"You said you were going to get help! I did not know it would be from an offworld murderer!"

"I am so very sorry. I tried to reverse the cast, but—"

"Iceheart stopped you, I know," Lightsprout sighed, her tone softening. "He told me everything when they came to me and the chief, offering their assistance."

"I am glad you refused their offer."

"Of course. I would never align myself with the likes of them. Unfortunately, the chief had different thoughts." Lightsprout turned to Felicity. "I am Lightsprout of Nightshore, by the way."

"Goldilocks. From the future."

"Iceheart's spouse, correct?"

Felicity rolled her eyes. "Did he tell you that too?"

"No. I just inferred it from his words and actions. Sometimes love can cause people to do some very irrational things," Lightsprout said, shooting Blackspore an irritated glance.

"All of this is actually your fault, Lightsprout," one of the other Wavemakers—the male native that had surrendered back up at the mountain—said. "You got the order involved in the war in the first place."

"Have you forgotten, Dirtmoss, that one of your villagers killed my brother—our colleague—right in front of me?"

"I have not forgotten, but still, that does not justify your actions."

"You could have stopped fighting at any time," another male shaman said. "Yet you persisted."

"I was only trying to defend what little was left of my village! You were the ones who persisted!"

"It was necessary to—"

"Dirtmoss, Eightarm," a different Wavemaker, a female, interrupted. "Enough. Instead of debating who was at fault in the war, right now we should be banding together to try to think of a way out of this predicament."

"Finally, a good suggestion," Felicity said.

"Thank you."

"What's your name?" Joel asked.

"Tanback. I am a healer from Bluecrest." She turned to Blackspore. "So, you are the master here. Tell us, what is the plan?"

"Give me a few moments," Blackspore said.

A few moments went by. When they were done, instead of Blackspore announcing a plan, the door to the hut opened instead. Thornleaf had returned.

"I almost forgot," the tall shaman said, "leaving all of you alone, unsupervised and able to converse, was probably not the wisest idea."

"Yeah, switching sides has made you stupid," Felicity said.

"You are beautiful when you are angry."

"Well, you're ugly when you're—"

Before Felicity was able to finish her quip, Thornleaf flooded the inside of the hut with a cloud of sleeping Aura.

But I just had a nap, was the last thing Joel thought before he passed out once more.

♪♪♪

This time there was no vision. No communing with Fireflower. Nothing but solid, dreamless sleep that was finally interrupted by the sound of Thornleaf's voice.

"Wake up," he said. "It is time."

Groggy and still bound, Joel pulled himself to his feet. He had a headache, his stomach was rumbling, and he had a horrible taste in his mouth. It was kind of like how he felt after sleeping in way too long on the weekend. Everyone else around him got up as well, each of them looking like they had been out for days. Blackspore even had a thin layer of facial hair that hadn't been there before.

"How long have we been asleep?" Eightarm asked.

"That is irrelevant," Thornleaf answered. "Now, outside."

All the shamans filed out. It was early morning. The sun was high and bright, hurting Joel's eyes. He squinted. The village was teeming with natives, all of whom had a dull, glazed look on their faces.

"Everyone, gather in the central courtyard!" Thornleaf barked. "Now!"

Slowly, Joel walked with the others toward the middle of the village. Ahead of him, he saw Thornleaf saying something in Felicity's ear; he found himself wishing he had some kind of super-hearing power to go along with the Sight.

A few minutes later—it took longer than usual because of the large crowd—Joel and the other Wavemakers arrived at the courtyard area. A giant stage, larger than any other Spectraland platform that Joel had ever seen before, had been erected near the far end. Atop it stood Fourfoot and Marshall. Thornleaf walked to the base of the stage and turned around, his wavebow still trained on the bound shamans.

"Welcome!" Fourfoot said, raising his hands. "I am so glad you were able to make it here on this fine, glorious day."

The assembled natives, except for the Wavemakers, cheered. Joel glanced around and realized that they were all now under mind control.

Okay, so yeah, we must've been asleep for at least a couple of days while Marshall went around the island performing his mass mind-control casts. Good thing Wavemakers are immune, otherwise—

"Hey."

Joel turned. Felicity had sidled up next to him.

"So," she said under her breath, "Jerkface told me to be ready."

"Ready for what?"

The cheering died down. Fourfoot resumed his speech, saying something about how Spectraland would be better off under a single ruler.

"After Fourfoot is officially coronated or whatever," Felicity said, "Marshall is gonna kill him, and then he's gonna kill all the other Wavemakers except for us and Blackspore. That's the last piece of history that needs to occur."

"Um, we can't let that happen."

"I know, duh. But what are we gonna do?"

"I dunno. But something cool will bail everyone out, I'm sure."

"I'm telling you, there are only so many times we can rely on a deus ex machina. Eventually, we're gonna have to bail ourselves out."

"Just think positive. I'm telling you, something will happen. I know it."

"Well, you're Mister Confident all of a sudden."

"I'm trying. Personal growth, remember?"

"Right, right."

Joel turned his attention back to Fourfoot, who was still speaking.

"Chief Raintree and Chief Twotrunk will remain at their respective villages as my deputies," he said. "And in due time, I will appoint a deputy to oversee Nightshore while I—"

"You murderous brat!" someone shouted from the back. Everyone turned. It was the beehive-haired lady, her hair now resembling more of a rat's nest than a beehive. She had a wild, crazy look in her eyes and a long spear in her hands. She looked like she hadn't slept or eaten in days.

"See?" Joel said to Felicity. "I told you something would happen."

"Ah, I had been wondering what became of you," Fourfoot said, grinning. "Nice of you to join us."

"Spectraland will never accept your twisted rule," the lady growled, jabbing her spear in Fourfoot's direction. "Rogue shamans or not, we will overthrow you!"

"Want me to put her under mind control?" Marshall asked Fourfoot.

"No thank you, Master Byle. Mind control would be—"

The lady, surprisingly strong, hurled her spear toward the stage like an Olympic javelin thrower. Before it reached its intended target, however, Marshall took aim and blasted it out of the air.

"You were saying, Chief?" he said.

"Yes, I was saying that mind control would be much too lenient for this particular individual. She deserves a slightly...stronger approach."

"As you wish."

Marshall turned his wavebow toward the lady and fired out a dark-Aura energy blast that blew a six-inch hole in her chest. After a moment, she fell forward on her face, and everyone cheered once more.

"So much for *that* giant eagle," Felicity muttered.

"Okay, maybe that wasn't it," Joel said. "I'm not sure what difference she would have made anyway. Something else will happen."

"I hope you're right."

Over the next couple of minutes, Fourfoot continued with his lengthy speech (Joel found himself wondering why people in Spectraland seemed so fond of long speeches) and then, when he was finally done, he turned to Marshall. "Now, Master Byle, if you would, please."

Marshall picked a large floral headdress up off the stage floor. "Right, then. I, uh, Marshall Byle of Earth, hereby declare you, Fourfoot of...of..."

"Nightshore," Fourfoot said.

"Of Nightshore, to be the new High Chief and overlord of all of Spectraland. May your rule be long, prosperous, and...all that rot."

Fourfoot looked askance at Marshall, but he was smiling nonetheless. Marshall placed the headdress on the young chief. Even larger than his former one, it nearly covered his eyes. He turned to face the crowd.

"Spectraland!" he yelled. "Rejoice!"

More cheers. Thornleaf turned and looked up at Marshall.

"Now?" Marshall said.

Thornleaf nodded.

Marshall raised his wavebow and aimed it, point blank, at Fourfoot's head.

"Master Byle?" Fourfoot said. "What are you—?"

Marshall strummed. Fourfoot's entire body turned a dark shade of purple. Then, with a second strum, it dissolved into a pile of tiny pieces, as if the young chief had been made of sand. The only thing left was the headdress. A few stunned gasps could be heard.

"All right, everyone, just relax," Marshall said. He picked up the headdress and placed it on his own head. It was a much better fit. "I'm in charge here now. That bloke was just a little kid, he would've made a terrible leader. In fact, he already was. But don't worry, I'll take good care of all of you."

A number of natives in the crowd looked at each other, seemingly unsure of what to do. Finally, one villager said, "What should we call you?"

"Call me...Chief Byle."

"You are not our chief!" Lightsprout shouted. "At least Fourfoot was one of our own. You are nothing but an offworld invader!"

"These people here may be mind-controlled," Blackspore said, "but we are not. We will find a way to make things right."

"The Elders will save us!" Tanback said.

"Yes, the Elders!" Dirtmoss exclaimed.

"Maybe that's our deus ex machina," Joel whispered to Felicity.

"The Elders?" Marshall laughed. "Ah, that is a good one. No—Iceheart, here, and I already took care of those geezers. They were barely even armed, can you believe that? It was like shooting fish in a barrel."

"Yeah, maybe not," Felicity muttered.

"I must admit, though, you little buggers might eventually cause me some trouble," Marshall continued. "Iceheart's already warned me. So, to make sure that doesn't happen, I'm afraid I'll have to say farewell to the lot of you. Now, which one first...?"

As Marshall paced back and forth across the stage, looking over the various bound shamans on the ground in front of him, Joel stood still, feeling desperate. With every passing moment, it was becoming more and more apparent that nothing was going to swoop out of the sky to save the day. He and Felicity, and maybe Blackspore, as the three who would be spared, would have to do it on their own.

But should they? he wondered, not for the first time. After all, this—the death of the other Wavemakers—is exactly what had happened in the original timeline. Maybe Mistress Moonear was right. Maybe the past really *couldn't* be changed. It was certainly beginning to seem like that, after everything that had happened up until now. Despite everyone's best efforts, Blackspore still got shot on the beach, the Fourfoot War still happened, Marshall still came over, and good people still died. The words of Mistress Moonear and the other Elders echoed in his mind: *The Aura is like water flowing in a river. It goes where it wants to go.*

"I know," Marshall said, coming to a stop. "How about"—he trained his wavebow on Lightsprout and shut one eye, as if he were looking through a gunsight—"you?"

We can place rocks in its path, maybe even change its course, but eventually it ends up in the same place.

Lightsprout looked up, defiant. "Kill me if you want, you miserable—"

"No!" Blackspore shouted. "Not her. Kill me instead."

You cannot change the past, nor should you want to. You can only accept it.

Marshall glanced over at Thornleaf, who shook his head *no.*

"My esteemed colleague here says that you are to be kept alive, for some strange reason," Marshall said. "But your little girlfriend is fair game."

You cannot change the past, but you can *shape the future. By taking what you have learned, and applying it to the present.*

"Please, I am begging you," Blackspore said. "If she dies, I will never be able to live with myself. Without her, my life will have no meaning. So please, please spare her and kill me instead."

It is not too late.

A puzzle piece fell into place in Joel's mind. He engaged the Sight, rewound the time of the scene, and looked around. After a few seconds, he saw what he was hoping to see: the image of a Nightshore warrior, carrying a bunch of wavebows, walking farther into the village.

"Now that is some world-class groveling, mate!" Marshall laughed. "Rather nauseating, though, I must say. Love—*pfft.* A worthless emotion that makes you do stupid things, like sacrifice yourself for a mere"—he glared at Lightsprout, his face twisted with contempt—"*woman.*"

Joel leaned over to Felicity. "I have an idea," he whispered.

"A good one, I hope."

"Actually, it's kinda crazy."

"So, the usual."

Joel glanced around. Blackspore was still pleading with Marshall, who was still responding with diatribes about the follies of love. Thornleaf was watching the proceedings with the air of someone who was waiting for a late bus to arrive.

"Yeah. Can you distract Marshall and Thornleaf? Like, really distract them?"

"Both of them? At the same time?"

"Uh-huh."

"Boy, you don't ask for much, do you?"

"Can you?"

Felicity rolled her eyes. "All right, all right," she exhaled. "I think I know what to do."

"You're awesome." Joel grinned.

"Tell me something I don't know." She looked up at Marshall. "Hey—scumbag."

Marshall broke off his dialogue with Blackspore and turned to Felicity. "Are you talking to me?"

"Yeah. You know your albums really suck, right?"

Marshall's eyes narrowed. "I beg your pardon?"

"I mean, 'Hang on Darkness'—pfft. Seriously?"

"What? I—first of all, that is the title of a *song*, not an album. Secondly, how do you even know—"

"I'm telling you, nobody likes your stuff. You're gonna fail, your label is gonna drop you, and, oh, I know that women don't like you, either. You're a total loser."

"How dare you!" Marshall aimed his wavebow at Felicity. "I'll show you who's a loser, you primitive, green-skinned piece of—"

"No!" Thornleaf shouted. He jumped in front of Felicity and created an Aura-shield just as Marshall shot out a dark-purple bolt. The bolt hit the shield, causing it to explode in a shower of multicolored sparks. The two then fired streams of energy at each other that collided with a cacophonous bang. The crowd reacted with a mixture of shock and awe.

Joel knew this was his chance. Amidst the noise and confusion, he took off running toward a hut that was located a few rows behind the courtyard, hoping that what the Sight had just revealed to him was accurate. Once he got there, he was relieved to see that the hut's entrance had no solid door or shield-cast, only a set of vine-ropes. He ducked inside and glanced around.

Where are they, where are they, where are—aha.

Up against the far wall of the hut was a large tarp draped over some unidentifiable objects. Joel dashed over to it and took an end of the tarp in his teeth. Then, with a yank of his head, he pulled the tarp off, revealing not only his and Felicity's supply packs, but also a set of wavebows that clattered to the ground.

Jackpot.

He located his wavebow—his very own, not the one the Elders had lent him—and knelt down next to it.

All right, how am I gonna do this? he wondered. *I can pluck the strings with my teeth, but how am I gonna make the right chord?*

He got down some more and twisted himself so that his face was over the body of the instrument while the toes of his left foot were on its neck. While in this awkward and uncomfortable position, he managed to play a note, but the only result was the appearance of a little Aura-globe that spun around and around, lighting up the hut's interior like a disco ball.

Dangit.

He was about to try again when he heard footsteps approaching.

Uh oh—who could that be? Thornleaf? Marshall?

But, to Joel's relief, it was neither; it was Blackspore, followed closely by Lightsprout, Tanback, Dirtmoss, and Eightarm.

“Hey, can someone help me with this?” Joel said.

Instead of responding, Blackspore closed his eyes and took a deep breath. A heartbeat later, one of the other wavebows played a series of notes on its own, and the binding casts on each shaman disappeared.

“Oh, right,” Joel said, picking up his wavebow and getting to his feet. “The hands-free thing. Cool. I really have to learn that one day.”

“This was a good idea,” Lightsprout said as she and the others gathered up the remaining instruments, “but even if we escape now, Byle will track us all down, eventually.”

“Not where we’re going,” Joel said, grabbing the supply packs.

“What do you mean?”

“You’ll see.” Joel looked into his pack. To his relief, his loudstone was still in it. “Where’s Fe—I mean, Goldilocks?”

“She is still in the courtyard,” Blackspore said. “With the other two.”

“Are they still dueling?” Joel asked.

“Yes.”

Joel ran out of the hut, the others right behind him. When he got back to the courtyard, he saw Felicity standing behind Thornleaf, who was engaged in an epic wavebow duel with Marshall; streaks of light and energy were flying everywhere, crashing into each other and creating what sounded like a dissonant EDM concert. The mind-controlled crowd was simply standing around, watching and emitting the occasional “ooh” or “aah.” No one seemed to take notice of Joel or any of the other shamans.

"Okay," Joel said, turning to Blackspore, "I'm gonna need to borrow as much energy from everyone as I can get."

Blackspore nodded and faced the others. "Link arms!" he said.

The Wavemakers all grabbed each other's wrists. Within a moment, Joel felt waves of Aura energy surge into him. Then, after letting go, he ran over to Felicity.

"I'm gonna time travel all of us out of here!" he shouted.

"You're gonna what?"

"Time travel! All of us! Back to the future!"

"Are you sure?"

"Am I sure of what?"

"That it's gonna work?"

That was a good question. The last time Joel tried teleporting this many people, he only succeeded in teleporting himself—and to the limbo plane, at that. Then again, that was space travel. This was time. He'd had more practice.

"I am!"

Felicity paused before responding. "All right, fine!"

Joel motioned to the other Wavemakers to gather around him. All of them did, except for Blackspore.

"Blackspore!" Joel said. "Stay close!"

"No," Blackspore replied, shaking his head. "I cannot go with you. I know what I must do." He turned and ran off.

"Blackspore!" Lightsprout called.

But Joel knew that the master shaman was right—he couldn't come with them. He had his own wave of fate to ride. "It'll be okay," Joel said to Lightsprout.

"Are you sure?" Lightsprout said.

"Trust me." Then Joel turned and looked at Felicity, who was looking at Thornleaf. It was hard to tell for sure, but judging from the expression on her face, it seemed as if she was debating whether to bring her estranged husband along with them, or leave him stranded here in the past, to deal with Marshall and whatever else would await him.

"Are you ready?" Joel asked.

Felicity hesitated, then nodded *yes*.

Joel played the time-travel cast. A queasy feeling set in. A ringing noise started up in his ears. As he continued to play, the noise got louder and louder. Then, just as the crescendo reached its peak, Joel saw Felicity reach out and grab Thornleaf by the shoulders. There was a *whoosh* sound, and then—

CHAPTER 22: DEJA VU

Everything was blurry. Joel blinked.

Did it...did it work?

It was hard to tell. He had a fresh memory in the front of his mind, one of Marshall declaring victory over Fourfoot and all the shamans who had opposed him, and a mass of natives cheering and chanting "Chief Byle!" Joel wasn't sure if the memory was a result of him actually being there to witness such an event, though, or if it was just a figment of his imagination. As he pondered which one it could be, his eyesight cleared up, and he realized that he was still in Headsmouth with the other shamans, but now Marshall, the stage, and all the villagers were gone. There was a strange but familiar sound way off in the distance...almost like music. He shrugged it off.

"Wow," Felicity breathed, "you did it this time. Good job."

"What...what happened?" Tanback asked, holding a hand to her head. "What did you do?"

"He has ruined everything, that is what!" Thornleaf barked, turning around and ripping off his antler-helmet. "All of you were supposed to die!"

“I do not think I like your tone,” Dirtmoss said, raising his wavebow.

“Neither do I,” Lightsprout said, also raising her wavebow. “It seems that now we have the upper hand, Iceheart.”

“Okay, okay, everyone calm down,” Felicity said. “First of all, his name’s not Iceheart, or Jerkface. It’s Thornleaf.”

“Thornleaf?” Eightarm said. “As in...Stoneroot’s son?”

“Yup.”

“How did he—”

“Look, it’s complicated,” Felicity said. “We’ll explain everything later.” She turned to Thornleaf. “And as for you, you’re lucky I brought you back with us. Heck, you’re lucky I don’t stun you right now and leave you for the elephant-sharks. I won’t do that, but only if you promise me that you’ll behave, listen to everything I say, and help us do whatever it takes to make things right.”

“But—”

“*Promise me!*”

Thornleaf took a deep breath. “Very well,” he said, his voice small. “But what I was going to say was—how is it that you are still here? We changed history by not letting Byle kill these other shamans.”

“I...actually, you know, that’s a good question.” Felicity turned to Joel. “Sightguy, care to explain?”

“Well, I realized that Mistress Moonear was right,” Joel said. “The results of the past can’t be changed. But you *can* alter the way you arrive at them, at least a little.”

“Are you gonna get to the point soon?”

“Um, yeah. Okay, so Fireflower didn’t actually know what happened to the other Wavemakers because she was in a coma the whole time. She only *thought* they had all died because when she got back, they were gone. Marshall also probably thought that he had killed them. But little did everyone know, they weren't dead, they just time-traveled twenty years into the future."

"Not bad, dude." Felicity nodded. "Pretty awesome, in fact."

"Thanks." Joel grinned.

"Guess we didn't need that deus ex machina, after all."

"Wait." Lightsprout held up her hand in a "stop" signal. "So you mean to tell me that Fireflower is still alive, and that we are now—"

"Twenty years in the future," Felicity said. "Yup, you heard him."

"And it's a good thing too," Joel said. "Because we're gonna need your help."

♪♪♪

Joel, Felicity, and a chagrined Thornleaf flew themselves and the other shamans up to Sunpeak. Once they arrived, they landed in front of the swordcat den.

"I have *so* many questions," Lightsprout said.

"I promise we'll sit down over tea and lifepods and answer all of them later," Felicity said.

With Joel leading the way, everyone got down and crawled into the tunnel. As he neared the opening on the other end, he saw the point of a spear aimed at him.

"Who is there?" a familiar voice—Yellowpetal's—demanded.

"Yellowpetal, it's me."

"Oh, Joel?" The spear withdrew. "What are you—?"

"Is Blackspore still here? Riverhand told me earlier that he was up here with the swordcats."

"Yes, he is."

"Okay, good."

Joel crawled the rest of the way into the den and stood up. The others followed behind him. Inside the den were Yellowpetal, Starpollen, Sammy, Seaberry, Blackspore (still unconscious), Doc, Platinum, Goldie, and the five sword-kits (three of whom were chasing Sammy around).

"I am afraid that something terrible has happened," Yellowpetal said. "The rest of the island's villagers were forced to go to the beach and"—she stopped, her gaze turning to the other Wavemakers—"Lightsprout? Tanback?"

"Yes, hello, Yellowpetal," Lightsprout said. "Dirtmoss and Eightarm are here as well."

"I—I see. But I thought that all of you..."

"Blackspore!" Lightsprout exclaimed. She rushed over to the fallen master's side.

"Master Sightguy saved us," Tanback said to Yellowpetal. "He brought us forward in time when we were about to be killed."

"Sightguy?" Yellowpetal said, looking confused. "Who is—?"

"That's me," Joel said. "My past name. Anyway, how's Blackspore doing?"

Yellowpetal paused, as if she needed a moment to process what was undoubtedly, to her, a bewildering turn of events. "Well, the swordcats are keeping him alive, but from what Seaberry has translated for me, he only has hours left."

"Then we're just in time." Joel turned to Tanback. "You said you were a healer, right?"

"I am," Tanback replied. "Still merely an apprentice, however."

"Oh. Well...can you heal Blackspore?"

"I can certainly try."

"Cool." Joel turned to Seaberry. "Can the swordcats help her?"

Seaberry looked at Doc, Platinum, and Goldie. All three of them issued little growls. Seaberry turned back to Joel and nodded. "They said they would be happy to."

"Wait," Felicity said, "If Fireflower and Doc couldn't do it, does Tanback even stand a chance? Even with all three swordcats?"

Joel glanced at Lightsprout, who was kneeling next to Blackspore's still form with her head bowed. "I'm hoping we have something extra this time."

Tanback and the swordcats got to work. Lightsprout, apparently digging deep, lent whatever energy she could to the healer.

"Please, Blackspore," she said, "you have to be all right. For me. For all of us."

"That's so corny it has to work," Felicity said, watching.

The healing cast and the purring went on for a while. At one point, even the sword-kits tried to get into the act, licking Blackspore's arms and legs while issuing little purrs of their own. After nearly ten minutes, Tanback ceased her healing cast, bent over, and exhaled.

"So?" Joel said. "How is he?"

"Unchanged, I am afraid," Tanback said in between gasps. "I tried my best. We all did."

"I am so sorry." Lightsprout buried her face in her hands.

"So much for the power of love," Felicity muttered.

"But he can't die," Joel said, clenching his fists. "There *has* to be something we can do!"

"Should we not be more concerned with what might be happening down at the beach?" Thornleaf said.

"You know," Felicity said, crossing her arms, "you've forfeited your right to have an opinion."

"I *am* concerned about that," Joel said, "but this is even more urgent. Plus, if we can revive Blackspore, he can use his far-vision cast to find out what Marshall might be up to, so we don't just go running into a trap. There must be some way to help him."

"Forgive me if this upsets you," Yellowpetal said, "but could you, perhaps, go back in time and...rescue Auravine? Like you rescued these shamans?"

The mention of Auravine's name once again made Joel's stomach turn cold, but he tried to retain his composure. "No. She died. I saw her die. We all did. We can't change that."

Goldie let out an exhausted-sounding growl.

"One Thousand and Four has an idea," Seaberry translated.

"We're all ears, kid," Felicity said.

"The Fourtails can help him."

"The who?"

"The Fourtails. Their ancestors."

Joel shook his head. "No, they all died in their own war against the Lightsnakes. Nineteen was the only survivor."

"Unless," Felicity snapped her fingers, "he wasn't."

"What do you—oh."

"Right?"

"He didn't necessarily know what happened to the others either, just like Fireflower," Joel said.

"Exactly. So you just have to go back and get them."

"That is not going to work," Thornleaf said.

Felicity rolled her eyes. "What did I tell you about not having an opinion?"

"All I am saying is that it took him multiple tries just to get to the correct part of the Fourfoot War. How is he supposed to pinpoint such an ancient time period?"

"Because I've been there before," Joel said.

Platinum growled.

"One Thousand and Seven says that he will accompany you," Seaberry translated.

"Okay, cool," Joel replied.

"And if he is going, I should go as well."

"Did he say that too?"

"No, I did."

"I dunno...it might be dangerous."

"You need someone to translate."

"But you're just a kid."

"I know. What difference should that make?"

"I go too!" Starpollen exclaimed. Sammy added a little affirmative-sounding chirp.

Joel nodded. "All right." He turned to the other shamans. "You guys stay here and lend your energy to Tanback so she can help keep Blackspore alive as long as possible. Hopefully we'll be back soon."

"Good luck, dude," Felicity said.

"Wait, aren't you coming?"

"Nah. Someone has to stay here and make sure this guy"—she pointed a thumb at Thornleaf—"stays out of trouble."

"Oh—okay."

♪♪♪

Platinum led the way to a large plateau a little farther down the mountain where he'd said—according to Seaberry's translation—they might be able to locate some Fourtails. Once they got there, Joel played the time-travel cast. There was a *whoosh*, and then—

Screeeeeeeeech!

"Whoa!" Joel exclaimed. Seaberry screamed. Platinum let out a ferocious growl. They had materialized not more than ten feet away from a giant dinosaur-like creature (who was quite possibly just as startled as they were).

"Big!" Starpollen said, Sammy cowering on his shoulder.

"Yeah, real big," Joel agreed. This creature was even larger than the one he had encountered by the Wavemaker Temple's location. "Um—everyone, just back away, slowly."

Everyone took a few steps back. The creature took a step forward.

"Seaberry, Starpollen," Joel said, "get on top of Platinum."

They did. The creature took another step forward.

"On three," Joel said, "turn and run. Ready? One."

The creature took yet another step.

"Two."

The creature parted its jaws.

"Three!"

Platinum turned and took off. Joel did as well.

Screeeeeeeeech!

Joel glanced over his shoulder. The creature, taking long strides, was right behind them.

"Teleport!" Joel shouted. "Go!"

With Seaberry and Starpollen hanging on tight (and Sammy hanging onto Starpollen), Platinum jumped, vanished, and reappeared some fifty feet ahead.

Screeeeeeeeech!

Just as the creature was about to bear down on him, Joel played the short-range teleport cast in midstride and reappeared alongside Platinum. They both kept running.

"Keep going!" Joel yelled.

They repeated the process twice more, after which the creature appeared to give up the chase. They paused to rest within a cluster of goldenorb trees.

"That was close," Joel puffed.

"Just a little," Seaberry said.

"That...that sounded like something Felicity would say."

Seaberry grinned. "She has been giving me the sarcasm lessons."

"Cool." Joel returned her grin.

"Do again," Starpollen said.

"Um, no." Joel shook his head. "Too dangerous. Plus, we have to find the Fourtails. A tracking cast won't work, so—"

Platinum interrupted him with a growl.

"One Thousand and Seven says that he can locate them," Seaberry translated.

"He can? How?"

Platinum growled again.

"By smell."

"Oh—makes sense."

Platinum sniffed the breeze, which was blowing gently from the west. He growled once more.

"That way," Seaberry pointed.

They set off, walking at first, but then teleporting once they had recovered enough energy to do so. The surrounding plateau seemed to be devoid of the ancient felines, so they kept working their way down Sunpeak, until they were traversing across the island at sea level.

The Spectraland of old didn't appear to be much different from the modern version; in fact, Joel recognized a number of familiar landmarks right away. There were a few more trees and a fair number of large creatures wandering about (Joel and Platinum made sure to steer clear of them or teleport away, as needed), but overall, the landscape was quite similar.

"I believe we are nearing the place where Spearwind village will eventually be," Seaberry pointed out during a walk break.

"I think you're right," Joel said.

Platinum growled.

"He says that the Fourtails are there," Seaberry translated.

"Cool."

"Tired," Starpollen complained.

"We are almost at our destination," Seaberry reassured her friend, who smiled in response.

"How long have the two of you known each other?" Joel asked, trying to make conversation.

"Starpollen and I?" Seaberry said.

"Yeah."

"About seven months. We met when he and his party were traveling to the north coast to deliver his sister's ashes to the ocean."

"Oh." *Kinda sorry I asked now*, Joel was able to keep himself from adding out loud.

"They had stopped off in Spearwind for rest and supplies," Seaberry continued. "I am very glad they did."

"Me too!" Starpollen said.

Despite the reminder of Auravine's death, Joel had to grin. It was nice that Starpollen had been able to find someone to connect with, especially now that the boy's sister was gone. Growing up, Joel had had a classmate who, like Starpollen, was mostly nonverbal, and the other kids would either tease him or just avoid him altogether (not unlike Joel's own experience in middle school). Seaberry, though, seemed like a gentle and accepting person who would never do anything of the sort. The two of them were probably very good for each other.

I could've used a friend like that at Starpollen's age, Joel thought.

After another short-range teleport, the group arrived near the valley where Spearwind village would be constructed one day. As they headed toward it, Joel spotted a group of creatures assembled atop the ridge that would, in the future, support a number of huts, tree houses, and various other structures.

"I think I see them," he said, squinting.

Platinum stopped in his tracks and growled.

"What's wrong?" Joel asked. "I'm pretty sure that's them."

"You are correct," Seaberry said. "But they are not alone."

Joel looked again. Sure enough, the creatures that appeared to be Fourtails were facing off with another group of creatures that were tall, upright, and reptilian.

"Uh oh," Joel muttered.

"One Thousand and Seven says that he smells something called Light...snakes?"

"Yeah, I think he's right. We'd better be careful."

They approached slowly, trying to stay out of sight by walking among some nearby seaweed-palm trees. It wasn't long before Joel saw that the other creatures were, indeed, Lightsnakes, and in fact, one of them looked a lot like the queen that Felicity had defeated in Prism Valley. Once they were within earshot, Joel could hear the two groups speaking to each other in languages that the translation cast didn't—or couldn't—parse.

"Does Platinum—I mean, One Thousand and Seven know what they're saying?" Joel whispered to Seaberry.

Platinum growled softly.

"He believes it is some sort of negotiation," Seaberry answered. "Over disputed territories."

"Oh," Joel said. "Then maybe we should try to find some others that aren't as busy."

Platinum growled again.

"He says that the Fourtail leaders are here," Seaberry translated. "If we are to request their assistance, they are the ones we must speak with."

"Um, okay."

Just then, the queen Lightsnake's head turned in Joel's direction.

Uh oh.

The queen started to quickly wave her pincers around in a sort of windmill motion.

"I think we'd better—"

Before Joel could finish his sentence, he and the others were swept up in a cloud of green Aura and levitated out from their hiding place. Joel tried to grab his wavebow, but he found that his arms were immobilized. As they floated toward the queen, she made some unintelligible shrieking sounds. The Fourtails responded with a series of noises that sounded like a cross between the growls of a tiger and the bleats of a sheep.

"The Lightsnakes are accusing the Fourtails of trickery," Seaberry said as Platinum growled. "They believe we are their allies and that we were going to ambush them."

"What are the Fourtails saying?" Joel asked.

"They are denying it."

The Lightsnakes and Fourtails conversed some more.

"The Lightsnakes do not believe them," Seaberry said. "They are going to...to destroy us."

The party continued to float toward the ridge. Joel redoubled his efforts to grab his wavebow, but to no avail. Then, suddenly, they came to an abrupt stop.

"What's happening?" Joel asked.

"The Fourtails are confessing," Seaberry replied.

"Confessing what?"

"That we are, indeed, their allies."

"Huh?"

"And they have offered to duel the Lightsnakes in exchange for our release."

"Um, they really shouldn't—"

Then just like that, the fighting began. As Joel and the others remained suspended in midair, the queen Lightsnake and two of her companions faced off against a pair of Fourtails.

"Hit them in the chest!" Joel called out, remembering how Felicity had managed to defeat the queen, but it seemed as if the Fourtails were either ignoring him or couldn't understand him, or both. Platinum also growled loudly, but no one looked at him either.

It was over within seconds. The Lightsnakes, using a variety of martial arts–style moves, carved up the two tiger-rams like expert swordfighters slaughtering livestock. Joel, feeling guilty and helpless, could only watch in horror. Then, once the queen Lightsnake was certain she had vanquished her opponents, she spoke again.

"She is honoring her agreement to release us," Seaberry said. "But she is also saying something about a truce being called off...and that the war will resume."

With that, the Lightsnakes turned and walked away. The levitation cast disappeared, and Joel and the others dropped to the ground. Then, while most of the remaining Fourtails rushed up to examine their fallen leaders, two of them cautiously approached Joel and his party.

"I am *so* sorry," Joel said. "We didn't mean for that to happen, I swear."

One of the Fourtails growl-bleated. Platinum responded.

"They are forgiving us," Seaberry said.

Joel was glad for that, but he wasn't sure it made him feel any better.

"And...they are asking who we are. Where we came from," Seaberry continued.

"Is Platinum explaining?"

"Yes."

After a few more moments of the creatures conversing, the two Fourtails looked at each other. Then, after a long pause, one of them turned back to Platinum and growl-bleated once again.

"She is inviting us back to their den," Seaberry said.

"Um...does Platinum think that's a good idea?"

"He thinks we do not have a choice."

CHAPTER 23: LUCKY NUMBERS

The Fourtails' den was a relatively short walk away. When they arrived, Joel counted an additional ten of the creatures, all of them practically identical. One of them, however, stood out slightly from the rest by virtue of the pattern of his coat.

"Nineteen...?" Joel said.

There was a lot of growl-bleating, so much so that Platinum and Seaberry didn't even bother to translate. Then, once things settled down a bit, one of the Fourtails—not the one who looked like Nineteen—waved its eyeball-tipped tails around, creating a series of tones. When it was done, it looked at Joel.

"Can you understand me now?" it said in a smooth, silky voice that sounded neither male nor female.

"Oh! Uh, yeah, I can," Joel replied.

"Good. My name is Forty-Two."

"I'm Joel. Nice to meet you. And, uh, this is Seaberry, Starpollen, Sammy, and Plat—I mean, One Thousand and Seven."

"I know," Forty-Two said. "And I have been informed that there is something you wish to ask of us."

"Yeah, there is. Are you...are you the leader?"

"I understand that our previous leaders have perished," Forty-Two said. "Therefore, yes, I am now the new head of this pride."

"Okay, well, did One Thousand and Seven tell you that we're from the future?"

"He did. I must say, that is an amazing accomplishment, to travel all this way."

"Thanks. Anyway, we know that you're in a war with the Lightsnakes. And we also know that...well, you're going to lose."

"I understand," Forty-Two said nonchalantly.

"There's hope, though. We can rescue you—take you with us to the future."

"I am not sure that is a wise idea," Forty-Two said. "As much as we value life, altering the fatewave in such a fashion could lead to even more disastrous consequences."

"But we wouldn't necessarily be changing anything," Joel insisted. "You see, no one really knows what actually became of some of you. There's a good chance that we'd be recreating history exactly as it happened."

"I cannot believe you are actually listening to this!" one of the other Fourtails said, sounding unusually emotional.

What the—Nineteen?

"What are your concerns, Nineteen?" Forty-Two said.

"First of all, their claims that they are from the future are ludicrous," Nineteen said, lashing all four of his tails. "It is more likely that they are offworld creatures employed by the Lightsnakes to deceive us!

"Furthermore, even if they are telling the truth, we cannot abandon our fellow prides. Especially not now, when we are on the brink of extinction!"

Joel's jaw dropped. Even though he was sure this was Nineteen (albeit a younger version), he certainly didn't expect him to have such a different personality.

All those years he spent wandering Prism Valley by himself must have mellowed him out. Like, a lot.

"I sense that they are telling the truth," Forty-Two said. "And even if we were to remain, we stand no chance against the Lightsnakes."

"So are you suggesting we should selfishly save ourselves, and leave the others to die?"

"If that is the will of the Aura, then that is what must be done."

"You would not be completely selfish," Seaberry said. "We actually need your help."

"Help," Starpollen repeated. Sammy, sitting on the boy's shoulder, let out a chirp that also sounded like "help."

Forty-Two cocked his head. "Oh?"

"Yeah, um, one of our friends is dying," Joel explained. "He's really important to the future of Spectraland, and no one else can heal him."

"Why should we care about that?" Nineteen said. "You are talking about an era that is hundreds, possibly thousands of years from now. And what kind of creature are you, exactly? Perhaps *you* were the original invaders of our land, and deserve everything that is happening to you right now!"

Joel opened his mouth, but then closed it when he realized he didn't really know how to respond to that particular accusation. *Were* the green-skinned humanoid inhabitants of Spectraland invaders? He never actually learned how they arrived on this island, other than being told by the future Nineteen that they basically just showed up one day.

"Whatever their origins, no one truly deserves to die if it can be helped," Forty-Two said.

"I disagree," Nineteen said. "The Aura makes sure that justice is served. One's misdeeds will always come back to them. Their friend must have caused harm to others during his lifetime."

Outside the den, it suddenly became dark. It sounded like a thunderstorm was brewing. Joel turned to look. Instead of a thunderstorm, though, what he saw was much worse: a gathering tornado of Aura energy.

"The Lightsnakes have started the end," Forty-Two said. "They have unleashed their final attack."

"Well, I intend to fight back with every ounce of strength I have left," Nineteen said.

"You will surely be killed," Forty-Two said.

"Then so be it. At least I will die with the knowledge that I am not a coward. Who is with me?"

All the Fourtails except for Forty-Two and one other roared their approval. Led by Nineteen, they charged out of the den and toward the onrushing tornado.

"I will help you," Forty-Two said to Joel. "But whatever method you use to travel through time, I hope that it is fast. We do not have much longer before everything here is destroyed."

"I, uh, I think we'll be okay," Joel said, even though he wasn't completely certain. He glanced out and saw the Aura-tornado sweeping up the Fourtails in its path. Behind it marched what appeared to be an entire army of Lightsnakes.

"We only have a few seconds left," Forty-Two warned in a tone of voice that lacked any sense of urgency whatsoever.

"Okay, everyone stand close," Joel said. He played the time-travel cast. For some reason, though, nothing seemed to be happening.

"Whatever it is you are doing," Forty-Two said, still sounding calm, "I would recommend that you do it a bit quicker."

"I—I'm trying," Joel said, puzzled and more than a bit panicked. Then he glanced at his loudstone: empty.

Dangit.

"You energy level appears to be low," Forty-Two said. "We will help you."

Forty-Two and the other remaining Fourtail wrapped their tails around Joel's arms and legs. They closed their eyes. The tornado was almost upon them. Then, after a moment, Joel felt a strong current rush through his body, so strong that it bordered on painful. After it was over, he felt even more powerful than when Blackspore had given him his energy from the limbo plane during their previous adventure. He started to play the time travel cast again. As soon as he struck the first note, there was a loud *whoosh*, and then—

To Joel's surprise, he and the others appeared not only back in the future, but right inside the swordcats' den. There were a few startled exclamations, but after that, mostly everyone broke out into applause.

"You did it!" Eightarm said.

"He did? Really?" Felicity said. "Because, you know, I couldn't tell."

"How long were we gone?" Joel asked.

"Almost three hours," Lightsprout replied. "To be honest, we were starting to get a little worried."

"Who are your new friends?" Yellowpetal said.

"Oh yeah, um, everyone—this is Forty-Two and...what's your name?"

"Twenty-Three," the other Fourtail answered. "I am Forty-Two's mate."

"Forty-Two and Twenty-Three?" Felicity snorted. "You've gotta be kidding me."

"Help!" Starpollen said, pointing to Blackspore's motionless form.

"Oh—right," Joel said. He turned to the Fourtails. "Can you guys heal him?"

"Healing him will be the key to saving this island, correct?" Forty-Two asked.

"Yeah, well, it's the first step. An important one."

"Then we shall do as you have requested."

Forty-Two and Twenty-Three got to work, weaving clouds of golden Aura by swishing their tails around. The swordcats and Tanback joined their efforts. Blackspore became bathed in a swath of brilliant, blinding light that made it seem almost as if the sun itself had been pulled into the den. The light began to shift from gold to silver to white and back to gold again. This went on for what felt like a very long time. Then, just as it seemed as if everyone was wearing down, something finally happened: Blackspore coughed. This was followed by exclamations of happiness, relief, and congratulations. Joel, for his part, simply exhaled.

"Thank you very much," he said to Forty-Two and Twenty-Three. "Now Blackspore will be able to"—he stopped, noticing something odd and different about the Fourtails' personal Auras—"are...are you guys okay?"

"Healing your friend required our entire life essences," Twenty-Three said, totally emotionless.

"Wait, what? Does that mean—?"

"I am glad we were able to assist you," Forty-Two said. Both he and his mate began to dissolve into tiny floating specks of energy.

"No! I didn't mean for you to sacrifice yourselves!"

"Do not feel sad or guilty," Twenty-Three said. "We would have perished anyway, had we remained back in our time. At least this way, we were able to perform one last noble deed."

"So thank you," Forty-Two said, "for giving us that opportunity. Best of luck."

And with that, the two Fourtails vanished completely. Joel felt his eyes well up.

"I'll make sure you didn't die in vain," he whispered.

♪♪♪

Several minutes later, after Blackspore's tearful reunion with Lightsprout and the other shamans, he asked Joel if he could speak with him outside, alone. Joel agreed, so they crawled out of the den, through the concealing bushes, and onto the mountain trail.

"Okay," Joel said as they stood up and looked out at the island's landscape, "so, what did you want to talk about?"

"Well, first of all, thank you very much for saving my life. And for trying, anyway, to honor my original request."

"You're welcome. It's too bad we didn't succeed. But I think that the past—"

"Cannot be changed, yes, I know that now." The master shaman turned and looked Joel in the eye. "Joel, I have a confession to make to you."

"Um, okay."

"There is a reason I asked you specifically to stop me from bringing Byle over, rather than any of the other myriad possibilities."

"Because you knew that nothing else would work? But wait, that didn't work either, so...I don't get it. What's the reason?"

"Remember how I used to be so bitter about love? How I spent all those years in exile, training myself to let go of that emotion and all of its distractions?"

"Yeah."

"But then when we returned to Spectraland, you told me that I was wrong?"

Joel wanted to pull a Felicity and say "are you getting to the point soon?" but he managed to refrain.

"Well, while I was dying, I realized that you were right—that maybe love is not so bad after all. I began to think, what if Joel could use his power to save everyone from Byle, including Lightsprout? And then, despite whatever punishment we would incur from the Elders for getting involved in the war, at least we could be together."

"That's actually what I told your younger self."

"I seem to recall that now, yes."

"You still didn't tell me why you asked me to do that, though, specifically."

Blackspore chuckled, setting off a fit of coughing. "I was just getting to that," he said once he had recovered. "You see, I did not ask you to prevent the Fourfoot War itself because the war is the reason Lightsprout and I got together in the first place. Prior to that, we were simply colleagues. But after the war broke out, she was impressed with my poise in keeping the other shamans out of the conflict as per the Elder's wishes, and so eventually she became receptive to my advances."

"Wait, so that means...you were willing to sacrifice lives for the sake of your own selfish purposes?"

"Indeed. The very thing I accused you of. So in addition to my confession, I would also like to apologize. Do you forgive me?"

Joel wanted to feel angry, but for whatever reason, he couldn't. "Sure, but the others..."

"Please do not tell Lightsprout yet," Blackspore asked. "I will find my own way to let her know."

"Okay."

"Thank you. By the way, that is quite an impressive shapeshifting job." Blackspore tugged on one of Joel's arm-leaves. "When I first met you and Felicity on that atoll earlier this year, I thought you both looked familiar, but it took me a while to realize that you were Sightguy and Goldilocks."

"Thanks. I mean, Fireflower did it."

"I assumed that was the case. She is a very talented healer and Wavemaker, truly deserving of her position as our leader. Anyway, we should go back inside now. I have a job to do."

The two crawled back into the den.

"I am ready," Blackspore said. "If I may borrow a wavebow, please."

"Are you sure you are strong enough to do this?" Lightsprout asked, handing her instrument to him.

"Of course," Blackspore replied, even though his reply was accompanied by a wheeze that made it sound as if his lungs were filled with screeching bats.

"You need to rest," Lightsprout said.

"Nonsense." Blackspore cough-laughed. "Having you back at my side has given me the strength of a hundred master shamans."

Felicity rolled her eyes and stuck out her tongue. "Bleh. Gross."

Ignoring the remark, Blackspore played a melody on Lightsprout's wavebow. Within seconds, a sphere of Aura energy materialized in the middle of the swordcat den. Soon after, an image formed within the sphere: a scene of the beach near Crownrock.

"What. The. Heck." Felicity said.

The whole area now looked like a giant concert festival—the kind that you would see on Earth, not Spectraland. There was a huge amphitheater, like the Waikiki Shell or maybe even the Hollywood Bowl, along with tents, trailers, generators, a perimeter fence, even port-a-potties. A band was playing onstage, and there were thousands—perhaps hundreds of thousands—of people in the audience.

"Are you sure you have the right place?" Joel asked Blackspore. "That looks more like Earth, I mean, the Bluerock."

"Quite sure," Blackspore replied. He moved the focus of the cast. "Look—Crownrock."

Joel looked. Sure enough, the little offshore islet where the Rift was located was there, although the golden shield of Aura that usually surrounded it was nowhere to be seen.

"Is the Ultracom still down there?" Felicity asked.

Blackspore moved the cast's focus around some more. As he did so, Joel spotted the Ultracom behind the amphitheater, surrounded by a fleet of trailers. He also saw hundreds of Spectraland natives—probably the entire population of the island minus whoever was here in the swordcats' den—all dancing in a group near the middle of the enormous crowd.

"Okay, that seems strange," Felicity said. "Wonder why they'd be dancing?"

“They don’t seem happy about it,” Joel said, noting the expressions on the natives’ faces.

“It is probably the effects of the Ultracom,” Thornleaf said. “They are being forced to dance.”

Blackspore zoomed in. Joel saw—among many others—Fireflower, Riverhand, Windblade, Redstem, and the five chiefs, all of them looking quite distressed.

“We need to rescue them,” he said.

Felicity looked at Thornleaf. “Were the Ultracom controls inside of the Ultracom itself?”

“No. They were housed separately, but still nearby.”

“Then they must be somewhere on the concert grounds.” Felicity turned to Blackspore. “We have to get in there.”

“That might be challenging,” Blackspore said. “There are guards from the Six States posted all along the perimeter barrier, and flying vehicles are patrolling the skies above the beach.”

“Can you teleport us in?” Felicity said.

“I suppose, but...”

“But what?”

“I am sensing something strange,” Blackspore replied, his brow furrowing. “There is a field of energy permeating the area inside the barrier.”

“Yeah, the Aura. Duh.”

“No, no—it is a negative energy, almost an antithesis of the Aura. It is like nothing I have ever seen. I suspect that it is meant to prevent the use of wavecasts within the concert grounds.”

“You think Marshall figured out how to do that?” Joel asked.

“I am not sure,” Blackspore replied. “It would have required some very advanced knowledge. In any case, I am afraid I will not be able to teleport anyone in.”

"Wait," Felicity said, "so does that mean invisibility is out too?"

"I would assume so."

"Well, that sucks."

"If the field is negating the effects of wavecasts, why are the Six States people still mind-controlled?" Yellowpetal asked.

"They are all positioned outside its area of influence," Blackspore answered. "Any security personnel within the grounds itself appear to be from the Bluerock."

"Marshall must've brought over a bunch of his own goons from back home," Felicity said.

"That gives me an idea," Joel declared. He turned to Tanback. "Are you able to reverse a shapeshifting cast?"

"I believe so," Tanback said. "But why would I need to do that?"

"Because she and I are actually offworlders," Joel said, glancing at Felicity. "Fireflower shapeshifted us to look like Spectraland natives. If you can reverse the cast, then at least the two of us can go down there and blend in with the crowd."

"Wait," Lightsprout said, "so your names are not Sightguy and Goldilocks?"

"They're not," Felicity answered. "My name's Felicity Smith."

"And I'm Joel. Joel Suzuki. The Virtuoso."

CHAPTER 24: THE FESTIVAL

After Tanback changed Joel and Felicity back into their normal selves, Blackspore teleported them to a spot about a hundred yards away from the concert festival. From there, they began walking.

"Why do you think Marshall is putting on this whole giant concert thing, anyway?" Felicity asked.

"I dunno," Joel replied. "To satisfy his ego, maybe?"

"Maybe. But I don't think his new goal in life is to become a promoter. Knowing him, there's got to be some other reason."

"Well, I assume he's gonna make a lot of money from this. What if he's trying to become an evil billionaire, like an anti-Batman or Iron Man or something?"

"Hmm, could be."

"That would be bad."

"Yeah, no kidding."

"Okay, well, after we rescue Fireflower and everyone else, we can try to find and capture him," Joel said. "With that anti-Aura field in place, he can't perform any wavecasts."

"Hello—neither can we," Felicity said. "And I'm sure he'll have security guards from Earth protecting him."

"We'll figure something out. We always do. Right?"

"Sure, yeah, why not."

They walked in silence for a while. Then Joel decided to ask something that had been on his mind ever since they returned from the past.

"So...what's gonna happen with you and Thornleaf?"

"Dude, let's talk about that kind of stuff later."

"I mean, shouldn't we be arresting him or something? After all, he helped Marshall."

"Yeah, I know."

"And are you sure the past Wavemakers are cool about hanging out with him in the swordcat den? You know, without you there?"

"We worked all that out while you were off fetching the Fourtails. I just...let's put that in a box for now, okay?"

"It's really been bugging me, though. I think we need to—"

"Hey, do you hear that?"

"Hear what?"

"The concert...it sounds like Sugarblood is playing."

Joel listened. Sure enough, he could make out the unmistakable voice of Lexi Anderson, Sugarblood's lead singer, belting out the chorus of "Heartrender," one of her band's many hits.

"Wow," he said. "I can't believe they're playing here, in Spectraland."

"So weird, right? It's like two worlds colliding."

The edge of the concert grounds came into view. The fence they had seen through Blackspore's far-vision cast was, upon closer inspection, almost twelve feet tall and topped with barbed wire. Soldiers from the Six States with rifles and countercoms were stationed in front of the fence at ten-foot intervals.

"Good thing there aren't any Earth guards out here," Felicity said.

"How come?"

"'Cause we're still wearing Spectraland clothes, which I'm sure would invite all kinds of unwanted questions. The only thing these Six States guys will see are two Earth-person energy signatures."

"Oh. Um...I don't get it."

"Just follow my lead." She started to jog toward the fence.

"Wait, what are you—?"

"Woo! This is place is so cool!"

Joel jogged after her.

"Stop!" one of the guards barked, aiming his rifle. Felicity stopped, and Joel pulled up next to her. "How did you two get out here? No one is supposed to leave the concert grounds!"

"We just wanted to explore this rad island, that's all," Felicity said. "I mean, have you guys seen this place? It's like Hawai'i, only better!"

"No, it is extremely dangerous. There are many deadly creatures here that would not hesitate to tear you to shreds. That is why we have this fence—to protect the concertgoers from the indigenous wildlife."

"Aw, are you serious?" Felicity turned to Joel. "I didn't see any deadly creatures, did you?"

"What? Oh—um, no. No, I didn't."

"Trust me," the guard said, "they are out there. Now get back inside."

"Okay, fine," Felicity pouted. "Man, you guys are no fun."

The guard moved to his side and opened up a gateway in the fence. Felicity walked in. Joel followed. The guard closed and locked the gateway behind them.

"How did you know that would work?" Joel asked Felicity when they were out of earshot. "We don't have tickets or hand stamps or anything. They didn't even search our supply packs."

Felicity shrugged. "I had a hunch the only ticket you need for this concert is to be a person from Earth. See how the barbed wire rows are tilted inward? I think the fence is to keep the crowd in, not to keep animals out."

"Hmm. You're probably right."

"I know I am. Now let's find out where the Ultracom control room is."

"My guess is that it's probably in one of the trailers. If we can get closer to them, I can use the Sight to rewind the time of the scene and figure out which one it is."

"What about the anti-Aura thing?"

"It won't affect the Sight."

"Are you sure?"

Joel cleared his mind and performed a quick test of his ability. As he expected, it seemed to work just fine. "Yup, I'm sure."

"Okay. On the way over there I'm gonna ask someone what's going on. I'm still curious as to why Marshall set this whole thing up."

"Sounds good."

The pair walked past a row of concession stands and into the crowd. Sugarblood had finished their set, and a crew of roadies was preparing the stage for the next band.

"Hey, excuse me," Felicity said to a dark-haired girl in leather pants and a lime-green halter top. "What's going on here?"

"You don't know?" the girl tittered. She had a lanyard around her neck, at the end of which hung a laminated card with the word *BYLE* printed on it in fluorescent letters. "This is the Biledriver reunion concert!"

"The what?" Joel and Felicity said at the same time.

"Yeah, I guess Marshall Byle faked his death as some kind of publicity stunt or whatever. So now he's back! Isn't that cool?"

"But how...why...where..." Joel stammered.

"Boy, you must be drunker than me!" the girl said. "They had a big radio contest where they gave away all these trips to this tropical island for the show. Don't you remember?"

"Right, right, the contest," Felicity said.

"What're your guys' names?" the girl asked.

"I'm, uh, Joel," Joel said. "Joel Suzuki."

The girl's eyes widened. "Joel Suzuki? You mean, like, from Joel Suzuki and the Wavemakers?"

"Yeah."

"That means you must be Felicity!"

"Ding," Felicity said. "Give the girl a prize."

"Oh, wow! I didn't recognize you guys. You're all dressed funny, like those green-skinned people serving the drinks. Is it cosplay or something?"

Joel wasn't quite sure how to answer that. "Um—"

"Wait," Felicity said, "did you say those green-skinned people are serving drinks?"

"Yeah. In between bands, they've been handing out free booze. Cool, right? Then when the bands play they just dance like crazy. It's so awesome."

"Hmm."

"Oh, and by the way, I *love* your guys' music."

"Oh, uh, thanks," Joel said.

"Wait," the girl gasped. "Are you playing tonight?"

"No."

"Oh. Just here as VIPs, then?"

"Sure, yeah," Felicity said. "Hey, look, I noticed you're wearing something there. Is that a backstage pass?"

"Yup," the girl giggled, fingering her lanyard. "All access, can you believe it? I got it extra because I could name most of the songs on Biledriver's first album."

Joel was tempted to roll his eyes, but he managed to stifle the impulse.

A tall, muscular guy in a Biledriver T-shirt and swim trunks sauntered up. "Hey, Jamie," he said to the dark-haired girl, "who're you talking to?"

"Joel Suzuki and Felicity Smith!"

"Who?"

"You know, from Joel Suzuki and the Wavemakers?"

"Never heard of 'em."

"Yes, you have," the girl—Jamie—said, slapping the guy on his arm. "They're in my Spotify feed."

"Oh, right!" the guy said. He too was wearing what was apparently a backstage pass. "Man, you guys rock!" he held up his hand in a high-five motion.

"Thanks," Joel said, sheepishly returning the high-five.

"Well, you know what?" Felicity said. "It's your lucky day. We have some copies of our new album and T-shirts to give away."

"You do?" Jamie gasped.

"Yup. They're back in the VIP trailer. If you guys come with us, we'll give some to you. We'll even autograph them."

"Sweet!" the guy said.

"What are you doing?" Joel whispered to Felicity.

"I think those backstage passes might come in handy."

"Oh. How are we gonna..."

"You'll see. Just let me know when you spot a villager serving drinks."

Felicity and Joel led the way through the crowd with Jamie and the muscular guy right behind them. It wasn't long before Joel noticed a Spectraland native—Windblade—holding a wooden tray of red plastic cups and walking in a slow, zombielike fashion.

"Over there," Joel said, pointing.

They went up to Windblade, who turned his head as they approached.

"Joel! Felicity!" he said, his eyes lighting up. "Thank the Aura you are here! We are all being forced to—"

"Shh, yeah, we know," Felicity said. "Do you know where the control room for the giant countercom is?"

"I do not. There are a number of large vehicles behind the amphitheater, though. My guess is that it would be in one of those."

"Okay, yeah, that's what we thought too."

"Are you going there now? Because I must warn you, that area is heavily guarded."

"I wouldn't expect anything less." Felicity turned. "Hey, uh, Jamie and..."

"Matt." The muscular guy grinned.

"Jamie and Matt. How about a toast?" Felicity grabbed a couple of cups off of Windblade's tray and handed it to the pair.

"Okay," Matt said, accepting the cup. "But what about you guys?"

"Yeah," Jamie said. "You're not playing, right? So drink with us!"

"Well, we're not twenty-one."

"The drinking age on this island is seventeen," Matt said. "The radio contest guys told us that."

"So c'mon!" Jamie said.

Felicity and Joel exchanged glances. Felicity made a face that Joel took to mean something along the lines of *just fake it*. She picked up two more cups and handed one to him.

"Okay, fine," she said. "To, uh..."

"To Biledriver!" Jamie raised her cup.

"Biledriver!" Matt echoed.

Joel hated the choice of toast, but he knew he had to play along. He raised his cup to his lips and pretended to drink the contents: a blue liquid that smelled like an unholy mixture of lifepods and gasoline. He was going to stop after one fake sip, but then he noticed that Felicity—who he assumed was also faking it—was keeping her cup raised, so he did the same. Jamie and Matt seemed to notice as well, so they both continued drinking. After a few long seconds during which Joel tried his best not to gag, Jamie and Matt drained their cups and tossed them aside onto the ground.

I'm sure we'll clean that up later, Joel thought.

"Woo!" Jamie exclaimed.

"Rock 'n' roll!" Matt pumped his fist.

Felicity placed her cup—which Joel noticed was still full—back on Windblade's tray with one hand and wiped her mouth with the other. "Wow, yeah, that was awesome. Okay, let's keep moving."

Joel set his own cup down on the tray and leaned toward Windblade. "Just, um, hang in there. We're gonna free you guys soon. I promise."

"I have no doubt." Windblade nodded.

Felicity continued to lead the foursome in the direction of the trailers. Along the way, as the next band's roadies were soundchecking their instruments, she stopped at every Spectraland native they came across, repeating the same toast over and over again. By the time they arrived in front of the giant amphitheater, Jamie and Matt could barely stand.

"Man," Matt said, "fer a coupla kids, you guys sure can"—he paused to let out a giant burp—"hold yer liquor."

"Well, we are rock stars, after all," Felicity said.

"I think...I think I hafta throw up," Jamie slurred, her lids heavy.

"Not here, that's gross," Felicity said. She took Jamie by the arm and led the girl toward a nearby row of port-a-potties. "Joel, why don't you bring Matt?"

"Um, okay." Joel grabbed Matt's arm.

"Oh—hey, no, bro," Matt said, weakly pulling away, "I'm good."

"Uh, well, Jamie might need someone to hold her hair up while she...you know. Is she your girlfriend?"

"Heh," Matt smirked. "Sorta."

"Well, either way, I'm sure she'd appreciate it."

"Yeah, all right. But don't hold me, dude. I can totally make it there myshelf." Matt stumbled forward. Joel caught him before he fell on his face.

"Totally," Joel said. He escorted Matt the rest of the way to the port-a-potties, where Felicity was waiting with a barely conscious Jamie.

"Take him into that one," Felicity said under her breath, "and swap clothes with him."

"Wait, what?"

"You heard me. We need to get out of these Spectraland clothes if we're gonna make it past the Earth security. Oh, and be sure to grab his backstage pass."

"Um, okay."

Joel went into one of the port-a-potties with Matt. He set the muscular guy down on the toilet and shut the door.

"Bro...wha...what are you doing?" Matt mumbled.

"Just, uh, just relax," Joel improvised. He reached down to take off Matt's shirt.

"Whoa, whoa," Matt said, "I'm not—you know, I'm not into—"

"It's okay," Joel said, "we're just switching clothes."

"I mean, I don't have a problem with it or anything like that," Matt said, seemingly oblivious to what Joel had just told him. "In fact, one of my best friends is gay. Super cool guy. He and his boyfriend, they, uh...they..."

Joel blinked, waiting for Matt to finish his sentence. He never did, though; after a few seconds during which some drool dribbled out of the corner of his mouth, the muscular guy closed his eyes and began to snore.

"Well," Joel exhaled, "I guess that'll make this a little less awkward." He finished up the wardrobe exchange and exited the stall. Felicity was already out there, wearing Jamie's halter top, leather pants, and backstage pass.

"That took you long enough," she said.

"I can't believe I have to wear this stupid Biledriver T-shirt," Joel complained. "And these shorts are way too big."

"Hey, how do you think I feel?" Felicity responded. "I can barely breathe in this outfit."

"You know, we probably just lost a couple of fans there."

"I doubt they'll remember any of this. Let's go."

The pair circled around the amphitheater toward where the Ultracom and its surrounding trailers were stationed. After a short walk, they came across a stretch of fence that was, as Windblade had said, heavily guarded. As the next band (Second Player Score, from Felicity's original hometown of Vancouver, Washington) started playing, Felicity approached one of the guards.

"Hey, can my friend and I get back there?" she said, holding up her backstage pass. "We don't like this band, so we just wanna chill out for a while."

Joel held up his pass as well.

"All right," the guard—an enormous, well-tattooed man who looked like he could be making better money as a professional wrestler—grunted. "You know where the guest trailer is?"

"No," Felicity replied.

"The fourth one on the left there." The guard pointed.

"Thanks."

"Re-enter through here when you're ready." The guard opened a gate in the fence.

"Gotcha."

The pair walked through. They arrived at the trailer, which had the number four on a sign on its door, and stopped outside.

"Okay, see what you can find out," Felicity said.

"About what?" Joel said.

"Where the Ultracom controls are. Using the Sight."

"Oh—right."

Joel engaged the Sight and rewound the scene. He saw trailers rolling off of some Six States ships, the fencing being erected, and a lot of soldiers and Spectraland natives walking around and working.

"Weird," he said, "they seem to have gotten a lot of stuff done in a really short period of time."

"Yeah, yeah, whatever. Did you see anything that tells us where the controls are?"

"Um—no, not yet."

"You might want to hurry up. The guard who let us in is looking at us."

"Okay, but it's hard to—" Joel paused. He didn't see the Ultracom controls, but he did notice something else interesting: Thinker, Keeper, Seeker, and another Six States soldier he didn't recognize being ushered by a human security guard toward a trailer—with a door sign labeled with the number twelve—located near the far end of the area. As they walked, the guard would occasionally slap or punch his prisoners for what appeared to be no good reason; finally, they entered the trailer, and the door closed behind them.

"You got something?" Felicity asked.

Joel described what he saw.

"Man, what a jerk," Felicity said.

"Are you talking about the guard?"

"Obviously. We'd better go help them."

"Who's the other Six States person?"

"Sounds like Catcher. He was the other soldier besides Seeker who Thornleaf and I administered the mind-control antidote to."

"Oh—so since they can't be put back under mind control, Marshall's just keeping them locked up in a trailer."

"Sounds about right." Felicity waved at the guard by the fence, who continued to stare. "All right, follow me." She went into the guest trailer. Joel followed. There was no one inside, just a couple of couches and a table with trays of food.

"How long are we gonna stay in here?" Joel asked.

Felicity grabbed a lifepod off the table and took a bite. "Just give it a minute or so," she said, chewing. "Then we'll sneak over to that other trailer."

"Okay. What are we gonna do when we get there?"

"Don't worry. I have a plan."

"I'm not worried." Joel gave Felicity an admiring glance. "You're really on a roll with your plans."

"Yeah, I know. I might've been distracted before, but I'm totally in the zone now." She put the half-eaten lifepod back on the table. "Let's do this."

Felicity opened the door a crack and peeked outside. The coast must have been clear, because she carefully slipped out. Joel followed. They made their way over to trailer number twelve, which, fortunately, was located behind the Ultracom and out of the fence guard's view. Felicity tried the door.

"Okay, yeah, it's locked," she said.

"So now what?"

"Just keep an eye out and make sure no one's looking." She knocked on the door.

"Wait, um—what are you doing?"

"You'll see." Felicity knocked again and put her face up against the door. "Catering!" she said.

A few seconds went by. Nothing happened.

"Catering is here!" Felicity said, knocking again. "We have sandwiches, tacos, beer...all that good stuff."

A few more seconds passed. This time, Joel could hear footsteps inside the trailer.

"Okay, stand back," Felicity whispered.

The door opened. The human guard that Joel had seen with the Sight was standing there.

"I wasn't expecting—"

Felicity threw a vicious right hook at the guard, connecting with his jaw. Before he had a chance to recover, she grabbed him, placed him in a chokehold, and dragged him back into the trailer.

"Joel, get the door," she said.

"Right."

Joel entered the trailer and closed the door.

"Felicity! Joel!" Thinker exclaimed. He, Keeper, Seeker, and Catcher were standing up against the far wall, all of them tied up with rope. The trailer's interior was mostly bare except for a small cabinet with several drawers.

"Are you guys okay?" Joel asked.

"A bit bruised, but alive, at least," Thinker replied.

Felicity dropped the guard, who was now unconscious, onto the floor. "We saw this guy hitting you. Why was he doing that?"

"He said it was because of our appearances," Thinker said.

"I believe his exact words were 'scary alien freaks,'" Keeper added.

"They were originally forcing us to dance and serve drinks along with the native villagers," Seeker said, "but then apparently a few of the concertgoers complained, claiming that we were too frightening. Several of them even threatened us with violence. That is when the guard had us removed, saying it was for our own safety."

"But as we left the area," Keeper said, "he proceeded to assault us anyway."

"Lame," Felicity muttered.

"Now that you are here," Catcher said, "You should check the cabinet drawers. I believe the guard placed some of your spouse's belongings in it."

"Oh?" Felicity walked over to the cabinet and opened one of its drawers. "Well, whaddya know."

"What's in there?" Joel said as he worked to undo Thinker's ropes.

"Buncha good stuff—the nullifier, the invisibility salve, and the mind-control antidote."

"None of that will really help us, though, since we're already inside the concert grounds."

"Hmm, you're probably right." Felicity turned to the Six States folks. "Would any of you happen to know where the Ultracom control room is?"

All four responded in the negative, with Catcher adding, "We would help you search for it, but we are all still under the Ultracom's influence and cannot move on our own."

"Figures," Felicity grumbled. "All right, tell you what—Joel and I will keep looking. Then, once we find it and get everyone freed up, we'll round up the villagers while you guys take this stuff"—she motioned at the salve, antidote, and nullifier—"and sneak out of here. If you head away from the amphitheater, you should be able to reach the perimeter fence, which is being guarded by Six States people. Use the salve or nullifier to get yourselves outside somehow and then un-mind-control all of your buddies. Think you can handle that?"

"Of course," Catcher said.

"We are not a group of amateurs," Seeker said.

"No, I suppose you're not." Felicity chuckled. "Hey, Joel—I'll finish up untying these guys. In the meantime, use some of that rope to tie up the guard, would ya? You know, in case he wakes up before we have a chance to reverse the Ultracom effects."

"Okay." Joel took the rope he had removed from Thinker and went over to the fallen security guard. As he bent down, he spotted some items on the guard's belt: a handheld countercom, a set of keys, and what looked like a Taser gun. "Oh, wow."

"What?" Felicity said.

"I found some things that might come in handy."

CHAPTER 25: ALL APOLOGIES

Back outside, Joel tried the Sight again. This time, he saw some Spectraland natives carrying what looked like a bunch of video game equipment into another one of the trailers, this one labeled with the number nine.

"Are you sure that's it?" Felicity said.

"It has to be," Joel replied. "Remember the deluxe countercom the Redivision used on us in The Vast Wasteland?"

"More like, the one that the Uniter's goons used on me and everybody else while you were off having fun with Blackspore in the limbo plane."

"Um, yeah, that one. Anyway, it had that joystick-like thing on it, which is how the user moved people around after they were under its control."

"So you're thinking all the video game components you just saw are actually the controls for the Ultracom."

"Yeah."

"Fair enough. Did you see if anyone else went in there? Like, guards, or whatever?"

"No." Joel said. "It's weird—after I saw the natives take the equipment in, the scene fast-forwarded itself. It was like time skipped ahead or something."

"Hmm. Well, let's check it out."

The pair snuck over to trailer number nine. As expected, the door was locked, so Joel took out the keys he had lifted from the guard.

"How do you know those are for the trailers?" Felicity asked.

"Well, there are thirteen trailers and thirteen keys, so, you know..."

"Gotcha. So, what, are you just going to try them all?"

"No, they're labeled." Joel held up one of the keys, which had the number nine emblazoned on its bow. "See?"

"Ah. How convenient."

Joel tried the key. He felt the door handle unlock.

"Okay, it's open," he said.

"All right," Felicity said, "just in case there are more guards than I can handle in there, you use the countercom, and I'll use the Taser."

"You know how to use a Taser gun?"

Felicity shrugged. "How hard can it be?"

"Um..."

"Fling the door open on three. Ready?"

"I guess, but—"

"One...two...three!"

Joel flung the door open. What he saw inside was definitely not what he had expected; instead of some obvious set of controls for the Ultracom, there were leather couches, a full kitchen, three wide-screen televisions, even a pool table. And instead of a bunch of guards or Ultracom operators, there were the members of Sugarblood and a couple of roadies, taking full advantage of their trailer's amenities.

"Hey!" the band's drummer, sitting on one of the couches, exclaimed. "How did you guys get in here? This is a private trailer!"

"We…we have all-access backstage passes," Felicity said, holding her pass up with one hand while quickly hiding the Taser gun behind her back with the other. "Security opened the door for us."

The band's bassist, standing over the pool table, banked the eight ball into the corner pocket. "You could've at least knocked first."

"Relax, guys," Lexi Anderson said, holding a large steaming mug with a tea bag tag hanging out of it. "It's not like we're entertaining groupies in here or anything."

"We could've been," the band's guitarist, playing *Diablo III* on one of the wide-screen TVs, muttered.

"Um, sorry for the interruption," Joel said, a bit starstruck. "We'll, uh, we'll just be going."

"Hey man, it's cool." Lexi smiled as she walked over. "Did you guys want an autograph or something?"

"Well…sure," Joel said.

Lexi pulled out a pen and signed Joel's backstage pass. "You know, you two look really familiar. I swear I've seen your faces somewhere before."

"Probably just at one of your shows," Felicity said. "We're big fans."

"Well, thanks," Lexi said, signing Felicity's pass. "We appreciate that."

"Wait, no, I know who they are," the bassist said. "They're from that band…Joe Something and the Waveriders. Right?"

"Joel Suzuki and the Wavemakers," Joel said.

"Close enough."

"Oh yeah!" Lexi exclaimed. "I love your music. Aren't you opening for us next month in Seattle?"

"Tacoma, actually," Joel said. "But, um, no, we're not."

Felicity turned to Joel. "You're not?"

"What?" Lexi said. "How come?"

"It's, uh...it's kind of a long story," Joel said. "You see, Felicity left the band, so then your management changed their mind. They only gave us the gig because she and I are both on the autism spectrum, and they thought it would be, like, a cool gimmick, or whatever."

"You're kidding," Lexi said.

"Nope."

"Did you find a new guitarist yet?"

"No."

"Tell you what—I'll talk to our managers when we get home and make sure you get put back on the bill. Then Jason here will learn the parts and fill in."

The guitarist—Jason—looked up from his video game. "I will?"

"You'd better."

"Fine."

"Oh—uh, wow," Joel said. "Thanks."

"Don't mention it," Lexi said. "Autism or not, it shouldn't really matter. I mean, it's cool if you guys are advocates for that community and all, but the bottom line is, your band rocks."

"That's what I always say," Felicity said.

"Just curious—why'd you quit?" Lexi asked.

"It's complicated."

"I hear ya," Lexi chuckled. "You probably already know this, but Jason's left Sugarblood twice before."

"It might be three times if you keep talking," Jason said.

"Jerk."

"Hey, um, by the way," Joel said, unsure if Lexi and Jason were flirting or arguing, "did any of you happen to see anything unusual about one of the other trailers?"

"Like what?" Lexi asked.

"I dunno, like, lots of people taking a bunch of video game or computer equipment into it."

"You mean, more than what we have here?" Jason asked, nodding at the generous array of game consoles and controllers that were laid out in front of him.

"I guess, yeah."

"Nope, I haven't seen anything like that."

"Neither have I," Lexi said.

"Actually," one of the roadies chimed in, "when we were setting everything up earlier, I saw a group of people carrying, like, a whole load of monitors and other hi-tech-looking stuff. But not into one of the trailers."

"Where, then?" Felicity said.

"One of the yurts, back out on the grounds. I figured it was for filming the festival."

"That must be the control room," Joel whispered to Felicity.

"Yeah, hopefully."

"Why'd you want to know?" the roadie said.

"No reason," Felicity replied.

"Uh...okay, then."

"So, do you guys want to hang out for a bit?" Lexi said. "We have drinks, food...oh, this island has this amazing little blue fruit that tastes like banana and watermelon, with a slight minty aftertaste. You have to try it."

"Actually, that's okay," Felicity said. "We're, uh, gonna go look for Biledriver now."

"You want Marshall's autograph, huh?" Lexi chuckled. "I don't blame you—dude's a legend. Good luck with that, though. He isn't in any of the trailers—I checked. I actually haven't seen him or anybody from his band since we got here."

Interesting, Joel thought.

"Maybe he's here now," Felicity said. "We'll go find out."

"Well, have fun," Lexi said. "And hey"—she pointed at Felicity—"let us know if you change your mind and rejoin your pal's band. They'll have the gig anyway, but we'd love to see both of you next month in Seattle—I mean, Tacoma."

"Yeah, and then I won't have to learn your guitar parts," Jason said, not looking away from his game.

"Ten-four," Felicity said, turning. "And thanks for the autographs."

"Anytime," Lexi said.

"So...are you gonna do it?" Joel asked Felicity once they were back outside.

"Do what?"

"You know...rejoin the band."

"What made you think I was gonna do that?"

"You told them ten-four."

"I was just acknowledging what they said."

"Oh."

"Let's go check out that yurt."

The pair headed out of the trailer area. When they reached the fence, the well-tattooed guard shot them a curious glance.

"Going back in already?" he said. "That band you don't like is still playing."

"Eh, that's fine," Felicity said. "We got bored back here."

"All right." The guard opened the gate.

Joel and Felicity exited and headed for the far side of the concert grounds, over near the concession stands. After looking around for a minute, Joel spotted an area with twenty-two yurts arranged in rows.

"Will the Sight show you which one it is?" Felicity asked.

Joel engaged the Sight. "Can't really tell...there's that weird time-warp effect going on again."

"Great. So we'll have to check all of them?"

"Well, my guess is...it's that one," Joel said, pointing at one of the yurts.

"What makes you think that?"

"It's a little larger than all the others. I figure they would need the extra space to house all the equipment."

"Makes sense," Felicity said.

They went up to the yurt. It had a wooden door, which was locked.

"I don't suppose any of those keys would work," Felicity said.

"I doubt it," Joel said, inspecting the keys. "The cuts on the blades don't match this keyhole. Can you use your catering trick?"

"Not if there's a lot of people in there." Felicity inspected the door. "This thing is made of some pretty soft wood, though, and it opens inward, so..."

"What are you thinking?"

"I can probably kick it open."

"Oh—cool."

"Be ready with the countercom. Once the door's open, freeze as many people as you can. Then I'll point the Taser gun at the rest. Hopefully that should take care of it."

"Got it."

Felicity took a couple of steps back. Then, after a deep breath, she gave the door a swift, solid kick. It flew open. Joel immediately pressed a button on the counter-com, causing it to emit a high squeal. Right after he did, he noticed something unexpected: inside the yurt, there appeared to be only a single individual, a person with long dark hair, sitting at a console desk and facing away from the door. The individual was surrounded by nineteen separate video screens that had been mounted to the walls, making the place look like a high-tech security monitor room. Joel and Felicity entered and closed the door behind them.

"Don't make a sound," Felicity snapped, holding the Taser gun up with both hands.

The individual remained silent and motionless.

"My friend here is gonna release you from the energy lock," Felicity said as she took a few cautious steps forward. "Then, after he does, you're gonna do the same for all the Spectraland natives. Got it?"

No response.

"Answer me," Felicity demanded.

"Um, you told her not to make a sound," Joel noted.

Felicity rolled her eyes. "I was talking about screaming or calling for help," she said. "Just turn her around, would ya? So we can talk to her face-to-face."

"Okay." Joel walked up to the chair. When he got there, he received yet another surprise: instead of a human woman, sitting in the chair was a bizarre alien being that, underneath its hair, resembled a cross between a star-nosed mole and a giant cockroach. Startled, Joel yelped and jumped back.

"What? What is it?" Felicity said.

"Um...see for yourself." Joel slowly turned the chair around, being careful not to touch any part of the strange being.

"Well, that's different," Felicity said. "Can you talk?"

"Of course I can," the being said in a female, south London–accented voice. "I am a highly intelligent engineer."

"And we're hearing you speak English," Felicity said. "That must mean someone implanted a permanent translation cast on you. Based on your accent, I would assume that someone was Marshall."

"I will neither confirm nor deny."

Joel looked up at the monitors. Each screen displayed various groups of Spectraland natives dancing, some of whom—primarily the very old and the very young—were obviously on the verge of dangerous exhaustion. "We don't have much time left," he said.

Felicity took another step forward, Taser gun still aimed at the strange being. "All right, mole-roach-lady, you're gonna do what I told you to do, or else you're in for quite a shock. And I mean that literally."

The being made a noise that sounded like a rattlesnake's rattle; its version of a chuckle, perhaps. "Very well. But, like you said, you will have to release me first."

"I, uh, I'm not sure that's a good idea now," Joel said to Felicity. "We don't know anything about her physiology. She might be immune to the Taser's effects."

Felicity frowned. "You might be right. She was a little too quick to agree there." She glanced at the console desk. "Think you can figure this thing out?"

Joel examined the controls on the desk. It was like looking at a giant video game controller with ten times as many buttons and joysticks. Fortunately, video games and countercoms were two things that Joel was quite familiar with. “Yeah, I think so,” he said.

“If you push the wrong button,” the mole-roach woman said, “you may end up hurting your friends instead of helping them.”

Joel grimaced. To his knowledge, countercoms didn’t have any harmful functions (other than, say, allowing you to place someone under energy control and then walk them off a cliff), but it was certainly possible that this one did. “I can probably figure out if any of these buttons match the ones on the small countercom,” he thought out loud, “but it might take a while.”

“Just use the Sight,” Felicity suggested.

“To rewind the time of the scene?” Joel asked, unsure of what good that would do or, given the strange time-warp effects he had just been seeing, whether it would even work at all.

“No, silly—to quickly find any similar buttons.”

“Oh, right.”

Joel engaged the Sight. Instantly, he was able to spot which buttons on the console most resembled the ones on the small countercom he was holding. “Okay, I found some.”

“Then what are you waiting for?”

“Nothing, I guess,” Joel said, although he was still a little apprehensive about possibly pushing the wrong button. “All right, here goes.” Hoping for the best, he pressed two buttons in the same sequence that would release someone from an energy lock produced by a handheld countercom. After a brief whirring sound, Joel glanced up at the monitors. The first eighteen of them still showed the natives dancing, but the nineteenth one displayed a welcome sight: a group of villagers regaining control of their bodies, some of them collapsing to the ground with weary relief.

"That's a good start," Felicity said.

"Yeah," Joel replied. He proceeded to repeat the process until all the natives had been freed from the Ultracom's energy-control effects.

"See if you can find the trailer that Thinker and the others are in," Felicity said.

Again using the Sight, Joel was able to adjust one of the monitors—changing its channel, in effect—until it displayed an image of Thinker, Keeper, Seeker, Catcher, and the still-unconscious guard. He pressed a couple of buttons, and then they too were released.

"Okay, cool," Felicity said, "now we just need to give them some time to un-mind-control the guards on the outside. Then we can get the villagers out of here."

"But by then it might be too late for some of them," Joel pointed out. "Even though they're not under energy control anymore, I'm pretty sure they still need some immediate medical attention."

"They're just gonna have to hang in there. I'm not sure what else we can do, unless you have any ideas."

"If you release me," the mole-roach woman said, "I can disable the anti-Aura field with these controls. Then you can use your magic to help your friends."

"Nice try," Felicity said. "Thanks for the info, though. Joel—think you can figure out how to take down the field?"

Joel looked back down at the console desk. "Well, that's not a standard countercom function, so I don't know if—" He stopped midsentence as a strange sight appeared: a ghostly image of his own hand reaching out and pushing a series of buttons, all of them different from the ones he had just pressed.

"Okay—you're seeing something, right?" Felicity said. "I can tell by that look on your face. Is it something from the past?"

"No," Joel replied. "I...I think it's from the future."

"Leveling up again, huh? What do you see?"

"This," Joel said. He reached out and began pushing the same buttons that he had just seen himself pushing.

"Whoa, whoa," Felicity said. "Are you sure that's a good idea?"

"Pretty sure."

Joel finished pushing the last button in the sequence. Then, after a moment, the strings on Felicity's wavebow lit up as it began playing a tune that sounded remarkably like "Firework" by Katy Perry.

"Dude," Felicity said. "I'm getting a call. That must mean the Aura's back!"

"Um...is that your new ringtone?" Joel asked.

"Shush," Felicity said. She plucked one of the strings on her instrument. "Hello?"

"Felicity, it is me," a voice—Thornleaf's—said. "Blackspore saw that the anti-Aura field has vanished. Did you dispel it?"

"No, I think Joel did. Don't ask me how. Anyway, we released the villagers from the energy control, and now we need to get some of them up to Tanback and the swordcats, pronto."

"Understood. I will have Blackspore set up a portal between here and the concert grounds."

"Have him open it inside of this yurt so it's not so obvious. Then we'll start bringing people back here."

"Very well. And, by the way...I just wanted to let you know that I am truly sorry for my actions in the past. I was only trying to do what I thought was right."

Wow, Joel thought. *Thornleaf is actually apologizing*.

"We'll talk about that later," Felicity said. "Smith out." The strings on her wavebow dimmed, and she turned to Joel. "Shall we?"

"Okay. We should get the older and younger ones first."

"Yeah, I know."

A small ball of Aura energy appeared a few feet away. It quickly grew into a large sphere, big enough for an adult person to fit through.

"And as for you," Felicity said, glancing at the moleroach woman, "we'll figure out what to do with you once this is all over."

"Oh, it will soon be over, all right," the woman said, "but not in the way you hope."

"What's that supposed to mean?" Felicity said.

"You will see."

"Geez, so ominous." Felicity turned to Joel. "Ready?"

"I am."

Joel and Felicity headed back out to the concert grounds and, with the assistance of the Sight, began locating Spectraland natives. They spent the remainder of Second Player Score's set escorting whomever they found back to the yurt and into Blackspore's portal. At one point, they ran into Ringneck.

"Hey, I have to ask you something," Felicity said to the island's justice minister. "What's the process in Spectraland for getting a divorce?"

"Why do you wish to know?" Ringneck asked.

"Just curious."

"It is fairly simple, actually. One or both parties merely has to present a formal request to the minister of justice—myself—and, upon my recognition of said request, the union is dissolved."

"How formal does the request have to be?"

"Typically it is written on parchment. But in some cases, I will accept a verbal request."

"Okay, then I'd like to divorce Thornleaf, please."

"You what?" Ringneck and Joel said at the same time.

"You heard me."

"Why?" Ringneck asked.

"It's complicated. Can you just do it, please?"

"I—well, yes, of course, but..."

"But what?"

"One condition of the separation is that the requesting party needs to relocate to a different village. With both of you being shamans and living in the Wavemaker Temple, that might pose a problem."

"It won't. After all this is done, I'm moving back to Earth. Permanently."

Joel's eyes widened.

"I...I see," Ringneck said. "Very well then."

"Cool, thanks," Felicity said.

"I really would like to know why, though," Ringneck said. "Was he not who you thought he was?"

"No," Felicity sighed, "he's pretty much exactly who I thought he was. It's just that I finally realized...that's not who I want to be with."

Joel felt a guilty thrill. He had been prepared for Felicity and Thornleaf breaking up due to a change in history, but now they would be breaking up anyway, and he would get to retain his friendship with Felicity back on Earth—and possibly more. Still, though, he felt bad for Thornleaf and for the dissolution of their marriage in general, since his parents' divorce had been such a traumatic event in his own life. At any rate, this turn of events seemed like a vindication of his earlier decision, at Felicity's wedding, to not try to be more like Thornleaf, but to just be himself—a good guy.

"I understand," Ringneck said. "Do you want me to let him know?"

"No, I'll tell him. Later."

"All right." Ringneck headed into the yurt.

"So, um," Joel said, "I guess now I know."

"Now you know what?" Felicity said.

"What's gonna happen with you and Thornleaf."

"Yeah, I guess you do."

"When did you decide that?"

"I really don't want to talk about it right now."

"Okay. Sorry."

"Don't be sorry. Be focused."

"Got it."

The next native they found was Fireflower.

"Thank you," the Wavemaker leader said after Felicity had given her a quick update on what was happening. "That was quite the ordeal."

"Sure looked like it," Felicity said.

"So Blackspore is fine?"

"He is," Joel replied.

"How?"

"Long story," Felicity said.

"And...what of Thornleaf?"

"He's with Blackspore."

"I see. We will need to deal with his transgressions later."

"Transgressions?"

"Yes. I now know that he was actually the one who brought Byle over to Spectraland."

"Okay, yeah."

"I also know that he was the one who attempted to kill Byle, not you."

"What? How did you find that one out?"

"I saw it in a vision."

Felicity smirked. "Can't keep anything from you, can I?"

Fireflower smiled. "I would like to apologize for what I said to you earlier, back at the Thirsty Tunnels. You are welcome to remain in the Wavemaker Order and in Spectraland, if you wish."

"You know, that's okay," Felicity said. "I was already mentally prepared to leave."

"Are you sure?"

"I am. Now we're gonna go find the rest of the villagers. You go on into the yurt. There are spare wavebows and some old friends waiting for you up at the swordcat den."

"Old friends?"

"Yeah. You'll see. Then, once everyone is ready, we've got one last mission to accomplish."

"Capturing Marshall?" Joel said.

"Ding—give the man a prize."

CHAPTER 26: THE HEADLINER

Once all of the Spectraland natives had been seen to safety, Joel, standing outside of the control yurt, tried using a tracking cast to look for Marshall. Oddly, it turned up nothing.

"Where do you think he could be?" he said.

"I dunno," Felicity said, "but knowing Marshall, he's probably planning some kind of grand entrance."

"Yeah," Joel agreed. "Still, though, I'm kinda worried."

"Don't be. I forget—what is that thing Art always says?"

"Worrying is a waste of time?"

"Right. That."

The countercom that Joel was holding beeped. He pushed a button to answer it.

"Hello?" he said.

"Seeker of the Sun here. We have successfully administered the antidote to our compatriots."

"Even Guider?"

"Yes."

Felicity leaned over. "And all of the air patrols?" she asked.

"Affirmative. Once the Governor was back to normal, she ordered them to land, and then we took care of it from there."

"That was fast."

"I told you, we are not amateurs."

"Never said you were. All right, just stay outside the grounds for now—we don't want to start freaking out any skittish audience members just yet. And let us know if you spot the Orchestrator anywhere."

"Acknowledged. Seeker of the Sun out."

"If the tracking cast didn't find him," Joel said to Felicity, "why do you think the Six States people might be able to?"

"Just covering all the bases," Felicity replied. "What about your new ability—can you look into the future to see where he might be?"

Joel tried, to no avail. "I don't think I'm quite there yet. I think I have to be under pressure, and even then I can only see short-term."

"So, kind of like a second-rate Spider-Sense."

"Um—"

"Have you managed to locate Byle?"

Joel turned. Fireflower had come out of the yurt, followed closely by the other shamans, Thornleaf included.

"Not yet," Felicity replied. "He must be cloaked, or some other weird thing."

Joel glanced back and forth between Fireflower and Thornleaf. "Is, uh, is he..."

"I am allowing Thornleaf to assist us," Fireflower said, apparently understanding what Joel had wanted to ask. "His fate will be decided later. For now, we need all the help we can get."

Joel leaned over to Felicity. "Are you gonna tell him?" he whispered. "You know, about the...ivorce-day?"

"Later. Can't afford any distractions right now."

"So, what is the plan?" Riverhand asked.

"The chiefs gave us permission to do whatever is necessary to capture Byle," Fireflower said. "Does anyone have any ideas?"

"I assume he will have to emerge, sooner or later, for his performance," Redstem said. "We could simply wait until then."

"And then stun him?" Windblade asked.

"Exactly."

"Or," Joel said, a mental puzzle piece falling into place, "I could make myself invisible, sneak up on stage, and then use the handheld countercom to freeze him."

"Why you?" Felicity said. "A lot of us know how to use one of those things."

"I, uh, I just figured I'd volunteer, that's all. Plus"—Joel adopted a serious look as he recalled what Marshall had done to Auravine—"I feel like I owe him one."

"Okay, well, no matter what we do, we're gonna have to wait until he's done playing."

"What? Why?"

"Half a million drunk people are here to see Biledriver," Felicity said. "If they don't get a whole show, I guarantee a riot will break out and people will get hurt, or worse. Like that 1991 Guns N' Roses show in St. Louis. You've heard about that, right?"

"Oh, yeah—or like when they played with Metallica the next year in Montreal."

"Exactly."

"If Joel knows how to operate the Ultracom," Blackspore said, "he could stay here instead and use it to freeze the audience members who are turning violent."

"The Ultracom's signal is not selective," Thornleaf said. "It affects everyone who is over twenty feet away from its control panel at the time of activation. I learned that while I was being held prisoner."

"And besides, whoever we freeze, we can't keep them like that forever," Felicity said. "We'd have to release them eventually, at which point they'd be even angrier. These are Earth people. Trust me, I know."

"But as long as the performance has been completed, they will not mind us apprehending him?" Lightsprout asked.

"Well, they still might." Felicity frowned. "We'd have to wait until Marshall gets off stage completely. But then that'll give him a chance to escape into whatever hole he's hiding in now."

"We won't have to wait," Joel said.

"We won't?"

"No. Because once he's under energy control, I can just use the handheld countercom to walk him off the stage. Everything will seem normal, more or less."

Felicity paused, as if thinking it over. "You know what—you're right."

Joel grinned. "I know."

"So, it sounds like we have a plan," Fireflower said. "Our window of opportunity will be right after he finishes performing but before he gets a chance to leave the stage under his own power."

"Yeah." Joel turned to look at the amphitheater. There was a huge black curtain with a giant *B* logo on it hanging from the rafters. Oddly, there were none of the usual sounds of instruments being soundchecked. "I'll start heading over there now."

"I'll come with you," Felicity said. "You'll need backup. Even if Marshall is under energy control, he can still call for help from his backstage security."

"All of us should go," Blackspore said.

Everyone agreed, so they ducked back into the yurt, stunned the mole-roach woman, and then fleshed out the details of their plan. The present-day Wavemakers, having been forced to help build the amphitheater, knew the layout of the structure and how to get behind it and up onto the stage. After briefing the others, they prepared to perform invisibility casts on everyone.

"Wait," Dirtmoss said, "I have a question. How will we know when the performance is over?"

"Oh yeah, I'm glad you asked that," Felicity said. "They're gonna stop once, but then they'll play a couple more times after that."

"Like an encore," Eightarm said.

"Exactly. We'll know when he's done for real when he says what he always says at the end of all his concerts, which is...Joel, what was it again?"

"Um"—Joel cleared his throat and prepared to speak in what he hoped was an acceptable English accent—"'Good night, everyone, you've just been *biledriven*.'"

Felicity laughed. "Man, that is *such* a lame line. No wonder I couldn't remember it."

"All right," Fireflower said, "Everyone, leave your wavebows open to communication so that we can speak with one another. Joel, please notify us when we should start heading up onto the stage. If necessary, we will take care of any guards who may be blocking the way. Then, after you have Byle under energy control and safely away from the audience's view, we will subdue him."

"Got it," Joel said.

"Does anyone have any other questions?"

No one did.

"Then good luck to all of us."

The invisibility casts were completed. Then the twelve shamans exited the yurt and headed toward the amphitheater. On the way there, Joel glanced around and saw that the outlines of Redstem and Tanback appeared to be holding hands.

Hmm. Maybe Redstem won't need online dating after all.

Finally, they reached the front. There, they waited.

Well, I couldn't stop Marshall from coming over to Spectraland, Joel thought, *but at least I'll get to help capture him now and put an end to his schemes once and for all.*

A minute ticked by.

And even though I couldn't change the past and save Auravine and all those other people who died, at least we'll all have a better future to look forward to.

Most of the surrounding lights went out. People started to push toward the front. Joel did his best to stand his ground and not get crushed. Fortunately, it seemed that most of the concertgoers were too drunk and/or distracted to care about bumping into something they couldn't see.

If Felicity never comes back here, then maybe I won't either. In a way, maybe that's what was meant to happen. Like she said, we mentally prepared ourselves for it, and even though it would be for a different reason, perhaps it was always inevitable. It's the direction the fatewave is leading us in.

Loud background music—"Mars, the Bringer of War" by Gustav Holst—began to play. The audience cheered in anticipation. The Rift sprung to life, its glowing silver sphere becoming so bright it looked like a third moon. The audience cheered even louder. Then, as "Mars" segued into "Welcome to the Jungle" by Guns N' Roses (a predictable preconcert song selection, Joel thought), something came flying out of the sphere. At first, Joel thought it was Marshall, but then he quickly realized it was someone else: a humanoid creature that looked like an orc straight out of *Lord of the Rings*, complete with a long, wild mane of greasy, jet-black hair. Joel squinted. It was carrying Redstem's original wavebow.

What the—

Wrapped in a cocoon of dark-green flying Aura, the orc swooped around for a while, performing several loops, rolls, and spins before it rose high up into the air above the stage and then went into a nosedive, ostensibly landing behind the black curtain. Pyrotechnics went off.

Okay, I wasn't expecting that.

"Welcome to the Jungle" segued into "Enter Sandman" by Metallica (another overused selection, in Joel's opinion). Then a second being flew out of the Rift. This one was a cross between a Ferengi from *Star Trek* and Po the red Teletubby, although not nearly as cuddly. Carrying Windblade's original instrument, it, too, did a number of aerial acrobatics before it landed behind the black curtain, setting off another round of pyrotechnics.

Where did these things come from?

The third being to emerge from the Rift (to the tune of "Smells Like Teen Spirit" by Nirvana) defied easy description; it was as if someone had put an octopus, a butterfly, a rainbow lollipop, a bunch of random machine parts, and three hundred pounds of clay into a huge blender, turned it on, and then spit the whole thing back out in a six-foot-tall, cone-shaped form that whirled around like a giant spinning top. Holding Riverhand's original wavebow in one of its tentacles, it repeated the same flying-landing-pyrotechnics process as the first two creatures.

"Is this his new band?" someone standing near Joel said.

"They're like Gwar!" another concertgoer exclaimed.

Marshall must have learned the portal cast and used it to find Wavemakers from other worlds or dimensions, Joel realized. *That's probably where the mole-roach woman in the control yurt came from as well.*

The fourth being—whose entrance song was "Hangar 18" by Megadeth—was not as complex as its predecessor, but it was no less bizarre; with a thin torso made up of equal-sized segments, it basically resembled a giant tapeworm with arms and legs. With Fireflower's original wavebow in its grasp, it soared around like a long-tailed kite for a while before it vanished behind the stage curtain.

"How are they flying like that?" someone said.

"It's all wires and stuff," another audience member replied. "I've seen plenty of shows like this before."

The Megadeth song gave way to "Live Forever" by Oasis. As the music swelled, the Rift became even brighter. An explosion went off, and someone zoomed out: Marshall. The cheers were deafening.

So that's where he was hiding. No wonder the tracking cast couldn't find him.

Marshall flew around for a while like a drunken honeybee, leaving thick trails of dark-green Aura in his wake. Finally, he too did a nosedive behind the black curtain. This time, there were no immediate pyrotechnics; instead, the music abruptly stopped, and for a few long moments, the crowd was as quiet as several hundred thousand people could possibly be. Then, just as a sense of restlessness began to set in, a number of things all happened at once. Columns of flame erupted all around the perimeter. Huge explosions went off. The curtain fell, and Biledriver—the new Biledriver, with

Marshall fronting a group of otherworldly beings—launched into their first song. Joel saw that, instead of normal electric guitars, each of the alien band members was playing its stolen wavebow (one of them was even somehow playing the drum parts on it), lending the song an additional layer of sonic *oomph* while also creating a spectacular light show right there on the stage.

"Joel?"

Joel glanced at his wavebow. Blackspore was contacting him.

"Yes?"

"I need to warn you," the master shaman's voice said.

"About what?"

"These beings—I encountered them during my search for help during the Fourfoot War."

"Um, okay."

"But I passed over them because I deemed them to be too evil."

"Worse than Marshall?"

"In retrospect, probably not. But they were more...forthcoming about it."

"All right, that doesn't sound good."

"It is not. So you need to be very careful when you use the countercom. Make sure you are able to freeze all of them simultaneously. Otherwise, we might be in for a bit of a fight—one that I am not sure we can win."

"Got it."

Biledriver finished the song. The audience cheered as if they had just seen and heard the greatest thing in their entire lives.

"Thank you, thank you!" Marshall said into his microphone. "How's everybody doing?"

More cheers.

"So glad you all could come to this lovely tropical island to witness the reunion—nay, the rebirth—of the greatest rock band of all time. Oh, are we going to have fun tonight!"

Marshall started up the next song. After that, the concert raged on for nearly two and a half hours (two hours, twenty-seven minutes, to be exact) as the band tore through material from all five of Biledriver's albums as well an extended guitar/wavebow solo by Marshall. This new lineup of musicians sounded so good together that, at one point, Joel even caught himself enjoying the show, before he remembered that Marshall was his hated enemy. Following the performance, the band took a short, screams-and-applause-filled break before returning for an encore that consisted entirely of cover songs. Then, during the break before the second encore (during which the crowd chanted *By-EL, By-EL*), Joel decided that it was time for him and his fellow shamans to make their move.

"Okay," he said into his wavebow, "let's go."

Following the directions provided earlier by Fireflower and the others, Joel made his way to the back of the amphitheater, where a short staircase was located. As he approached, someone bumped into him from behind. He turned and saw Felicity's outline standing there.

"Who's this?" she said, reaching out.

"It's me—Joel."

"Oh. You know, you're the third one of us I've collided with so far. You're lucky you can see us with the Sight—the rest of us are winging it. We probably should've all just held hands in a line, or something."

"I, uh, I can hold your hand now," Joel offered. "I mean, if that's okay."

Felicity paused before responding. "Not like we haven't done that before, I guess."

"I guess." Joel reached out and touched the outline of Felicity's hand, which grasped his in response. "Ready?"

"Yeah."

With Joel leading the way, the pair continued on. There were a lot of human security guards—thirty-six of them, to be exact—standing around, but fortunately, none of them were directly blocking the stairway, so Joel and Felicity were able to sneak through. After a minute, they arrived at the back of the stage area. In front of them, Marshall and his alien bandmates were in the middle of covering "Paranoid" by Black Sabbath.

"This is usually the last song Biledriver plays at their concerts," Joel said into the outline of Felicity's ear. "So our chance is coming up."

"I know. Are the others here?"

Joel looked around and saw the outlines of the other Wavemakers standing nearby.

"Yeah, they all made it."

"Cool."

Joel leaned toward his wavebow. "Get ready," he said into it, hoping everyone could hear him clearly.

Finally, after an extended cadence that seemed to last forever, the song came to an end. Lights flashed. Fireworks went off. Marshall stood at the edge of the stage, basking in the glory and adulation of the roaring crowd. Joel raised the countercom and placed his finger on the button.

All right, he thought, *as long as I'm aiming it in this direction, it'll put Marshall and all four of his band-mates under energy lock. Then I can just turn them around and walk them off the stage. Clean and simple.*

Marshall turned. For one scary moment, Joel thought that the Biledriver singer had noticed him and his fellow Wavemakers. But then the moment passed, and Joel breathed a sigh of relief.

This is going to work, he told himself. *It's going to work, because the good guys always win in the end. It's destiny—the will of the fatewave.*

Marshall moved back over to his microphone.

Here we go.

"Good night, everyone!" Marshall shouted, raising his stolen wavebow in the air. "You've just been...*biledriven.*"

There was a loud, hideous squeal, like a cross between the Emergency Broadcast System tone and guitar feedback on steroids. But it wasn't coming from the countercom in Joel's hand. In fact, his finger had been frozen before it was even able to push the button on the device. No, this sound was coming from everywhere. Joel wanted to put his hands up to his ears, but his arms were frozen as well, along with his entire body below his neck. After four excruciating seconds, the sound stopped.

"Blimey, that's annoying," Marshall said. He too appeared to be frozen in place. From the audience, there were sounds of concern and mass confusion.

That was the Ultracom! Joel realized. His eyes darted around. *Did the mole-roach woman wake up and free herself somehow? Or did the Six States people enter the concert grounds and activate it? We did forget to tell them what we were doing...*

"Well, anyway, thank you, Darkeye, for doing that," Marshall said.

What?

"Feel free to turn the wavecast-negation field back on as well."

A moment later, Joel became fully visible, as did Felicity, along with the rest of the Wavemakers.

"Ah, there you all are," Marshall said, turning his head. "Bloody good show, you lot. You managed to get a lot closer than I expected."

"Um—you're under arrest!" Joel shouted.

Marshall laughed. "Oh, I am, am I? Well, I suppose in that case, I have no choice but to go quietly. Aren't you going to read me my rights?"

"You have the right to remain stupid," Felicity snapped. "You may have frozen us with the Ultracom, but you're stuck too, along with your creepy new band members."

"True, true. But don't forget, Darkeye is still mobile. And yes, I did say Darkeye. Don't be shocked—the bloke knows a winning team when he sees one. I had him retake the Ultracom controls. He also provided me with the space- and time-travel casts from your archives. That's how we were able to get all of this set up so quickly."

That explains the strange time-warp effects I was seeing, Joel thought. "But...what's the point of all this?" he asked.

"Yeah, if this is your idea of an awesome evil plan," Felicity said, "then I gotta say, you're starting to lose your touch."

"Seriously now, kids, do you really expect me to explain everything?"

"Might as well, since you're already such a cliché."

"The old get-the-bad-guy-to-talk-so-he-can-buy-you-some-time trick, eh?" Marshall chuckled. "Okay, why not, I'll play along. You do realize, though, that the Ultracom has frozen everyone on the island—you, me, the crowd, the Six States folks, even all the other villagers who escaped through your silly little portal. No one will be able to stop it from happening."

"Stop what?"

"Eh, hold on—Darkeye, could you clear everyone off, please? Can't have anyone else soaking up my glory."

Joel felt his body start to move involuntarily. Apparently, Darkeye, at the helm of the Ultracom controls, was going to make him, the other shamans, and even the alien band members—all four of whom were protesting loudly—walk off the stage.

"All right, now where was I?" Marshall said. "Oh yes, the plan. Well, you see, this amphitheater has been specially designed to reflect and contain sound waves—sort of like that stadium in Seattle that I know you and Joel are familiar with. The acoustics of it are such that if an enormous amount of Aura energy is released nearby, that energy will become trapped within the structure's shell, bounce around, and eventually focus upon whomever happens to be standing on the stage at the time."

All the Wavemakers and the aliens descended from the stage and came to a stop in front of the crowd barrier.

"Now, you may be wondering, 'are you talking about all the energy that was generated by your amazing performance just now'?" Marshall said. "Well, we certainly did produce quite a bit, I must say, but it was nowhere near the amount that's required for my purpose. It was important, however, as it served to magnetize this area, if you will, so that the massive energy that is eventually released will be attracted in this direction."

"So you used us!" the orc-being shouted. It had an English accent, making it seem even more like a character from the Tolkien classic. "You promised us power, but you were lying!"

"He does that," Felicity muttered.

"Hmm, yes, I suppose I was," Marshall said. "Anyway, the question you need to be asking now is 'where then, exactly, is this massive amount of Aura energy going to come from?' Well, I'll tell you. It's going to come from all—of—you."

Confused mumbles rippled throughout the enormous crowd.

Marshall grinned. "Yes, you see, buried beneath the ground throughout this entire area are explosives. Giant, powerful explosives, courtesy of the Six States military, all rigged to go off at once. When that happens, half a million people will blow up at the same time, releasing their energies into the air. All of that energy will then migrate toward this structure, where I will be waiting."

"That will kill you as well!" Blackspore shouted amidst scattered boos from the audience.

"Ah, but that's where you're wrong," Marshall responded. "Well, sort of wrong. It *will* kill me, but because I am basically indestructible, I will come back to life as an omnipotent being—sort of a superwraith, to put it in terms that you can understand."

"You do not know that for sure," Fireflower said. "You are taking an extremely large risk, Byle."

Marshall nodded. "Perhaps. But then again, I've always been a gambling man. And really, I like my chances. You see, I'm not a scientist, but I do have the knowledge and wisdom of creatures that know a thing or two about Aura explosions."

He's talking about the Lightsnakes, Joel realized.

"So you are just going to kill all of these innocent people?" Lightsprout shouted.

"No one is truly innocent," Marshall scoffed. "Everyone deserves to die for some reason."

More boos.

"Do not do this, Byle," Thornleaf said. "I am warning you."

"Oh, a threat from Master Iceheart! How terrifying."

"Please," Joel said, "please don't do this. I'm begging you. If anything, just kill me."

"Joel, shut up!" Felicity said.

"No, really," Joel said, not shutting up. "I'm the one you hate. So kill me. Spare everyone else."

"So valiant of you, Joel," Marshall sneered. "Such a hero, sacrificing himself! What a boring, stereotypical good guy. You know, I'll tell you a secret. A long time ago, I used to be like you. A nice guy. Or, at least, that's what I wanted to be. I tried to be. But I wasn't any good at it. I'd offend people, make them angry, and I wouldn't even know why. But then I realized that nice guys really *do* finish last. Nobody likes them, especially women. I'm sure you've noticed that. Everyone loves the bad boy. The world respects you—rewards you, even—for being a tosser. And on top of that, it's *so* much easier."

Joel clenched his jaw, hoping against hope that some kind of deus ex machina—Starpollen, Seaberry, the swordcats, or anyone else who had been in the swordcat den when the Ultracom went off—would somehow be able to get down here in time.

"At any rate," Marshall continued, "do you really think that after all this work and planning, I'm going to turn back now? I don't think so. Besides, once I become all-powerful, I'll have the ability to bring these people back from the dead, if I so choose. In fact, you know, I just might do that, because—despite how it may have seemed—I was never really into the whole killing-just-for-the-sake-of-killing business. Besides, who wants to eliminate such a large chunk of their loyal fan base, eh?

"But as for you, Joel, and Felicity, and everyone else from this bloody little island...I'll have to think that over. Well, enough talk. Darkeye, push the button."

Joel felt a rumbling sensation start up beneath his feet, as if he were standing on a massage chair.

"Actually," Marshall went on, "I think for you, Mr. Suzuki, I'll bring you back as well. But just you. Partly because I feel like I owe you for helping me fulfill my destiny, but also because keeping you alive means you'll probably try to come back to stop me, which will make for all sorts of entertainment. A cat plays with his meal first, you know?"

The crescendo of the rumbling continued. Joel turned his head to look at Felicity, his eyes wide and full of panic.

"Bye, babe," she said. She was talking to him. "It was fun while it lasted."

"No...no!" Joel exclaimed. "You can't die. You can't!"

Felicity flashed a small, sad smile. "It's all right. Tell Victoria...tell her I love her, okay?"

"I—you—this can't be happening! I swear, I'll find a way to fix this. I promise!"

"Oh, this is going to be so much fun!" Marshall cackled. "I'll be like Q, or Mr. Myxzptlk, or Dr. Manhattan..."

Joel looked back up at the stage. "I'm coming for you, Byle!" he shouted.

Marshall grinned. "I'm counting on it."

The ground was positively shaking now. It felt like an earthquake. Against his will, Joel's Sight engaged, and he saw an image of the very near future—one in which everyone and everything around him would be destroyed in a deafening eruption of smoke, fire, and rubble. He closed his eyes in a futile attempt to shut out the horror. Then, a heartbeat later, the world exploded.

CHAPTER 27: KARMA

Joel awoke with a tune in his head. He didn't recognize it; it was a simple melody, just a few notes repeating over and over. Sometimes he'd get ideas for songs this way. He'd wake up in the middle of the night, pick up his guitar, and recreate the melody as a riff, or maybe a vocal line. He'd play it again and again until he was sure he'd remember it in the morning, thinking that anything you had to record to recall wasn't worth keeping.

As the notes continued to repeat, Joel's vision cleared up, and he saw that he was in the limbo plane once more. This time, though, there were no ghostly images floating around; there was only empty teal-colored space as far as the eye could see. He thought for a moment that perhaps he was dead, but, recalling all of the near-death experiences he had gone through so far in his relatively short lifetime (and the fact that Marshall had said he would bring him back), he quickly replaced that thought with another one: *How can I get out of here?*

That thought was soon joined by others that mostly revolved around the emotion of concern. Concern for Felicity and the rest of his friends, concern for the hundreds of thousands of people who were at the concert, and, most of all, concern about what was going to happen next. Was Marshall really now an all-powerful, omnipotent being?

Joel air-swam around for a bit, hoping to find some sort of exit. *I'm gonna stop Marshall,* he swore to himself, concern quickly morphing into anger. *I'm gonna undo everything he did, and then I'm gonna put an end to him, no matter what.*

After nearly ten minutes of wandering, Joel finally spotted something other than nothingness: a vague, hazy wisp of energy floating about twenty feet away. Encouraged, he propelled himself toward it. As he approached, it began to take on a humanoid shape.

"Fireflower?" he said.

But it wasn't Fireflower; once Joel got close enough, it coalesced into someone else familiar.

"Um...Mistress Moonear?"

"Yes. Hello, Joel."

"Thank goodness. Can you help me get out of here? Marshall—he killed everyone and I think maybe he's turned himself into some sort of superwraith who's going to do who-knows-what, so I need to go back and undo what he did and then stop him because I'm the Virtuoso so it's my job to—"

"Joel," Mistress Moonear said, holding up her hand. "Calm down, please."

"Oh—sorry."

"I know what you want to do, and I am afraid I cannot help you with that."

"What? Why not?"

"I sense great anger within you. You want to kill Marshall Byle for everything that he has done."

"Well, he needs to be stopped, once and for all," Joel said, a bit taken aback. "And no one else seems to be able to kill him. I think I have to be the one to do it. I almost did it before. I should've gone through with it."

"I know, you want justice. And justice will be served when it is deserved. But leave that to the Aura. The Aura will decide on true justice."

"But I can't just let him go. I can't just sit back and wait for fate to destroy him, or whatever. He just killed half a million people. He might be omnipotent now. Don't you see? I have to do something."

"First, you need to let go of this anger," Mistress Moonear replied. "Remember, all energy is interconnected. When you do something that creates suffering, it degrades your own Aura." She took a deep breath. "To help you understand, I will try to use expressions from your homeworld. Ever notice that when you hurt someone, even though it may feel good or satisfying in the moment, it leaves a...a bad taste in your mouth?"

Joel blinked.

"And conversely," Mistress Moonear continued, "when you do something that creates happiness in others, you get that...warm, fuzzy feeling inside? That is not a coincidence. What you call karma is real. It is all about the energy of the universe and how it stays in balance."

"I'm still not sure I get it," Joel said. "Are you telling me that if I kill Marshall, I'll be hurting myself?"

"Essentially, yes."

"But what if it's justified? Like, on Earth, we have laws that say you can legally kill people in self-defense."

"People can make whatever laws they want," Mistress Moonear said with a Spectraland shrug. "We can make it legal to kill, but any suffering that you cause others will harm you over the long run. Just as holding a grudge will."

"Honestly, I don't think anyone will suffer if Marshall is gone."

"Oh? How do you know that? You just came from a concert where hundreds of thousands of people were professing their positive feelings toward him. Before he blew them up, of course."

"I guess..."

"What if there is some young fan somewhere who does not know Marshall Byle as an evil murderer, only as a talented and inspirational musician? And that fan becomes so distraught at his death, especially after thinking that he had returned from the grave, that he or she does something to harm themselves or others?"

Joel pursed his lips. She had a point. After all, not too long ago, he himself was that distraught fan.

"Let me take a step back," Mistress Moonear went on. "Aura energy gets recycled. So, when you die, your energy becomes part of the whole and is eventually used somewhere else...possibly even for a new incarnation, or whatever you wish to believe. So the stronger your Aura is in this life, built up from helping people and creating happiness for others, the more likely you are to live on in some form of immortality. But if you cause harm and unhappiness and pain and suffering, your Aura decays, possibly to the point where you will be snuffed out, no longer exist, like a flame that has been extinguished. Even if what you do may be considered legal and moral by your culture, the misery you create always comes back to you eventually."

"Now you're starting to sound like Art," Joel muttered.

Mistress Moonear smiled. “I know that all of this may be a little hard to grasp right now, but in time, it will come to you.”

“So then what should I do? Just float around here and hope for the best?”

“Follow your fatewave. It will guide you to where you need to go.”

“But what does that really mean, anyway? I’ve always thought that we’re the ones in charge of our own destinies.”

“In some ways, you are. Do not get me wrong—you do have free will. When you are riding the wave, you are free to get off at any time. But it is important to remember that you and the Aura are partners. If you consider getting off the wave, first stop and look around. Will you be jumping into calm waters, or onto a reef of sharp rocks? You need to feel, to sense within the Aura that it might be the wrong thing to do, or perhaps the wrong time. The Aura is not forcing you to remain on a single path, but it does provide guidance. When you are doing the right thing, it will feel easy and comfortable. You just need to breathe, believe, and let the Aura take you where it will. Or, as you say in your world, ‘go with the flow.’”

“I’m getting more confused.”

“I assume you do not know how to swim.”

“Um, yeah. But what does that have to do with anything?”

“Joel—your destiny, your fatewave, is shaped by you. It is shaped by your dreams, goals, and desires. The Aura then works with you to get you to your destination. It will tell you when you are headed the right way, and when you are not. You just need to listen to it.”

“And so...the Aura is telling me that killing Marshall is the wrong thing to do?”

"Actually, it is I who is telling you that."

"Oh—right. So if it's the wrong thing, then...wait, I think I got it. All I have to do is return to Spectraland and then go back in time to before when Biledriver started playing. Then, instead of killing him, I could come up with a different plan to capture him—one that works. But hold on, though...if he's omnipotent, won't he be able to stay one step ahead of me? And haven't you told me that the past can't be changed anyway?"

"Well, there is more to being the Virtuoso than just traveling through time and space."

"I know, I know, it's about knowledge, wisdom, and growth. You told me that already. But how is that going to help?"

Mistress Moonear nodded. "It is about those things, but there is something else as well. Something I learned of only after my death."

"What is it?"

"A fully realized Virtuoso has the ability to shape reality as he or she sees fit. You know how, with a basic wavecast, you envision the particular outcome that you want?"

"Yeah."

"Imagine that ability multiplied exponentially, possibly to an almost infinite amount, giving you the power to manifest anything that you visualize. That is what a true Virtuoso should be able to do."

"You mean I'd be omnipotent? Like Marshall?"

"Correct."

"Cool! So how do I become—what did you call it—fully realized? Can you train me? Is that why you're here?"

"Unfortunately, I lack the knowledge to help you achieve your potential. You will need to find your guidance elsewhere."

"What? From where? Blackspore died in the explosion, along with Fireflower, and everyone else...who else can help me?"

"Like I said, follow your fatewave, and you will find your answers." With that, Mistress Moonear's image began to fade. "Farewell, Joel. And good luck."

"No, wait! Don't go yet! I just thought of another question. If causing pain and suffering degrades someone's Aura, then why is Marshall—"

Ding.

Joel suddenly found himself sitting in the elevator of his apartment building. He had his backpack on. He looked inside of it. No wavebow. He checked his pocket. No loudstone.

What the heck?

He stood up and pushed the button for the nineteenth floor. After what felt like a very, very long time, the elevator stopped and the door opened. Joel walked out and headed down the hall toward his family's apartment.

So I need to become a complete Virtuoso if I'm going to stop Marshall and undo everything he's done. But how am I supposed to do that? Who or what is going to help me? I don't even have my wavebow or my loudstone anymore. Did he take them away and then send me back here? If he's already omnipotent, what chance do I even have?

Joel stopped in front of his door, took out his key, and opened it. He walked inside and glanced around. Based on what he saw, it was still Thanksgiving, and he couldn't have been gone for longer than fifteen minutes.

"Hi, honey," his mom said, putting the last of the dishes away. "How was your walk?"

"Um, good."

"Are you sure?" Taylor said. "You look even more depressed than when you left."

"C'mon, Joel, join us for some video games," Art said. "I'm sure that'll cheer you right up."

"No thanks." Joel went into his room, closed the door, and sat down at his desk.

What am I going to do? I don't even know where to start. I—

The intro riff to "Slo-Mo Kikaida" by The Dambuilders sounded. It was the ringtone on Joel's phone. He took it out of his pocket and looked at the screen. He nearly choked when he saw the caller ID name: *Felicity Smith.*

www.joelsuzuki.com

CPSIA information can be obtained
at www.ICGtesting.com
Printed in the USA
FSHW021056101118
53647FS